The Duet Dilemma

BOOK 1 OF THE DUET DIARIES

MAGGIE EVANS

SYLVANA SKIES PUBLISHING

To the 13-year-old girl who stayed up all night writing Harry Potter fan fiction, read books during math class, and dreamed of being an author.

You did it. :)

A Smile

Dear Diary,

Did you know it's considered bad luck to put your purse on the floor? I read somewhere it means you're disrespecting the bag that holds your money and your wealth along with it.

A purse on the floor is money out the door.

Of course, I had to test it myself.

I'm already a broke college student on scholarship, so it's not like there's any risk involved. Secretly, I hoped it had the opposite effect on people with no money.

The setup was easy enough, since all I had to do was put my money in my backpack and leave it on the floor. I even dragged it around campus to summer courses and coffeehouses.

After two weeks, I haven't had a single stroke of bad luck. My measly wad of bills still happily fuels my daily coffee runs.

Teresa called the whole experiment a waste of time on a baseless superstition, which only put her at risk of losing the Best College Roommate in the World award.

Can you believe she said she didn't care about "that stupid award"? Her words, not mine.

But maybe I should stop putting so much weight on superstitions.

Sweet Dreams,
Emma

I T ALL STARTED WITH A SMILE.

Monday began with room temperature coffee and underwear that paid homage to Hello Kitty since I'd deferred anything laundry-related over the weekend. During my two months on campus for college prep courses, I'd probably done laundry a total of three times.

Fine, two.

But I was a college girl now, which was both exhilarating and terrifying. I'd finally traded in my puppeteering parents in Kansas for the warm, welcoming sun of Southern California. One could only hope it was far enough away.

My Music Theory class was set to start any minute, and my sole focus was on avoiding Charlie Davenport's gaze from a few desks over. It wasn't that he was creepy—no, he definitely bordered on something more akin to adorable—but a girl could only take so many cow eyes before she caved. We'd gone on what I'd dubbed "the Date from Hell" this past weekend, and I was convinced the only thing that could've made it more awkward was if I'd discovered we were brother and sister.

From the goodnight kiss alone, I would've believed we were at least cousins.

Now we were stuck in the same class of forty students for four months, and I considered how pathetic it would be to drop a class because of a guy I'd been on a few tepid dates with over the summer. Music Theory wasn't exactly high on my list of preferred classes this semester, but it was a necessary sacrifice to major in Westcroft University's competitive piano program.

If only the class wasn't slated first thing on a Monday morning.

Breakfast was regretfully skipped, my only hygiene for the day consisted of freshly brushed molars, and I gave Sleepy Susan in the back row a run for her money on who could yawn the most before 8:00 a.m.

Yet, I'd still shown up ten minutes before class started for fear of getting lost, which would've been more than enough time to stop at the coffee cart by the quad to get something that didn't scream *instant-mud-water*.

In fact, if I left now and took the stairs, I could make it back with about a minute to spare.

"Is this seat taken?"

If the stairwell was empty, I could slide down the railings. That'd shave off another thirty seconds or so.

"Hey, is someone sitting here?"

My mouth watered in anticipation of a caramel macchiato, and my heart thumped at a quickened rate—much too fast for the simple joy a freshly brewed coffee would bring.

"Yo, Blondie? You high or something?"

The thumping beat increased, pounding faster and faster until I rubbed a hand across my chest in alarmed confusion.

Maybe I had indigestion.

That was when I noticed a blue pen tapping against my desk and the grimy fingernails on the hand gripping it.

"Huh?" My morning articulation had what the college counselor referred to as *room for improvement*.

"Is. This. Seat. Taken?" the gruff voice said. I blinked before allowing my gaze to leave his tapping pen and trace up a hairy arm and broad shoulder to annoyed blue eyes glaring back at me.

I eyed the empty seat beside me.

"Well, it looks empty to me," I said, fighting back a frown. "But I'm not exactly the desk police."

The grimy-fingered boy sighed, and from the way both his eyes narrowed to slits, I could tell he was not thrilled with my theorizing.

"No need to be a bitch. I was just making sure you weren't saving it. Forget it." He continued down the aisle, the scent of something putrid lingering behind.

I bristled at the unnecessary name-calling.

Then I noticed the room had really filled up while I'd been daydreaming. The only regret I felt was that I'd lost my chance for a hot coffee.

"Don't take it personally," I muttered to the empty seat he'd abandoned. "You're better off without him. I'm pretty sure my gym socks smell better than he does."

A few snickers hinted that my whispering could use a little work, but Cheyenne—a dark-haired girl I'd met during the summer intro courses—turned around with a conspiratorial grin as she pinched her nose. I couldn't resist beaming back. Still sporting that half-crazed expression, I glanced at the weathered clock looming above the door.

Unfortunately, this was also the moment a well-dressed upperclassman decided to waltz in. He stepped directly into my line of vision, surveying the room with a pair of hazel eyes that locked on mine. From the arch of his brow, it was safe to assume this new arrival thought my smile was meant for him.

And from the small frown gracing his otherwise expressionless face, I'd guess he wasn't used to it.

A Pen

THE NEWCOMER'S gaze held mine captive in a way that had the psychotic grin fading faster than it'd appeared. My heart kicked into a gear four times more rapid than the smelly hooligan's pen-tapping earlier.

It had started with a smile—an albeit deranged one—and sometimes I really wished Cheyenne hadn't turned around. If she hadn't, then I never would've smiled, and a surprisingly refined-looking college guy wouldn't have spared me a second glance.

But life was never so kind. I couldn't stop sneaking glances as he strolled toward the only remaining seat... right next to mine. I regretted getting snarky with Smelly Boy earlier; I'd take smelly boys over heart palpitations any day.

Then the new guy was sitting down, arranging his note-taking supplies, and focusing on his sleek ebony phone as if he hadn't just incinerated my concentration.

Was he a freaking wizard?

Wearing a dark blazer complimented by a white dress shirt, he made me look like a slob in my casual skirt and top. He looked older than the rest of the class, too—at least early twenties. More man than boy. His angular jaw was a distraction by itself.

"Laptops and phones away," a new voice said from the doorway. All thoughts of the new guy screeched to a halt as I turned to gape at the middle-aged maestro striding into the room.

Atticus Slade.

My parents and I had attended his concert on campus during a vacation, and I'd handed in my application for Westcroft's piano program the following morning. It was every piano student's dream for Slade to choose them for an independent study. He was a legend.

If composers were flowers, he'd be the *Rafflesia arnoldii*. His music was big, bold, and beautiful from far away, but when you were close enough to truly decipher the tonality of his masterpieces, you'd be haunted by the scent of rotting flesh. I found him utterly fascinating.

I couldn't stop staring.

Professor Slade didn't spare us a single glance as he approached a podium in the front of the room; hard eyes, tall, and imposing. He owned the professor look with his tweed jacket and glasses.

"I'm Atticus Slade, and I'll be your Music Theory instructor. Blaise Rousseau is my teaching assistant. She's sitting in the front here."

A pretty redhead with a wild mane of curls swiveled in her seat, offering a quick wave.

Slade cleared his throat, scanning the room through a pair of horn-rimmed glasses. "You or your parents are paying good money for me to teach you, so if I find that you're slowing us down for even half of a note, I won't hesitate to drop you from this course. It's very possible—and even more likely—there will be ten empty seats in this room by midterms. Don't let one of them be yours."

Apparently, coffee was unnecessary, because that woke me right up.

"Pens and paper at the ready. Our lecture will begin following attendance," he said before uncapping a pen and glancing down at the podium. "*Zamora, Brennan?*"

Pens and paper at the ready.

"Crap." I scrambled for my bookbag and dug through every available pocket to verify I really was stupid enough to not restock my pens after the summer courses. Nothing. "Double crap."

After a quick glance to the right confirmed the girl beside me had one pencil that was on its last leg, I nibbled on my lower lip and scoped out Mr. Blazer's impressive roster of writing utensils while he was already distracted writing on a piece of paper. There were at least five pens lying there in a straight line. Surely, he wouldn't miss just *one*?

I attempted to clear my throat in a hey-you-look-over-here kind of way, but maybe it sounded like I had a tickle, because his attention remained firmly on his paper as Professor Slade read the next few names.

So, I tried again. But then a tickle actually did catch in my throat, and I coughed hard enough that my eyes watered. I tried swallowing, but the coughing wouldn't stop. Before I knew it, I was smacking a hand against my chest and hacking up half a lung —not to mention dying of mortification.

"Miss, we would appreciate it if you could move to the hallway as opposed to disrupting roll call," Professor Slade said from the front.

Great first impression, Emma.

Blinking back the moisture clouding my vision, I scooped up my now-favorite cup of coffee I'd swiped from the teacher's lounge and swigged back a mouthful.

"I'm okay!" I stumbled to assure our professor before my stubborn body coughed once more just to discredit me. With another clearing of my throat, I was good to go. "Really, I'm all right to stay. Sorry for the interruption."

With one more look—to make sure I wasn't going to die or interrupt him again—Professor Slade returned to his list.

Time for Plan B.

"Hey," I whispered. I slid my pink-Keds-clad foot across the linoleum until I could nudge my new neighbor's chair leg. "Hey, you. Excuse me."

Still nothing.

"*Milton, Maura.*"

I sighed, smoothing down my skirt. While keeping my eyes on Professor Slade, I scooted my chair the tiniest bit toward my target—wincing when a shrill *squeak* echoed around the room.

"*Kincaid, Noah,*" the professor's booming voice called, not looking up from the roster.

Mr. Blazer's voice was deep and sure beside me as he answered. "Present."

I paused in my approach. Noah Kincaid. Noah. *No-ah.* From the way his dark brown hair brushed away from striking features, and how his lips pinched together as he wrote in his notebook, I decided the name fit.

I leaned closer, banking on his peripheral vision being up to par.

Leaning in had its own advantages. Noah smelled... fantastic. Like the air after a rainstorm.

"Noah," I whispered, then watched as his purposeful hand froze midstroke. "Noah?"

It was only a momentary lapse in his concentration, though, because his pen continued flying across the paper a heartbeat later.

I raised my voice, showing him I meant business. I'd already disrupted the class once, after all. "Noah Kincaid."

"Yes?" he asked, voice low and steady, with eyes focused on the paper before him.

"Could I borrow a pen, please?" I purposely kept my tone completely platonic. Knowing how attractive he was, the last thing I wanted was for him to think I was trying to get an opening to flirt with him.

Hazel eyes framed by dark lashes met mine with a flicker of surprise.

"A pen?" he asked with the most miniscule amount of surprise. "You'd like a pen?"

"I forgot mine," I said, tacking on a sheepish smile. He still hesitated, both unrelenting eyes locked on mine as I fought the urge to fidget. What was the big deal? It wasn't like I'd asked for his underwear. "I just need to borrow one, and I promise to return it after class."

Slowly—as if he were doubting my intentions—Noah picked up the shiny pen closest to him before holding it out in a wary offering. Completely weirded out by this point, I snatched it out of his hand with a quick word of thanks and turned to my open notebook.

Doodles of hearts and treble clefs took over the page. I added a quick note of the date as Professor Slade barked out a few more names. Noah's pen glided smoother than butter, and I considered myself thoroughly impressed.

"*Fox, Emma.*"

Showtime.

"I'm here," I said confidently while raising a hand, despite knowing he wouldn't look up. My focus was concentrated on Noah anyway, watching for his reaction.

It was a whole lot of nothing—he didn't even glance over—and the Jane Austen side of me wasn't very impressed.

I focused on doodling a new heart, still amazed by how easily Noah's pen glided across the page. It registered with me why he'd been so skeptical to share such an instrument.

I was tempted to keep it.

"That's everyone. Thank you for doing yourselves a favor and showing up today." Professor Slade stole my attention back as he surveyed the room. "Make no mistake, that was the easiest step. During your time with me, we'll be studying the melody, rhythm, and diatonic tonal harmony both in four voices and in instrumental textures. There will be an emphasis on rudiments of music, voice leading, harmonic progression, and elemental melodic forms. This is a required course for all music majors, and you'll be seeing me again next year for the second part of this theory sequence."

A couple quiet groans sounded from the back row, and I fought not to join in. Music Theory wasn't exactly my forte. I usually just played whatever songs I liked the sound of. All of the mumbo jumbo technical stuff sounded like a foreign language... probably because a good portion of it *was* foreign words.

"By the end of this course, you'll be expected to identify and write all elements of the fundamentals of music," Slade said. He flattened both hands against the podium. "We'll cover the seventeenth through nineteenth centuries. Grading will consist of quizzes on the text material as well as ongoing projects. Your final exam will be a performance with an emphasis on your composition and execution of an original thirty-two-measure work."

I glanced around the room along with everyone else, nibbling on a fingernail. Performances wouldn't be a problem; I'd been raised to perform. My parents sold my soul to the piano gods before I'd lost my first baby tooth. As a child, I could jam to Beethoven and Bach with the best of them. But playing my *own* work in front of others? Slight problem, Houston. My fingers produced a lovely sheen of sweat as they clung to the pen like a lifeline.

Slade smiled and crossed his arms. "But this music program is also known for its collaboration, so we'll be introducing a unique new aspect to the project this year. You'll be composing and performing in pairs."

My stomach dropped.

A duet?

Oh no.

"Partners will be posted at the end of class. Now, please open your *Tonal Harmony* books to page ten, and we'll begin..."

Dread pooled in my stomach. How was I supposed to articu-

late my musical thoughts well enough to compose a piece with
someone, let alone work with them for an entire semester?

Flipping open the textbook, which weighed more than a
bowling ball, I managed to dutifully follow along with the class for
the first four pages before finding a topic worthy of taking notes. I
stopped nibbling nervously—not the best habit—and turned to a
blank page in my notebook. Pen poised, *Tonal Harmony* opened
to a chapter on the elements of pitch, and brain one hundred
percent focused on all things music. I couldn't refrain from jolting
in horror as I trapped Noah's pen in a death grip.

Holy macaroni.

Teeth marks glared back at me from where I'd chewed on two
inches of the beautiful instrument. Little dents and saliva coated
the cap, and I focused on deep breathing as my hands shook. My
fingernail looked barely touched. I was officially the idiot of the
century.

Something told me Noah Kincaid wouldn't appreciate his
fancy pen being turned into a chew toy.

A Coffee

It wasn't what I'd expected from my first Music Theory lecture.

For one thing, I thought I'd actually be paying attention to the professor I idolized. Instead, I spent the next forty minutes vaguely listening to a legendary composer's wise words while internally freaking out over the bite marks on Noah's prestigious pen. Unfortunately, I'd been so distracted wondering if those deadly hazel eyes of his would glare me to death that I'd unintentionally nibbled on it a few more times out of nerves.

Luckily, Noah didn't glance my way even once during the entire lecture.

I tried not to take it personally.

"Here are your partners for the duet project," Professor Slade said as class ended. He let his textbook fall shut with a *thump* and pulled up a spreadsheet on his projector. "Pairings were randomly generated and are final. I don't want to hear about how badly you need to be paired with your best friend."

I scoured the list for my name, unsure which I was dreading

more between Noah and Smelly Boy. Finding Cheyenne's name next to mine was a welcome relief. I could breathe again.

My eyes unwittingly sought out Noah's name and found it next to Blaise Rousseau, Slade's teaching assistant.

That didn't seem fair.

"For next class, make sure to study up on your inspirators. You'll be doing an in-depth analysis on the composers you've been influenced by," Slade said when there weren't any complaints. "That'll be all. I'll see you on Wednesday."

There was a mad dash for the door, but I remained behind. My toes wiggled and my weight shifted restlessly while I tried to get my apology straight.

"Emily?" The voice that would surely haunt my dreams was closer than before, and I peeked up from under my lashes to see Noah waiting beside my desk. He was too self-possessed to hover, and accusing the man of loitering felt like a crime.

Time to face the music.

"Oh. My name is Emma." I tried not to grimace at the fact that he'd forgotten my name when I'd already doodled his a total of three times in my notebook. My grip tightened around his glossy pen as I clutched it behind my back. A tiny delusional part of me hoped he'd stopped by to ask something as mundane as what shampoo I used instead of demanding his precious pen back.

"You have something that belongs to me." He showed no acknowledgement of whether he'd retained my name or not.

"Right." I pursed my lips as I used my free hand to straighten my skirt, then scooted out of my chair. It'd be easier to run away if I was standing. I took a deep breath and faced him, wincing when I saw his frown. "Your pen."

"Yes, my pen," Noah said slowly, presumably in case I didn't understand someone speaking at a normal rate. "The one you promised to return."

"You see, that's the funny thing about pens." I giggled a little hysterically as his eyes impatiently scanned my person and desk.

The pen remained firmly behind my back in a grip that would battle any laboring mother's. "They start out as just a pen, right? But then you hold it for the first time, and you realize 'maybe this is what I've been missing all my life'—"

Oh God. *Shut up, Emma.*

"—and I know I said I'd return it, but I was wondering if you'd be interested in a trade or—"

He cut me off with a narrowed look that proved words were unnecessary. "I allowed you to *borrow* my pen with the promise that it would be returned following this lecture. I'd hate for you to go back on your word."

"... Okay." I took a deep breath and straightened my spine until it threatened to bend backward. "Can I just preface this by saying that I didn't eat breakfast this morning? I'm a growing girl, you know, and first day of class always makes me a little nervous. Also, I can't really be blamed for—"

A pale, polished hand appeared palm up in front of me with more authority in its pinky finger than I had in my entire body.

My shoulders sagged.

"I'm *really* sorry," I muttered in defeat and pulled the pen from behind my back. It took effort, but I dropped the casualty into his outstretched palm before snapping back to clasp my fingers together. "I'll pay for a new one. I promise."

Silence fell as Noah's posture went rigid. He looked down at the mutilated pen with a face that would rival any poker champion. My foot shuffled anxiously against the linoleum as I waited with bated breath.

"This can't be sanitary," he finally said, allowing a single blink at the offending writing instrument.

"Yeah," I mumbled, then offered what I hoped was an apologetic smile. I shifted my weight to the other foot. "But it kind of adds a little character, too, don't you think?"

Not to mention it completely destroyed the sophistication and elegance of the pen.

Noah didn't deign to respond. He just slipped the pen into his slacks pocket and shook his head before heading toward the door.

I blinked. No bloodshed?

"Wait!" I scooped up my backpack and made quick work of stuffing my notebook and planner inside. Slinging the bag over my shoulder, I ran to catch up. My skirt didn't appreciate the rush, and it took both my hands holding it down to keep things decent. "Noah!"

Part of me wanted to turn the other way and forget our mortifying exchange ever happened, but guilt overpowered that urge. So, I flung myself down the stairs at a speed that was bordering on suicidal—clinging to the sides of my skirt and doing something that resembled a penguin skipping—and caught the back of Noah's head as he started down the second flight.

With my bookbag thumping against my back on every step, I wove through the littering of students in front of me.

Noah made it out of the building before I caught up, and I tried to ignore the way I was panting for breath as he appeared unaffected by a whopping three staircases.

The late morning sun bathed the campus in warmth, making the quad look like we were heading into summer vacation instead of just starting a fall semester.

"Noah, wait!" I wheezed as I squeezed past a couple upperclassmen to reach him. I matched his stride, waiting to speak until I caught my breath. "I'm so sorry! Really. Can I at least get you a cup of coffee or something to make up for it?"

Noah's lean legs stopped midstep, and I looked up as a flare of suspicion broke his Alcatraz-level exterior. "Was this your plan? Vandalize my property so you could spend more time with me?"

I stopped in the middle of the sidewalk as well, before getting jostled to the side when the boy behind me didn't get the memo. But my disbelieving eyes were drawn to Noah, and I began to understand why a genuine smile threw him off so much earlier. "Wow. There's no way someone can be that cocky."

"Being perceptive isn't the same as being cocky," Noah said, and he didn't even spare a glance to the side as the grumbling flow of students parted around us.

"Listen. I accidentally chewed on your pen a bit. I admit it's not the best habit, but it's not like I filled your sock drawer with sardines or hacked your phone." I enunciated each word to make sure he didn't misinterpret them and think I was proposing. I shrugged before letting my arms fall against my sides. "It was an honest mistake, and I just want to make it up to you."

"By asking me out?" Noah asked with no small amount of disdain. If I hadn't known what my hair looked like that morning, I would've taken offense.

"I'm talking about buying you coffee from a cart as an apology until I can replace your pen, then going our separate ways," I said just as slowly. "It's not a date, and before you get any ideas—no, it's not a marriage proposal either."

He shot me a dry look at that one.

"I don't see how coffee is an acceptable form of apology," Noah said, starting down the sidewalk again. I rushed after him— God knows why.

"Because coffee can make anything better." I pushed to keep up with his freakishly long legs. "Besides, it's not the coffee itself; it's the gesture. I owe you for ruining your pen—at least until I can replace it. What do you say?"

My traitorous hand reached out of its own accord, resting on his upper arm like I would do for any friend whose attention I wanted. Why was this a bad idea?

For one, Noah wasn't my friend. So, the move surprised him as much as it did me, and he jerked to the side as if I'd taken a swing at him.

Secondly, I'd never been the most coordinated person. I fumbled to catch my footing as my body automatically counted on Noah's arm providing a steady hold for my hand.

Lastly, there's no limit to how many times one can be embarrassed in a day, so I really should've seen it coming.

I found myself careening toward the pavement. My hands smacked against the sidewalk to take the brunt of the fall as my backpack dug into my skull.

I groaned, blinking at the concrete below me. My palms tingled from the impact, too numb to move. I let the rest of my weight from my makeshift push-up fall against the ground in defeat. "Crap."

My thighs met the ground, and I realized with growing dread that there was no skirt separating them from the warm pavement. I heard a few muffled snickers and snorts. My hands scrambled to yank down the fabric over my butt as I remained belly down on the walkway.

Double crap.

If I'd known a modest amount of my peers would see my Hello Kitty underwear today, laundry *definitely* would've been on the top of my list of priorities this past weekend.

A familiar pale, polished palm appeared in front of my red-tinted vision. I dusted the small pieces of gravel and dirt off my hands before accepting Noah's help. He pulled me up in a graceful move reminiscent of dancing.

"Hello Kitty?" Noah asked quietly as he let go, and I could've sworn I caught a glimpse of amusement in his eyes. Something about the way those words rolled off his tongue had my cheeks flaming. "Are you all right?"

"I'm fine. It's laundry day," I said past a dry throat, feeling defensive as a wave of fire rose up my neck until it reached my hairline. My hands made quick work of smoothing down my skirt before brushing bits of dirt off my knees. "I don't normally wear such juvenile underwear. Honestly."

The students milling around us had already moved on from watching the girl who'd eaten pavement, and I only caught a few lingering looks from boys who were probably hoping for a second show. The towering oak trees bordering the quad were a nice distraction to avoid looking at Noah. I prayed my candid mouth would remain tightly shut until he said something first.

My mortification grew the longer the silence stretched.

"I take my coffee black," Noah finally said, and my gaze shot to his at the abrupt change of subject. I squinted back at him, trying to determine if he was having a stroke. "No cream, no sugar. And it's not a date."

Oh.

Oh!

"I knew I'd break you!" I grinned and hoped my cheeks weren't as pink as I knew they were. "I just didn't know it would require flashing you."

His gaze definitely held a pinch of amusement. "What can I say? I grew up in the South. It's deeply ingrained in us not to let a girl make a fool of herself for this long. My grandmother would find a way out of her grave if I left without making sure you could walk."

"Oh." I blinked, wondering if I should be insulted. "Well, isn't that... sweet."

I spun around to face the coffee cart located a few yards away, happy to see there wasn't a line. I didn't want to risk Noah bailing if we had to wait in line together. I also didn't trust my mouth to stay quiet. I subtly fanned my cheeks before marching toward the cart on a mission and sparing a quick glance over my shoulder to verify Noah was following at a slower pace.

At least he hadn't taken off running.

"Hi, Scott." I offered a small wave to the coffee attendant. The coffee cart was my favorite place on campus. It was big enough to fit two people, with a green-and-white striped awning held up by gold poles, and a display case of pastries that made my mouth water.

"Hey, Emma." Scott grinned from behind the register as he plucked a new cup off the stack. Scott Holliday still lived in a world where guys used globs of hair gel, and his brown hair formed something close to a fauxhawk. I thought it did a great job of drawing attention to his big brown eyes—the same rich color as the delicious coffee he served. "One caramel macchiato with extra caramel syrup and a scoop of sugar, right? Or is it a two-scoop day?"

I winced as he recited my usual, wondering what straight-black Noah thought of my completely-under-control addiction. "Um, no, actually. Just a black coffee for me today. No sugar or anything. Not sure if there's a special name for it?"

The coffee boy paused with a frown. "You just want a regular coffee?"

"Yep." I nodded and pulled a few crumpled bills loose.

"No sugar?"

"None," I said with a shake of my head. "Not even a little bit."

"But, Emma, are you sure...?"

"She's sure," Noah said firmly from behind me, and I glanced up from the wad of dollar bills to see Scott sizing him up. I found that cute, because Scott was closer to my height while Noah was well over a head taller than both of us.

"Yes, I'm sure." I winked at Scott to show him there was no harm meant as I smoothed down my traitorous skirt again.

"One regular coffee, coming right up," Scott said with no small amount of confusion before pulling on the coffee lever. It took no time at all to fill the cup, and he handed me back much more change than I'd expected. Maybe if I made the switch to black coffee, I'd be carrying twenties instead of ones.

"Here you go." I handed Noah the coffee with a smile before straightening the straps of my sagging backpack. I shifted my weight and glanced at the ground. "One fresh black coffee. Just a small token of my apology for ruining such a beautiful writing instrument. I'll pay for it, I swear. But the coffee helps, right? Actually, you know, they usually have these nifty little cup sleeves. Not just for looks, but the coffee is *really* hot when you first get it.

I probably shouldn't have just handed it to you like that. Your hand must be on fire. Hold on—hey, Scott, got any sleeves?"

I wanted to slap a hand over my mouth to stop the incessant babbling—and from Scott's raised brow, it looked like he agreed—but Noah's expressionless face when I'd handed him the cup wasn't offering me anything, and I just couldn't seem to stop.

"Thanks." I huffed a breath as Scott handed over a cup sleeve. I fiddled with the paperboard and focused on him before I had to face a stoic Noah again. Laughing Hello Kittys swam across my vision, and I found it easier to face the customer-friendly coffee boy. "You know, fun fact about these little guys. Coffee sleeves were invented in the early nineties because a coffee spill burned a man's fingers—"

"Uh, Emma?" Scott nodded at something behind me. "You know he left, right?"

I spun around in time to see the back of a blazer as Noah wound his way through the sea of casually-dressed-at-best students before disappearing around the corner.

Okay, then.

I turned back around with a sigh and offered Scott the wad of bills. "What was that you were saying about a two-scoop day?"

A Debt

Dear Diary,

I met a cute boy today.

Then I promptly ruined any chance I had by muti-lating his pen beyond recognition. Oh, and I showed him my underwear. On accident, but still.

Kill me now.

You can probably guess which pair it was, too, because my mortification wouldn't be complete without everyone at Westcroft knowing I wear fictional cats with pink bows on my backside.

In other news, Scott gave me an extra drizzle of caramel in my coffee today. If my guardian angel ever took human form, he'd be Scott Holliday.

Great start to the semester,

Emma

"Holy macaroni!"

My eyes bugged out, and my jaw was dangerously close to hitting the comforter on my bed as I clutched the sides of my laptop. "Ninety-nine freaking dollars!"

I squeezed my eyes shut and muttered a quick prayer under my breath to whichever god would listen, before opening them tentatively. My eyelids fluttered, and I scrutinized the picture of an exact replica of a certain Aurora Ipsilon I knew quite intimately—just without the teeth marks.

"What kind of pen is worth ninety-nine dollars?" I asked the empty dorm room in disbelief, but Mr. Elephant—the trusty elephant plushie I'd had since primary school—just stared back at me from my mountain of pillows with noticeably less incredulity. "What a rip-off—it didn't even taste that good."

That was a lie; it tasted like sunshine and happiness.

But my heart sank, and the guilt for ruining Noah's pen quadrupled. I wasn't exactly well-off. My parents kept a tight leash on my recital earnings, and the only reason they'd approved of Westcroft was the scholarship I'd received.

There was no way my side-gig of tutoring kids in piano would pay for such a work of art. The sessions were sporadic, and that money went straight to food... and coffee. How was I supposed to afford a pen that cost more than all my shoes added together?

A soft click of a key in the door interrupted my musings, and my roommate strolled in, soaked in a post-workout sweat.

Teresa Ruiz was a force to be reckoned with. Her 5'10" frame made me feel like a hobbit at 5'2", and she somehow fit in three workouts a day during summer courses while I considered a walk to the cafeteria a hike. It didn't help my self-esteem that not only was the girl an All-American soccer star who played a handful of other sports on the side, but she was majoring in Criminal Justice *just in case* the National Women's Soccer League didn't work out.

And to think last night I'd been proud of twisting both sides of an Oreo apart without breaking up the creme in the middle.

It was double-stuffed, to be fair, but I digress.

"Hey, Emma." Teresa smiled as she tossed her gym bag to the floor and kicked off her sneakers. Our dorm was a modest double room with two twin beds on opposite walls, matching dressers, tiny desks we never used, and two bookcases already cluttered with knickknacks. The shared closet was smaller than the one my mother used for her scarf collection, and the room perpetually smelled of honey berry hula Febreze to cover up what we suspected was moldy carpet, but it was more of a home than Kansas ever was. "Did I hear you yelling about buying penises?"

I blinked back at her. How thin were the walls in this joint?

"I wish that's what I was replacing. Then I'd be getting a bargain," I said, grumbling as I scrolled through the list of pens for sale. But then I would've had to do something to the original one to replace it.

Great, now I was thinking about teeth marks on Noah's—

"Well, aren't you grouchy today?" Teresa laughed and pulled out the ponytail her dark brown hair usually lived in. My own blonde locks reached past my shoulders and couldn't decide if they were curly or straight, but Teresa had at least four inches and a bucketload of shine on my hair. "Let me guess, the coffee cart was out of sugar?"

Little did she know, I carried individual sugar packets in my backpack just in case *that* atrocity ever happened again.

"No. I'm just low on cash and letting myself wallow for a bit." I snapped the secondhand laptop shut instead of giving in to my growing desire to hurl it across the room.

"Low on cash, you say?" she asked with a smug-sounding hum. "Maybe you shouldn't have left your backpack on the floor so much."

A purse on the floor is money out the door.

I sent her an unimpressed look before glaring at my bag sitting innocently on the floor, but my gut was yelling the same thing. What if I'd done this to myself? It was stupid to test that superstition. What did I have to gain from it? "It's considered poor sportsmanship to rub things in, just so you know."

"Oh, I wouldn't dream of it. Have you checked the job posts on campus?" She slipped on a pair of flip-flops and grabbed her shower caddy. "Or I could ask Mr. Everton if he has an open spot in his catering crew. His pay isn't great, but it'd be fun to work together."

It took effort not to grimace. Mr. Everton was a caterer Teresa worked for on weekends when she didn't have a game scheduled, but the hospitality industry wasn't my cup of coffee.

"You know how clumsy I can be. The last thing I wanna do is spill champagne or snails all over a guest." A flashback of tripping in front of Noah bombarded my sensitive memory, and I wished it wasn't frowned upon to donate perfectly good underwear to Goodwill. Maybe I would just burn it instead.

"First of all, we're not catering the Oscars," she said with a laugh, heading for the door. "There's some ritzy stuff occasionally, but the majority is birthday parties and class reunions. Besides, we can just put you on buffet duty."

I glanced at my discarded laptop, knowing there was still an open tab with a picture of a super expensive pen laughing at my face.

"Let me think about it," I said. I used my big toe to nudge the pink ankle sock off my foot. Teresa shrugged before disappearing out the door, and I fell back against my pillow in defeat.

Catering didn't pay much, but it was more than I had now.

"Ninety-nine freaking dollars." I sighed in dismay. "I'm never questioning a superstition again."

I wondered how Noah Kincaid felt about payment plans.

A Quiz

WEDNESDAY ARRIVED with a brilliant blue sky to welcome my next Music Theory class. Breakfast was off the table again, as I hadn't trusted my stomach to keep it down.

I'd arrived early and laid claim to a seat in the front. Being so focused on staying far away from Noah, I barely avoided sitting right next to a certain doe-eyed Charlie Davenport.

Just like Monday, the guy I was indebted to strolled through the door with barely a minute to spare. My spine straightened in reflex as I took in his getup, which was as tasteful as the last time we crossed paths. White dress shirt, navy blazer, and shiny brown loafers. He took a seat four rows away without even a glance my direction.

Fortunately, I was able to pay attention during this lecture. Professor Slade put us into small groups to discuss the composers that influenced our own playing, and I earned more than a few eye rolls when I mentioned Claude Debussy. It was painfully cliché, but *Clair de lune* resonated with me early as a child. I'd found a comfort in the piece that was warmer than any lullaby, and it'd quickly become my equivalent to any other child's security blanket.

All it took was one concert my family attended on vacation where we heard Oliver Bishop—a young prodigy turned piano god —play Debussy's *La Mer*. He'd opened a door for me with that song.

Debussy's style was so heavily sensory-focused that goose bumps enveloped my arms any time I listened to his work. After months of begging my parents and getting nowhere, I practiced in secret and played back what I could remember by ear.

The subterfuge didn't last long, but being on the receiving end of my father's ire was worth it when my parents allowed me to play Debussy.

Clair de lune was the crowd-pleaser and the reason my father accepted my new obsession. It provided a soothing balm during decidedly brutal recitals.

When I'd had a particularly rough day—when Father yelled himself hoarse between lessons, Mother *forgot* to set my plate at dinner for the fourth time that week, or when my father decided words didn't send enough of a message—I would play *Reverie*. It never failed to work some sort of magic, warming me from the inside out until my worries melted away with the chords.

And on rare days, the ones where everyone got along and I didn't need to force my smile—when family actually meant something more than public relations and people who drove me to recitals, or a father who made me practice until the sun rose because I missed *one* stupid note—I would play *Arabesque*. My favorite.

I didn't share all of this with the group, of course. They were too busy trying to one-up each other by naming composers so scarcely known that their pieces were the equivalent of made-for-TV movies. Instead, I focused on doodling a cupcake in the corner of my notebook and tried not to notice the abysmal quality of my writing tool.

Now that I'd seen how the other half lived, my little blue pen left a lot to be desired. It only worked half of the time, and it tended to smudge on parts of the paper without rhyme or reason.

But I'd say that wasn't too shabby for a fifteen-cent pen.

Halfway through class, Slade called us back to our seats. Blaise walked across the front of the room and smiled much too happily as she handed small stacks of paper to each row of desks. This couldn't be good.

"On Monday, I mentioned this is a highly intensive program, and we have neither the time nor resources to help students who lag behind," Slade said. "Music Theory isn't for everyone, and some of you, frankly, aren't cut out for it. Now that you've helped your classmates understand why you're here, it's time to show *me* what you can handle. Blaise is passing out your first quiz."

The boy in front of me handed me a stack of papers, and I grabbed one before passing them back. Clicking my pen, I scanned the first page of questions with a smile. It looked easy enough.

"These questions cover theories and terms you should already be familiar with as a pianist. You have thirty minutes to complete this quiz," Slade said as he surveyed the room with sharp eyes. "If anyone fails, I strongly recommend you postpone taking this class until you've built a solid foundation."

A sliver of unease crept up my spine, and I nibbled on the end of my cheap pen. Dropping the class meant losing my scholarship, and that definitely wasn't an option.

The first section of basic notation was a breeze, and putting dynamics in the correct order from quietest to loudest was child's play. The second section was tougher, with diagrams of harmonic intervals. I tapped my pen against my lower lip, wishing I hadn't zoned out every time my piano teacher back in Kansas opened her mouth. This stuff never made sense to me, though. When it came to music, I liked keeping things simple. If I heard a piece I liked, I'd fiddle around with the keys until I could replicate it. It was a sound strategy that'd gotten me this far. I never had to mess with the boring technical side of piano.

Slade's quiz was on a whole other level. Skipping over the third section—which must've been written by aliens—I flipped to the last page. Short-answer questions on music analysis stared back at me, and I swallowed hard. How was I supposed to analyze someone else's work on a piece of paper? Either I'd feel something when listening to it, or I wouldn't. This wasn't what music was about for me.

I sucked in a deep breath and scribbled down my first impressions of the examples before making a few educated guesses on the third section. Thirty minutes later, I was one of the last students to hand my quiz to Blaise. That didn't sit well in my stomach.

"Your homework is posted online, and I expect everyone to have the reading completed before Friday. That'll be all," Professor Slade announced at the end of class. I lingered as nerves pinballed around my stomach at the thought of confronting Noah about his pen—before realizing he'd already left.

Well, there went my opportunity to ask about a payment plan.

But the nerves were persistent, and I decided to rip off the Band-Aid by approaching our teacher's podium, where Professor Slade gathered his papers and talked to Blaise.

He looked up and raised an expectant eyebrow.

I offered a hesitant smile, not wanting to overdo it even though it felt like I was in the presence of a renowned celebrity. "Hi. I'm Emma Fox."

He checked his watch before his hawklike eyes took my measure through horn-rimmed glasses. "And how can I help you, Miss Fox?"

I leaned against a desk in the front row, hoping it looked nonchalant. "I was curious about that quiz we took. Just wondering when we'll get them back? I'm not feeling too confident about mine."

Slade cleared his throat and held a hand out to his side. "Miss Rousseau, if you would?"

Blaise stepped closer, brushing back her auburn curls and shuffling through a pile of papers before handing one to the professor. "Here you go, sir."

Slade ducked his head and pushed up his glasses as he skimmed the page. I shifted my weight, feeling my palm get clammy against the desk's wooden surface. My heart dropped with each millimeter his frown deepened as he read.

He flipped through the pages for a torturous minute, putting me at risk of an ulcer, before sighing and fixing me with a hard stare. "Forgive me for being blunt, but your answers on the first page indicate that you *have* indeed played piano before. Is that correct, Miss Fox?"

My cheeks warmed at his patronizing tone, and I wanted to die from mortification. "Yes, I've played."

He flipped the pages closed and set the quiz down atop his stack of papers. "The other sections show a severe lack of understanding. Didn't your high school program include Music Theory?"

"I wasn't involved in any school music programs. I only took one required class—choir. My piano lessons were outside of school."

"And none involved learning these terms?"

I bit my lip, vaguely recalling my old piano teacher droning on about things I didn't care about. "Not exactly."

Slade sighed and traced one of his thick eyebrows with a finger. "These include fundamentals you'll need in order to follow my curriculum."

"I realize that, but I know I'll get it," I said, not needing to fake my confidence as I held his gaze. "I just don't have much practice with composing, so I've never really needed to learn this stuff. I was unprepared. It won't happen again."

"Well, I hope that's true, because the knowledge shown here barely qualifies as an *F*."

Ice filled my veins, combating the fire burning my cheeks. An *F*? I'd never gotten an *F* before in my life. And what did he mean by *barely qualifies*—was there something below an *F*?

I let loose a long breath as my stomach sank. "Oh, okay. That's... not so great. I was definitely hoping for a different letter there; preferably higher on the alphabet."

Professor Slade simply raised a thick brow.

"I can play, Professor. Just put me behind a piano, and you'll hear what I can do—"

He waved a hand. "That's the last thing I'm concerned with. Theory is about the study of music and the fundamentals of building it. Understanding the composition methods, not just running in and pressing keys. When you perform your duet, I won't be grading even a single point on how *well* you play. This isn't the class for that. You'll be evaluated on the techniques you utilize to compose the piece and how well you show your understanding of the material."

I was at a loss for words and bit my cheek as he sighed and pointed at the papers. "This quiz showed me you aren't prepared for my curriculum, Miss Fox. I strongly recommend postponing this class until next year and using the time to take a course we offer on fundamentals."

Postpone the class? My teeth dug into my cheek a bit too far as panic set in, and I winced at the sharp sting. "But I need this class for the music program. If I push it back... I just can't do that. It's against the rules of my scholarship."

Slade nodded, straightening his brown tweed suit jacket. "I can't force you to drop the class, but it would be a disservice to my other students to spend valuable time getting you up to speed when they're already there. Miss Rousseau holds tutoring sessions twice a week, but I'm afraid it'll take too long for her to catch you up this semester."

"Then I'll learn it myself and put in extra time. I know this looks pretty bad, but I'm a fast learner." I waved at the papers in his hand. "*That* is not an accurate indication of my skill."

Slade leaned back and looked me over. I stood straighter on instinct, as if that would help.

"Let's see how fast of a learner you are, then," he said. "You can retake the quiz on Friday."

My lips parted. "This Friday?"

"The day after Thursday," he said absently before walking from the podium to his desk and sliding some folders into a briefcase.

I swallowed back a protest for more time and forced myself to nod. If holing myself up in the library for forty-eight hours was what needed to happen, then that was what would happen. "Thank you, Professor."

"It won't be the same questions, so don't try looking up the answers and memorizing them." Slade gave me a pointed look. "Another *F*, and it'll be extremely difficult to salvage your grade."

At risk of turning into a bobblehead, I kept nodding enthusiastically. "I understand, sir. Thank you again, and I won't let you down."

He grasped the briefcase with a sigh. "You won't, because the only person you'll be letting down if you fail is you."

He handed my quiz back to Blaise, and they walked out together while I trudged back to my desk to gather my things. My shoes dragged like they were made of lead. I kept replaying Slade's smooth baritone voice over and over in my head as he told me I'd gotten an *F*.

An *F!*

This called for a pick-me-up, but it was too early for a cheeseburger Happy Meal. I settled for the next best thing: visiting the music room across the hall to fully distract myself with the piano stored there.

And if I happened to brush up on some fundamentals that would help me with the next quiz, all the better.

Westcroft's music room was the size of an average classroom. Reserved for students in the school's music programs, it was a hidden-away practice room that required badge entry to keep out undesirables.

The room easily would've fit forty students comfortably at desks. But instead, there were rows of chairs set up for a practice choir, a teacher's desk, and a smattering of instruments and music stands. One lonely orange couch sat off to the side next to a small mountain of sound equipment. Bookcases filled with music sheets, books, and binders lined the walls. The main event was the black baby grand piano sitting off-center from the rest, bathed in sunlight.

I peeked down both sides of the hallway while swiping my card. The subterfuge made me feel like a secret agent on a mission, but a loud chime interrupted from my backpack. I fumbled for my phone, and my lip curled back when I recognized the email's sender—my mother.

Dear Emmaline,

How was Music Theory this morning? I spoke with Rita in Admissions, and she mentioned you aren't signed up for a piano independent study this semester. She must be mistaken, but please verify.

I do hope you're keeping up with your piano practice. Your father still isn't convinced you should take the time off for college, but he's distracted with a new merger at work for the moment.

Call me when you read this,
   Mother

.   .   .

My jaw dropped, and I froze on the spot. She'd called the Admissions Office? That was so... *so* beyond inappropriate!

I scowled at my phone before stuffing it in my bag and shoving the door open. I'd worry about that later. There were bigger fish to fry.

There would be plenty of time before Friday to hit up the library. Right now, I needed to remind myself why I was taking something as dreadful as Music Theory in the first place. I needed to play.

What I didn't expect was to see a certain pen connoisseur I owed money to. Noah stood next to the corner of bookshelves, flipping through one of its binders. He glanced up as I stepped over the threshold, before looking back at the binder like I didn't exist.

Well, that did wonders for a girl's self-esteem. I hovered uncertainly, eyeing the piano sitting innocently beside him before sucking up my courage.

"Fun class today," I said to break the silence as I let go of the door. It clicked shut behind me, the sound echoing ominously in the still room. "Slade sure knows his stuff."

Noah flipped to another page, and my confidence wavered.

"So, what kind of pen costs ninety-nine dollars?" I asked, before hastily adding, "Plus tax."

"The kind that I should've known better than to lend out," Noah said flatly without lifting his gaze.

Ouch.

"Does it have magical powers or something?" I nibbled on the tip of my thumbnail before catching myself and pulling my hand down. "Or come with a membership to some secret society?"

"If it did, do you really think I'd be allowed to tell you?" he asked, earning a stare. Did he just make a joke? "The only magical power it holds is very fine quality."

"If the quality was so great, you'd think it would be more dent-resistant," I said under my breath as I traced the hem of my shirt with a finger.

Noah snorted and flipped the page. "I'm afraid the creators may not have accounted for such determined canines having their way with the pen," he said, but I caught one side of his lips twitching as he scanned the page, and it gave me hope. "Or maybe they just didn't account for you."

Another joke? I let out a slow breath, not wanting to push my luck.

"What kind of college student carries around fancy pens? Aren't you afraid of getting mugged?"

His lips definitely flirted with a smile at that. "There's a very short list of things I'm afraid of, but I can't say mugging made the cut."

I sighed, itching at the side of my nose. It must've been nice not having to carry pepper spray around in your backpack.

"Listen, Noah. I'm here on scholarship," I explained, cutting to the chase. "And not just because they like the way I play piano, but because I literally couldn't afford to buy a single textbook, let alone pay tuition. But don't worry, I'm going to pay for the pen."

"I don't need your money." Noah waved a hand dismissively, as if girls chowing down on his yacht-equivalent pen was an everyday occurrence.

I blinked back at him, not understanding how someone could be so blasé about this. If a stranger chewed on something as trivial as my fifteen-cent pen, I'd want to punch them in the face.

Wait—could that be a sign of undiagnosed anger issues?

I cleared my throat, feeling like a broken record. "That's great, but I *do* intend to pay you back. I just can't do it all at once. Honestly, I've got about seventeen dollars to my name right now."

Seventeen dollars already allocated toward food and my coffee budget.

He had that look on his face again—the one that warned me he was going to turn down my money and probably make me feel like dirt because he could so easily write off a pen that cost more than my nicest dress—so I held up a hand before he could unwittingly degrade me further.

"Hold your horses. I was just wondering if maybe... well, okay, this makes me feel really poor—but maybe we could set up some sort of payment plan?" I asked hopefully and offered him my best smile. "I'm not very liquid right now, but I could pay you back ten or maybe fifteen dollars every week? At that rate, it'll be settled by Thanksgiving."

Two and a half months to pay a guy back for his pen. Did this sound ridiculous to anyone else?

"I don't need—"

"Please stop telling me you don't need the money. I ruined your pen, and I'm paying you back for it."

Noah raised a brow, and the sharp line of his jaw tensed. "All right. If you want to pay me back—fine. If you don't, that's also fine. But you've apologized enough for an honest mistake. Now, I need to be somewhere, so the room's all yours."

At a loss, I nodded and shrugged in tandem. He slipped the binder into his messenger bag before slinging the bag over his shoulder and making to walk past me.

Chewing on my lip, I glanced back at the empty spot on the shelf where he'd taken the binder from. "You're not really supposed to take those with—"

Noah's raised brow cut off any further comment, and I bit my tongue as he brushed past me. When the door clicked shut behind him, I sank onto the rigid piano bench.

Out of all the pens in the world, why did I have to chew on his? I was just grateful Music Theory didn't have assigned seats.

A Cupcake

Dear Diary,

Why is it so hard to make money?

Seriously. I ate a Pop-Tart for lunch today, and I'm convinced my stomach will stage a revolt if I don't give it proper nourishment soon. My scholarship covers the bare minimum—tuition and housing. Yet my mother won't even entertain the idea of giving me access to my recital earnings to buy something as basic as food. "It was your decision to go off to college, Emmaline. This wouldn't be an issue if you stayed home with us."

Who exactly decided it would be a good idea to create trust funds people can't access until they turn twenty-five? I want names.

Then I was supposed to tutor the Sterlings' son in

piano this week, but they cancelled because it overlapped with his riding lesson. That's forty dollars I'll never see.

At this rate, there's no chance I'll pay Noah back. ~~Unless I stop buying coffee?~~

Wait. Pretend I never wrote that. How do I erase pen?

Sincerely Starving,
Emma

IMAGINE my surprise when my History of Opera professor called Noah Kincaid's name during our first night class Thursday and he was nowhere to be found.

Then when Music Theory rolled around Friday morning and the guy I was obligated to repay was conveniently missing, I entertained the possibility that my overactive imagination had fabricated him out of thin air. Common sense didn't stop me from going straight to WebMD and reading up on schizophrenia when I got back to my dorm after retaking Slade's quiz.

I'd spent most of my free time the past two days—minus a few hours distracted by games on my phone and a hot new crime show—studying for that quiz, and Slade decided to make the questions five times harder on the retake. It was painful to get through, and my concentration was shot for the weekend.

Or at least, that was how I explained why I'd agreed to tag along on Teresa's catering gig when she claimed Mr. Everton could use the extra hands.

"We're not expected for another twenty minutes, but it won't hurt to get there early for your first night," she said while rifling through her side of the closet. I hovered beside her and picked lint off the black shirt she'd just handed me. "I picked up a uniform that should fit you. Just make sure to put your hair up and wear black shoes."

My nose scrunched as I took in my meager selection of footwear. "They don't have to be heels, right?"

"Not unless you want to trip straight into the buffet table and get fired before the night is over." She snorted before pulling on her own simple black shirt. I quickly tugged mine on, keeping my back turned away from Teresa so she didn't see my father's handi-work. The scar on my shoulder blade was a nice reminder of what he thought of second place at recitals.

"Good call." I slipped on a pair of black ballet flats. While not as practical for walking around with food all night, I didn't exactly have combat boots lying around. "What kind of party is it?"

"One full of five-year-old terrors on sugar highs." She rolled her eyes. "Upper-class birthday parties are a great test run, because the parents are happy as long as food is there for the kids and booze is there for them. They couldn't care less about professionalism."

Kids? My stomach churned. It was safe to say that children and I didn't exactly get along. I'd put a minimum age requirement on the students I tutor after a three-year-old went all *Exorcist* on me when I tried to teach her *Chopsticks*.

"Let's go!" Teresa practically cheered, before I shuffled consid-erably less cheerfully behind her.

I wondered if there was time to stop by the coffee cart.

It didn't take long to see Mr. Everton ran a tight ship. We'd loaded the catering van with food, driven to suburbia, promptly unloaded the food into a kitchen, set up six buffet tables, and gone over assignments, all in less than forty minutes.

Mr. Everton had assigned me buffet duty—something both

Teresa and I had hoped for—and I'd spent the last thirty minutes refilling macaroni and gourmet dino-nuggets.

"How's it going over here?" Teresa asked as she rounded back from the adults' tables, weaving her way through a game of short-people tag. I had to actively remind myself to keep my mouth closed, because the hosts' backyard was gorgeous—filled with paper lanterns, a humongous pool, *three* hot tubs, two tennis courts, and a freaking garden maze.

"Well, the food has remained off the floor, my feet haven't tripped over themselves, and the sky hasn't fallen yet. I'd say it's going pretty well," I said with a proud nod. I scooped another helping of mac and cheese into the silver chafer. "How're the parents doing?"

Teresa grimaced. "Two drinks away from Margaritaville."

A shudder racked through me. "I don't think I'll ever get that drunk."

"You haven't even been tipsy," she countered with a snort before leaning down to pry open the cooler and dish out a few juice boxes to add to my award-winning table. "*Yet.* Just wait until I get you to a frat party. If you can get past the questionable music and people humping on and off the dance floor, it's worth it just for the free kegs."

"That sounds awful." I frowned, hoping she never actually tried to drag me to one. Another date with Charlie Davenport sounded more pleasant.

"I've only been to one so far with the soccer team, but it wasn't so bad." Teresa hummed, and she gave me a thoughtful look. "Even if you end up hating it, at least you tried, right?"

The same could be said for jumping off a bridge, but I kept my mouth shut and zoned in on arranging the dino-nuggets to look like the dinosaurs were climbing out of the chafer. Surely a frat party wouldn't *kill* me. I hoped.

Teresa sighed and balanced the tray against her hip. "Fine, I guess I'll have to talk you into it later. Wanna help me bring out some desserts?"

"Yes!" My head shot up with an eager grin. Cake at birthday parties may have been a given, but I hadn't caught a single glimpse of one yet. "Yes, *please*."

"No samples, Emma." Her eyes narrowed in warning before she led the way toward the house. I kept up, hot on her heels through the back door and wondering if we were lucky enough to have an ice cream cake. Surely the kids were stuffed from eating twice their body weight in dino-nuggets, and now they wouldn't have enough room for sweets. Right?

Mr. Everton's voice boomed as we passed the kitchen. "Bring those knives over here! I don't want someone knocking them off the counter and taking off a toe. Where's the rest of the Riesling? Are we out already?"

"This way," Teresa whispered, pointing toward the dining room as we passed a frazzled server.

Turning the corner, I had to suck in my stomach to hold in a gasp of awe.

Right in the center of the table, a princess-themed three-layer cake dominated the show. It was elegant and covered in roses and *very* pink, but it only held my attention for the initial glance. Because around that fantasy cake?

Cupcakes upon cupcakes upon cupcakes.

There must've been dozens of them lined up beside each other, stacked over four trays high. All fitting the pink-and-white theme, but with different toppings like cherries and Oreos and sprinkles.

I wiped a bit of drool from the corner of my mouth.

Teresa whistled in approval. "Damn, that's a lot of cupcakes."

Heaven. This was absolute, honest-to-God heaven.

"Come get me when the party is over," I heard myself say as my legs took a purposeful step closer to the mouthwatering morsels before me. "I'll be here."

"Nope! No way. Don't even *think* about it." She wrapped her fingers around my arm and tugged in the opposite direction of my babies. "No way am I getting in trouble for recruiting the girl who ate her way through half of the desserts. I'll knock you out first."

"Is there a problem here, girls?" The new voice cut through my anticipatory haze, and the cupcake spell was broken as we both spun around to see Mr. Everton wiping his burly hands with a wrinkled dish towel. The middle-aged man towered over both of us, his green eyes sharp. A monstrous brown beard outshone his equally thick mane of hair. He could easily be mistaken for a lumberjack with his blue flannel shirt and broad shoulders.

Narrowed eyes noted Teresa's hand on my arm, and Mr. Everton's beard twitched.

"No, we were just getting started on bringing the desserts out," Teresa explained. Her hand dropped from my shirt like she'd been burned.

"Don't worry about that. Seamus and Trent will take care of them." He shook his head before jerking his chin toward the hallway. "But we could use some help with the napkins and utensils."

"We're on it." Teresa nodded before hustling out of the room. I lingered, unable to stop myself from sparing one more wistful look over my shoulder at the lonesome cupcakes. My taste buds ached.

The older man followed my gaze and grunted. "You're Emma, right?"

"Yes, sir," I said, trying to focus on my new boss instead of the sweet smell of sugar calling out to me like a siren from the table.

He gave me a considering look. "You like cupcakes?"

I snorted. "Does a fish like water?"

Thin lips twitched into the semblance of a smile, and my toe scuffed against the hardwood floor as he glanced back at Cupcake Mountain.

"I think it's just about time for your fifteen-minute break," he said before crossing his arms over the flannel shirt. "Why don't you run down to the van and find the extra Tupperware of cupcakes for the staff in the back? Help yourself to one."

It took effort not to let my jaw drop. "Wait, really?"

"Really."

"Thanks, Mr. Everton!" I beamed and made a beeline to the door before he changed his mind.

"Only one!" his sharp voice called after me.

Warm evening air kissed my cheeks as I heaved the massive door open. Mr. Everton's van was sitting inconspicuously next to the neighbor's fence. I forced my walk to stay casual so the neighbors wouldn't think I was some small-time burglar looking for easy catering prey.

The van's back doors were trickier to open than one would expect, with more handles and levers than any door should need. But I managed to pry one open far enough to peek inside—feeling like a badass spy—and... *there.*

Two Tupperware containers sat innocently beside a case of iced tea, neither of which could hide their sweet aroma from tickling up my nose. Without further ado, I grabbed the nearest one and licked up a dollop of sweet pink buttercream icing before stumbling away from the van. My head rocked back from the individual sugary bursts overwhelming my unprepared taste buds, and both eyes drooped closed. Pure heaven. The icing was a treat in itself, but I wanted the full effect. With a deep breath to prepare, I opened my jaw to unforeseen lengths and went in for the kill.

"Whoa! Slow down there, cupcake!" The urgent voice startled the stuffing out of me, and I spun around midbite.

Maybe the icing was laced with fast-acting LSD, because I'm pretty sure I was hallucinating a guy that'd walked straight out of a magic show.

A red cape billowed out behind him, and an honest-to-God top hat sat atop short chestnut-brown hair. The only things missing were a magic wand and white rabbit.

"Huh?" I said inarticulately around the cupcake. I had an

excuse, though, because the guy was so handsome my brain stalled. He had cheekbones that could cut glass. Skin kissed by the sun. Wide eyeliner-framed eyes, and a chin that could run for president. He was straight out of my dreams.

The new arrival jogged across the driveway with a growing grin —blinding pearly whites, of course—as I experimentally blinked my eyes.

Yep. He was still there.

"Not you," he dismissed me easily, focusing a little too intensely on my mouth. There was a twinkle in his eyes that reminded me of Christmas morning or the last day of school. "I was referring to this little beauty."

Nimble fingers nabbed the precious cupcake out of both my hand and mouth with such finesse I almost didn't believe it was happening. If I hadn't seen it with my own eyes—or LSD-inspired imagination, as I hadn't ruled that out yet—then I doubt I'd have felt the cupcake being taken at all.

"You can't just rush into someone's mouth like that. They need to appreciate every granule of your sugary goodness," he lectured while giving my cupcake a stern look.

I gaped, recalling my earlier web search on schizophrenia and deciding it couldn't hurt to get a doctor's opinion. Hallucinations were one of the main symptoms.

Then I watched in a dumbfounded mixture of revulsion and fascination as this cape-wearing baked-goods thief proceeded to make love to my cupcake with his mouth.

His tongue eased out before slowly licking across the same dollop of buttercream icing I'd had my own tongue against just moments earlier. In third grade, we would've considered that kissing.

From the way his eyes turned half-lidded as he took the slowest bite known to man—with a moan that made my toes curl—I'd go ahead and say we might as well have cleared second base.

"Oh my God." I wasn't sure if I breathed it or prayed it, but nothing about this felt real. Maybe Teresa had knocked me out when I'd tried to attack the cupcakes, and this was a concussion-inspired dream.

My borderline moan snapped Mr. Magician out of his baked-goods-lovefest as he finished off the last bite and sucked on a piece of the wrapper. His gaze shot up, and he had the audacity to look surprised that I was standing there to witness such an intimate scene. But realization hit as he lowered the empty wrapper and gave me his full, far less risqué attention.

"Actually, the name's Finn," he said, accompanied by an icing-covered smile. Playful green eyes took in my face, and something told me this was honestly the first time he'd really taken notice of me since confiscating his new lover. "But you can call me whatever you want, as long as it keeps including 'oh' and 'my.' 'God' was a nice touch, too."

I was beginning to wonder if arrogant males were native to Southern California.

"What about 'cupcake' and 'thief'?" I asked calmly while eyeing the empty wrapper in his hand and trying to remind myself that there were other cupcakes in the world. It wasn't worth getting attached to just one. "Would those be suitable?"

"Oh, shot to the heart." Finn clutched his chest theatrically. Smiling eyes gleamed down at me. "Dessert *and* the most flattering of pet names. Is your name, by any chance, 'The Perfect Woman'?"

My blood boiled.

"My name is none of your business. The only thing you should be worried about right now is that you stole my cupcake," I said, trying not to raise my voice but feeling entirely validated in my growing anger. "A cupcake that I was very, *very* much looking forward to."

"As you should have." Finn smiled before licking the last crumbs of fluffy white cake off his fingers. I wanted to cry.

But another part of me was itching to lick them off myself. I blamed my sweet tooth. Or hormones. Maybe both.

"I'm so happy you enjoyed it," I said flatly. I leaned back against the van in defeat as I tried to recall the difference between self-defense and cold-blooded murder. Maybe I could claim he was attacking me instead of reaching for the cupcake? "How... how did it taste?"

I didn't want to punish myself further, but I had to know.

The handsome magician grinned, so open and happy that I kind of wanted to punch him in the face. "Absolutely divine. Possibly the best cupcake I've ever had in my life."

Definitely wanted to punch him.

I settled for frowning. "Yeah, well, you have icing on your lips."

"Really?" Finn's brow rose, and he leaned forward as his eyes dipped to my mouth. "Care to help me get it off?"

Anger overrode the hormones.

"Oh, so *now* you're willing to share some of the cupcake?"

He shrugged innocently, but there was nothing virtuous about the glint in his eyes. "What can I say? I'm a giver."

"You are absolutely shameless," I said with a half-hearted scoff. But he was more impish than creepy, which made part of me want to come out and play. "Don't let the cupcake overhear you talking to me like that. You might hurt her feelings."

"Don't worry, she's in a better place now." His grin was all male as he patted his stomach. "And I think her last memories were fond ones."

"Yes, I'm sure being licked to death is a wonderful way to go," I said. Then the words caught up to me and my cheeks heated. I cleared my throat. "What are you doing here?"

"Just in the neighborhood for a little magic show." Finn lifted the rim of his hat and pulled a deck of cards out from under the rim before wincing. "But turns out I had the wrong house. My party's down the street a bit." He sighed and glanced around. "I was on my way out. Rabbits don't pull themselves out of hats, you know."

"Just like cupcakes don't make themselves disappear," I said with a touch of bitterness.

One side of Finn's mouth quirked up, and he stuck his hands in his pockets. "Maybe I should stick around. We could make a few more disappear."

My heart thudded loudly in agreement with him, and I cleared my throat to tamp it back down.

"Nah, you better get a move on. I called 911 to report a burglary while you were busy chowing down," I lied, using a hand to shoo him off. Finn smiled.

"I've never had a girl call the cops on me before," he said, sounding thoughtful. With a tilt of his head—pushing the hat back up when it started to fall—he slowly walked backward across the driveway. "I think I like it."

"Maybe I'll write to you in prison, then."

"Maybe I'll find you when I get out. Does my pen pal have a name?"

"She did before you stole her—"

"Cupcake."

"Yeah."

His bright eyes danced before he pivoted on the spot and strolled away. I told myself not to look at his butt.

I didn't listen.

"Oh, and Cupcake?"

My eyes shot up at his call. Finn stopped on the grass, half turning with a smile that showed the tiniest hint of dimples. Of course he had dimples. "You weren't wrong about that 'thief' part earlier."

"I wasn't?" I frowned and scooted to the side so I was blocking the back doors to the van. If he thought he could steal more cupcakes and stick me with the blame after Mr. Everton said I could only have *one*, he was sorely mistaken. I used to watch inspirational sports movies as a kid, and if there was one thing I'd learned, it was the underdog always won.

"In the magic industry, I have what some might call sticky fingers," Finn said. He wiggled all ten fingers at me. "It goes with the whole sleight of hand thing. But I just want to warn you, because once I set my eye on something, I tend to take it."

His words made my hackles rise, but I put on my best innocent face. "I guess it's a good thing I'm fresh out of cupcakes, then."

His grin turned downright devilish, and my lips parted as he gave me a once-over. "That's never a good thing. Something else caught my eye tonight, though."

Oh dear.

And with a parting wink, he jogged around the neighbor's fence—disappearing before I could do anything but gape at his forwardness.

And to think I'd been worried about this job being boring.

A Mother

IT WAS safe to say the rest of my weekend was much less eventful than the week before. No Noah sightings. No cupcake thieves. No unintentional panty flashing—or *intentional*, just to make that clear. Just me, Teresa, and a couple dozen hours spent down a crime show rabbit hole while screening calls from my mother.

I think there was food involved. Possibly.

There was definitely coffee.

On the plus side, I was sixteen dollars closer to replacing Noah's pen. After setting aside money for meals and coffee, plus failing to walk away from a few dozen delicacies in the dorm lobby's vending machine, I hid the rest of the money in my sock drawer where one of my green polka-dot socks was now officially known as The Noah Fund.

Teresa's groan woke me on Monday morning. "Emma, if you don't shut that stupid alarm off, I'm going to shove it down your throat."

"Oh." I blinked through the fog of sleep, barely registering the sound blaring from my phone. I heaved a breath for strength before leaning over to the nightstand. "That would be unnecessarily violent."

"Mondays were made for violence," she said, voice muffled by her pillow.

My fingers fumbled for the phone, expecting to hit the snooze button, only to end up accepting an incoming call with *Queen of All that is Evil* flashing across the screen.

"Crap." I sprung up in bed and pushed my rat nest of hair out of my face. My Mr. Elephant plushie went flying off the bed from the movement, and I winced.

"Mother?" I croaked into the phone.

"Emmaline," my mother said with all her usual decorum. Charlotte Fox was a proud woman. She'd been raised on a farm in the Midwest, but one would've never guessed if they saw her garden parties and daily brunches now. She'd somehow wrangled herself a marriage with one of the banking elite, and milking cows was so far back in her past, she hadn't consumed dairy in decades. "You sound tired. Are you staying up too late?"

"It's not even eight o'clock here. I'm two hours behind your time zone."

She made a dismissive sound, and I could perfectly picture her twice-done nose turning up. "How's your class with Atticus Slade going?"

I rolled my eyes. "Did your new friend Rita in Admissions tell you he's my professor?"

"Yes, and she sent me a copy of your schedule. His assistant told me there was a quiz last week."

"You're talking to Slade's assistant?" I wasn't sure whether I was mortified or furious.

"Well, what am I supposed to do? He won't respond to my emails." She had the nerve to sound offended, while I could only gape.

"Emails? As in *multiple*?"

She sighed. "Emmaline, your father and I are putting your

prime recital years on hold because you begged to run off and learn from that man. I'm simply making sure this is a worthwhile investment."

"But you can't just email my teacher like that!"

"You're my daughter. Of course I can," she said airily.

I was at a loss for words, and Teresa's brow rose in question.

"Have you secured an independent study with him, yet?" my mother asked.

I stifled a scoff. If only she knew I was failing Slade's class. "That's impossible. He doesn't accept freshmen."

Another sigh filtered through the earpiece, and my eye twitched. "I'm sure there are ways around that."

I closed my eyes and fought to keep my voice even. "Please tell me you're not planning on bribing my teacher. I'll get kicked out of the program."

"I'm saying it's an option." Her tone was a delicate one she used when talking to her precious houseplants, and it grated on my ears. "Now, enough about that. One of the ladies in my garden club said Oliver Bishop is doing a concert in LA in November. Why don't your father and I come visit; we'll invite Atticus and make a night of it?"

Blood rushed to my ears at the mention of my father, and I swallowed around a lump forming in my throat. I was counting on not seeing my father until at least summer, and the thought of inviting my professor to a concert made me want to puke.

"I'll have to let you know," I said to stall. "I'm really busy with school and tutoring."

"It's one night, Emmaline."

My fingers clutched the phone tighter at her patronizing tone. "I know. You two should still go, though. It sounds like fun—"

"Darling, I have to run," she said in a rush. "The landscapers are overwatering my hydrangeas again. Roberto—*hey, Roberto!* What have I told you about—"

The line clicked as she hung up, but my relief was minimal

compared to the worry over her ruining the happy little life I'd made here.

"That sounded nice," Teresa said dryly from her bed.

"My mother is truly one of a kind." I dropped the phone back onto my nightstand and rubbed at my eyes. "At least I'm awake now."

Teresa snorted and rolled over to face me. "I don't know what possessed you to sign up for an 8:00 a.m. class. How have you not dropped it yet?"

"Probably some misplaced childhood crush on an accomplished composer, or the fact that I need it for my major."

"You had a crush on Professor Slade?"

"Had, have. Same thing." I sighed before pushing into a full-body stretch against the sheets. A bone cracked somewhere in my back, and I melted into the mattress. "Though I must admit, the grey hairs have only done him favors."

"Aren't piano players kind of pansies, though? Or pretty lackluster in the romance department, at least? I think I read something about that in Cosmo."

"If a guy can tap out a sonata, it's pretty much guaranteed he's good with his fingers," I said like it was obvious—which it was. Oliver Bishop's handsome face crossed my mind, and I held back an adoring sigh. With how well he played piano, I'd bet my whole scholarship *he* was good with his fingers. "And don't trust Cosmo. They write articles about things like giving your butt a facial."

Seriously. Why would you *ever* want to do that? They were called facials for a reason, not buttals.

Sure, it made your skin feel silky smooth, but it wasn't worth getting avocado in places that avocado should never be.

To be fair, I'd been testing it for scientific purposes, and afterward I made sure to tell my dentist's office that maybe Cosmo wasn't the most appropriate reading material for their waiting room.

Though, I didn't have any excuses for the second time I tried it.

"Well, shoot. Maybe I need to find myself a pianist," Teresa said. "What time does your class get out, again? I can meet you at the cafeteria for breakfast."

I sighed. "Nine o'clock. Right about the time my caffeine high starts fading."

"Seriously? I guess that explains why the coffee cart is always on the opposite side of the quad at nine now," she said with dawning realization. "Which is *so* not fair. For most of the summer, Scott would stay on the south end the whole day and I could stop by on my way to food."

I blinked against the sleep still fogging my eyes, which widened as her words caught up to me.

"Wait a second. You think Scott moved his coffee cart for me?" I asked incredulously as I leaned up to gape at Teresa's groggy face nestled against her pillow.

"I think he would," she said through a yawn. "You're obviously his most consistent customer. I'm surprised they don't make a membership card just for you. *Emma's Earnings*, or something else ridiculous like you."

I was oddly flattered, and I practically floated my way to Music Theory.

A Monday

From the butterflies racing around my stomach, you'd think it was prom night instead of my fourth Music Theory lecture.

Mind you, on prom night I'd been waiting for Eric Hanson—a completely harmless goofball—instead of the decidedly less goofy guy whose pen I'd horribly mutilated beyond recognition.

And yet here I was, double-fisting my favorite caffeinated beverage as I waited awkwardly beside the classroom's open doorway.

Maybe I was being too forward again. Noah very explicitly said he didn't want payment. But there was nothing wrong with a little coffee to sweeten the wait before the unwanted payment I was still going to pay him.

But the last thing I wanted was for Noah to assume me bringing him apology-coffee was my newest strategy in seducing him. It was so silly of him to think I'd been asking him out the other day. I mean, sure, the whole blazer thing he had going on was kind of attractive. And the flecks of gold in his eyes made me feel all warm and gooey. If he happened to ask *me* out, I would probably give it some serious consideration.

But, alas—this was a debt, not a date.

I quickly rubbed the back of my hand across my lips to scrub off the strawberry lip gloss I'd talked myself into wearing this morning, managing to only spill a few drops of coffee. Luckily, that was Noah's cup.

Not a date. Just getting a little kick start on this debt thing. I'm showing initiative.

After all, we were going to spend an hour sitting through a college course together. There wasn't anything romantic about that, *and* that was assuming he'd even sit next to me.

Oh God, what if he felt pressured to sit next to me now that I was waiting for him outside the door like some sort of stalker?

This was a bad idea.

Abort. Abort. Abort.

Whirling around, I hustled into the classroom to find only a handful of open seats left. My plan to abort the mission was quickly foiled when I noticed that each empty seat had another empty one next to it. There was no way Noah wouldn't make assumptions if I was sitting with two cups of coffee and an empty seat next to me. That somehow seemed worse than waiting by the door.

I hustled down the rows before slipping into a particularly squeaky desk in the middle of the room to play it safe. Neutral territory.

Professor Slade gave me a pointed look when the chair squeaked as I settled down, before returning to his papers up front. I sneaked a peek at the door to make sure Noah wasn't moseying into the room as I contemplated hiding the evidence.

After a beat of hesitation, I smoothly slid the regular coffee onto the desk beside me and nudged the cup around until its logo faced the front of the room. Maybe it would just look like the cup of coffee meandered its way into the classroom all on its own. Like a Brave Little Toaster type deal. It wasn't like my name was written on it anywhere.

No one would ever know.

Another beat passed, the toes of my white Keds tapping impatiently against the desk's legs, until I frowned at the coffee cup. Was it still obvious? The other students probably saw me put it there... they might snitch to Noah.

I snatched the coffee back and nibbled on my lower lip while testing its weight in my hand.

This was a stupid idea.

Eyes straying to the classroom clock, I stifled a groan when it showed exactly one minute left before class began. The cup felt impossibly heavier in my hand, and I finally accepted that Noah would find me beyond desperate if he found me bringing him coffee.

I was pathetic.

Glaring at the to-go cup in my hand, I almost missed the guy in question slip into the room. My breath caught, my heartbeat working itself into a frenzy as I waited to see if he'd choose the seat next to mine—but he settled into an open desk in the front without even a glance in my direction.

The butterflies in my stomach weren't sure if they should be relieved or disappointed, but my shoulders deflated a touch.

"Miss Fox, a word before class begins?" Professor Slade called from the front, and I jolted in my seat.

Feeling called out, I may have dragged my feet a little while walking up the center aisle to his desk. "Yes, sir?"

"I graded your retake from Friday," he said, holding up a packet of papers. His voice lowered, and I leaned in to catch it. "I'm afraid I don't have good news."

A bright red *F* glared at me from the top of the page, and my heart lurched into my throat.

"It's a small improvement percentagewise, but you're still not grasping the material," Slade said as he flipped through the packet before pointing out slashes of red covering half of the third page. He met my gaze through horn-rimmed glasses, and the pity swimming in his eyes froze my feet in place. "This isn't a coveted position to be in. I've already given you my recommendation, but the best I can offer is if you can somehow reach and maintain a C average by midterms, you'll have improved enough to get through the semester. If you don't feel that's attainable, it would be best to seek out a different program now rather than later."

I blinked hard to hold back unexpected tears, nodding on autopilot as Slade skimmed through the rest of the quiz. He shared comments that went straight over my head.

I'd failed.

Again.

I was a failure.

My mother's laughter rang through my head as I imagined telling her I'd lost my scholarship. My father's knowing smirk wasn't far behind. They would enjoy this far too much, reveling in my return home. Mother would make some excuse about me getting homesick to her socialite friends, and father would book me for recitals every week. I'd be stuck again.

Slade handed over my quiz when he finished obliterating what little confidence I had left, and I trudged back to my desk with carefully measured breaths. It wouldn't do to burst into tears in front of all my classmates. Pretty sure I'd had nightmares about that before.

I took a sip of my sugar-loaded coffee and slumped back in the chair. My eyes sought out Noah of their own accord, and I officially regretted buying the second cup of coffee when I saw him talking to the beautiful redhead sitting next to him. I did a double take, recognizing Blaise Rousseau, his partner for the duet.

Blaise scooted her seat closer to Noah's desk and reached over to pick up one of his fancy pens. I braced for the impending blowout, but he simply gestured a hand at the pen and said something as she inspected it with a look of admiration. Then she laughed, brushing a bouncy red curl out of her face, and my throat closed up.

What the hell?

Hadn't Noah learned his lesson about lending out expensive writing utensils? I would've thought chew marks the size of Texas would be reason enough to keep his precious pens under lock and key for the rest of eternity.

Blaise laughed again, which only proved that Noah was being purposefully nice, since he wasn't *that* funny. She said something with a smile and twirled the pen around her finger like some sort of incredibly talented pen-wielding circus performer before handing it back to him. My eyes narrowed when their fingers brushed.

I caught myself before a scoff slipped out and snapped my gaze forward to watch Slade take attendance. What did I care if Noah flirted with a girl?

Didn't matter one bit to me.

Nope.

He could flirt with all the girls he wanted to. Especially pretty ones with hair the color of lucky pennies and legs that made mine look like stumps.

I glanced down at the daunting red *F* on my quiz, and my stomach somersaulted in protest. Trying to force down the growing panic, I gripped my coffee like a lifeline and chugged it back.

Bad idea.

Coffee sprayed forward, sideways, and vertically as I got the traitorous cup as far away as possible from my horrified mouth.

That was *not* my coffee.

"Holy mother of crap!"

"*Miss Fox.*" Professor Slade's commanding tone cut through the quiet chatter of the room as the students around me leaned away from the shower. I blanched, scraping tongue against teeth to try to limit the scalding damage to my delicate taste buds. "I ask that you refrain from distracting my class, if it wouldn't be too much trouble."

My face burned hotter than the coffee in my hand, and I shot up from the chair as if my butt was on a fire just as scalding.

Leaving my bag and supplies where they were—sacrifices had to be made—I mumbled an excuse about accidentally grabbing the wrong cup from the coffee cart and needing to return it before flying out the door.

I dunked Noah's cup into the first wastebasket I could find, and my feet kept walking straight ahead of their own accord.

Down the stairs, through the lobby, out the door, and onto the grass in the quad.

I collapsed next to one of the oak trees students enjoyed eating lunch underneath and curled up into a ball of regret on the dew-covered blades.

I was ready for the ground to swallow me whole if it felt so inclined.

What felt like ages later but was probably an hour tops, I lay sprawled across the grass and impatiently waited for a much-needed epiphany.

The one that would say Noah was a stuck-up jerk who *A*, had made no attempt to be nice to me, and *B*, didn't find any of my humor actually humorous.

Which begged the question, why was I trying so hard? What was so special about some guy in my Music Theory class? Was Noah really that attractive?

Yes.

Hands down, he was handsome. There was no denying my level of attraction toward the guy, even if it felt like I was receiving a painfully-slow-thawing cold front in return.

But was it worth the stick seemingly shoved up his slacks-wearing butt?

... Maybe.

"Why do I do this to myself?" I asked under my breath, sliding my arms back and forth across the ground, as if I were making a grass angel instead of just getting grass stains on my clothes. I closed my eyes to the cruel world and mentally relived my coffee catastrophe from upstairs over and over. "He's just a guy. Who cares if he loaned me his pen or made me laugh that one time? If he wants to ride off into the sunset with another girl who touched his pen, more power to him. I'm fine. I wish them and their future piano genius babies the best—"

The clearing of a throat interrupted my quiet ramblings, and I froze mid-angel-making.

I glanced up to let whoever it was know that I wasn't giving up my prime spot on the quad's grass just so they could play Ultimate Frisbee with their frat bros or make out under the tree like adorable little lovebirds while I was destined to be a decrepit old spinster.

My lips froze when I saw Noah Kincaid watching me expectantly from the sidewalk, standing a mere few feet away from my pity party.

Holding two to-go cups of coffee.

Not frowning.

He wasn't smiling either. But still, not frowning. A girl had to take her victories where she could.

"Mind if I join you?" Noah asked with a nod toward the ground.

My head started shaking of its own accord. Hoping to any god who would listen that he hadn't heard me talking about his future babies, I pulled my knees up before scooting across the grass to give him more room against the oak tree. "Not at all."

He held out one of the coffee cups in offering, and I tried not to hesitate too long before accepting it. The cup was toasty against my palms, warming each finger as I watched Noah set his own cup and messenger bag on the grass. Then I noticed another bag on his shoulder—*my backpack*. He set it next to the tree as I gaped. Then he peeled off his charcoal blazer and laid it on the even ground.

I could only continue to sit and stare stupidly as he settled cross-legged atop the blazer. Noah's posture was as rigid as an ironing board, and he looked wholly out of place sitting in the university quad beside me.

His eyes were focused on the handful of students milling around or heading to their next class. I watched him sip his coffee, feeling decidedly like a stalker but still absurdly confused at what had possessed him to bring me coffee.

Warm, thoughtful coffee.

My eyes finally tore themselves from Noah's immaculately styled hair, and I eyed the cup skeptically. A boy in high school once gave me herbal tea while insisting it was coffee. When I accidentally spat it out at his face in surprised disgust, he claimed both drinks contained caffeine and got the job done. Needless to say, I did my best to avoid said boy through the rest of my years at school. It was a petty grudge, but I'd clung tightly to it, proven even further when I'd chosen the definition of coffee as my senior quote for the yearbook—followed by "not to be confused with herbal tea."

And my counselor said I lacked drive.

"It's not going to bite you," Noah said, and I realized I'd been frowning at the cup in my hand as I recalled that stupid tea boy. I looked up to see Noah's head tilted curiously. "I thought you liked coffee."

"I do..." I hedged. I worried my bottom lip before sparing the cup another wary glance. "I'm just picky about what type I... Never mind, it's not important. This is great. Thank you."

I offered a shaky smile and gathered a breath for courage before going in for a cautious sip of the warm liquid.

Followed by a gulp.

Then another gulp, and I looked at Mr. Black Coffee in surprise. "There's sugar in this."

Noah spared me a cool glance before looking back at the students milling around. "There is."

It was true. The otherwise plain coffee held a tiny bit of sweetness to it. Not nearly enough, but it was something. I was floored that the thought of adding sugar had even crossed his mind, but that didn't stop me from diving a hand into the front pocket of my backpack.

I dug around through the mess of school supplies I'd restocked after the pen-tastrophe in Music Theory, but it didn't take long to fish out three sugar packets. I made quick work of ripping them open and pouring each one into the steaming cup.

Ah, much better.

Noah shook his head in exasperation, and his eyes lingered on the sugar packets.

I could only offer a sheepish smile. "I always carry extras. Just in case, you know?"

"I'm starting to understand," Noah said with an amused tilt to his lips. "I was afraid of going overboard, but it looks like that was never a risk."

I snorted a laugh and took another gulp of the magical substance. "Was that another joke? Careful. I'm beginning to think you aren't as prickly as you seem."

He drank his coffee, hiding what I hoped was a smile as he returned to people watching.

I tossed the empty sugar packets into my backpack before pulling out a few crumpled dollar bills. They were wrinkled in the worst way, and I used my palm to hastily iron them out as smoothly as I could against the grass.

"Here. For the coffee," I said. I leaned over and lightly placed the bills beside Noah's knee.

He barely spared the money a glance before shaking his head

and moving the bills to rest next to my thigh. "Consider us even on this one. You looked like you could use it today."

... Be still, my beating heart.

He knew I needed coffee.

Was it possible to swoon while already sitting down?

I tried to suppress my stare of amazement, but the truth was staring me in the face as I felt my cheeks warm.

I definitely had a crush on Noah Kincaid.

"Mondays are rough," I whispered.

Noah's lip curled up on the side, his sharp eyes meeting mine and holding. "You don't seem to have the best track record with them."

Mutilated pens and laughing Hello Kittys danced across my vision.

I cleared my throat and took another sip of coffee as he held my gaze. He was still here, and it kind of felt like we were hanging out. Was that even something Noah did—hang out? Did he feel even a smidgen of the attraction I felt for him?

I offered him a small secret smile, and glanced at my coffee cup before meeting his eyes. "Not all of it was bad."

I held his stare, watching the tilt of his lips slowly disappear until he was simply studying me.

Okay, so maybe I was the only one planning which patterns to use in our future scrapbook.

"So, does that make this pity coffee?" I asked, trying to brush off the fact that he'd completely disregarded my attempt to flirt.

"It's truce coffee."

My lips parted in surprise, and I glanced down at the coffee with renewed interest. "Can't say I've had that brand before."

He chuckled and brushed at the knees of his slacks. "I was a little short with you last time we spoke, and I don't want that overshadowing the rest of the semester."

That almost sounded like an apology.

"Which brings me to the real reason I stopped by." Noah

cleared his throat. "Slade wanted me to fill you in on a change in plans."

My gut clenched. Had Slade sent Noah to tell me I was cut? *What sort of monster*—I stopped that line of thought and swallowed around the lump forming in my throat. My eyes couldn't seem to stop blinking. "What plans?"

He leaned back on his hands, watching for my reaction. "Cheyenne dropped the class."

That wasn't what I'd expected to hear, and my mind raced to remember what little I'd seen of Music Theory this morning. There'd been a handful of empty seats when class began, but I hadn't given them a second thought. "What? Why?"

"She failed the first quiz."

It hadn't even crossed my mind that others might've failed, too. A wave of nausea hit so suddenly, I jerked up straighter. "I thought she—wait, but she's my partner for the duet!"

Noah offered a tight-lipped smile. "That's where I come in. Say hello to your new partner."

I blinked back at him.

... Oh dear.

"But you already have a partner," I said, remembering just how happy Blaise had looked to be paired with Noah. Not to mention how not-unhappy he'd looked with her.

"Slade put me with Blaise because the class size was uneven. She was simply filling in," Noah explained. He didn't seem to care that he was trading in a frontrunner for a potential flunkout. And he had no idea I'd failed the quiz, too.

Oh boy.

"That's... great," I squeaked out.

"We can meet Wednesday after class to go over a plan of action and make arrangements. I booked the music room for an hour," Noah said before getting to his feet and gathering his bag. He slung the blazer over his forearm and paused long enough to check his phone. "Bring your own pen."

He disappeared amongst the sea of students crowding the sidewalk before I could process what he'd said, and I slumped back against the tree, speechless.

Noah was my new duet partner, and I couldn't think of a single superstition to blame this on.

A Music Room

Time sped by much too fast for my liking, and it wasn't long before I found myself unable to sit still in the music room on Wednesday. My leg took it upon itself to get the jitters so badly it kept wobbling about like a newborn fawn. I clamped a hand down on it, determined to get through this session with as much poise as possible.

I settled on the piano bench while Noah stood and flipped through a binder of music sheets.

"First things first, we need to pick a direction," Noah said without looking up from the binder. "Who did you answer for Slade's question on inspirators?"

"Debussy," I answered, then frowned at my leg when it shook again.

Noah is just a boy, I reminded myself. *Try to be normal.*

Noah paused in his flipping, and his gaze cut to me. "An impressionist?"

I shrugged under his shrewd stare, telepathically ordering my overzealous leg to behave. "I don't think he liked being called that, but yes."

"I lean toward neoclassical," Noah said, and I bit my lip to hide a smile. Of course he preferred a style associated with order, balance, and emotional restraint. Who would've guessed? His judgement of impressionism made more sense now, too, considering it put such a strong weight on mood and emotions.

"I'm sure we could find a sweet spot somewhere between the two," I said. My leg finally settled against the bench, and I breathed easier.

Noah's brow rose, and the room felt a little smaller. "You'd rather have two competing styles? Why not choose one and create the strongest piece with that style?"

I frowned, wondering if that was a trick question. "I take it you're not big on compromise?"

He mirrored my frown. "Not when there's no reason to."

"So, you'd be okay with us choosing impressionism, then?" I asked while crossing my ankles. "Since I'd rather not do pure neoclassical and you see no reason to compromise."

Noah's eyes narrowed to slits, but he wasn't going to steamroll me in all our decision-making when I had a scholarship riding on this. Then again, since I was the one failing, maybe I shouldn't be so vocal. That didn't stop me from holding his stare until my eyes watered. But he didn't cave.

I sighed. What was the point of disagreeing on this if we weren't even partners in the end? I took a deep breath for courage, deciding to rip the Band-Aid off.

"Don't worry, it's a moot point since you probably won't have to put up with me much longer. Once I fail out, Slade will match you back up with Miss Legs-for-Days," I said, then winced at my own pettiness when I realized I'd called her that out loud. "Blaise, I mean. I'm sure you two will be very happy together."

That didn't sound bitter at all.

The skin between Noah's brows pinched together. "You're failing?"

"Slade officially recommended I drop the class."

I dropped my gaze to the ivory keys to avoid looking at Noah while he digested that. At least I was honest, even if it meant he thought I was an idiot now.

"Are you?" Noah broke the silence, pulling my eyes up. He eased the binder closed and rooted me in place with a hard gaze. "Dropping?"

I took a deep breath and let it out. This part I was sure about. "No."

Just saying the word infused a new surge of hope in my veins, and a knot eased in my stomach. I wasn't giving up.

"Then I don't see why we shouldn't continue what we started," he said. He flipped the binder back open and set it atop the piano before turning a few pages. "Let's work with what we know now."

I scratched my knee, more than a little surprised by his attitude. Okay, then.

Noah's eyes didn't waver from the page when he spoke again, as if it was an afterthought. "And I could see something along the lines of Ravel's style doing well."

Something warm and fuzzy unfurled in my stomach at his suggestion. I told myself not to smile smugly, repeating it twice in my head when my lips didn't listen.

Maurice Ravel was a compromise.

Knowing how impossible it would be to stifle, I ducked my head to block Noah from seeing my grin. "Sounds good to me."

He nodded and pulled out a sleek black phone before checking the screen. "I need to cut this short, but let's meet for another hour after next class?"

Again? "You do know this project isn't due until December, right?"

Noah slung his messenger bag over one shoulder and

smoothed down the front of his tie. "I'd rather be proactive about it. You never know what'll happen later."

"You sure it's not because you want to see me again?" I smiled cheekily. He didn't say anything, but his flat stare was answer enough. I held my hands up to show I was kidding. "Fair enough. All right, another hour on Friday."

"See you then."

He walked out the door, disappearing almost as quickly as he'd come.

A Thief

THURSDAY WAS EVEN LESS fun than Monday.

Why I agreed to cater an event that required me to show up before eight in the morning on a Thursday, I'd never be sure. It was some sort of breakfast hoopla for a corporate conference. I regretted everything.

Teresa wasn't scheduled for this one since she had a working brain and was smart enough to say no. But she was also kind enough to drop me off so I wouldn't have to take the bus and be late. One of the many reasons I'd nominated her for the Super Cool Roommate award.

It felt pointless since I could only be there for an hour before I had to rush back to campus for Philosophy class, but apparently Mr. Everton was desperate after some volunteers cancelled, and yours truly made the cut as a van unloader.

Unfortunately, there hadn't been enough time for coffee before our little road trip began, and I passed out with my face smooshed against the passenger window before Teresa could pull away from the curb.

Twenty minutes later, I wasn't faring much better as I tugged boxes of croissants out of the catering van's side door.

If I had ever thought van unloading sounded like a fun job, that was quickly corrected within the first five minutes of unloading.

Croissants weren't very heavy; *logically* my brain understood that. They weren't, really. So why did it feel like I was carrying a box full of miniature bowling balls as my noodle arms continued to drag closer and closer to the dew-covered grass I trudged across?

This totally wasn't worth the money it was adding to The Noah Fund.

"You okay?" one of the other highly valued van unloaders asked as he sidled up beside me. I tried not to gape at the two crates of fruit in his bulging arms.

Show-off.

"Yeah." I shuffled toward the side of the building as he strolled leisurely beside me.

"You look tired," Mr. Muscles said, even going so far as to point a finger at my face while balancing the crates with one hand.

Brawny bastard.

"I'm fine," I said through a tight smile before setting my box down beside the building's side door.

Okay, so it was actually three feet away from the door, but it was close enough. My arms tingled as I shook them out.

I was still floating in a hazy sleep fog as Mr. Muscles and I trudged back toward the van—which felt football fields further away than it had when we'd first gotten here.

I wondered how much jail time one would get for killing a roommate who signed them up for a catering job.

"Why don't you pull some more items to the back of the van?" my partner suggested as we reached the back doors. He jerked a thumb over his shoulder toward the building. "I'll take another load in and grab us some coffee."

Maybe guardian angels really did exist.

My shoulders sagged in relief, and I sent the super van unloader the warmest smile I could manage—which I usually reserved for saints like Scott and the barista at Starbucks who put enough extra shots into my Americanos to fuel a small army. "Thank you, thank you, *thank you.*"

He laughed—maybe a little uneasily—before scratching the back of his head and picking up more crates of fruit. I debated collapsing onto the grass but convinced myself to hop in the stuffy van and pretend I was doing something productive until he went inside. I fiddled around with nothing and stealthily watched his progress toward the building over my shoulder.

The very second his shoulders disappeared behind the side door, I stumbled out of the van and leaned against its warm side as my burning eyelids fluttered closed. Resting my eyes for just a quick minute sounded like a swell idea. Then I'd be refueled enough to get back to the grind.

Mornings sucked.

Manual labor sucked more.

Unloading vans was hard work, and I felt for all the other van unloaders out there in the world.

Maybe we should form a union.

"Sleeping on the job, Cupcake?"

I snapped my eyes open, startled by how close a pair of emerald green eyes were to mine.

I gaped. *The Cupcake Thief!*

His magician getup had been swapped out for jeans and a yellow hoodie, but I only missed the eyeliner for a moment. He had quite some nerve showing up here.

I scoured every crevice of my memory for the sticky-fingered thief's name, before embarrassingly coming up blank. Nothing rang a bell. *Jeremy? Isaac?* Maybe he'd never actually told me.

Seriously, Emma? I scolded myself, blinking away the grogginess. *Are you really holding that strong of a grudge that you forgot his name?*

... But it was such a beautiful cupcake he'd stolen from me. It deserved a dedicated grudge.

"Excuse me?" I stammered, surprised by the force of my residual anger toward the guy who'd stolen my cupcake.

"Just wondering if you're getting paid to snooze against the van?" He leaned a shoulder against the van beside me, with a cheeky smile that seemed permanently glued to his face.

Did he work for Mr. Everton, too? But I couldn't picture this company inviting a magician to their breakfast, plus he wasn't wearing the cape.

"Well, technically yes, I suppose," I said with a frown. After all, I *was* getting paid while snoozing, despite what Mr. Everton intended for me to be doing. But that didn't mean he needed to call me out on it. I racked my brain for the thief's name. *Spencer?* No, that didn't sound right. "What are you doing here?"

"I was just wondering if you had another treat for me today?"

Well, that hit a sore spot.

"I guess I could treat your face to my fist." I picked at a piece of dirt beneath my nail.

"Already thinking outside the box, I see." His eyes widened and his smile morphed into a grin as he leaned closer. I welcomed the scent of maple syrup. Had he eaten waffles for breakfast? "Tell me, Cupcake. What other treats can you think of that don't involve food?"

He was close now—way too close for someone who'd not only touched my food but devoured it in front of me before bragging about it. My grudge felt like a living, breathing entity. His teasing words fueled it. He'd broken the cardinal rule.

Don't touch Emma's food.

"I can think of an old favorite." My eyes lingered on the thief's smiling lips. Maybe that was a bad idea, though, because they looked all too welcoming. Like freshly baked donuts sitting behind smudge-resistant glass on a Sunday morning. My stomach rumbled. "A swift kick to the balls for guys who don't know the meaning of personal space?"

The rogue dimple made an appearance as he laughed, but he also backed off a few steps until he was just outside kicking range.

"Listen... uh," I said, hesitating when I counted on my brain to somehow magically remember his name if I went to say it. Didn't work. "Cupcake Thief." I shook my head to clear the cobwebs residing there, then coughed before soldiering on. "It's not—"

His hand flew up, and he motioned for me to shut up as his smile fell for the first time this morning. Big green eyes blinked back at me in adorable bafflement. "Hold up. Did you seriously forget my name?"

Flames licked my cheeks, and I shuffled my foot against the ground.

"It's nothing personal." I gestured pathetically with one hand as the other one tapped out a tune against the van. "I mean, I *was* a little distracted the last time we met."

He gaped at me, chestnut hair ruffled by the breeze the only thing not frozen in shock.

The building's side door burst open before I could dig myself into a deeper hole, and Mr. Muscles came lumbering out with two steaming to-go cups. My mouth watered on instinct, and I straightened up from the side of the van, clenching my hands into fists to stop myself from sprinting over and busting both coffees from his hands.

Mr. Muscles smiled as he reached us. He handed me one of the large cups. "Here you go."

"Thanks," I said appreciatively, trying to tame the smile taking over my face as the blissful scent of espresso accosted my nose.

Ah, heaven.

Mr. Muscles hesitated, and I paid enough attention to see him eyeing the thieving magician with unease.

As he should. You never knew when he would take a sweet, helpless, generously icing-ed cupcake straight out of your—

"Coffee?" Mr. Muscles offered to the charming vagrant, holding out the other steaming cup before nodding over his shoulder. "I'll go grab another."

Cupcake Thief perked up a bit. He nodded easily and accepted the coffee. "Thanks, man."

Well, at least that meant he probably wouldn't try to steal my coffee now.

I held the cup closer to my nose while Mr. Muscles lumbered away—as close as I could without burning my lips on the edge. The scent of maple syrup grew stronger, and I looked up to see Cupcake Thief stepping closer while sniffing his own cup.

He caught my eye with a smirk, and his gaze darted toward Mr. Muscles' back before he focused back on me. "That your boyfriend?"

I blinked at the question, not expecting it. But the answer was easy. "Nope."

It shouldn't have made my stomach pool with warmth when his smirk widened.

"It's Finn, by the way," he said, reintroducing himself before holding his cup out in a toast. "I could always tattoo it on my forehead, in case you forget again."

Finn.

It sounded a lot better than Cupcake Thief.

I mimicked his toast, and we both ceremoniously lifted our coffees. I threw caution to the wind, going for a gulp because it'd been too long since I'd tasted the sweet release of a caffeinated beverage—

—before promptly spitting it out at the same time coffee sprayed from Finn's lips like a fountain.

"*Ugh!*" He scowled, shoulders jerking as he shook his head.

I spat again—very ladylike—before letting out a whimper.

"Black coffee," I spat like a curse before squinting into the lid's tiny mouth hole. The view wasn't great, but sure enough, the liquid was on the seriously darker side of the brown scale.

Finn's face crumpled. "Also known as the devil's brew."

I tried my best to hold back tears.

"This is such a waste," he muttered and turned his coffee upside down over the grass.

"Wait!" I cried, leaping forward to stop him. Finn jerked back, startled—which made sense since I was a practical stranger jumping toward him. "Don't just pour it out!"

Finn stopped and flipped his cup back the right way as his eyebrows shot up. "It's fine, Cupcake. I'm not even a huge fan of coffee. I just wanted him to leave so I could spend more time with you."

I blinked, my hand still in midair as I processed his admission. "But that doesn't mean you should pour it out. We can still salvage this."

"How?" Finn glanced at his cup with a grimace. "Honestly, we'd be doing the world a favor if we got rid of it."

"Just—wait! Trust me." I hurried to the back of the van and pulled my bookbag out. Going straight for the front zipper, it didn't take me long to find our saving grace. I curled them inside my fist before hiding it behind my back as I faced Finn—

Only to find him pulling a silver flask out of his hoodie pocket.

"You're right. It's worth a shot," he said while holding his flask up in a cheers motion.

I frowned. "What's that? What are you doing?"

He glanced up, grinning wide enough to show off his dimples. "Just making this coffee a little Irish."

My lips parted. The sun had barely risen, and he was suggesting hard liquor? "You carry alcohol around with you?"

Finn cradled the cup in his elbow while unscrewing the flask, not looking the least bit bothered. "It comes in handy."

"Hold up. How old are you?"

"Nineteen."

"That's not legal... Wait, I wasn't talking about alcohol!" I took a calming breath before opening my fist and showing off the sugar packets. "I meant *sugar*."

Finn's eyes lit up. "Good call. That's even better."

I tried to shake off the unease at seeing the flask and ripped off the corner of a packet while cradling the travel cup in the crook of my elbow until I could get the lid pulled off.

"Guess we don't need this after all." He tucked the flask back in his pocket, as if he hadn't just pulled out alcohol before most people left for their morning commute. "Where'd you get those?"

"I always carry extras with me." I smiled and tried my best to wink. "Just in case. You never know when you'll need a little sugar."

Finn's dumbfounded gaze shot back to mine from the cup, and I couldn't suppress a snort at the way his jaw dropped comically.

"You... I... sugar..." Finn trailed off, at a loss for words as he wiped a hand over his mouth. His head turned, eyes darting all over the surrounding area before his incredulous gaze turned back to mine.

I started to feel concerned, wondering if this was the part where I called 911 because he was having a stroke.

"Will you marry me?" Finn asked abruptly. He looked as straight-faced and earnest as I'd ever seen him.

I froze, the smile fixed on my face as my hand held the now empty packet of sugar over my steaming cup of coffee. *Did he seriously just—*

Finn sucked in a sharp breath and smacked a hand against his forehead. "Shit. I forgot to get down on one knee."

I snorted before covering my mouth as he scratched the back of his head. The laughter started deep in my belly and completely caught me off guard. It rose quickly, and I was in a fit of giggles before you could've spotted the flush washing over my cheeks.

"Hey, it's rude to laugh when you're being proposed to," Finn said before sniffing in affront. That dimpled smile spread across his face as he watched me try to tame my laughter—which was futile. "Pretty sure you should be crying happy tears and hugging me and talking about flower arrangements or something. But never mind that, we can save it for later. Now about those sugar packets..."

The giggles only grew as Finn sat his cup on the van's bumper and nabbed a packet from me. I watched in unbridled amusement as he ripped it open before pouring the sugar contents straight down his throat.

Not exactly what I'd had in mind...

"Hey!" a gruff voice called behind us, followed by the *bang* of a door swinging shut. I tried to smother my laughter. A glance over my shoulder showed Mr. Everton jogging over with a frown gracing his weathered face.

"Think on it," Finn murmured in a rush. His lips twitched into a shameless smile as he winked. I was at a loss for words, but he was already backing away toward the sidewalk without breaking eye contact with me. "I'll see you around, Cupcake."

He was gone before I could wave, disappearing like a magic act while I was left with a grumbling Mr. Everton approaching my side.

"Bye, Finn," I whispered before my boss sidled up beside me. He crossed both arms over his chest. His eyes turned to me with a gravity I didn't expect.

"You seem like a nice girl, Emma," Mr. Everton said, but he let out a heavy sigh. "And I want to keep you nice. So, do me a favor and stay away from Finn, okay? It's for your own good."

I frowned. A sense of unease crawled across my skin as I shifted my weight to the other foot. He knew Finn?

"We were just drinking coffee."

Mr. Everton shook his head. "Please trust my judgement on this one, okay? That boy is bad news."

He offered me a sad smile before opening his mouth, then he hesitated before closing it again. Without another word, he grabbed a box of muffins and headed back toward the building.

I gazed at the sidewalk Finn had disappeared down, wondering what could possibly be so bad about a boy who loved cupcakes and snuck up on van unloaders in a non-nefarious way. With no answers in sight, I found a renewed strength that helped me haul an entire bag of apples into the company building.

When I left less than an hour later, I searched for my bookbag and found it settled nicely between the two front seats. Odd. I could've sworn I'd left it in the back.

My arms were ready to fall off by the time I crawled into bed that evening. Classes were a blur—Noah slipped out a mere ten minutes into History of Opera and never returned—and my muscles ached from carrying croissants. It was a miracle I'd been able to keep walking.

Teresa was out with friends, while I was in bed before the early bird dinner special at Denny's was over.

Cuddling Mr. Elephant close, I was right on the edge of dozing when my phone vibrated between the sheets. I groaned and prayed to every higher power I could think of that it wasn't Teresa saying she'd forgotten her keys or ID and was locked outside the building.

Then I backtracked, also praying it wasn't my mother texting about another recital. Or my practice schedule. Or reminding me not to even *look* at a boy.

I grumbled, fumbling for the phone before squinting as my eyes adjusted to the harsh glare.

UNKNOWN NUMBER

Wanna know a secret?

I blinked and brushed a loose strand of hair off my forehead as I gazed blankly at the text. My lips dipped into a frown as I typed back.

EMMA

Who is this?

I'd barely sent the message when my phone was vibrating again, and a text appeared underneath mine.

UNKNOWN NUMBER

I haven't been totally honest with you.

I shared a look with Mr. Elephant and tried to remember who I'd given my number to lately, but it hurt to even think. I hesitated, chewing on my lip as I tested the weight of the phone in my hand. But they didn't even wait for a response as another text popped up.

UNKNOWN NUMBER

I didn't get the houses mixed up that night you were catering. I stopped by because I saw you at the van.

My heart stuttered in surprise, and my bare legs shifted against the sheets as I scrambled to sit up. Finn? But how did he...? I'd never given him my number.

My skin heated, but I managed to save his number in my phone while trying to decipher what this warm feeling meant. And once again, I was too slow to respond before my phone vibrated again with a new text from him.

FINN

I just knew I had to meet the girl who looked at a cupcake like it was the Eighth Wonder of the World. Hope I didn't scare you off.

... Crap.

A Song

Needless to say, I never responded to Finn's text. And to be honest with myself, I wasn't sure *how* to respond. So, I made the logical decision to simply avoid it completely, and the next day I renamed his contact info in my phone to something that reminded me of his true motives: Cupcake Thief.

Noah and I spent an hour after Music Theory in the music room working on our duet project. His work ethic was downright inspiring. If it were up to my procrastinating butt, we wouldn't have met until a week or two before the performance.

But I had a fresh cup of coffee, courtesy of Scott's cart, and I was more than happy to spend time with the guy I'd been crushing on.

Even if I was indebted to him.

We spent the hour researching Maurice Ravel and comparing his techniques to what we'd learned in Slade's class so far. Being in the same room as Noah was distracting, but I quickly got lost down an internet rabbit hole reading the history between Debussy and Ravel.

Juicy stuff.

I was just getting to the good part when Noah flipped his binder closed.

"We should call it for today," he said before checking his phone and starting to pack up his things. "I have plans I need to get to."

"Oh. With your girlfriend?" I asked, the words slipping out of my mouth before I could catch them. I blinked in shock at myself, wondering what had possessed me to ask that. I took a sip from my cup to hide my mortification. Maybe Finn was rubbing off on me.

Noah's lips twitched into what looked like a reluctant smile. "I don't remember mentioning a girlfriend."

"Really?" I hummed and lowered the cup. I was going for nonchalance, but failed horribly if the growing smile on his face was anything to go by. My fingers picked at a loose corner on the coffee sleeve. "Interesting. Does that mean you don't have one?"

Noah's smile worked the butterflies in my stomach into a tizzy, and he looked so pleased with himself that I narrowed my eyes. "Boyfriend, then?"

That wiped the smile clean off his face.

"No boyfriend," Noah said with an unimpressed look.

I let out a slow breath, and my heart beat forcibly against my rib cage. He was single. But my stomach clenched when I remembered the way he'd made Blaise laugh. Just because they weren't together *yet*, didn't mean he was available. "Redheaded friend?"

His brow pinched. "No? No redheaded friends."

"Very interesting." I wondered if it made me a bad person to feel so relieved by that, but I tried not to show it. Instead, I took another sip of coffee to hide my smile.

Noah wasn't fooled. "Why do you ask?"

I shrugged, pursing my lips against the rim of my coffee cup. "Just wasn't sure how a significant other would feel about these little study dates."

"Dates? These aren't dates. They're mandatory for a project."

Ouch. Time to rewind.

"Of course." I quickly recovered and set my cup on the piano. "It's just... I mean, they *could* be dates, right? If we were both single... and interested."

Noah blinked back at me, momentarily stunned, before his stoic expression was back with a vengeance.

"You're pretty forward, Emma," he said, studying my face.

"I'm also pretty single," I quipped. *And interested*, I added silently. Once again, the words left my mouth before I could catch them—not that I was entirely sure I wanted to.

Surprise lit the mix of gold and green in his eyes in a way that had my stomach tightening, and I could've sworn he was fighting down a smile. The way the left side of his lips tilted up sent a thrill down my spine that was way too satisfying for my liking.

"Incredibly forward," he said softly, the sound barely traveling to my ears. But he didn't wait long before shaking his head and focusing back on the binder. "I'm not looking to get involved right now."

Ouch again.

"Right," I said just as softly. I kept a firm hold on my fingers so I wouldn't start chewing on my nails. "But for the record, I wasn't saying we needed to take off to Yemen or anything. Just something casual."

Noah's breath escaped him in a way that almost could've been considered a laugh as he met my gaze.

"I don't do anything lightly," Noah said with a shake of his head. "Ever. There's more to consider than just the logistics."

... What?

"Okay," I said, and the smile froze on my face as I gave him a puzzled look. A drop of doubt crept in, but I assured myself that even though he may sound like one sometimes, Noah wasn't actually a robot. "That sounds... not weird at all?"

He snorted quietly—a very human sound, I noted—before the buzz of his phone broke the quiet. Noah shook his head as he read over the screen. "About those plans I mentioned. I have an appointment on campus with someone, and they just arrived."

I bit my lip and slid off the piano bench. "Well, I guess that's my cue. Plus, I'm late for my midmorning coffee cart stop."

Noah tapped away on his phone, only sparing me a glance. "You already have a coffee."

I looked down at my cup. "This was from my *morning* stop, to tide me over until the midmorning one, which will last until my lunch cup with my roommate."

He shook his head, clearly not as big a fan of caffeine. "Meet again after class on Monday?"

I grinned, unable to resist teasing a little as I edged toward the exit. "It's a date."

My laughter chased me out the door and drowned out Noah's muttered protests.

Go figure I'd forget my bookbag back in the music room. It only took an eight-minute walk, then ten minutes of catching up with Scott on the coffee bean harvest this year, and a few minutes of debating what to order before deciding on the same thing I got almost every other day before I noticed a distinct lack of weight on my shoulders. Particularly the bag's front and side pockets, which held my cash.

Maybe I was too distracted wondering who Noah was meeting with on campus.

I offered Scott my most apologetic of smiles before promising to be back before the prelunch rush and hightailing it out of there.

It was a long hike back up to the piano room, and I took my sweet time on the stairs. I'd been up and down them enough times today that it could almost be considered a workout.

That must count for something, right?

Those stupid butterflies in my stomach scrambled awake at the possibility of Noah still being in the music room. I'd just seen the guy thirty minutes ago, but God forbid the little flying creatures didn't freak out on the off chance we crossed paths again. I may have even run a hand through my loose hair and practiced what I believed a sultry pout would look like as I hopped up onto the last landing in the stairwell.

The door to the music room was cracked open, and I bit back a smile as notes from *Pachelbel's Canon* in D Major floated through.

I'd never heard Noah really play before—aside from a few notes he fiddled around with working on the duet—but he was nothing short of incredible.

My steps slowed in a show of reverence, and it was easy to tell he played better than professionals I'd seen on stage. The way his major notes blended so seamlessly together with the minor ones, while weaving in a technical precision I could only dream of attempting one day... It was phenomenal. I could practically hear his sophistication pouring through the piece.

I'd spent over ten years practicing almost every day, rain or shine, and I knew I didn't sound even half as good. My insides clenched, and I couldn't stop my feet from picking up their pace as I craved getting even a short peek of what Noah looked like as his fingers swept across the keys.

I was two steps into the room when my shoes skidded to a halt, squeaking against the linoleum floor as my world tilted on its axis.

I blinked. Then blinked again. Then blinked a third time because I had slight OCD tendencies as a child when it came to blinking. I must've been hallucinating or experiencing a stroke.

Either that, or Oliver Bishop was sitting on the piano bench my boney butt had been warming not even half an hour ago.

"Cheese and fries." I let out a breath, grabbing the back of a chair for support and blinking one more time just to be safe. He

hadn't noticed my hasty entrance, and I took a moment to come to terms with the reality of the situation.

Oliver Bishop looked the very epitome of an icon. His heart-shaped pale face was almost painfully handsome. Thick honey blond hair brushed back from his eyes, looking smoother than silk.

His fingers danced across the keys like tides moving in and out from the ocean, striking me with warring pangs of jealousy and awe.

I couldn't believe we were the same age. He played with an ease I could never achieve, shoe pressing fluidly against the pedals like they were old friends. The boy was a legend—a revered prodigy from practically out of the womb—and he was almost close enough for me to reach out and touch.

Instead, I could only stand there stupidly and gape as my mouth caught flies for much too long. It wasn't just that this was Oliver Bishop—I mean it *was*—but he also looked... different. In place of the usual tux for recitals were jeans and a T-shirt. Boots replaced polished loafers, and he was even wearing a freaking leather jacket. But I'd seen that same face splashed across dozens of magazines, and I'd recognize it anywhere.

What felt like seconds later, the smooth cadence of music regrettably stopped, and he turned toward me. A pair of pale grey eyes snared mine from across the room. The same eyes I'd seen on magazine covers.

"Oh. Hey." Oliver Bishop's equally smooth voice filled the quiet.

Internally, I screamed like a twelve-year-old fangirl who'd just gotten front row seats to her idol. Oliver Bishop was *talking to me.*

My jaw was still working on a recovery strategy, so all I could do was stand there and gawk stupidly.

"Hello?" He stood up from the bench and caused my brain to short-circuit as he ran a hand through his silky hair.

I regularly dreamed of doing the same thing myself.

"I..." My voice trailed off into an empty abyss, and I cleared my throat of the butterflies battling each other to fly up it. I was out of my depth. "... Hi."

"Sorry if you reserved the room," he said. He stood so perfectly poised that my shoulders pulled back in reflex. He'd had a growth spurt since I last saw him perform, and he was almost a foot taller than me now. "I thought I'd test the tuning and get a little practice in."

"But you're *you*," I whispered, wide eyes locked on his slim body walking nonchalantly toward my scrawny one. I hadn't blinked since finding him in here. Why wasn't I blinking?

Oliver Bishop's head cocked to the side, and one light eyebrow deviated from the other as an unsure smile formed on his surely soft lips.

"Do we know each other?"

A laugh of disbelief escaped before I could stop it, and I blurted out the first thing that came to mind. "I know *you*."

Wow. Get it together, Emma. That wasn't creepy at all.

I pointed an accusing finger at his chest. "You're Oliver Bishop."

Any start to a smile dropped from his face, and I panicked when he pulled a phone out of his pocket.

Oh my God, he was calling for backup like I was some crazy stalker chick.

"You're actually the reason I'm here!" I wrung my hands together. Where was a pen to chew on when you needed it?

His finger froze on the screen, and he glanced up at me. "Huh?"

"Not like in a stalkery way," I said, because I definitely didn't need him calling any bodyguards on me. I sighed through my teeth, trying to pull myself together and show him how nonthreatening I was. "I mean, I didn't know you'd be here right *now*. And I didn't mean *here* here, in this room. I'm *here* because I forgot my backpack. But you're the reason I'm going to school for piano."

A hint of the smile was back. "I'm not sure I'm following."

I couldn't blame him. Even when I wasn't blabbering, I made little sense.

"I'm sorry, I guess I'm a little starstruck," I admitted, then winced at the understatement. "I just meant you're a huge inspiration to me."

Oliver Bishop shook his head and slid the phone back into his pocket. I held my breath as he walked to the piano and sat back down.

"Well, I'm going to need more details than that," he said before patting the piano bench beside him. "Come on. Have a seat."

I gaped, hardly believing it. Oliver Bishop wanted to *talk* to me? This couldn't be real. I took a step forward before stopping with a frown. "Seriously? You sure you didn't secretly text your bodyguards and now you're trying to keep me calm until they arrive?"

He chuckled, and the sound sent a shiver down my spine. Even his laughter sounded melodious. "You're safe... for now."

I shuffled closer before perching on the far end of the bench and smoothing out my skirt. I was within touching distance of Oliver Bishop, and it showed in the way my heart flipped over itself with each beat. I took a deep breath to center myself, and my nose caught a subtle whiff of smoke and leather. "Are you always like this with fans?"

"Just the cute ones," he said with a smile, and the twelve-year-old girl inside of me died a little bit at that. *Oliver Bishop thinks I'm cute?* He chuckled again, and I warned myself I'd have to stop staring eventually. "I'm kidding. I don't really get out enough to see fans in the wild."

Wait. Did that mean he didn't think I was cute?

"Or they don't recognize me." Oliver pulled a grey beanie out of his pocket and tugged it on before adding a pair of sunglasses to complete the look. He smirked. "See? Totally incognito."

And still as handsome as ever. The disguise worked wonders, but I thought it was a travesty to hide eyes as lovely as his.

"Definitely a different style than we're used to," I said while rubbing my palms on my skirt. Everything felt clammy. "Well, I promise not to freak out on you and try to steal a lock of your hair. I'm not that kind of fan. Like, I don't have a shrine of you in the back of my closet or anything."

Crime shows taught me closets were the first place people checked for shrines. Smart stalkers knew to put them at a secondary location.

"That's reassuring." He slipped off the sunglasses and hung them on his shirt. "So, you said I inspired you to go to school for piano?"

I cleared my throat and looked down at the ivory keys. I was struggling to believe I was sitting next to piano royalty. I didn't know what to do with my hands. "Yeah, I did. My parents took me to one of your concerts when I was eight, and the next day they bought me a piano."

My finger tested out the resistance of one lonely key, giving the nerves racing through my body something to focus on. It molded down easily, and I started a lingering melody between two keys before throwing in a third to offset the others. There was hardly any rhyme or reason to it, but fiddling with the notes was a balm to my frazzled nerves.

"Not in the spoiled brat kind of way," I said. I offered him a sheepish smile before focusing back on the keys in front of me. "But because they saw someone so young accomplish so much, and they'd decided I was inadequate in comparison."

He cleared his throat. "Excuse me, but your name..."

I cringed before laughing at my rudeness. "Wow, I'm sorry. It's Emma Fox. And I'd been taking piano since I was four years old or so, but I wasn't anywhere near your level of talent. So, my parents pulled out the big guns with a baby grand and twenty hours of piano lessons every week. Ten years of lessons and recitals later, and here I am."

"Here you are," Oliver Bishop said. One of his fingers reached toward a black key and pressed it intermittently between the first two keys I was fiddling with. Of course it harmonized with my tune beautifully.

"When I heard you play..." I trailed off and shook my head before holding down all three keys at once. The noise was sharp and daunting at first, until it faded away and Oliver's key was the only remaining sound. "I was entranced. I'd never heard the pieces in your set, and you played so beautifully."

I stalled, stroking a finger over the nearest black key before I turned to the handsome, talented guy sitting next to me. It was so hard to face him, but almost impossible to look away at the same time. He was a celebrity to me, someone unreachable and practically gold-plated. "It was Debussy, really. When... Well, when every other song was boring my brains out, or recitals weren't up to my father's expectations, or I felt like I was suffocating, I had Debussy —because of you. You played *La Mer* at that recital when I was eight, and I guess it kind of made an impression?"

Oliver Bishop nodded and breathed a laugh. "His works are pretty powerful."

That was an understatement. "Yeah, they really did a number on me. Especially *Arabesque*. It's what made me fall in love with music, and now I'm here."

"Now you're here," Oliver Bishop echoed again, voice soft. His thigh was dangerously close to mine, and I swallowed around a lump forming in my throat. "What is it that you like about *Arabesque* in particular?"

"I like that it's soft." I traced my finger along the keys as he pressed down on more. A soft tune picked up, and he took his time working through it. It wasn't something I recognized, but it was lovely. "It's gentle. It builds you up with it, but then doesn't leave you hanging by yourself like so many other pieces do. You can practically taste the emotion through it, and it sounds like home. Or what home should be."

His fingers danced across the keys as his eyes closed, and he was so polished I had trouble finding even the tiniest hint of mistakes or finger misplacements.

Because there were none.

My eyes kept bouncing between his face and hands, unable to reconcile the sight before me. I had the best view in the house, and a pang of guilt hit low in my gut that others weren't here to hear it. But there was a touch of intimacy at being the only two people in the room. I could pretend he was playing just for me.

Time to stop that train of thought.

"I know you have no clue who I am, but it really meant something to me. So... thank you." I lightly touched the leather sleeve covering his arm. The melody stuttered for a beat, but then recovered as if I'd just imagined it. It sounded lame as heck, but I'd been dreaming of one day saying that to this boy. I was just happy I'd had the chance. "Thank you, Oliver Bishop."

I looked up as his fingers continued gliding across the keys. His eyes met mine, and I was blown away by how striking they were.

"You're welcome, Emma. But you can call me Oliver, you know."

Oliver.

I swallowed before nodding and dropping my hand from his arm. Everything about this felt like a dream. "Okay. I, uh, I will."

He looked back at the keys, not realizing how much his friendliness meant to me. I was surprised myself with how choked up I was getting, which meant it was time for a change in subject.

"Why *Pachelbel's Canon*?" I asked, referring to the piece he'd been playing when I walked in, and Oliver glanced up in surprise.

"You know it?"

I gave him a weird look. "Everyone knows it. Does this mean you're trading in sold-out auditoriums to play weddings now?"

He chuckled, and his fingers fell from the keys. "No, no. Nothing like that." He lifted a shoulder and looked away. "It's lame as hell, but the song reminds me of graduation. And being on campus here reminded me I've never had my own."

"You never graduated?" Not that I was surprised. With skills like his, I couldn't see his parents putting him through traditional schooling.

"I went to a boarding school, but never got to walk," he said before taking off the beanie and scratching the back of his head. "I shouldn't complain, though. Most guys at my school would've traded graduation for a concert in Italy any day."

I blinked at the reminder of just who I was sitting next to; a legend who'd traveled the world during the time I struggled through high school with braces and a tie-dye obsession. "Yeah, doesn't sound like a very tough decision."

My phone rumbled to life in my waistband, surprising the stuffing out of me. I jumped before fishing out the culprit and seeing my roommate's name flash across the screen.

TERESA

We still meeting up for coffee? I'm at the cart.

Son of a monkey.

"I should really get going." I slid off the piano bench not so gracefully. "You probably have way more important things to do, and I promised I'd meet up with my roomie. Either that, or I'm pretty sure I'm going to wake up from this super awesome dream any minute now."

Oliver chuckled, and his smile stretched wide enough for two deep dimples to peek out. I didn't recall seeing those on the magazine covers. "I promise this isn't a dream."

"Really?" I eyed him doubtfully. "So, you're saying if I tried to kiss you right now, I wouldn't wake up right before our lips touched? Instead, you'd be pushing me away and calling your bodyguards to get rid of the crazy stalker chick?"

Oliver's jaw dropped in the most comical fashion, and I took great pride in the way his cheeks flushed.

"I..." He straightened the leather sleeve around his wrist before his stark gaze met mine. A slow, far too handsome smile appeared. "Who says I'd push you away?"

A warmth spread through my belly, but I shook it off with a laugh.

"Don't tempt me." God knows I used to fantasize about pecking the heck out of him as a child, long before I'd learned what real kissing was like. "Just a preteen dream of mine, that's all. Probably for the best I don't. Even in a dream, it's not really fair to the guy I'm talking to."

It may have been wishful thinking, but I thought I saw a glint of disappointment before Oliver chuckled and shook his head. "I'm beginning to think my manager lied to me about the perks of stardom. He didn't mention anything about girls turning me down."

"Not used to it?" I smiled and picked up my backpack. "I really do need to go, but maybe I'll see you around, Oliver."

I spun around on the spot and headed toward the door as I shot off a text to Teresa to let her know I was on my way.

"Emma?" I looked over my shoulder at the sound of Oliver's voice. He'd gotten up and was leaning against the piano, offering a small smile that felt like we shared a secret. "I'm glad you're here."

My smile mirrored his. "Me too."

I floated the rest of the way to the coffee cart.

It was a good thing Scott had my regular order memorized, because my mind was still up in the fourth-floor music room.

A Deal

Dear Diary,

It's been almost a week since I met Oliver Bishop in the flesh, and I've dreamed about him every night since. In last night's episode, we were considering investing in a rustic coffeehouse together (I'm guessing he was footing the bill?) but got lost on our way to tour it. There were winding roads and abandoned gas stations and maps written in hieroglyphics. We stopped for coffee and cheeseburgers, then his car got stuck in a ditch and I spilled my coffee.

That can't be a good omen, right?

Maybe it was a fluke since I only slept a few hours after tutoring Little Miss Demon Spawn Angela Avarde in the ways of piano. After spending most of the night wrestling her Dubble Bubble out of my hair, I wrote

Mrs. Avarde a very stern, official warning that if I didn't desperately need the forty dollars they paid me per hour, I'd quit in a heartbeat.

The email is still sitting in my drafts folder, but it made me feel a little better to type it out.

Oh crap. If I don't leave now, I won't have time to get coffee before Music Theory.

Bye!
Emma

WALKING into Music Theory Wednesday morning in a brown bucket hat wasn't ideal, but it was the only hat I could find—courtesy of my hall's resident assistant, who went fishing with her father. My hair was nowhere near ready to be seen after a night's long battle with gum and peanut butter.

I feared it might never recover.

Slade was quickly losing his legendary aura in my presence, especially when he surprised us with a pop quiz. Was I ready for a quiz? No. Should I have been ready? Probably. Had I been too busy getting gum out of my hair and cursing a child, who still had her baby teeth, to study? I'd rather not comment.

So, it shouldn't have been a surprise that my mind completely blanked after Blaise handed out the quizzes. Musical terms were basically a foreign language, and I struggled my way through three pages of somewhat educated guesses. Fifteen minutes later, Blaise walked around to collect them, and I focused on my coffee. I couldn't even look at Slade when he took to the podium; I was too embarrassed. Hadn't I promised the man I wouldn't let him down?

Professor Slade cleared his throat as he accepted the quizzes from Blaise. "You can use the rest of lecture today to meet with your partners for your duet project. I strongly advise you establish a plan to meet outside of class as well, since allotted class time to work on your duet will be rare. I'll grade your quizzes during class, and Blaise will hand them back as they're ready. You're free to leave once you have your quiz back and a plan in place."

I let my head fall to rest against the cool wood of the desk as dread pooled in my stomach. Noah was the last person I wanted to see my current hair predicament, but it wasn't long before I heard the sound of a chair squeaking against the floor in front of me.

"Late night?"

"You could say that," I mumbled against the desk.

Noah hummed. "I didn't take you for the partying type."

I frowned and got an unwelcome sniff of disinfectant. "What's that supposed to mean?"

There was a weighted pause before he answered. "Nothing."

I groaned, sitting up and rubbing at the desk's indent on my forehead. I pulled on the bucket hat to make sure it was secure before facing Noah. "Well, it's only true if you consider seven-year-olds and gum in hair a party."

One corner of Noah's lips tilted up in amusement. "Do you make a habit of hanging out with children?"

"Only for work. I was supposed to be studying last night, but instead I was up until four in the morning trying to get the gum out with peanut butter and ice cubes."

"Kids never learn, do they?"

My frown deepened. "It was *my* hair."

His brow pinched, and he leaned against the chair's back. "This may be an ignorant question, but how did you manage to get chewing gum in your hair?"

"*I* didn't do it," I said as my head jerked back. That was just insulting. "The little brat I tutor in piano did when I was teaching her note values."

If it was possible, Noah looked even more lost. He smoothed a hand down the front of his grey blazer. "I didn't know you tutored."

"Yeah, you know—molding young minds and all that jazz."

"And you let these children put gum in your hair while you tutor?"

I grumbled and crossed my arms. "I mean, I didn't *let* her. But I couldn't exactly stop her without using bodily force, either."

"And you'd never hurt a child...?"

"I'm not saying I didn't try." I fought not to let the anger rise to the surface again. "But do you know how hard it is to move on a marble floor while wearing socks? It's not a walk in the park, and she's a slippery little demon spawn. I couldn't get a good shot at her."

"That sounds... challenging."

"Well, it wasn't all for nothing." I uncrossed my arms and stretched the sore limbs. Cleaning gum out of hair really did a number on the arms. "After taking out the money for a cheeseburger and budgeting for food, plus buying a pack of gum I couldn't resist, I'm ten dollars closer to buying you another pen."

Noah did a double take, and his lips parted. "You took a job just to pay me back?"

I looked at him like he was crazy. "I took *this* job to avoid starving. I took the *catering* job to pay you back. It just ends up I break things a lot, which isn't fun for my paycheck. Speaking of, do you think they'd still be allowed to dock my pay if we unionized?"

"I already told you I don't need the pen—or any money," Noah said, completely ignoring my question.

I shrugged. "Tough luck. A debt's a debt."

Noah's mouth opened—I'm guessing to argue again—when Blaise appeared beside us with impeccable timing. I never thought I'd be happy to see her, until I noticed the papers in her hand.

Blaise dropped my quiz on the desk without a word, and a bright red *D* was circled on the front for all to see.

My stomach dropped.

I got a *D*.

And this time, I could only blame myself. I hadn't studied enough.

That didn't stop my eyelids from working overtime to block an unwelcome rush of tears. I took a deep breath and flipped the quiz over—but not before catching Noah's eyes staring at the top of it.

Lovely.

"Tough luck again," Blaise said to me as she tucked a curl behind her ear. "I offer study sessions on Tuesdays and Thursdays, and Slade recommends them for struggling students. I think he mentioned them to you? You'd do yourself a favor if you stop by."

"Thanks," I muttered. I offered a smile that was surely more of a grimace.

A hint of a smirk teased her lips. "Oh, and tell your mom I said hi."

I blinked back at her as my cheeks heated, really wishing Noah hadn't heard that. Pursing my lips, I absolutely wanted to die on the spot when she turned to him and smiled.

"Hey, Noah," she said as she handed him his quiz. "Great job, as always."

"Thanks, Blaise," he said while setting it aside.

"You're easily top of the class," she added, and I slid further down in my seat when she lingered near his chair. "Well, I'll see you later."

Noah offered a thin smile before looking at his quiz, and I watched her watch him a moment before she clutched the stack of quizzes to her chest and turned away.

I bit my cheek as she sashayed down the aisle, trying to fool myself into blaming my tight chest on the quiz.

"I'm screwed." I forced out a slow breath and lowered my forehead back down to the desk. The bucket hat got in the way, and I readjusted it. There wasn't enough coffee in the world to handle this. "It's over. I'm done. There's no way he'll let me stay in the class now. Not with a *D*."

"It could be better." Noah's voice was far more even and pacifying than mine. "But it's not the end of the world."

"It really is, though." I squeezed my eyes shut. "I'm going to lose my scholarship and get shipped back to my parents in *Kansas*."

Noah chuckled, and his chair shifted closer. "It's not that dramatic."

I popped my head up and blinked at him. "Yes, it is. My parents are insane. Like dictator-level insane. I *can't* go back there. I won't."

"Take a deep breath." He held out a hand. "Let me see your quiz."

I slid the sad excuse for a quiz across the desk before turning away so I didn't have to watch the train wreck head-on. He glanced over the first couple pages while my stomach twisted itself into knots as I imagined my mother throwing a welcome home party.

She'd probably make me play Beethoven.

I hated Beethoven.

Noah cleared his throat, and I looked over to see his brow pinched as he flipped a page over. "I don't understand. You play piano, but you never learned this? A third of the quiz is defining terms."

I winced, vaguely recalling Slade saying something similar. "I never *had* to learn this stuff."

"Didn't you take Music Theory in high school? Or *any* music class?"

"My parents thought school-sanctioned programs were juvenile, so I only took private lessons—which I mostly zoned out during, I'll admit."

"Then how'd you learn to play?"

I half smiled as I thought back to how I'd mess around with the keys. "Playing was the easy part. I just listened to a song then copied it. My tutor never noticed I wasn't learning the book side because I played fine."

His gaze shot up to mine. "You play by ear?"

Did he have to sound so shocked? It wasn't that rare. "I guess. Yeah."

He nodded slowly before setting the quiz down and sliding it back across to me. I made a face at the *D*, but didn't bother to flip it over this time. Noah tilted his head and gave me a considering look before nodding again. "I'll help you."

I froze, staring at him. "What?"

"I'll help you study," he said with his gaze locked on mine.

"What?" I asked again before shaking my head. He was talking crazy. "But—no. I'm already in your debt. I can't afford to pay you to tutor me, too."

Noah lifted a shoulder and packed his own quiz away. I couldn't help but think he did it so I wouldn't have to look at his *A*. "I don't need money, but you need help."

"And you're going to help me... why, exactly? Out of the goodness of your heart?"

He smiled at that and leaned back in his chair. "You help children learn to play. Why shouldn't I help you learn the technical jargon? Playing by ear is no small feat. There's just a disconnect with the text material."

I was unsure if I should feel insulted. "Are you comparing me to a kid?"

Noah quirked a brow. "Weren't you the one wearing Hello Kitty underwear?"

My cheeks warmed. So, he hadn't forgotten about that. "You should know that I don't tutor because I'm a good person. I do it to make money."

Noah's lips tightened like he was holding in a laugh. "I don't think there's enough money in the world to tolerate children sticking chewing gum in your hair."

There had to be a catch. Nobody just offered help to someone who destroyed their property. "You seriously don't want anything in return?"

His eyes focused on mine, and his finger tapped against the desk between us in a steady beat that matched the thumping of my heart. "I want our project to do well, and that'll be a little difficult if my duet partner drops out of the class."

I held in a groan, glancing over to where Blaise sat talking with Slade. "But if I drop out, you'll be paired back with Blaise. I don't think you'd have to worry about failing with her."

"Probably not," Noah said, and the skin between his brows pinched. "But who would that make me if I stood aside when I could've helped? I've spent most of my life studying this instrument and everything about it. Let me help you."

I looked around the room, and other students were still working in pairs with their partners. Two were packing up to leave already, and Slade was still grading quizzes up front.

It was tempting—unbelievably tempting and an absolute godsend to my sinking scholarship. But the etiquette classes my mom forced me to attend every summer of my childhood reared their ugly heads and wouldn't let me say yes that easily. "I don't feel comfortable with this. It's not fair to you."

"Life isn't fair," Noah shot back lightly. "The only reason I went to a private high school was because of a scholarship. I don't know where I'd be without it, but it sure as hell wouldn't be anywhere near here. Why should you lose yours because you're brilliant enough to play without knowing what's in a textbook?"

His words made me pause, and I swallowed back a laugh of surprise—almost choking. "You think I'm brilliant?"

That teased a half smile out of him. He leaned forward. "I suppose that's still being determined. I haven't heard you play yet."

I swallowed. Screw etiquette. Maybe Noah Kincaid was my guardian angel. "Okay. I guess—I mean, if you're really okay with helping me out, then okay. I'd appreciate it. *And* I'd still owe you one. No arguments."

He sent me another half smile before standing and slinging his messenger bag over one shoulder.

"Good choice. Come on. We can study in the music room." He walked off without a backward glance.

"Wait, we're starting right now?" I called after him. I winced when I summoned Slade's reproachful glare.

I lagged behind, slowly packing up my things and having trouble believing what'd just happened.

The music room's ugly orange couch was surprisingly cozy as California's warm sunlight filtered through large windows. I made myself at home on one side of the sofa, and Noah took the other.

The hour we'd usually dedicate to our project quickly passed with Noah explaining the basics, but he didn't once make me feel stupid for not knowing something.

Then lunch came and went, and neither of us made any move to leave. He didn't mention having to leave for any classes, and I happily skipped Philosophy.

I wasn't the best student, but Noah was an amazing teacher. When I got distracted, he played a piece on the piano that related to the text. When the text wasn't clear, he explained things in a way I could understand. And when I felt like my brain was going to implode from overstimulation, he even called a coffee break. Noah was nothing short of professional the entire time, but I couldn't help falling just a little harder for him.

A Text

Dear Diary,

I think Noah was sent to this world to kill me. It's been one week since he started helping me study, and my normal evening life of bingeing crime shows and playing the coffee café game on my phone is now a distant dream.

The guy is a studying machine, and his determination rivals that of a bull. Honestly, I should be honored that he's putting this much effort into my academics.

We met up every day to go over all the piano terms and practices I'd never bothered to learn. He even made me go to Blaise's study session on Thursday before deciding he could do better just teaching me himself. And what did his teaching involve?

Flash cards.

Lots and lots of flash cards. I see them in my dreams.

There was some coffee involved in our sessions, and they definitely leaned toward the realm of study dates, but Noah was very firm about not calling them dates. Even platonic ones.

Which is probably for the best, because he kept accepting calls and taking them in the hallway so I wouldn't overhear. That'd be rude on dates, but as it was, I just kept wondering who the heck was calling him.

Turns out spending hours studying with an expert every day can quickly catch one up on years' worth of fundamentals, because we just wrapped up studying for today, and Noah thinks I'm ready for tomorrow's test.

I tried not to preen.

Shoot, I'm late for my night class.

Wish me luck tomorrow!

Emma

SELECTING History of Opera as a night class during registration wasn't one of my brightest moments. Maybe they should've named it History of Lullabies, because by the end of the first hour, I was digging both elbows into the top of my desk in an effort to keep my chin propped up on both palms.

And we were only halfway through the class period.

I couldn't even distract myself by looking at Noah since he'd sat a few rows behind me.

"In contrast, the 17th century opened new doors for Italian opera," Professor Whidden droned on as she flipped through slides on the projector. She wore a blue dress that reminded me of a plump peacock, and her grey hair was pulled taut in a low bun. "This occurred when Christoph Willibald Gluck introduced reform operas in the 1760s. This semester, we'll be taking a closer look at how he broke the stranglehold Metastasian opera held for the bulk of that century."

As Whidden continued down a monotone path that I didn't much care to follow, my phone vibrated from its snug home in the waistband of my shorts and startled me enough I jumped an inch off the chair.

I cleared my throat and tried to tamp down the blush that rose as a few bored students glanced over. After waiting a few seconds for them to look away, I covertly slipped the phone out of my shorts without flashing my panties at the jock on my left. My hands darted underneath the worn desk, and I made quick work of opening the text as I slouched further.

CUPCAKE THIEF

Why do they call the little candy bars "fun size"? Wouldn't it be more fun to eat a big one?

I pursed my lips to contain a snicker. Where had this boy come from?

My thumbs flew across the screen.

EMMA

Depends. What kind of candy are you eating, and how much are you going to share with me?

Oops. Is it bad to say I already ate it all? And it was a Milky Way.

> Milky Ways are fun in all sizes. Unlike opera. Opera is never fun.

CUPCAKE THIEF

> At the opera now? And texting? You wicked girl. ;)

> History of Opera class, and I never claimed to be good.

> Stealing cupcakes from a catering van and snoozing on the job. You always were a wild one.

> My boss said I could have that cupcake! And I still haven't had a chance to taste one because of you.

> I'll make it up to you.

> By rubbing it in and telling me how yummy it was again?

Finn didn't respond right away, and I bit my lip as my eyes remained riveted to the screen. I wasn't sure why I enjoyed his bantering so much; I just knew I did.

Not a minute later, a picture came through. My eyebrows rose, but I opened it with only a hint of hesitation. I almost snorted when I saw a fun-size Milky Way sitting innocently on his sun-kissed palm.

CUPCAKE THIEF

> I lied. There's one left. I'll save it for you.

I slouched further against the seat, unable to stop a smile from forming. Opera was completely forgotten, and I tapped the toes of my white Keds together as I typed back.

EMMA

That's a start. It's not a cupcake, but I'll give you brownie points for trying.

CUPCAKE THIEF

Brownie points? Really? How many?

Five.

Wow, five whole points. How many do I need for a brownie?

At least fifty. Plus a replacement for that cupcake.

You drive a hard bargain. When's your next gig?

Butterflies took off in my stomach. He wanted to see me again? I locked the screen and flipped the phone over in my hands as I took a deep breath before responding.

No clue. I don't really have a set schedule.

New to the whole catering business?

Newer than you are to the sneaking business. How'd you get my number?

A magician never tells. ;) The things I do to talk to a pretty girl…

I chewed on my lip. He was such a flirt.

Did it involve my defenseless backpack left all by its lonesome in Mr. Everton's van?

Let's just say you aren't the only one capable of pilfering through catering vans, but otherwise my lips are sealed.

I pursed my lips to hide a smile as my thumbs flew over the screen.

EMMA

Mr. Everton warned me about you.

There was another pause—longer this time—and Professor Whidden managed to go through six presentation slides before Finn texted back.

What'd he say?

He said you're bad news.

You're a big girl, Cupcake. You can make your own decisions.

I chewed on my lip, deciding to be direct.

… Are you bad news?

For rabbits who don't like confined spaces, maybe. But for you? Never.

Never.

Well crap, he was definitely somewhat interested. Which was already about ten times more interested than Noah was. Finn may have stolen my cupcake, but I'd already seen that he was fun and could take a good joke. Not to mention incredibly easy on the eyes. I felt like I already knew more about him from two meetings than I did the guy I'd been crushing on for weeks now.

Finn was handsome and playful and loved sweets. Why *wouldn't* I go for it?

Then Mr. Everton must be wrong. Up for teaching me how to pull a rabbit out of a hat? :)

I cringed a bit after sending it, hoping I wasn't too lame, but the three little dots on Finn's side popped up instantly.

CUPCAKE THIEF

Mark my words, I'll turn you into a master magician in no time, sweets.

An anticipatory smile bloomed as I pictured him showing up with a cape and top hat at the next party I catered.

I tried paying attention to the class, but the slides sort of all blurred together as I replayed the texts over in my head. Was I really going for it with Finn? It wasn't like Noah and I were dating. It was more of a one-sided crush on my end. The butterflies fluttered when I remembered him calling me brilliant, though.

Professor Whidden finished up her slideshow before projecting the homework for next class, and then we were free to go. I slipped my phone back into its spot in my waistband, surprised by how quickly the second half of class flew by. Maybe I'd make a habit of texting a certain cupcake-loving magician.

Noah was packing up his bag as I passed his desk, and he looked up with a half smile. I returned it with a bigger one, partly to show him up but also because I was trying to condition him into his own full smiles.

There weren't any noticeable results yet.

"Not thrilled by the history of opera?" Noah asked in a way I almost would've called teasing, and I came to a stop beside his desk. His blazer was brown today, and it did amazing things for his eyes. "I thought I saw you dozing off a few times."

I swallowed with a wince and looked over my shoulder to pretend I was making sure my backpack was zipped. Somehow the way he said it sounded reprimanding. Then it hit me like a train, and my head snapped back up. "You were watching me during class?"

Noah's expression didn't change, but I could've sworn his

cheeks tinted the lightest shade of pink I'd ever seen. Maybe my crush wasn't as one-sided as I'd thought.

"Emma..." He trailed off before gathering up his exquisite pens. "You were sitting a few rows in front of me. My eyes may have strayed from the board a few times. It's straining on the retinas to watch a screen for this long."

But it was too late for any excuses; I already felt like I weighed lighter than air.

He'd been watching me.

It didn't escape my notice that maybe I should've been creeped out that a guy was watching me during class, but honestly, I just hoped I hadn't picked my nose while he'd been doing it.

"Hey, I'm not judging," I assured him. "Actually, I was wondering if you wanted to get some coffee and hit up the library for one last study session?"

I crossed my fingers behind my back in hopes he'd say yes, just in case it actually worked.

"Not tonight," Noah said, proving my fingers wrong. "I have plans with a friend, but don't worry about tomorrow. You're ready."

I might've preened a little this time.

"Thanks. Rain check, then." I shrugged, trying to play it cool as I fiddled with the strap on my backpack. Now that I'd opened up to the idea of getting to know Finn better, it felt a little easier talking to Noah. The pressure was gone. "Well, have a good night."

I offered a nod and an equally awkward wave before starting for the door.

"You too." Noah's voice trailed after me.

I wove through the desks, wondering if I should mosey on over to the music room and tap out a couple tunes. I had a few hours to kill before bed, and if I went back to my dorm, I'd end up bingeing crime shows or eating my way through a box of Pop-Tarts.

My phone set off another vibration. I held my breath as I pulled it out of my shorts and hungrily scanned the screen.

Next question for the magician-in-training. Why
do round pizzas come in square boxes?

The way my heart rate sped up at something as simple as a text
scared me a little, but not as much as the smile that spread itself
across my face.

"Hey, Emma?"

I froze before pivoting toward the voice and finding none
other than Charlie Davenport a few desks over. His smile was
cautious, and he shuffled forward as if he were approaching a
cornered animal.

I didn't bother to hide my surprise as my eyebrows shot up.
"Hi, Charlie."

He cleared his throat and set his bag on the desk between us.
His gaze darted around the room before meeting mine, and he
pushed up his glasses with a smile. "Hey. Are you busy tonight? I
was wondering if you wanted to hang out again."

"Oh," was my genius reply. He wanted to hang out? Oh no.
No, no, no. I shuddered, and my butt clenched from nerves.

I wasn't sure if that was a normal nervous habit, but clench
it did.

"Like a date." His lips spread into a hopeful smile. "You
know... like last time."

So maybe the kiss-of-cousins hadn't been as nightmare-
inducing for him as it was for me.

Pity.

My brain kicked into overdrive to think of a way out of this
without hurting his feelings. "Well, it's a school night."

"It's only eight o'clock. We could just grab a drink and hang
out at the Student Union. You still like coffee, right?"

"I do..." I trailed off and nibbled on my lower lip. Maybe I
just needed to be more direct, while still being nice. But mostly
direct.

Unfortunately, all I could do was stand there as uselessly as chopped liver while he gazed at me with his heart on his sleeve.

"Oh. Okay." Charlie's eyes dropped when I'd been quiet for far too long. "I get it."

"No, no. It's not... no. Listen, Charlie. You're *great*," I started enthusiastically, and Charlie cringed back against the desk behind him. "No, really! You're a *really* awesome guy."

Why did that sound so sarcastic?

He avoided my gaze, and I licked my lips while floundering for a better excuse.

"I mean, really. It's not you." I gestured toward him, then back at myself. "It's me—"

Oh God. *Shut the hell up, you stupid girl.*

Charlie opened his mouth, but his eyes widened as he focused on something over my shoulder. I frowned, thrown off by the change until an arm wrapped around my waist and a broad blazer-covered chest appeared beside me.

"Are you ready to study?" Noah Kincaid's voice was closer and softer than I'd ever heard it before, and I quickly lost the ability to breathe.

"What?" I choked out. My eyes widened to saucers as I gaped up at him. "Ah. Um, yes? I mean—wait, what?"

My gaze ping-ponged back and forth between the boys before they settled on Charlie's shocked face, but his eyes were glued to Noah's arm resting around my waist.

"I'm sorry for making you wait." Noah gave my hip a gentle squeeze that had my confused heart fumbling for purchase. "Shall we?"

I didn't understand what was going on, and it must've shown on my face.

"I guess I'll see you around, Emma." Charlie recovered first and nodded quickly. He swung his bag over his shoulder as I cringed.

I floundered for something to say. "I... Okay. I'm sorry, Charlie..."

"No problem," he said with a tight smile. And if we were in a Saturday morning cartoon, dust would've flown up behind him at the speed he zoomed out the door.

I kind of wished this was a cartoon so I could hit myself over the head with a frying pan without causing permanent brain damage.

Noah's arm dropped from my waist as Charlie cleared the doorway, and the hair on the back of my neck stood on end as reality sank in. Had he just tried to scare Charlie off? I wanted to be angry, but the front-row view of Noah's feelings on display was sweet karmic payback.

"Just how many students are you getting coffee with?" Noah asked once we were alone.

"One." I pinched my lips to stop from grinning at him. "But I thought you 'had plans with a friend'?"

"My plans have changed," Noah explained simply, as if he hadn't just staked a claim.

I wetted my lips, unable to resist teasing him a little. "Was that fun for you?"

Noah's lips parted, and he looked down at me. "Pardon?"

"You just peed all over me in front of Charlie," I explained while pointing at the empty doorway he'd disappeared through.

The skin between Noah's brows pinched, clearly not following. "I never... What are you talking about?"

"Your little show. I should be angry with you, you know." I crossed my arms and wondered why I *wasn't* upset. "You really overstepped a line there—one you had no interest in crossing just a few days ago."

Noah's eyes lit with realization, and one side of his mouth turned up.

"You didn't appreciate me interrupting his bumbling attempt

to ask you out?" An eyebrow quirked. "Are you interested in him?"

"No, but you didn't even let me turn him down nicely." I conveniently ignored the fact that I'd been putting my foot in my mouth before Noah stepped in. "Instead, you embarrassed Charlie *and* me by marking your territory as if I were a freaking tree. And I'm not even your territory to mark!"

He frowned, glancing at the door. "You looked like you needed help, but I didn't mean to... urinate on you."

I gave him an incredulous look, my lips twisting into a scowl. "Geez, what is wrong with you? Don't say it like that! Are you kidding me?"

"It was the same metaphor you used!" Noah defended hotly with an accusatory finger pointed at my chest. I wanted to be angry at him for overstepping, but it was difficult when he honestly looked absolutely adorable with that little scowl on his face. I smiled in reflex and let out a surprised laugh before lightly smacking his hand away.

The butterflies took a twisted pleasure in his admission, curling up together in my stomach for a little catnap. He may have gone about it the wrong way, but this was probably the first time Noah had genuinely shared his feelings with me.

Maybe Finn had some competition after all.

"And it wasn't about that boy. I just thought you'd like to improve your grade," Noah said. "We made a deal, after all. I'm holding up my end."

My cheeks hurt from grinning. "Sure. You were concerned about my grade. That's all."

"Stop smiling."

I laughed, rubbing at my sore cheeks. "Stop lying, and I'll stop smiling. I thought you said I was ready for tomorrow's test."

He pinched his lips together and paused before answering. "It can't hurt to overprepare."

I leaned closer and dropped my voice to a stage whisper. "If you wanna ask me out, just ask me out."

Noah's eyes narrowed to slits, and such an action shouldn't have made a thrill shoot up my spine like it did.

"Do you want to study or not?" he asked.

I pretended to think about it a little, as if I hadn't already asked him to study a few minutes ago. But now I had something else in mind. "Actually, my brain is too overloaded to even think about looking at books right now. How about a coffee? Since it looks like your schedule opened up and all."

He considered it before his eyes narrowed further. "It's not a date."

I rolled my eyes and started for the door. "I wouldn't dream of calling it a date."

A Reason

Dear Diary,

Today's the day. The dreaded Music Theory test.

This test could decide whether or not I have to drop the piano program, yet somehow, it's the last thing on my mind.

I'm still working my way back down to earth after my not-date with Noah last night. There was coffee and talking and walking around until Noah said he had to drive home since he lives off campus.

But now I'm at a crossroads. I just decided not to friendzone Finn, and now Noah is acting all interested?? Throw in the recurring dreams about Oliver Bishop—the most recent of which involved us playing a duet atop an elephant—and, Houston, we've got a problem. Is this the universe's idea of a joke? Teresa thinks it's *hilarious, and she teased about setting up a calendar for me to keep my dating schedule straight.*

It wasn't funny.

What am I supposed to do now? Maybe this is one of those situations where I shouldn't put all my eggs in one basket. I've heard that's good advice. There's nothing wrong with playing the field, right? Not that I know anything about sports. Or is that saying about farming? I don't know anything about that, either. Or relationships, apparently.

And I thought Slade's test today was supposed to be my biggest worry.

Help me, Diary!
Emma

MY STOMACH WAS in knots when I walked into Slade's classroom on Friday. I was so distracted thinking about boys and fields and tests that I'd actually *forgotten* to stop by the coffee cart before Music Theory. But what I really wasn't prepared for was walking into class and finding Noah had beaten me there for the first time all semester.

He met my gaze just as I cleared the threshold, then nodded toward the desk beside him. I faltered a step, not believing my eyes.

A lone cup of coffee sat waiting on the empty desk.

My Keds dragged on the hardwood as I worked my way down the aisle. I didn't want to assume anything.

"I thought you'd be a little preoccupied this morning and

forget," Noah said when I reached him, guessing correctly. "Scott threw in an extra scoop of sugar for good luck."

I swallowed around an unexpected lump in my throat before easing myself into the empty chair beside him and staring at the innocent cup.

"You got me coffee?" My voice was still hoarse from waking up.

I glanced over in time to see Noah's lips tilting up into his signature half smile. "If that's how sharp your brain is this morning, drink as much as you can before the test."

It took me a moment to realize he was making a joke, and I pretended to scoff before popping off the cup's lid. Light-brown coffee and its wonderfully rich aroma greeted me, and the cup was still warm. I took a sip, finding everything about it *just right*.

Slade strolled into the room as I drank, and I glanced at Noah out of the corner of my eye. He was already focused on the front of the room, completely unaware of the butterflies he'd awakened in my stomach.

"Pens at the ready," Slade announced as he placed his briefcase on his desk and unsnapped it. He pulled out a stack of papers before gazing across the room. "Test day. You'll have the full hour of class to complete this test, and the questions consist of what we've covered so far."

I tipped the cup back, drinking faster.

Slade handed the tests to Blaise, who waltzed down the aisles as she passed them out. I finished my coffee, set it aside, and took a deep breath to center myself.

I could totally do this. I hadn't just wasted a week of Noah's time to bomb the test. Music Theory was my thing now. I knew this stuff.

My fingers trembled—whether it was from nerves or caffeine or butterflies, I wasn't sure.

Noah cleared his throat beside me and held out his arm. "Here, use this."

A sleek black pen rested in his fingers. The same style of pen I'd gnawed on less than a month ago—just missing the bite marks.

My jaw threatened to hit the floor. He was loaning me his fancy pen?

What.

"I can't," I said in reflex, unable to move or look away from the pen. "What if I chew on it again?"

"You won't." The right side of Noah's mouth turned up, and he wiggled the pen, but I still didn't take it. He sighed before leaning across the aisle. "You know what you're doing, Emma. You're ready."

I blinked down at the pen, hesitating before I reached out and took it. It was smooth and cool to the touch, and all kinds of wonderful.

I'd missed it so much.

"Thank you," I muttered, surprised by the gesture.

Blaise pushed her way through our arms, almost knocking the pen out of my hand. I grasped it tighter and pulled back as Noah settled into his seat again. Blaise smiled and handed us each a test.

"Good luck," she crooned before continuing down the aisle.

An hour later, when Blaise came by to collect my test, I decided I could at least be proud of myself for not chewing on Noah's pen. The writing instrument was still sleek, shiny, and oh-so-perfect.

And I hadn't been as nervous as I'd thought I'd be.

I was even cautiously optimistic.

"Thanks," I whispered to Noah after he'd handed his own test in. I passed the pen back, and he took it with a half smile.

The room began to clear since class was over, but I couldn't seem to look away from Slade's desk long enough to even consider leaving. How was I supposed to spend a whole weekend not knowing what my grade was? If I'd failed, I needed to know now—not three days from now.

"I'm just going to see if he has time to look at mine now," I said to Noah, already out of my chair and starting down the aisle. His low chuckle followed me, but I didn't think much of it as I reached Slade's sturdy desk. It wasn't like I was a teacher's pet; my whole college education was kind of riding on this.

I cleared my throat, then waited until he looked up from his papers.

"Hi, Professor Slade." I offered my best smile, the one that wasn't overly toothy but hopefully reached my eyes without seeming creepy. "I'm so sorry—I know you're busy, and I really don't want to be a nuisance—but is there any way you could take a look at my test now? I studied really hard, and the idea of waiting all weekend to find out my grade makes me want to puke—"

Slade cut me off with a sigh. "One moment, Miss Fox, I'll grade it now."

I hovered quietly as he found my test and skimmed down the first page. He marked a few spots, but not enough to work my heart into a tizzy.

He flipped the page. Another mark.

Next page. No marks.

By the time he reached the last page, my heart surged with hope.

"Well, it appears you might yet turn this semester around," Slade said when he reached the last page and flipped it back over. He scribbled at the top before holding it out to me with a clearing of his throat. "Your studying paid off."

I spotted a green *B* circled at the top of the test, and I sucked in a breath.

A *B*!

"A *B*? You're sure?" I checked myself when it came out suspicious. "Not that I doubt you or anything. Or myself. I just mean, it's not some other student's test you accidentally graded instead?"

"I'm always sure, Miss Fox," Slade said as I triple-checked my name on the paper. "Congratulations."

"A *B*!" My lips parted in awe as my chest filled with warmth. "That's passing."

"It is, indeed," Slade said before pushing up his spectacles. "But the road to redemption isn't fully paved yet. Even if you manage to maintain a *B* or higher on the remaining quizzes, you'll still need an *A* on the midterm for me to be confident you can handle the material and pass my class."

He may as well have been serenading me for all the good his warning did, because I was too overcome with relief to process much of anything beyond the test in my hand. Slade simply shook his head before focusing back on his scattered papers.

I practically vibrated on the spot in front of his desk, and my face threatened to split in two from the force of my smile. A *B*! I hadn't failed!

"Is it okay if I take this with me?" I asked, lowering my voice in case he didn't want to be disturbed. Slade nodded and waved me off without looking up from his papers.

I grinned and spun around on the spot, barely refraining from jumping in excitement. Every nerve ending in my body felt alive. I settled for a little skip down the aisle to my desk, where Noah waited against his own desk with his hands in his pockets.

"I got a *B*! I did it!" I said, and I barely suppressed the urge to fling my arms around him in a hug. He was the main reason this had even happened, and I was just so dang *happy*.

And relieved.

I wasn't losing my scholarship!

Noah grinned—the biggest one I'd seen from him yet—and my own cheeks hurt from smiling. "Of course you did. This calls for a celebration."

"It does! This is totally three-scoops worthy." I licked my lips at the idea of splurging on two coffees instead of just one. The occasion kind of called for it.

"No." He pushed off the desk to stand, still smiling. "We should go to dinner."

The sound of a record scratching pulled my brain to a halt, and every muscle in my body froze. I replayed his words over three times in my head, but no amount of repetition helped them make sense. "Dinner?"

Noah remained ever poised. "Yes, the meal."

"You and me?" I asked, to make sure. Was this a prank? I glanced around us, but the room was emptying and there weren't any camera crews around.

"Yes, both of us."

"*Together?*"

He breathed a laugh as he slid his hands out of his pockets and crossed his arms. "I'm sure we could sit at different tables, but that would ruin the—"

"Noah!" I groaned, tempted to hit him. My eyes narrowed dangerously. "I can't believe I'm saying this to you of all people—but can you please be serious for a second? Are you asking me to dinner?"

A smile cracked through, and his eyes were entirely too warm as they took me in. "Yes. Dinner. You and me. What do you say?"

I shifted my weight and pursed my lips as I searched for a catch. "And is this a not-date dinner?"

His smile widened. "Not unless you want it to be."

I took a deep breath, and my knuckles turned white from how tightly I clutched the test. "You're really asking me out?"

"Only if you say yes."

I guess that settled it. "I could eat."

Noah's lips quirked, and he didn't seem the least bit surprised. "Good. I'll pick you up at seven. Wear something nice."

He turned down the aisle, but I reached out and grabbed his arm before he could take more than a step.

He didn't jerk away this time.

"Wait." I swallowed over a lump forming as he turned back to me. Who knew a test could make me so emotional? "You helped me so much this week, and I just want to say thank you. I owe you. Again."

Noah glanced down at where my hand gripped his sleeve. "This was all you. You're the one who took the test."

If I'd thought the butterflies in my stomach couldn't grow more smitten with Noah Kincaid, I was wrong. They were throwing a party in the guy's honor.

A Lily

Dear Diary,

Ignore everything I told you this morning.
Noah asked me out. We're going on a date tonight.
Is smiling supposed to hurt this much?

Hope I don't throw up!
Emma

P.S. I passed the test! My life isn't over.

First lesson in all things magic: always have a first aid kit handy.

Just how dangerous is this magic I'll be learning?

Paper cuts from card tricks are common in the field, and some bunnies bite.

I have a box of Hello Kitty Band-Aids. Does that count?

It's a start.

"ARE you seriously going out with a guy you're indebted to?" Teresa asked later that night while sprawled on her bed. "Isn't that like prostitution or something?"

"Not if I don't sleep with him." I used one hand to keep a fluffy white towel wrapped around my torso as I ran a ratty pink comb through my drying hair. "And it's not like we're lowering the amount of money I owe him based on this date, so there's nothing nefarious about it."

The comb snagged on a knot, and I cringed back from the floor-length mirror with a muffled curse.

"It kind of feels like dating your boss or something, though. Is it really that guy I saw you with at the coffee cart?" she asked, sounding doubtful as I pulled harder on the comb. "The one wearing a *blazer*?"

I hummed and gave up on the knot before moving on to the other side of my head. "That's him."

Teresa whistled, eyes going wide. "I never expected you to go for a blazer."

"What's wrong with blazers?" I frowned, feeling defensive. "Besides, it's not about the blazer. It's about what's underneath it."

"*Emma!*"

"The *person*." I raised my voice and sent her a glare over my shoulder. "It's about the *person* underneath the blazer. God, Teresa."

She snorted a laugh and pulled out her phone. "Can you blame me? And I thought you were gonna go out with a magician instead? Or that Oliver Beebop guy. I can't keep up with your love life."

"It's Oliver *Bishop*." I pointedly ignored her comment on Finn because I had no idea what to say to that one. "And that's never gonna happen. Oliver is like the celebrity you crush super hard on and dream about marrying in a field of lilies surrounded by woodland creatures, but you'll never get even a smidgen of a chance with him. You're just destined to doodle wedding plans in your diary and cut out magazine pictures of him to tape to your mirror."

"That's oddly specific. But you actually *met* him. It's not like people meet celebrities every day, so that must've upped your chances to at least a speck over a smidgen," Teresa said. "Besides, he can't be that famous if I've never heard of him."

"Oh, he is. But I bet he already forgot my name. He *might* vaguely remember me as one of the girls he almost had to sic his bodyguards on, if I'm lucky." I pursed my lips as I focused on untangling my hair. "Noah, on the other hand, isn't famous—that I know of, at least."

"Fair enough, but it's not like you and Noah are exclusive. You could test the waters with all three of them. There's nothing I'd love to see more than you juggling dates with multiple guys!" Teresa laughed. I gave her a flat look in response. "Okay, geez, I'll drop it. But how long should I wait up for you to get back?"

"I won't be that late." I flipped my head down so I could try to get a better angle on the hair at the nape of my neck. "It's our first date, and I don't see anything too crazy happening. Remember, he wears a blazer."

She hummed thoughtfully. "How did he even ask you out?"

"He held a knife to my throat and said 'go out with me or you're gonna get it, punk,'" I said flatly before flipping my hair up and taking another stab at the knot near my ear.

She sighed and tossed the phone onto her comforter. "Sometimes it's hard to tell if you're joking or not. Hopefully he's into whatever kind of humor that's called."

"Who wouldn't be into me?" I joked before frowning at my reflection. Why *were* three guys showing even a semblance of interest in me? Sure, I looked like your average college girl with certain *assets*. Guys liked butts. And breasts. But lots of girls had those.

My elbows were on the boney side, my knees were knobby, and my hair lost battles with combs more often than not. Personally, I'd always been a fan of my delicate earlobes, but no one else ever seemed to notice them. I just assumed guys were charmed by my personality.

Now, I was leaning more toward the butt and breasts theory.

"Well, keep me on speed dial, just in case," Teresa said. "If things go south, text me and I'll call with an emergency or something."

I loved Teresa.

"What kind of emergency?" I grimaced as my comb remained firmly stuck in the unconquerable knot. I tugged harder, and my head jerked from the movement as I keened.

"Maybe a car accident?" Teresa suggested quickly, almost a little *too* excitedly.

"Life threatening? No way." I shook my head but yelped when that pulled harder against the knot. I rubbed my scalp in apology for the pain I'd caused it. "He might offer to drive me to the hospital, and it'd get awkward real quick when you're not there."

She sighed and pulled her hair back into a makeshift ponytail. "How about I call you crying about someone breaking into our dorm? I can mess things around a bit in case he follows you in. I'll hide my laptop, and we can say someone stole it."

"If Noah even bought that, we'd need to report it to campus security, and they'd check the security cameras." I shook my head, being careful of the comb this time. "It's a good idea, but they'd be able to prove it wasn't real."

Teresa puffed out her cheeks in thought before I saw the metaphorical lightbulb flash on above her head.

"Aha! I'll say I started my period and can't move because of the crippling cramps, and I need you to stop by the store for some Midol." She looked wholly too excited for someone who was going to fake bleeding out of her vagina in copious amounts.

But who was I to judge?

"Perfect," I agreed, thoroughly impressed. "It's just uncomfortable enough to make him too embarrassed to question it."

"Make sure to pick me up some Twizzlers, too. I'm running low."

"Wait, am I actually going to the store? And we're a Red Vines dorm, Teresa. You know that."

"If you need a fake emergency, yeah. Noah might drive you to the store on the way back if I say I need Midol, right?"

"True. Maybe I can pick up some more toothpaste while I'm there," I added thoughtfully. "Mine's almost out. It takes me like five minutes to squeeze a drop out of it each time now."

"And we need more Pop-Tarts. I finished off the last of them yesterday."

"Well, now I really want to go to the store." I frowned and turned to face Teresa. "Even if it goes well, I might just tell him you texted me anyway."

"How romantic." Teresa ran a hand through her long dark

hair, and a small smirk blossomed. "Then you can hold hands while strolling down the tampon aisle and—"

A knock sounded on the door. Teresa and I turned toward the clock.

7:00 p.m.

I dropped the comb I'd been running through my hair.

"What the heck?" I whisper-shouted before turning and gaping at Teresa as I wrapped the towel tighter around my chest. "He's on time. Why would he be on time? What college guy shows up to a date exactly when they say they will?"

Oh, right. This was Noah.

"Should we pretend you aren't here?" Teresa was just as confused.

"How will that help?" I asked. I'd rather not have to jump out the window and sneak up behind him. One of my goals for the night was to *not* break any bones.

"I don't know, but you look like you're freaking out right now!" Teresa's arms flew around in a way that I didn't understand.

"That's because I *am* freaking out!" My heart galloped into overtime as I started mindlessly flipping through hangers while clutching the towel securely around my chest. "Holy macaroni, what am I going to wear?"

"Jeans," Teresa said in another whisper. "They're safe date clothes. Nice ones, though. Fancy jeans."

"You think I have fancy jeans?" I continued the whisper-yelling match as my heart threatened to beat out of my rib cage. I thought I had at least ten more minutes. "He said something nice. Maybe a skirt—"

Another polite knock sounded on the door.

"Coming!" My voice bordered on hysterical as I fished a bra out of a pile on the floor.

"Oh my God, you can practically tell there's a stick up his ass from the way he knocks," Teresa said with wide eyes.

I pierced her with a glare as I stumbled for the door. "He can hear you, Teresa!"

She shrugged before rummaging through the closet. "Just saying. He's not exactly the laid-back, surferesque, bongos-playing, hipster-coffeehouse-squatter, homeless bum I pictured you with."

I froze in front of the door before turning on her with a scowl. "Excuse me? Teresa, let me make this *very* clear. I would never, ever, in a *million years*, go out with a guy who prefers *hipster coffeehouses* over cozy cafés. Never. *Do you understand me?*"

Wide-eyed, she nodded. I followed it up with a meaningful look before tightening the towel around my chest and turning the knob.

I was met with perfection.

Dark grey suit, elegant black tie, and brown hair styled with a precision that made my eyes cross.

Let it be noted that Noah Kincaid didn't mess around when it came to polishing his shoes.

"Hey," I breathed out, clutching the towel in a death grip as his eyes dropped to it. A dark brow rose. "Just give me two minutes to get dressed. I'd invite you in, but it's a small room and I think we'll just stick to dinner without the show for tonight."

His eyes lingered on the towel before meeting mine again, and a lump caught in my throat at the interest in his gaze. "Take your time."

Did I imagine his voice sounding lower than usual?

I forced a smile before shutting the door in his face.

"Shit," Teresa hissed from the closet as she flipped through hangers at super speed. She threw something that smacked me in my face before wilting to the floor. It did a great job of shaking off the trance Noah's darkened gaze had put me into. "Put that skirt on. I'll find a nice top."

"I need shoes," I whispered as I slipped a random pair of panties on underneath my towel before wiggling into the floral skirt.

Cheese and fries, it was short. But I felt better since I wasn't wearing Hello Kitty underwear today. If I happened to eat pavement again, Noah would get a peek at some nice little pink lace boy shorts.

"One thing at a time." Teresa tugged a light pink top off its hanger. "Bra, then this. I'll find shoes."

"Thanks, Teresa." I dropped my towel and struggled into the strapless bra before pulling the top over my head in a show of superhuman speed. My hair was starting to frizz from the hassle, and I threw it up into a bun.

"Shoes!" Teresa cried a little too loudly for my liking as she tossed some low wedges onto the floor at my feet. I was counting on flats tonight, but the floral pattern on the wedges went so well with my skirt that I decided to risk it for the cuteness.

I didn't bother looking in the mirror, just slipped my feet into the shoes and trampled toward the door before flinging it open.

Noah was still there.

He sent me that familiar half smile and held out a flower I hadn't noticed him holding. "I hope you're not allergic."

My eyes lingered on the flower as I fidgeted with the doorknob. A Stargazer lily.

Light pink.

My favorite.

"Nope, definitely not allergic. Thank you," I murmured. I accepted the lily, unable to resist giving it a sniff no matter how cheesy it was. I rarely got flowers outside of recitals. "They're my favorite."

"I'm glad you like it." Noah stepped back and gave me a once-over that did all sorts of fluttery things to the butterflies. "You're beautiful."

I basked in the compliment and cleared my throat in case it decided to do something stupid like purr. "Thanks. You too."

His smile widened into a grin, and I grimaced at the slip. But it was true, he really was beautiful.

"I almost forgot." He reached into his pocket and pulled out a stack of index cards. "I made flash cards for Slade's midterm for you. There's still plenty of time, but it doesn't hurt to be proactive."

As a serial procrastinator, I tended to disagree, but I was touched that he'd gone out of his way to help me again. I bit my lip to fight back the smile that was fighting to get out and accepted the cards. "Very thoughtful of you. These might even be better than the flower, and that's no small feat."

One side of Noah's mouth quirked as he slid his hands into his pockets, and I carefully placed the lily and flash cards on my dresser. Adjusting the pins in my hair, I tightened them enough to stop the front strands from falling out for now.

And with a quick wave to Teresa, we started down the hall.

"What time is the reservation?" I picked up my pace to match his longer strides as we passed a few freshman girls walking the other way. Their eyes lingered on Noah, and something warm sparked to life in my chest. I liked people seeing us together.

"Seven thirty. They have private parking, so we have plenty of time to get downtown."

"I'll be ready to eat a cow by then," I said mostly to myself, which raised the question of how many cheeseburgers could be made from a single cow.

Passing by a few groups of students in the lobby, Noah and I made it out of the building while I focused on not saying anything embarrassing—which translated to not speaking at all. It wasn't until we reached the bottom of the concrete stairs that he looked my way again.

"This way," Noah said as we reached the sidewalk, and he used a light touch on my elbow to steer me toward a sleek black car parked at the curb. He walked with an undisputed air of confidence that made me feel important walking beside him.

I liked that feeling.

I went to open the passenger door, but he beat me to the

handle and pulled it open. I bit my lip at the gesture and slid less than gracefully into the seat before tugging on my belt as he clicked the door shut.

The luxurious interior drew my eye, and rich leather overpowered my nose as Noah strolled around the front before sliding in beside me.

My fingers trailed over the soft leather of my seat as I let out a low whistle.

"Gorgeous car." I tried not to gush as I admired the paneling and navigation system. Noah started the ignition, and the car made a sound that could only be described as purring. "Don't worry, I won't chew on it."

He let out a quiet laugh as the car pulled out from the curb, and I hid a smile.

"I don't want to risk tempting you," Noah said with a half smile, eyes focused on the road as his palms rested at ten and two on the wheel, "but I have a feeling my Audi would have a better chance of withstanding your bite than my pen did."

"I do like a challenge," I said under my breath while risking a peek at him.

Noah's smile doubled in size.

A Date

THE RESTAURANT WAS STUNNING.

Like, seriously beautiful.

Drop-dead, top-of-the-bucket-list gorgeous.

Providence, the sign on the outside said. It looked like a relaxing bungalow resort, hidden away from the bright lights and noisy streets of downtown Los Angeles.

The interior was decadent. Candles shaped like swans. Three forks next to your plate. A smaller bread plate that sat next to your normal-size bread plate.

I was Alice in Wonderland.

Or Wendy in Neverland.

Or Emma in You-Don't-Belong-Here-Land.

And the menu didn't have any prices on it.

This was where Noah took girls on first dates?

"Noah..." I sucked in my lips as my head shook dubiously. My legs fidgeted underneath the table, and I wondered if I was even sitting correctly. "I don't know about this."

At a place this fancy, I was bound to make a fool of myself.

"Not a fan of seafood?" Noah lowered his menu to the table-cloth, which had a higher thread count than both my main bedsheets and my backup bedsheets combined. "They have turf options as well."

"Right." I chewed on the inside of my cheek and went back to reading the list of luxury appetizers.

They had *multiple* options for caviar.

My stomach rolled, and I inched down further in my seat. I felt like a kindergartner trying to read for the first time.

What in the world was uni egg? Or foie gras?

Was that even English?

"Do you know what *abalone* is?" I peered over the top of my menu. I was wound tighter than a spring, and Noah looked ready to work on his tan.

"It's a type of sea snail with a chewy texture," he said. "The natural flavoring is buttery with a hint of salt."

Snails? Hard pass.

"What about, umm, *iwashi*?" I asked again, sounding out the foreign word as carefully as I could. "And... uni egg?"

"Sardines," Noah answered, as if he was discussing ham sand-wiches instead of seafood delicacies I'd never heard of before. "And uni egg is sea urchin."

What the hell? I mouthed behind the menu, wondering what sort of alternate universe I'd dropped into.

Where were the cheeseburgers?

I tried to hum pleasantly in acknowledgement, determined to fake it until I could make it. "They sure do give you lots of options."

Odd, stomach-churning options with no prices listed next to them.

"If you're not sure what you'd like, we could do the tasting menu?" Noah offered, and I peeked over the menu to see him looking my way. I couldn't help but notice his suit looked good—*really* good—against the fancy chair and backdrop. "They bring samples of different popular appetizers, main dishes, sides, and desserts. We'd each get nine courses, so there's plenty to try. If there's something you really enjoy, we can order a full platter as well."

"Uh, okay. That sounds good." I set the menu down. The sense of relief was small, but at least I didn't have to worry about embarrassing myself while ordering. I reached out and gripped the water glass tightly, feeling the condensation cling to my fingers as I took a quick sip for my nerves.

Even their water tasted expensive. Did they charge for it?

God, I hoped not.

Noah was still browsing his menu, so I took a chance to slide my chair back. "I'm just going to take a quick trip to the restroom."

"All right." Noah set down his menu and got up as well.

I panicked, freezing halfway to standing as my brain raced into overdrive. Did he intend to go to the ladies' room with me? Was this some sort of fancy restaurant protocol?

I stumbled the rest of the way out of my chair and cleared my throat as I tried to figure out a polite way to say I was old enough to pee by myself.

But apparently it was for naught, as Noah sat back down as soon as I was standing. I shook my head, convinced I would never get a handle on his manners.

I plastered on a polite, closed-lipped smile as I began my newfound mission to find the powder room. Three wrong turns and an almost disastrous collision with a waiter carrying a tray of lobster tail later, I was swinging open the shiny bamboo door, which was at least fifteen feet tall.

What exactly was the point of having doors as tall as giraffes? I couldn't think of a single reason for that.

The scent of potpourri invaded my nostrils as I strolled as delicately as possible into the ladies' room. I purposely triple-checked the female sign next to the door, because I wasn't about to willingly walk in on any dudes making friends with urinals again.

Five times was more than enough.

The bathroom was as opulent as the dining area. Relaxing music streamed from unseen speakers, complimentary perfume sat on a mirrored table with pastel mints resting beside them, and there were even little packets of toothbrushes, floss, and feminine hygiene products.

"Cool," I whispered, impressed, as I trailed a finger over a bouquet of carnations. I may or may not have wondered if I could fit three of the floss packets into my bra. My dentist always said I needed to floss, and now was as good a day as any to start.

Laughter sounded behind me, and I turned to see a familiar redhead touching up her makeup at the vanity with another girl. Dressed in what looked like a couture cocktail dress—looking absolutely glamorous as I fingered the hem of my cotton skirt—Blaise Rousseau was rocking some heels that looked perfect for stabbing a man through the heart with.

Her eyes met mine in the mirror, and she handed a tube of lipstick to the brunette girl with her.

"Oh good, the bathroom attendant is here. Miss, you're running low on towels," she said before tacking on a little smirk. At least I assumed she was talking to me, since I was the only other one there.

Her friend laughed, and I blinked back at them. "Blaise?"

She did a double take. "Do I know you?"

Kill me now.

"I'm Emma... Emma Fox. You're my TA for Music Theory."

Blaise stared for a long beat before recognition lit her eyes and they widened. "Oh. Sorry, I thought you were the help. Your outfit sort of... blends in."

Lovely. Just lovely.

"Easy mistake. Excuse me." I sent her the tight-lipped smile I usually reserved for my mother's parties before I escaped to the furthest stall. Muffled giggles followed me.

My fists clenched as the stall door slammed shut behind me, and I had to repeat the chemical properties of sugar three times—a little trick I usually reserved for times my parents would lecture me—before I had properly bored myself and calmed the swelling temper that was telling me to punch Miss Legs-for-Days in her very-pouty-lipped mouth.

She was gone by the time I finished my business, and I took extra time washing my hands to make sure I'd calmed enough to return to the table.

A bathroom attendant?

Really?

Really?

It got worse when I wove through the smiling couples and smell of oysters back to our table.

Noah wasn't alone anymore. Blaise hovered next to him, leaning over the table and putting him eye-level with the top of her dress—a dress that surely cost more than my best recital one back in Kansas.

My eyes barely registered Noah's expression, as I was too busy seeing red. I pursed my lips as I approached.

"Ah, there you are." Noah stood up from his seat and pulled my chair out in what I could only assume was another attempt to confuse me.

My temper screeched to a halt. This proved to be a conundrum for me. I had no clue how to sit down while a guy was holding out my chair. Was I supposed to let him scoot it in? Or pull it in myself? Were we supposed to work together like some sort of chair-tucking-in duo?

There must be written instructions for this somewhere.

I moved forward cautiously and tried to squat over the chair—which felt awkward as heck—and Noah pushed it in until the seat knocked against the back of my knees. I sat down, still way too far from the table, and tried to subtly scoot closer as he found his way back to his seat and smoothly slid in. I gave up a good seven inches from the table.

I frowned, envious of how easy sitting was when you did it yourself. Steeling myself before looking up at the hovering girl, I tried my best to look relieved.

"Oh good, you're back! I think we're ready to order," I simpered, trying to sound grateful. Blaise's jaw dropped, and I sent her the smile of a shark.

It was very toothy.

Her pale skin blossomed with red as she spluttered, and Noah cleared his throat while I preened.

"Emma, she isn't a server. You remember Blaise Rousseau from Music Theory?" Noah asked before turning to Blaise. "Was there something else you needed?"

Her wide eyes turned to Noah before ping-ponging back to me with such stupefied disbelief I should've felt insulted.

"I just recognized you from class and wanted to stop by to say hi," she finally said to him, recovering spectacularly and sending Noah a bright smile. "How's your night going?"

"It's fine, thank you," Noah said before taking a drink of his iced tea. "Yours?"

"Same. Well, if you ever need help with Music Theory, just let me know. It's a shame we aren't partners anymore." Blaise's gaze settled on me, and her smile turned wooden. "And I'm sorry you had to drop the class, Emily. If you put in the work, I'm sure you'll be ready to try again next year."

I cleared my throat and warned myself that stabbing her in the eye with my fork would only bring bad consequences. I wasn't built for prison. So, I pasted on a smile. "Actually, I didn't drop it."

Her lips parted, but there was no surprise in her eyes. "I'm sorry. Professor Slade was convinced you would, but that's really big of you to hang in there. It takes guts."

It took all my self-control not to grab my fork. "I've actually learned a lot since that first quiz. Noah's been helping me."

Blaise's gaze cut to Noah and narrowed. "I'm sure he has." She cleared her throat and clutched her purse to her stomach. "Well, I better get back to my friend. Have a good night."

"You too, Blaise," Noah said before turning his attention back to me, and his hand inched closer to mine on the tablecloth. I bit the inside of my cheek to stop myself from saying something stupid, and I was positive he noticed when one side of his lips quirked up. "Did you see the view on your way to the washroom? There's a balcony on that side of the restaurant. I'd love to show it to you after dinner."

I swallowed before shaking my head to his question as I felt my ruffled feathers settle. "I'd love that, too."

I didn't even notice Blaise leave, but then again—as Noah's fingers splayed out on the tablecloth less than an inch from mine— I barely remembered seeing her in the first place.

I found myself relaxing a smidgen when the waiter delivered our first course. The food looked like tentacles, but I'd never really been a picky eater, so I gave it a go.

Surprisingly delicious.

Then there were scallops, crab, salmon, steak, oysters—gag me —and numerous other things where I worried the chef forgot to remove the eyeballs before serving them.

Noah assured me it was intentional, which scared me even more.

But the chocolate cake was to die for. Literally. I would've stabbed myself in the neck with my butter knife if it meant I could eat another one. Luckily, Noah shared most of his with me.

I was tempted to ask if we could order a couple more cake

slices, then figured it'd be safer to wait until at least the third date for him to realize my unorthodox eating habits were more befitting a hungry, hungry hippo.

Or maybe the fifth date. Just to be safe.

Noah made good on his promise to show me the balcony, and we spent a while peacefully watching the city pass us by in the chilled night air.

It was getting late, so we headed downstairs and made our way out to the cozy parking lot.

"So, do I get to plan the next one?" I swung my arms at my sides as we strolled along, trying to sound nonchalant.

"The next one?"

"Our next date." I winced when I realized how forward that sounded. "If there is one, I mean. I don't want to assume."

His lips twitched. "All right. You can plan the next one."

I smiled in relief. "Good. Clear your schedule for tomorrow night."

"Pardon?"

"I'm calling a redo. No blazers or ties allowed. I'll let a sweater slide, but only if you insist. Otherwise, it's casual all the way."

"Hold on." Noah sliced his hand through the air as he stopped midstride. I skidded to a stop next to him and teetered dangerously on my wedges. "A *redo*?"

"Yes. Not in, like, a *bad* way." I put my hands up and tried to backtrack. "But just because this was a little much. You know? Overwhelming for a first date. Maybe redo was the wrong word."

Tonight reminded me more of a ten-year anniversary date, and I wouldn't be surprised if each week a few girls ended up choking on engagement rings hidden in their desserts.

As Noah's face turned to stone, I winced at my lack of tact.

"Shoot, Noah. I'm sorry." I touched his wrist lightly before dropping my hand. "I'm putting my foot in my mouth. I really enjoyed tonight. Truly. It was just a little hard for me to relax, I guess?"

"So, you're calling a *redo*," Noah said slowly, as if testing out the words to see how they tasted.

"Okay, that was obviously the wrong word to use." I scuffed my shoe against the concrete. "Poor taste on my part. I'm calling a... a second date. All right? Another date, in *addition* to this one, because this was a lovely date."

Noah puffed out a breath, and the silence gnawed at my stomach.

"Please don't hate me," I pleaded, my voice dropping to a whisper.

"I don't hate you." His hazel eyes ensnared mine before he nodded toward the restaurant. "I'm just trying to understand. This is one of the top-ranked establishments in LA. They collect more awards than they have room to display."

I shrugged and warned myself to tread lightly. "Maybe a few dates—or years—from now, that would've been my dream date. Like, movie-worthy. Right now, I just want to hang out. But I still had an amazing time. Seriously, five stars. Or ten, depending on your scale."

Noah breathed out a laugh before placing his fingers on my lower back and leading me through the parking lot. "It's fine. Just remember that I'll be the one critiquing tomorrow's date, hm?"

I chewed on my lip as I enjoyed the warmth from his hand seeping through my light top as we strolled up to the car. "Oh, I will. Trust me."

He once again opened the passenger door for me, and I quickly slipped in.

I pulled my seat belt on and fidgeted in the leather seat as he swung around the front.

"One more thing," I said as he slid into the driver's seat. "Can we stop by the store on the way back? Teresa's Aunt Flo is visiting."

"Sure. What does her aunt need from the store?"

I gave him a weird look, wondering how on earth someone

could miss a reference to menstruation. "Umm, some Red Vines and Pop-Tarts. And toothpaste."

Noah's brow furrowed as he pulled out of the parking spot. "Interesting."

"And maybe some fuzzy socks," I added, just to be safe. They were an impulse buy I could never seem to resist.

"Teresa's aunt sounds like an intriguing lady," Noah said as he turned out of the lot. I watched the way his hands gripped the wheel so self-assuredly.

"One could say that." I thought about the last time my Aunt Flo visited. I'd spent hours curled up on the bathroom floor in a psychotic haze of pain, praying for some higher power to give me the mercy of a swift death.

I swore to myself that was the first and last time campus security would ever be called on me.

Noah's phone buzzed in the middle console, and since he was driving, I reached for it. "Want me to answer—?"

"*No.*" He grabbed my wrist. I stopped short, lips parting. "I'll call them back later."

I barely heard him as I eyed the way his hand grasped my wrist. In different circumstances, it would've felt nice. His grip was firm, but not overpowering. Instead, I cleared my throat and tried to play it cool. "Touchy about your phone?"

"What?" Noah took his eyes off the road long enough to realize what his hand was doing, and he dropped my wrist like it'd burned him. Reaching for the still-vibrating phone, he silenced it and focused back on the road. "No. My job can be invasive, and I don't want it interrupting our evening."

I swallowed and stuck my hand under my thigh while trying to ignore the way my wrist tingled. "Right."

Note to self: Don't touch Noah's phone.

A Question

WHEN A KNOCK SOUNDED on the door at promptly five o'clock the next evening, I was ready for it.

I swung the door open with a smile and nodded in approval as I took in Noah's dark green sweater. He'd taken my instructions seriously. The nice slacks were still there, but I wasn't trying to change the guy... just help him chill out a bit. "Hey. Got a free hand to help carry?"

"What's all this for?" Noah asked as he offered a hand. I passed a bag to him and swung the backpack over my shoulder before heaving up a box with both arms.

"Date supplies."

Noah weighed the bag in his grip. "Such as?"

"Oh, you know. Tarp, duct tape, rope. That sort of thing." I gave him my best innocent look. "Also, very, *very* sharp knives. Why do you ask?"

Noah returned my look with his own unimpressed one as we made our way down the dorm's deserted hallway. It made me wish

I had said the box was filled with kinky sex toys just to see his reaction.

Outside, the weather was gorgeous, and most students were taking advantage by eating outside or hanging out on the grass. Noah headed for the street parking, but I nudged his shoulder and nodded toward the classroom buildings before he could go further.

"This way, actually," I said, and his eyebrows shot up. "We're staying on campus."

It was a quiet walk, filled with small talk asking about each other's days—which I didn't have much to contribute to because Teresa and I'd binge-watched crime shows all day.

The music building was unlocked when we arrived, and an onslaught of air conditioning welcomed us.

I readjusted the box in my arms before starting up the steps. "Follow me."

Noah followed dutifully, and I led him toward the music room where I'd met a certain Oliver Bishop.

I shook my head to rid myself of that baffling memory.

Balancing the box on one hip and only briefly risking its contents, I swiped us into the room and flicked on some lights as we moseyed in. There was a small stagelike platform just one step up from the floor, and I decided to make that our home base as I plopped down the box and slid off my backpack.

"Get comfortable?" I suggested while pulling a blanket off the top of the box and laying it out. He eyed it uneasily.

I stifled a smile and turned back to rummage through my bookbag.

"Listen, last night was nice," I said as I pulled out a board game and set it beside our blanket. "The restaurant was absolutely *beautiful*, and fancy, and you seriously know how to treat a girl. So, I'm not trying to take anything away from it. I just wanted to take some of the pressure off. Give us a chance to get to know each other without dead fish staring up at us, you know?"

Noah settled onto the blanket and glanced over the items I pulled out. A bottle of sparkling grape juice came next, followed by two red Solo cups, a bag of chips, and some portable Bluetooth speakers. "By sneaking into the music room?"

"It's not sneaking if we have swipe access." I grinned. I decided to overlook the fact that it was generally frowned upon to use the class buildings after five o'clock on weekends. "I thought we could eat this Chinese I ordered and hang out. I brought some games but left Monopoly in my dorm because I didn't think we were ready to show our true colors and hate each other just yet."

Noah chuckled. "Good call, and Chinese sounds great."

After connecting my phone to the speakers, I started up a classical station.

The light melody that could only be *Waltz of the Flowers* filled the room, and I went back to unpacking.

"I ordered almost all of their recommended meals, but don't worry—most of this will be leftovers. I don't expect you to eat all of it." I pulled out four cartons of takeout and a few containers of rice before stacking them between us. Garlic and all sorts of spices filled the room, and I took a deep inhale. I might've splurged money I didn't really have to spare, but I wanted this to go well. "You mentioned you like dumplings, right?"

"I do. I'm not a picky eater, though."

"Well, I got those." I pulled out the last container in the box and scooted it toward him. "And I brought forks, just in case you're not a chopsticks person."

"I don't mind chopsticks," Noah said as he accepted the offered container.

I grinned. "See? We've practically doubled the number of things I know about you."

Noah laughed dryly and flipped open the cartons before claiming one of the rice containers as his own. "You know a little more than that about me by now."

"One would hope." I claimed my own take-out container of rice and picked out some beef and broccoli to lay over it.

"Which game would you like to start with?" Noah asked as he swiped up a dumpling.

"How about Twenty Questions? Taking turns asking questions to get to know each other. We can skip over any if they're uncomfortable, and it's easier to play while eating."

Noah picked through his rice for a beat before nodding. "All right, that sounds fair."

I beamed before nibbling on my lip as I debated a safe-yet-telling question. Caution was key at the start of this game. "What's the last show you binge-watched?"

"Binge-watched?" Noah echoed with a hint of confusion. "I don't watch anything in excess."

I blinked, but his words didn't compute inside my brain.

"Seriously? Nothing? Not even..." I trailed off and racked my brain for a show he would enjoy. "... C-SPAN?"

"Not even C-SPAN," Noah said with amusement. He twisted open the sparkling grape juice and poured each of us a cup. "Why the love for coffee?"

I shrugged, not even sure if there *was* a significant reason. "I've never been a morning person. It's hard for me to wake up, so discovering coffee was a godsend. At first it was awful—I tried something way too bold—but eventually I found the right balance of sweetness. After a while, I just started enjoying it. Also, it doesn't hurt that coffee goes great with chocolate chip waffles."

"You add chocolate chips to your waffles?"

I made an honest effort not to frown at him. "You don't?"

"I'm more of a pancake person."

I barely refrained from gagging. "I hate to say it, but this might be a deal breaker."

His lips twitched. "Waffles are that important to you?"

"Yes," I said, deadpan. "With chocolate chips."

Noah's brows pulled together—he was probably waiting for me to say I was joking. Too bad for him, I wasn't.

"Moving on. Who's the first composer you ever played?" I asked, not wanting to let his uncultured preference for pancakes sour the date. "Not counting pieces like *Chopsticks* or *Mary Had a Little Lamb*."

"The first classical composer?" Noah asked. I nodded before taking a bite of my spring roll. He sat back and leaned on his hands as he thought about it. "Stravinsky. One of my instructors adored Stravinsky, and for a while it was all I ever played. You?"

"Beethoven." I tried pursing my lips to hide a grin threatening to break. God, it was such a predictable answer. "My parents didn't know much about piano, but they knew he was popular. So, they had me learn so many of his songs, I heard them in my sleep. A real crowd-pleaser."

"What's the first piece you played that you actually liked?"

This time I didn't fight the grin. I searched for the song on my phone and started it up before answering. Soft notes trickled into the room. "*Dawn* by Dario Marianelli. It's so delicate and enchanting, and you feel like you're holding your breath at the start so you can hear it. It's cheesy, but it made me feel like I was taking in air for the first time."

"It's a beautiful piece, especially when accompanied by strings," Noah said, and we took a moment to listen to the soft melody before I took my turn.

"What other classes are you taking?" I asked.

"Music Theory and History of Opera are my only classes."

I blinked, and my spring roll hovered halfway to my mouth. "Wait, *what*? How? That's only six credits."

"Actually, it's zero since I'm auditing." His lips curled up into an amused smile. "I'm not enrolled at Westcroft. I take classes in my free time when I have an interest in one."

My lips parted in surprise. "Hold on. Is that why you've been skipping classes or leaving early?"

Noah's smile grew, and he gave me a knowing look. "You've noticed?"

I gave him my best glare, trying to ignore the way my cheeks burned.

He chuckled.

My *best*, most *fierce* glare, and the guy chuckled.

"My job is a little unorthodox," Noah explained. "The hours aren't fixed, and I'm almost always on call."

I thought back to the call he hadn't answered last night. I hadn't wanted to seem nosy then, but if there was ever a time to ask questions...

"What do you do?" I asked, aware that I had hijacked all the questioning, but this was too interesting for me to be patient with.

"I'm in consulting. Mostly financial," Noah said, and the blazers and ties suddenly made a lot more sense. "It's for a private firm. We focus on commercial consulting, but sometimes we'll assist with private matters."

That threw me for another loop. I'd half expected him to say he was part of an orchestra somewhere, or even part of a wedding band, but *financial consulting?* "Wow."

"I attend classes on the side in things that pique my interest. Piano has always been a favorite of mine."

"That's really cool," I said, more than a little jealous.

"I'm happy with the arrangement. Is it my turn, yet?"

"Yes—of course, sorry. It's definitely your turn now."

He hummed and tilted his head as he peered at me. "What do you want to do after college?"

I paused to consider it. That far into the future wasn't something I usually allowed myself to think about. "I'm not really sure. I was thinking about Music Therapy, but I don't want to limit myself to just one thing right now."

The way Noah's brows rose shouldn't have warmed my chest as much as it did. He looked impressed.

"Admirable," he said. "That field isn't nearly as supported as it should be."

"I think so, too," I said as I fished around for a delicious dumpling. It kept slipping through my chopsticks, but I refused to give up. "What you said about it not being supported, I mean. The two main paths I'm looking into are mental health issues and abuse, and I'm hoping to get an internship next summer with a behavioral health institute nearby."

Music was more powerful than a lot of people thought, and I knew it was responsible for getting me through most of my child-hood. Plus, the internship would give me an excuse not to go back to Kansas over the summer.

Noah's eyes were all too knowing as he gazed back at me, and my heart leapt into my throat. Even though I *knew* he knew noth-ing, it was almost like he knew everything.

"What's with the blazers and dress shirts?" I asked before he could comment, using the first out I could think of.

Noah didn't immediately answer, and it took effort to hold his gaze as soft music played in the background. Then he blinked, and I could breathe again.

"They're what I like to wear."

"No specific reason why?"

"They're formal." Noah ran a hand down the front of his sweater. I smiled when I realized that was where the lapel of his blazer would've been. "I like formalities and routines."

"No kidding," I muttered through a smile. "Okay, your turn."

He took his time thinking, and he watched me with a curious look as I ate. "So far, I've learned that you're clumsy, you can down enough coffees to put anyone else in a coma, and you have an affinity for playing piano. What other talents do you have?"

I snorted a laugh, and the butterflies tittered along with me at him referring to my clumsiness as a *talent* of all things.

Would it be too forward to tell him I was a really good kisser?

It was tempting.

I tapped my chin as I thought, since I honestly had no clue what would qualify as a talent. Putting on socks with my eyes closed?

Somehow, I didn't think that was what Noah was looking for.

"I can roll my tongue?" I stuck out said tongue and rolled it into a cylinder shape as my eyes crossed to watch it. Attractive, I know.

"That's inherited genetically. Nothing to do with skill, I'm afraid," Noah said, dismissing it easily.

I scoffed and sat up straighter. "Okay. Let's see, I can play a mean game of Hungry Hungry Hippos. I was the hula hoop champion in sixth grade, and I've still got it. I can't cook worth a dime, but I can heat up the best pepperoni pizza rolls you've ever tasted in your life. I can solve a Rubik's cube. It'll take me like a week, and I'll probably end up looking up videos on the internet for instructions, but I can do it."

Noah's brows rose, and I'd say he looked pretty close to impressed. "Sounds like you have some tricks up your sleeve."

"And what are your tricks, Noah? Besides piano."

"I have a few things. I'm proficient in academics," Noah said evenly. "I still play soccer with a local league occasionally, and we won the under-thirty championship last year. I can cook a few tiers higher than pizza roll level, but I'm no gourmet chef. And I have a tendency to solve unsolvable problems."

It was my turn to raise my brows. "Like math problems?"

Noah chuckled, and the sound bordered on patronizing. "People problems. More like personal problems. Qualms. Or even company issues. I have a level head when it comes to times of crisis, especially when it involves the people I care about."

That was cryptic, to say the least. Definitely intriguing.

The people I care about.

"People you care about, like... friends? Will you tell me about them?" I asked, trying not to sound too eager.

"What about them?" Noah's chopsticks froze in the air, and he sounded decidedly defensive.

"Noah, I know literally nothing about your friends. Or family. Or whoever it is you usually hang out with." I shrugged. "Anything. Tell me *anything* about them?"

His gaze dropped to the takeout container, and he slowly took another bite as he weighed my question. I tried to sit still, hoping I didn't start fidgeting in anticipation.

He wasn't biting, though.

"How many are there?" I asked. *Dawn* had finished on the speakers, and the silence between songs hung in the air.

"Five," Noah answered, throwing me a bone as a Chopin piece started up.

"Five." I whistled, since I'd expected maybe one or two. Before, I might've assumed Noah was antisocial to a degree. Turns out he had more close friends than I'd ever had in my life. "That's a solid number. And you're all close? I can't imagine keeping up with five people's lives, but maybe that's because I'm an only child."

Noah laughed, and some of the tension dropped from his shoulders as he set his container down. "It's easier than you'd expect. They're all so different, and we've been through a lot together."

The smile on his face was an odd one I hadn't seen yet. One that held stories and emotions and memories of a world I'd never been a part of. It was almost suffocating to see.

I wanted to smile like that.

I nudged his foot with my own. "Like what?"

"I don't want to get into my past right now, but simply put... I didn't have the best childhood. I don't speak to my parents anymore." Noah's voice was as quiet as my own. "I have a sister, but we don't talk either. My friends were in similar situations, and that fused us together from the beginning. It's why we've stuck together since."

I swallowed around a lump in my throat, wanting something

like that so badly it made my stomach ache. "I'm glad you found them."

Noah sat still for a moment. His eyes refused to leave mine as he studied me for five full heartbeats. "I'm glad I found *you*."

Well, shoot.

"Julian is one of my friends," Noah continued, as if he hadn't just said something so sweet it gave me cavities. *Julian*. I filed the name away, determined to remember his friend. "You remind me of him, actually. He makes it his mission to exasperate me to no end."

"Hey!" I scowled and gave his ankle a harder nudge.

He laughed again, but this time his smile was only for me. "I'm sorry, that sounded worse than I meant it to. You both keep me on my toes."

I rolled my eyes and nibbled on my spring roll as I considered Noah. "I'd love to meet him, then."

Noah's smile slowly faded until I second-guessed if it had ever been there in the first place. "I'm sure he'd love to meet you, too."

It was odd, but from the way he said it... it almost sounded like that was a *bad* thing.

"How'd you find yourself out in California?" Noah asked, and I took the hint that all talk about his mysterious friends had now passed. I was just happy to have gotten a taste. "You said you're originally from Kansas?"

"I came out here for the Arts program. For Slade specifically." And to get as far away as I physically could from my parents, but that was a bit more than I planned on sharing tonight.

"He's a talented musician."

"He is. What about you?" I asked. "You're more Southern gentleman than surfer dude. Where are you from?"

"Texas. My friends and I moved here several years ago."

I itched to ask more. Who were his other four friends? Had they moved together for school? But I felt I'd already asked my allowance of friend questions.

"I've got another one for you," Noah said as he leaned back on his hands. He paused a long moment, cocking his head to the side and studying me. "Why'd you pretend Blaise was our server last night?"

A flutter took off in my stomach that turned into a nervous laugh, and I winced, not wanting to relive that part of the date. "Oh. You noticed that?"

"It was difficult to miss, considering our server was male."

I braced myself, figuring there was no better option than the truth. "I was being petty. She said something in the bathroom, and I just... I don't know. It got to me."

Noah's jaw tightened before he asked, "What'd she say?"

Yeah, I wasn't about to admit she'd mistaken me for a bathroom attendant.

"It doesn't matter. Actually, I think that's enough of this game." I cleared my throat and dusted off the front of my skirt. "What do you say to a little Pictionary?"

"I say you're avoiding the subject. You can tell me, Emma."

My lips twisted in protest at his knowing gaze, and I wondered if it was worth pleading the fifth. But it couldn't *hurt* to tell Noah the truth, and I didn't want him thinking I was hiding something. "Blaise didn't recognize me from class, okay? She thought I worked for the restaurant."

Noah's brow rose, and he shook his head slowly. "I'm not sure I'm following. You were upset about being mistaken for a server?"

"Well, a bathroom attendant." I tried to hold back a grimace. "But it wasn't that. It's stupid, but she was making fun of my outfit."

He cocked his head to the side, and if it were any other topic, I might've enjoyed the struggle he had grasping what I said. "So, you pretending Blaise was our server was a way of shaming her the same way she did you?"

I winced, wishing he hadn't made it sound so juvenile.

"You know, for being an academic, you sure could use a few

lessons in female social interactions," I muttered under my breath before tilting my chin up. "It was childish, but it made me feel a little better at the time."

"The list of things that cheer Emma Fox up is getting longer," Noah said as he counted off on his fingers. "Coffee with two scoops of sugar. Getting back at redheaded bullies. Waffles—"

"Chocolate chip waffles," I corrected. There was a big difference.

His lips twitched, and he dropped his hand back to the blanket. "And Pictionary?"

I swallowed at the warmth in his gaze and picked at a piece of lint on my skirt for something to focus on. "Yeah. Pictionary, too."

Noah meticulously folded his take-out container closed and brushed off his hands before responding. "Game on, then."

A Duet

I BLINKED. Then shook my head and blinked again, because I must've been hallucinating. Either that, or I could've sworn Noah was drawing a... a *certain part* of the male anatomy that surely wouldn't be included in the family-friendly game of Pictionary.

Then he added another circle next to the existing one on the whiteboard, and it was a miracle I didn't choke on my sparkling grape juice.

Noah's intense gaze turned to mine before he glanced at the timer for the eighth time. He tapped the marker pointedly against his unfinished drawing.

I could only sit there gaping.

"Uh." I stalled as Noah tapped against the whiteboard more urgently. His eyes were pinned to mine, and he was doing some sort of meaningful dance with his eyebrows, as if he could telepathically send the answer to me.

But surprise, surprise—Noah Kincaid wasn't telepathic. And it still looked like a penis to me. A bit of an oddly shaped one, but I'd never been one to judge.

I stalled again, pinching my arm in case this was a dream and I was about to wake up. No luck. "Noah... I, uh... are you sure you're drawing the right thing?"

Surely, it wasn't actually a penis. Even if the card said penis—which I was positive it didn't because this was kid-friendly game—there was *no way* Noah would've purposely drawn a penis on our date.

But it really, *really* looked like a penis. There were even small dots coming out of the top to resemble—

"*Mmmph!*" Noah mumbled emphatically through closed lips, taking the whole 'no talking' rule to heart as he continued to tap the marker rapidly against his drawing.

He gazed so steadily and pointedly at me that I gulped. For such a formal guy, he sure took Pictionary seriously.

I swallowed around the growing lump in my throat and winced in pre-embarrassment as I threw caution to the wind because there was honestly nothing else my brain could even fathom to guess.

"Is it... is it a penis?" I asked before cringing back in embarrassment.

From the way Noah's eyes widened and his lips parted in shock, I could tell my first assessment was correct—the drawing was indeed *not* a penis.

"No." Noah scowled, sounding decidedly offended. His tone made it seem as if it were crazy of *me* to even make that guess, when *he was the one who drew a freaking penis on the board.* "No, of course not. You think I would—"

I cleared my throat before nodding pointedly toward the very clearly penislike drawing.

Noah followed my gaze and took a moment to study the masterpiece as his head tilted slightly to one side and then the other.

A long, slow breath escaped him.

"I'm sorry," Noah said as he took in the drawing with new

eyes. My heart melted a bit at how chagrined he looked. He picked up an eraser and wiped off the board with quick, harsh movements, as if his drawing personally offended him. "That's not at all what I intended. Let me choose a new word."

I bit my lip to stifle a growing grin. "It's fine. What was it supposed to be, though?"

"An elephant, I'm afraid."

I blinked at the cleared whiteboard as the corner of my lips twitched. "But what were those... What was the line of dots coming out of the trunk?"

Noah rubbed at his temple, and his lips twitched with a reluctant smile. "Peanuts. I thought they'd be a helpful clue."

"Oh." I clapped a hand over my mouth to stop the bubbling laughter from escaping. Were the circles supposed to be eyes or ears?

Noah noticed my predicament, and he let out a strained chuckle. "Drawing isn't my forte, all right?"

He chose a new card, and I couldn't hold in my laughter anymore.

He sounded so embarrassed, but I was thrilled.

I'd finally discovered something Noah Kincaid sucked at.

The night was flying by, and my harmless crush on Noah was blooming into something warm and dangerous. The butterflies in my stomach felt far too content for my liking.

I'd almost given myself a hernia from laughing during the rest of our Pictionary game, and Noah finally threw in the towel when his drawing of a giraffe resembled more of a lava lamp.

The sun had long since set before my smile ever would, and an eerie glow cast itself through the room's wide windows as I settled back and nibbled on one of the chocolate chip cookies I'd packed.

Noah moved over to the piano bench, and I couldn't help noticing how at home he looked there.

"I grew up learning technique," Noah said as he folded back the cover from the piano's keys. "Every lesson was about note measures, finger placement, posture, and the right amounts of pressure."

I shuffled further down against the wall into a delightful slouch, really wishing I had some milk for this cookie. "Looks like it paid off," I said, wincing when a stray cookie crumb flew out of my mouth. I dusted it off of my thigh, hoping Noah wasn't as observant as I knew he was.

His back was almost ramrod straight, with his shoulders in resting position as he started a slow classical waltz with the keys. The butterflies came to life, wings fluttering sluggishly against my stomach as they awoke.

"For years, I played the same set of pieces targeted toward refining my technique and fine-tuning the foundation until it was unquestionably perfect."

Yep, definitely paid off. Noah's eyes focused on the keys before him while mine were riveted to him. His melody picked up, weaving through the room like a physical dance as I watched his hazel eyes remain centered on the keys. It was no wonder he'd helped me pass Slade's test.

"Until one day when the organist at my local church called in sick and wasn't able to perform," Noah said in a softer tone, and the notes followed suit until they were whispers crawling throughout the room. "Most of the parishioners were our neighbors and knew of my lessons, so they asked my mother if I could fill in.

"It was... new," Noah said unsurely before nodding his head at the word choice. "Something fresh and exciting."

His eyes shot up to mine, and I sucked in a breath at the warmth in them.

"It's just like you said with Marianelli. I felt alive in a way I hadn't before. It was simple gospel hymns, but they were different from the box I'd been confined to—even borderline cheerful. They weren't about keeping my fingers spaced perfectly or pressing on the pedal with *just* enough pressure. They were about the feeling behind it."

I understood. I understood in a way that had the hairs on my arms rising from how freaky it felt to hear someone else voice the words. Voice my own feelings. Before I could second-guess myself, I set down the rest of my cookie, turned off the classical playlist on my phone, and heaved myself up off the blanket.

It was a short walk to the piano, and I didn't waste any time joining Noah.

"I get it," I said just as softly before nudging Noah's shoulder until I could clumsily join him on the bench. He moved to the side, sliding so gracefully I kind of wanted to throw up a little bit. My hand reached out, and my middle finger hit the same happy note three times in a row. Then I tapped it again, as well as the next two to the left. Switching again to the right, I took turns tapping the next three keys in a row with an extra amount of fervor until I threw an extra tap in on the last one. "Do you know this one?"

"I do." Noah moved both hands back to the keys. His right one rested close to mine, and I chuckled.

"No." I swatted his hand away instead of grasping it like I itched to. "I meant as a duet. Not by yourself."

He blinked back at me, and I'd never seen Noah look more ruffled. "But—"

"You do the low notes, and I'll do the high ones," I explained in layman's terms, unsure why he looked so confused right now. It was just a beginners' duet. Most kids knew this one by heart. "Okay?"

"I don't do duets," Noah said, and he moved his right hand next to mine again. I raised a challenging brow at it, not backing down. "In fact, I've never played a duet."

It was my turn to blink, but he didn't seem to be joking. "You do know our partner project is a duet, right?"

Noah chuckled and ran his tongue over the front of his teeth. "I realize that."

"Then it sounds like we have quite a dilemma here," I said with mock-solemnness. "There's two options. Either you can keep being the guy who plays solo, or you can learn how to share. Do you need some time to think about it? It's a big decision."

That got another quiet chuckle out of him. Noah shook his head with a rueful smile and glanced down at where our hands rested next to each other. "I don't think it's quite as dire as you make it sound."

The hushed way he spoke—like we were sharing a secret—spread a warmth through my stomach at its intimacy. I tried to play it cool and licked my lips.

"What kind of guy are you gonna be, Noah?" I asked quietly, not wanting to break the sudden stillness settling into the room.

His eyes trailed up to mine, and he studied me with an intensity that made my hands tremble against the keys. Up close, the hazel in his eyes was ringed with a warm gold.

"The kind who plays duets with a beautiful girl, apparently," he finally answered, and I had to drop my gaze to the keys to stop myself from spontaneously combusting. The hand next to mine retreated as his other one took up its appropriate spot on the bass side. His first note filled the place of the beat my heart skipped, and my toes tapped along as he worked through the opening. Then I joined in with those three happy treble notes, and a moment later we were creating something that was only meant for the two of us.

I didn't care that my face was flushed from the pleasure of playing Noah's first duet with him, or that I was nervous my fingers would fumble over such a simple, repetitive melody. It didn't faze me that we were in the middle of a college campus, and that anyone with swipe access could barge in at any moment.

Because when Noah's free hand rested atop his slacks as we

played, his knuckles grazed against my thigh in a way that awakened goose bumps all the way down to the tips of my toes. His hand stayed there for three whole iterations of the duet, until it slid down and cupped my knee.

I stumbled over a note, but then he did too—and "Heart & Soul" quickly became my new favorite song.

A Tutor

Second lesson in all things magic: Be a performer, not a showoff. Nobody likes a showoff.

Nobody likes people who steal their cupcakes, either.

Touché.

SUNDAY ARRIVED FAR TOO SOON, and the happy haze from my date with Noah had almost completely worn off within the first ten minutes of my piano tutoring job.

"Miles Preston Fitzgerald Sterling the Third, I swear to God— I mean, I swear to the creator of sugary breakfast cereals everywhere—if you don't sit your boney little butt down on this piano bench, you'll regret it."

Miles stopped midstrike with his lightsaber and frowned. He was my most rambunctious student—out of the two who hadn't quit on me yet—but I'd take him over a certain gum-chewing demon spawn any day. It didn't hurt that his parents were loaded, and I only had to switch buses once to reach their neighborhood.

The Sterlings' marble-covered parlor was dedicated to the most gorgeous Steinway grand piano I'd ever laid eyes on. An expensive-looking rug lining the floor made me a little antsy, but the whole room was the embodiment of opulence. Floor-to-ceiling windows looked out into the garden. An odd assortment of plants filled each corner, softening the vibe. There was a shapely white couch, plus poofy chairs I was pretty sure weren't for sitting on. Even the air smelled higher quality.

How did someone achieve that?

"I mean it, Miles. Sit your butt down," I said while patting the bench beside me, "or I'm going to hide that lightsaber somewhere you'll never, ever find it."

His blue eyes turned to me in alarm, blond hair windswept from battling invisible adversaries.

"Miss Emma, you wouldn't!" He batted those big, beautiful eyelashes—which were much too thick for an ungrateful little six-year-old brat who was spoiled to the point of turning rancid.

I snorted and patted the bench again. "Oh, trust me. If you don't start showing me your progress on 'Twinkle, Twinkle, Little Star,' I most definitely would, little man."

We were ten minutes into the little menace's tutoring session, and I could guarantee that Mr. and Mrs. Sterling weren't paying me to watch their young jedi-in-training pulverize couch cushions.

"But that song is for babies," Miles said as he let his state-of-the-art lightsaber toy drop to the Persian rug before dragging his feet over to me. "I don't wanna play it."

"Well, tell me which piece would you like to learn instead," I said, testing out my patience. It was already shorter than usual this morning. I'd been dozing in bed daydreaming about my date with Noah, when I remembered I had a session with this little hooligan.

"The opening to *Star Wars*!" He pumped both fists into the air and beamed up at me. I had no idea how his mother kept his suits perfectly tailored to fit such small shoulders plus legs that seemed to grow more each day.

"Uh..." I stalled and tried not to wince as I thought of how complex that could get. "How about the music that plays in *Jaws*? When the shark is in the water?"

Miles blinked up at me. "Miss Emma, I'm not allowed to watch *Jaws*. That's a grown-up movie."

"Right." And *Star Wars* wasn't? "Well, Miles, we need to start by learning the different notes our fingers can play. That's why we practice beginner songs first, and then we work our way up to the more fun songs. Does that make sense?"

"But why do *I* have to play? Why can't I just give someone money to play for me?" Miles whined as he held his little palms out to his sides.

He was such a treat.

"Because it's a good skill to learn," I said, mostly to give myself more time to think of a better reason. My mind blanked. "Learning a musical instrument is fun, and it teaches you things like discipline. It's always good to try different things so you can find out what you like."

"Please don't lie to me." Miles rolled his eyes. "This is *not* fun."

I glanced at the *Piano for Kids - Beginner 101* sheet music on the piano's music shelf with a frown.

My breath escaped me in a sigh before I put on my best camp counselor voice. "All right! How about this? For every correct line you play, I'll give you half of a cookie. That sounds fun, doesn't it?"

Apparently, I wasn't above bribery.

Miles put a couple stubby fingers to his chin in the very aristocratic picture of thinking as he considered it. My heart sank when he shook his head. "No cookies. But I'll counteroffer a *whole* scoop of Jell-O for each line, *and* if I get everything right, we stop playing piano and you play jedis with me."

I considered his offer, but I didn't bother putting a finger to my chin, as I couldn't pull it off the way his munchkin-self did. The boy obviously hadn't practiced a single note, and he detested the song itself. Plus it would take the rest of our hour for me to go through how to read the sheet music and play the first few lines. It was the easiest bet I'd ever made. "Those terms sound fair. One question before I agree, though."

Miles nodded sagely for me to continue.

"Do you already have Jell-O in your refrigerator, or will this require me to make it?" I wasn't sure how far along my cooking skills were. I could've gotten store-bought cookies, but I wasn't sure if I trusted Jell-O molds.

"Miss Louisa made Jell-O yesterday." Miles waved off my concern. "There's a *really* big bowl in the fridge."

"All right." I held out my hand to the little bugger. "I agree to your terms, Mr. Sterling."

"Lovely," Miles's little voice proclaimed as he slipped his hand into mine. The self-satisfied smirk on the rugrat's little face should've clued me in.

That little devil.

That ungrateful, conniving, psychotic little menace.

I sat stewing on the curb outside of the Sterlings' gated mansion. My session ended fifteen minutes ago, but I was still fuming at the nerve of that little brat.

Turns out he *had* been practicing since the last time I'd seen him. Enough so that he was able to perform "Twinkle, Twinkle,

Little Star" perfectly the first playthrough, without a single error.

I'd been hustled.

By a six-year-old.

I should've been proud of him.

My arms and legs ached after being swatted with a plastic lightsaber more times than I could count. I was tempted to whack mine over the kid's head, but child abuse wasn't really my thing.

Once he'd defeated his fellow jedi twin sister—the role he'd oh-so-graciously given me—enough times that I spent the last two fights lying uselessly on the floor while he attempted to decapitate and dismember me, Miles called in his Jell-O winnings.

I assumed he would eat it nicely while sitting at the immaculate kitchen island like a good little preppy boy.

I'd been wrong.

The Jell-O was green, and in Miles's mind that meant it was perfect for an intergalactic space battle. All five scoops were lobbed at me as soon as he got his eager little hands on the giant bowl. With superstrength unexpected from a twiggy little ankle-biter, he made his last stand on top of the island—pouring the entire bowl over my head.

Children are our future, indeed.

And that was how I found myself stranded in the middle of the Stepford Wives' summer subdivision, with mansions as far as the eye could see. Part of me was surprised no one had called the cops on my disheveled, Jell-O-soaked appearance yet.

Now I just had to find a way back to campus.

The bus driver would have my head if I tried to get on his beauty while shedding globs of green Jell-O and smelling like a hospital cafeteria.

I tried calling Teresa, but she was busy with something that didn't involve checking her phone.

That left me in a precarious situation.

I glanced down at *Cupcake Thief* on my contacts list, but something about asking a practical stranger to come pick me up from the other side of town while I was covered in Jell-O felt wrong.

My thumb scrolled back up through the list, and I hesitated at a name near the top that was recently added but hadn't been put to use yet.

Noah Kincaid.

I hovered over it, debating the pros and cons of reaching out to a guy I'd been on two dates with for a ride—before I realized the biggest con of all was Jell-O reaching into places it should never be as I fidgeted on the curb.

Tapping the button before I could overthink it any further, I held the phone up to my ear and took a deep breath.

I immediately regretted it and wondered if there was time to hang up before my name showed up on his phone.

Noah answered after the first ring, voice so deep and sure I had to take a moment to make sure I was still capable of breathing. "Kincaid."

"Hey, boo," I cooed, and immediately shook my head in self-disgust as I mouthed *what the fudge?* to myself.

What. The. Hell.

I had *never* in my life called someone *boo* before.

"Pardon?" Noah sounded just as confused as I felt. "Emma?"

I grunted and pushed back a wayward strand of hair covered in the green globs of sugary gelatin. "Hi. Sorry about that. Just ignore me. There was a ghost—you know what, never mind. It's not important. Listen, you like me, right?"

His response was less than enthusiastic. "Yes?"

"Great. That's good." I chewed on my bottom lip. "Next question. And I'm just curious, so no pressure. But if I was stuck at a house across town in the scorching heat and with very little food in my belly, do you think you happen to like me the appropriate amount to come pick me up? Totally hypothetical, by the way, and I would absolutely hypothetically reimburse you for gas money and mileage."

Noah's quiet snort reached through the phone, and I leaned my head down until it rested on my bent knees. My skin fused together with leftover stickiness from the Jell-O, making them become fast friends.

"Since this is purely hypothetical," Noah said, "I'd have to know how you managed to get stranded before I decide if I like you the appropriate amount."

I sighed and nudged the toes of my white Keds—which were now tinged green—together. "I heard they had some really good coffee over here?"

Noah chuckled. "Well, as long as you aren't out hunting for innocent pens to gnaw on, I suppose."

"Hey, that was one time!" I pointed an accusing finger at the ground as my head shot up. "*One time.*"

"One time too many. What's the address? I'm heading out the door now."

I rattled off their address and wrapped a strand of sticky, Jell-O-stained hair around my finger out of habit. "Thank you. Seriously. You rock."

I winced.

You *rock?*

What is wrong with you, Emma?

"Um, and Noah?" I hesitated, a finger pushing gently against my cheek as I tested it for stickiness. "Bring a towel or two? I don't want to get your car dirty."

"Emma..." Noah trailed off before letting out a breath. "Never mind, I don't want to know. I'll bring towels."

"Thanks." I sighed, and a weight lifted from my chest as I flicked a piece of Jell-O off my knee. "You're the best."

"I'll see you soon," Noah said, and I got a quick goodbye in before he hung up.

It was a hot, sticky, uneventful wait until I saw Noah's black Audi pulling around the curb like my knight in shining Armani.

I winced as I approached the rolled-down window of Noah's passenger door. "Would you believe me if I said this wasn't just an excuse to see your car again?"

"Considering that would mean you willingly doused yourself in a mysterious green substance, I'd say I believe you," Noah said before hopping out of his side of the car. He circled the front without taking his eyes off me, and all sorts of questions were brewing in his gaze.

"It's Jell-O," I said as he opened my door. Towels covered the front seat, and I felt a smidgen better about asking Noah to bring his fancy car to pick me up. If I stained his car green, I didn't think any sort of payment plan could help me.

"Of course, it is," Noah said, as if Jell-O-covered girls asked him for rides home every other day.

I used the tips of my fingers to balance on the towel while crouching into the car. There was nothing ladylike about how I lowered myself onto the seat, but I wasn't willing to risk ruining his car just to save my modesty.

And if I happened to angle my butt in an eye-pleasing manner while I maneuvered myself through the door—in hopes of Noah possibly checking out how much junk I had in my trunk—then the Jell-O was fully to blame.

Not me.

He propped the door open and looked down at me. "I'm trying not to ask."

"You're failing," I said as I leaned carefully against the towels and let my eyes fall shut in much needed rest. The door closed with a *click*, and shortly after that, Noah was sliding into the driver's seat.

The silence lasted a total of ten seconds as he pulled away from the curb.

"So, was this particularly good coffee you heard about in a residential home?" Noah asked. "And does it explain your current state of... disarray?"

I winced again as I opened my eyes, and I tried to fight off the blush that was rising from my neck. I *really* didn't want to share this particular story with Noah. "It's kind of embarrassing."

"I wouldn't expect anything less."

His eyes were still stealing glances at my sticky face, so I heaved a breath and dove right in.

"I was helping to shape young talent when my piano student morphed into a possessed demon child and did *this* to me," I said succinctly before throwing in a careless shrug to drive it home. As if it didn't bother me that Jell-O was getting into the nooks and crannies of my body.

The shrug was a bad idea, though, because it caused a glob of Jell-O to fall from my nest of hair and land with a *plop* on my shoulder.

I could only stare at it in betrayal.

Noah's side of the car was quiet, and I told myself not to look, but of course I did—only to find his face turning red from the effort of holding in laughter.

"It's fine, you can laugh." I crossed both arms over my chest and turned to look out my window.

Air burst from Noah's lungs with a laugh joining it, and I got whiplash from the force of my head turning back to him. He laughed with his full body, hands shaking on the wheel as his stomach constricted. A smile stretched from ear to ear, and his hazel eyes were pools of warmth when he spared a glance at me.

He looked happy. Really happy.

At my expense, but I was too flabbergasted to really care.

I couldn't resist joining in, and laughter bubbled to my lips until I was smiling just as widely as he was.

It was a few blocks before Noah's laughter eased off and settled into a handsome smile while he smoothed a hand down his blazer. "Did you end up getting any coffee while you were there?"

"No. The Sterlings said I could help myself to their coffee, but they have this espresso machine that you need a bachelor's degree in machinery to know how to operate."

"Not worth the risk of trying in case it blew up?" Noah teased as he turned onto the highway.

"Oh no, I still tried. I just couldn't get it to work. It kept yelling at me."

Noah chuckled again, and I decided he was feeling particularly carefree today. At least as carefree as someone who wore blazers and nice slacks could feel.

"How about I drop you off at your dorm to clean up, then you meet me back at the car and we'll go for some coffee?" Noah asked casually. Almost *too* casually. "I know of a new café that just opened up a few blocks from campus."

The butterflies were back, and it felt like they were vomiting happiness inside my stomach, because it was quickly pooling with a warm kind of pleasure.

"Sally's Café?" I prompted before clearing my dry throat. Noah nodded. I cleared my throat again to give myself a chance at sounding like I wasn't hyperventilating on the inside. "That sounds great. I heard about it, too, and I've been wanting to try it."

"We could grab lunch, too," Noah said as he switched lanes. "They serve sandwiches."

The butterflies in my stomach roared into a frenzy. "I'd love to."

Noah spared me another smile before focusing on the road again, and I'd lost count of how many he'd sent my way this morning.

I just knew I wanted to see a thousand more.

Maybe Miles Preston Fitzgerald Sterling the Third wasn't so bad after all. In fact, I think I owed the little bugger a few rounds of lightsaber battles.

The kid was officially my wingman.

A Group Project

CLIMBING out of bed the next day was like waking from a dream. I managed to rouse before my alarm, and there was a stupid smile permanently etched onto my face. I didn't even care that it was a Monday.

I was in such a state of post-hanging-out-with-my-crush bliss, I felt like sitting cross-legged on my bed and humming Kumbaya while making a daisy chain crown.

So that was exactly what I did.

Teresa didn't appreciate the humming very much, and a bee stung me while I was plucking daisies in front of our dorm building, but my smile was still going strong when I strolled into Music Theory at promptly eight o'clock with a freshly brewed cup of coffee in hand.

And it didn't leave when I spared a glance at Noah, only to catch him returning my look before we both twisted toward the front of the room like naughty children.

I was beginning to think the butterflies in my stomach would never leave, and I resolved to start charging them rent.

But karma was a female dog, which was quickly proven when class began.

"Break up into your assigned groups of four and work on the project I've outlined," Professor Slade said to the room before backing off the podium and taking a seat at his desk. "I'll be grading papers but available for any questions."

My eyes stared at the projected list, where my name was woefully crammed between Sleepy Susan and Aaron Richards.

Okay, so her name didn't *literally* say Sleepy Susan, but we were all thinking it.

Unfortunately, she was the one I was least worried about. I was a little more concerned with the boy I may or may not have snarked back to when he was looking for a seat the first day of class.

Blaise's name above Susan's was another kick to the gut, and I held my breath while shuffling over to Susan's desk. Neutral territory.

A red notebook dropped onto the desk with an echoing slap as I sat down, and Susan jerked awake. I'd recognize the grimy fingernails holding that notebook anywhere.

"Aaron," I said politely before looking up to see his blue eyes glaring down at me. Déjà vu hit with the force of a train, and I gulped on instinct.

It appeared he remembered me, too.

"Blondie." His lip curled up in a sneer as he dropped unceremoniously into a chair.

Blaise appeared behind him, red curls pulled back in a high ponytail and enough resentment in her gaze to fuel an army when she looked at me. "Emma, how's mother dearest doing? I haven't heard from her in a few days."

I stifled a groan and tried to ignore the way her sneer rivaled Aaron's. "Hi, Blaise."

She sat without another word and quickly lost interest in me.

I glanced around the room, officially jealous of every other group in the class, since they were all actively working together. My eyes spotted Noah's table quickly, and it was obvious he'd immediately taken over as lead of the project. From the way his sharp eyes darted between the other group members as he spoke, and the commanding finger pointing at the paper sitting between them, I wasn't too proud to admit that I may have swooned in my seat a little bit. He looked like an army commander, and the others in his group nodded along—riveted to every word.

My own eyes were riveted to the way his hands rolled up the sleeves of his white dress shirt, causing the muscles in his forearms to flex as he motioned around. It reminded me of when we'd eaten lunch together yesterday and I'd gotten caught staring at his wrists when he'd taken a bite of his turkey sandwich.

I wasn't sure Noah believed my little white lie when I'd told him I was inspecting the turkey to make sure it wasn't raw, but seriously—it wasn't fair for a guy to have such attractive wrists.

Telling him would only inflate his ego. So really, I'd been looking out for him by making a fuss about the turkey.

The subject of my scrutiny met my gaze across the room with those piercing hazel eyes, and I was officially caught creeping as an amused smile curved his lips.

I just stared stupidly back as my heart rate ramped up.

Blaise cleared her throat, and I focused my attention back on our little gang of misfits.

"I can't believe I have to do a project with you losers," Aaron said, and it took all of my willpower not to kick his chair. Blaise raised an eyebrow while Susan just blinked wearily.

"I guess we can start with picking a piece to discuss?" I offered in hopes of getting the ball rolling. "Then we just need to figure out how to present on it for ten minutes."

My suggestion was met with one blank stare, one glare, and the back of Aaron's head as he ignored me.

"And why exactly should we be taking your suggestions?" Blaise's glare turned glacial. "The other students with your grade dropped out, you know."

My jaw dropped, and even Aaron fell silent at her sharp tone. "I've been improving."

"Yes, of course." She offered a tight-lipped smile and lowered her voice to a stage whisper. "If only all problems in life could be solved by sleeping with the smartest guy in the class, right?"

I blinked, and Aaron let out a snort of surprise on my other side.

What. The. Hell.

"Blaise," I said, completely uncomfortable with where this was going. My face was hot enough to fry an egg. "Noah helping me study has nothing to do with the dates. I'm not using him for my grade."

"Oh, so it's *dates* now?" She leaned back in her chair. "Whatever. You guys have fun doing the project. It's not as if I have a grade relying on it."

"Great. This is just great. Of course I get paired with the psychos." Aaron stood up abruptly from his chair. "I'll ask Slade if we can go to the music room to work in case you two decide to go at each other's throats."

Blaise dragged her feet but followed his lead. I sighed and stopped by my desk to grab a notebook before trudging out of the room behind them.

Against my better judgement, I snuck a glance over my shoulder at Noah's group. They were all focused intently on the paper between them as Noah scribbled on it. The boy beside him said something, and they all nodded encouragingly.

I frowned and started out the door again before a large lump at my group's desk caught my attention.

"*Susan.*" I shuffled back over to her desk and gave her shoulder a quick shake. "Wake *up*. We're going to the other room."

A Two-Scoop Day

Steam must've been coming out of my ears by the time class mercifully ended and I stomped out of the music room. Blaise knocked into my shoulder from behind, her bright red ponytail bouncing as she strode past. I made a face at her back.

Seeing Noah leaning against the wall in the hallway when I'd finally escaped the bloodbath did little to calm the aggravated tic I'd developed, but he still managed to make me crack a smile when our eyes met.

"Emma." Noah nodded and offered me an arm as he turned toward the stairs. "I hope you don't mind. I found myself in need of a little caffeine and thought you might, too."

I frowned at his arm and instead slipped my hand into his before we started down the hallway at a leisurely pace. His fingers wrapped securely around mine, and the butterflies in my stomach perked up.

"That's odd, because I find myself in need of a baseball bat to knock someone over the head with." My smile turned thin.

"Would it be concerning if I suddenly found the bad guys on my crime shows inspirational?"

Noah took my bloodthirsty thoughts in stride and only spared me a side look. "Well, I'm glad to see your day is going well."

I groaned and leaned my head back with a sigh. "Sorry. This morning just sucked. Like really sucked. Big time."

"What happened?"

"It's just the stupid group project." I scoffed. My blood pressure rose just thinking about it. "When that jerk wasn't making dumb blonde jokes, he kept laughing at everything that witch said! I wanted to punch him in the throat."

Noah led us down the stairs, which were a little crowded. Students heading the opposite way jostled my shoulder, so I leaned a little closer to Noah until we got to the last staircase. He looked down at me, eyes understanding. "What can I do to make it better?"

I rubbed a finger across the soft skin between his thumb and forefinger and thought it over. "Depends. Do you have any opposition to removing articles of your clothing while dancing provocatively to seedy music?"

Noah gazed back at me blankly, and I pulled a face when he didn't laugh.

"I'm kidding. Mostly. Heading to the coffee cart ASAP would be a good start, though, so I think we've got it covered," I said with a cheesy grin.

He nodded warily and gave my hand a quick squeeze. "Is it a two-scoop day?"

A two-scoop day.

I ducked my head to hide the instinctual smile at him remembering, but there was no way Noah could've missed it.

"Yep." I gave his warm hand a return squeeze as we reached the bottom step. "It's definitely a two-scoop day."

And Noah Kincaid was very much a two-scoop guy in my book.

September's weather was gorgeous as we headed toward the quad, and the breeze was gentle enough to only force the occasional strand of hair to block my line of vision. Oak trees lined the open grassy area surrounded by school buildings, and students were littered all across the quad. Girls playing Frisbee. Guys hogging the hammocks. Small pods of students studying or goofing around. I closed my eyes and tilted my head back to soak in the sunlight.

"If you want to grab that table, I'll get our coffees," Noah said as we approached the coffee cart. He pointed out the only open table left on the patio of the Student Union before looking at me. "Caramel Macchiato with extra caramel syrup and two scoops of sugar, right? Or did you want something else today?"

"Oh, I'll grab the coffees." I reluctantly pulled my hand from his and scratched at an itch on my elbow. He knew my order? To think I'd thought remembering the two scoops was impressive.

"That's all right. I've got it covered."

"But I still owe you for your pen..." I trailed off and gave him a pointed look.

Noah frowned. "Emma, we're dating now. I don't expect you to pay me back. And I'd like to pay for your—"

"Noah," I said firmly, not backing down. "I need to pay for it. Please."

My stomach was entirely too pleased about the way he said *we're dating now.*

We're. Dating. Now.

I didn't recall an official conversation going down, but I was ready to roll with it.

Obviously, my old gymnastics teacher didn't know what she was talking about when she claimed I wasn't flexible.

His lips thinned, and I prepared myself for a staredown.

"Can I at least pay for yours, then?" Noah asked.

I snorted a laugh and shook my head. "That completely defeats the purpose! My order goes for four times the price of yours."

"I'd like to pay for it," Noah said, and a tinge of command inched into his tone that did seriously weird things to me. "My job pays well."

"That doesn't matter, because I don't feel comfortable with you paying right now. You've already paid when we've gone out. Let me handle the coffee until I can reimburse you for the pen, and then we can renegotiate, okay? If... you know, if we're still dating then. Not trying to be presumptuous or anything."

Noah's determined expression morphed into one of amusement as I tried to backtrack. He eyed the coffee cart again before his gaze flickered over my own determined face.

"Presume away," he said, and his lips twitched. "All right, I'll reserve the table... this time."

"Thanks." I smiled before reaching out to touch the soft material covering his forearm. He tensed a little, but it was progress since the time he'd jerked away and I'd face-planted into the ground. "Sorry, I swear I'm not going all super-feminist on you. I just need to do this."

Noah managed a small smile back, followed by a soft sigh as the hard lines of his jaw eased. "I understand. I even respect it, but that doesn't stop me from disliking it."

"It just rubs all those Southern manners deeply ingrained in you the wrong way, doesn't it?" I teased with a smile as I let go of his arm.

Noah's smile widened, and he shook his head. "You have no idea."

I tried and failed to fight down another smile before shooing him away. "Hurry, before someone takes the table. I'll be right over."

Noah's eyebrow rose effortlessly. "Someone's feeling bossy today."

"Less talking, more walking." I clapped my hands together twice for emphasis before making a beeline for the coffee cart.

"Hey, Emma," Scott said as I stepped up to the counter. He threw away a handful of paper towels and offered a smile.

"Morning." I smiled back before pulling out my trusty wad of dollar bills and freeing several from the bunch. "The usual for today with two scoops, plus a regular black coffee, please."

"I thought a regular black *was* part of your usual order now?" Scott's smile widened, and he plucked a cup off the stack to fill.

"Maybe." I smiled like a boy-band-obsessed schoolgirl, beyond pleased that he'd noticed. I glanced over my shoulder—making sure Noah was well and distracted at the patio table—before leaning closer to the cart and lowering my voice. "He's cute, right?"

Scott handed me Noah's cup before starting on my masterpiece, and I didn't miss the flat look he sent my way. "Don't even start that. I'll make as many coffees as you want, but checking dudes out for you isn't on the menu."

I huffed, having to stop my mouth when it reflexively went to drink the black coffee. "Whatever. He's cute. How's your day going?"

"Can't complain," Scott said as he dropped a couple scoops of sugar in my drink. He covered the mixture with a splash of whipped cream before topping it off with an extra drizzle of caramel. My mouth watered. "I have classes this afternoon and a test I'm not ready for, but it's been a slow morning."

I frowned as I gave his cart a considering look. "Slow enough for them to think we don't need a coffee cart on the quad anymore?"

Scott's brow rose in amusement, and he snapped a lid on before trading the caramel macchiato for my money.

"Don't worry. My cart is staying right where it is," he said as he rang up the order. "And who is *them*?"

I shrugged and set my cup down so I could accept the change before slipping it into my backpack. "I don't know. School administration? Starbucks? The coffee gods?"

Scott rolled his eyes and waved me off. "Never change, Emma."

"Never stop providing me with my energy source, and I won't have to," I said just as an upperclassman came up to the cart. I picked my cup back up and scooted away, trying to give Scott a finger wave while holding both coffees. "I'll see you tomorrow?"

"Bright and early, unless the coffee gods smite me first."

I wove my way through the throng of students switching classes before reaching Noah's table in the middle of the Student Union's patio.

His sharp eyes followed my approach, and I wondered just how long he'd been watching me.

"Your coffee, sir," I announced. I reached the table and placed the cup in front of him with an accompanying bow.

"Thank you," Noah said as I slid onto the stone bench across the table from him. "I was wondering about your piano tutoring over the weekend. How long have you been doing that?"

"Oh, I've been tutoring for years," I said. "It's the only job my parents let me do in high school, since it involved the piano."

"They're fairly strict, I gather?"

I snorted. He didn't know the half of it. "You could say that."

"How do they feel about you attending college so far away?"

I fought a smile and attempted to quirk a brow. "Is this another game of twenty questions?"

"Sort of. I've been wondering a few things."

I hesitated before answering, not sure how much I wanted to share. "My mother is totally on board with Westcroft. She thinks Slade walks on water and couldn't have dreamed of getting a better mentor for me. I don't think she realized I'd only see him during lectures."

Even if it'd finally gotten through to my mother, she certainly didn't accept it.

"And your father?"

I tried to hide my wince. If my father had his way, I would've stayed home and continued doing recitals. "He came around."

Noah pulled the lid off his coffee to let it cool faster. I wanted to do the same but didn't want to seem like a copycat, so I just sat there and let my coffee take its own sweet time.

"Are you close with your family?" he asked as he looked up.

I blinked in surprise at the personal question. "No, not really. You said you don't talk to yours, right?"

"No," Noah said easily, as if I hadn't been pulling teeth to get answers from him a few days earlier. "My mother and I in particular never got along, but I like to think she's happy with where I've ended up."

I swallowed, not sure how to interpret that.

Did he mean happy with me or his life in general?

"Are you happy?" I asked.

"I am," Noah said with sincerity, not even taking a moment to think about it. "Although, one thing has been troubling me lately."

"What is it?"

"You," he said, pulling my gaze back up to his. His usual unyielding demeanor was cracking, and a flash of frustration peeked through. "I can't seem to figure you out."

I swallowed. "What's there to figure out?"

"Why aren't you close with your family, Emma?" Noah squared off his shoulders toward me—as if preparing for battle. "Or anyone truly, for that matter. That's what I can't understand about you. You're the most easygoing person I've met, yet aside from your roommate and the boy at the coffee cart, you tend to keep to yourself."

I blanched as my hackles rose. Where was this coming from? "Hey, I talk to a lot of people!"

"There's a difference, though. You're always friendly, and you have a big heart. You'll talk to a *squirrel*, for god's sake—and I know this because I've seen you do it—but you aren't friends with anyone aside from Teresa. I'm the only other person you spend time with."

I inched my coffee cup across the table as I struggled for words.

How was I supposed to explain to him that college was the first time I'd really had a chance to spread my wings without worrying about the backlash? The first time I didn't spend most of my waking hours playing the piano or dreading what my father would do the next time I messed up. That not having friends wasn't for lack of trying, but because I wasn't exactly sure how to go about doing it. After meeting my parents or having me bail on plans too many times because of piano, my so-called friends eventually just stopped asking me to hang out. Getting Teresa as my roommate was the luck of the draw, and it was easy to talk to Scott—he was the coffee cart guy.

I cleared my throat. "I didn't know you paid that much attention."

"It's difficult not to." Noah tapped his fingers against the table-top. "Some days you seem like an open book, but then I'll turn around and you'll surprise me again. You're funny. You're intelligent. You're beautiful. Emma... you're very easy to pay attention to."

A blush warmed the crests of my cheeks. He'd shared his feelings so easily, while I floundered for what to say. "I guess I'm just not that good at making friends?"

"That's not it," Noah said with a shake of his head. "I've seen you be very charming. But you don't usually approach people. You wait for them to come to you."

"I don't understand where you're going with this."

Noah paused and considered me for a moment before doing what I assumed was the fancy equivalent to a shrug. He simply lifted his shoulders in a very graceful way. "To be honest, I'm wondering why you decided to talk to *me*, of all people."

I blinked back at him. "You mean besides the fact that I mutilated your fancy pen and pretty much *had* to talk to you to make things right? Well, since we're being honest, that's exactly why I did it. I don't think I ever would've approached you otherwise."

"Why not?"

"You're pretty intimidating." I waved a hand at the way he was leaning forward with his body tensed. "And very polished, not to mention way out of my league."

"That's not true."

"Of course it's true. If I hadn't damaged your property, you probably never would've talked to me either. I had to chase after you."

Damn him for making me exercise.

Noah's silence spoke volumes. We both knew he hadn't been the most receptive to me.

"Why are you asking?" I pressed again and leaned forward the same way he had. I wasn't above trying to intimidate him back, but I had a feeling my shorter stature and much-less-broad shoulders weren't having the intended effect. Not sure what to do with my hands, I picked at the sleeve on my coffee cup.

"I'm not used to being approached like that." Noah cocked his head to the side. "And you're a puzzle that I can't seem to make sense of."

I snorted. "Well, good luck figuring me out."

Three school therapists had already tried and failed.

I stopped fiddling with my cup's sleeve and laid both hands flat on the table. Noah tracked the motion, and his hand reached out until it cupped mine. I stilled underneath his touch before meeting his gaze again.

He lowered his voice. "It's difficult for me to let people in without understanding their motives. I can't recall the last time someone tried to get to know me. I know with my prying it may not seem like it, but I'm glad that you chewed on my pen that day."

I was all too aware of each nerve ending connecting his hand to mine, and the hackles that'd risen packed up and went home after his confession.

He was *glad* I'd defaced his property?

"I'm glad, too," I said just as softly, then used my free hand to risk taking a sip of the steaming coffee just so I wouldn't start serenading the guy.

The coffee wasn't scalding anymore, and it warmed me all the way down to the butterflies frolicking in my stomach.

"Are your parents—" Noah cut off midsentence. He let go of my hand and pulled his phone out from the inside pocket of his blazer. He glanced at the screen before apologetic hazel eyes cut back to mine. "I'm sorry, I need to take this."

I waved him off. "Oh, you're fine."

"Kincaid," Noah said shortly as he turned away. There was a severity to his voice that I didn't recognize, and it sent a wave of chills down my spine. He walked toward the end of the patio while sending me a signal that it'd be a minute.

I sighed and fiddled with the sleeve on my coffee cup. Noah called me a puzzle, but he was the mysterious one making private phone calls.

He was back a moment later, and from the edge to his pursed lips I already knew it would be a short visit.

"I'm sorry. There's somewhere I need to be," Noah said with an apologetic smile as he picked up his cup from the table.

"Work?"

He nodded as he collected his messenger bag.

"Okay. I guess I'll see you on Wednesday, then?" I tried not to sound too disappointed.

Noah paused after slipping on his bag. "Ah, I'm heading out of town today for work. I'll be gone the rest of this week."

He held up his sleek phone as if it were Exhibit A during a murder trial, before sliding it into his pocket.

"Oh." My lips parted in surprise. "You travel for work?"

"Occasionally. Some of our clients are local, but we have accounts all over the country. I'll be in Seattle until Friday."

"Oh. Wow, okay. That's neat."

My mouth didn't have anything else to say, and Noah was just standing there while I sat awkwardly.

"Emma." Noah squinted and faced me head-on. "I'd like to see you when I return on Friday."

He'd like to see me on Friday.

"Oh," I repeated like a broken record as warmth spread through my body. "You'd like to see me. Okay, sure. Yeah. That sounds... fun."

A smile was fighting its way onto his face, but he won the battle before I could see it fully formed.

"Friday, then," Noah said firmly before turning and making quick work of weaving through the students mingling about on the patio.

"Friday," I whispered to his back before slumping over the table.

It was going to be a long week.

I took a sip of coffee to try and relax after that impromptu interrogation. The restlessness got to me, and I pulled out my own phone as Noah disappeared around the corner. I was surprised to see a text that had come in unnoticed during class.

CUPCAKE THIEF

> Why do men have nipples? Seems kinda pointless, don't you think?

The smile was quick to take, and my cheeks ached slightly from the force behind it. Was this boy serious?

EMMA

> I don't know... They seem kind of pointy to me? At least when it's cold.

> No. Nonono. Please don't tell me you like puns, Cupcake! Please?

> Okay, I won't tell you I like puns.

CUPCAKE THIEF

Puns are the lowest form of humor, I'll have you know. They aren't even funny.

EMMA

But they're punny!

This brownie you owe me better be worth it.

Only 45 more points to go.

Any chance I could get an advance on those?

Tell me a pun, and I'll see what I can do.

…

I'm waiting.

Cupcake, don't do this to me… I thought we were gonna be magician buddies?

Still waiting.

I stifled a laugh and scooted to the edge of my seat in anticipation. It was stupid, and I felt like such a dork, but there was something compelling about texting the cupcake-stealing magician I'd met.

Three little dots appeared to show Finn was typing before disappearing. Long seconds passed while I sat stupidly staring at the cracked screen in my hand and sipping on coffee. Finally, those three little dots appeared again with a vengeance.

CUPCAKE THIEF

You're baking me crazy, but I will stop at muffin to get that brownie, Cupcake.

I snorted into my cup, and little drops of coffee flew over the edge as I clutched my phone. Some students at the table next to me glanced over, but they quickly dismissed me as the stupid girl who didn't know how to consume liquids correctly.

I was too busy watching the dots that said Finn was still typing to care.

CUPCAKE THIEF

God, I hate myself for doing that. Transfer the brownie points to my account, then delete all evidence pls.

EMMA

Screenshotted, printed, and framed. +10 points added to your account.

A new text popped up almost instantly.

CUPCAKE THIEF

Worth it.

I was smiling so hard my cheeks ached, and I flipped the phone over a few times in my hand from restlessness.

See? I could totally make friends. Noah didn't know what he was talking about.

But I warned myself to be careful, because texting Finn worked the butterflies up just as much as talking to Noah did.

A Storm

THE REST of the week flew by uneventfully, and by some miracle my group survived our project in Slade's class. I did my best to shove the memory of that disastrous presentation to the back of my mind where I would never have to relive it again.

Let's just say Blaise and I would never be BFFs.

Teresa and I spent some quality time watching my favorite cooking show on Netflix Tuesday night—*Baking with Babushka*—but she'd made a new friend from her soccer team and I barely saw her the rest of the week. I didn't see *any* of Noah since he was off being a big hotshot consultant up in Seattle, and it was a decidedly lonely week. I spent most of my free time studying, practicing piano, or hanging out with Scott at the coffee cart, and even *he* commented on how unpopular I was.

Mr. Everton called with a new catering job for Saturday, and I pounced on the opportunity, happy I'd be back on buffet duty. While van unloading was an honorable calling, I wasn't too proud to admit it just wasn't for me.

Noah called me once from the Emerald City, but he wasn't

really the chatty type, and I didn't want to put my foot in my mouth, so our phone call was short and sweet. He told me he'd be back in town Friday evening, and as soon as I saw his smiling face outside my dorm room, I took it upon myself to drag him to Teresa's soccer game.

He came willingly, and he even traded in his blazer for a cardinal-red sweater.

I tried not to stare.

"We don't have to stay long," I said to my trusty soccer buddy as I tugged him toward the stands. "Just enough for me to see Teresa run around a bit so I can be a supportive roommate and all that jazz."

"I don't mind going to her game." Noah's grip tightened on my hand, and he sounded amused. He kept walking at a casual pace, no matter how much I tried to pull him along faster. "I told you I like soccer."

That was right. He even played, which was way more than I did.

I pulled Noah along behind me until we reached the bleachers of the student section. Teresa was standing around by the goal near us, and I tried waving to get her attention.

"Clouds are rolling in," Noah said, and he gazed up at the greying sky as we settled into the third row of bleachers. "Looks like rain."

"Oh good, maybe they'll have to play in the mud." I looked at Noah hopefully. "That'd be a little more thrilling to watch, don't you think? Players slipping and sliding all over the field."

His lips twitched again, and I found it fascinating that such a handsome creature had agreed to date me. There were probably scientists out there itching to do a study on us. "I think it'll get rained out before they're forced to do that."

"Pity." I set my water bottle on the bench beside me and practically vibrated in my seat as I watched Teresa run after a girl kicking the ball. "So, uh, how was Seattle?"

Noah lifted a shoulder, and his hand pulled mine closer to his thigh with the movement. "Not too interesting. It was work."

"You didn't do anything fun while you were there?" I asked, mostly to distract myself from the way our thighs pressed together. "Nothing touristy?"

Noah shook his head and looked back out to the field as Teresa kicked the ball away. Attagirl. "Nothing worth mentioning."

Well, okay, then.

I was officially out of conversation topics. According to my plan, talking about his trip was supposed to take up at least a quarter of a game's worth of conversation.

I twiddled my thumb against his to help myself think through the list of topics it would be safe to bring up.

I could ask him how his classes were going? *Pass. I'm in all two of his classes, so I already know that.*

Talk about the weather? *But he already mentioned that. Clouds. Rain. Yada yada.*

Bring up the declining salmon population in California? *Honestly, it's such a downer to even think about. Really don't want to put a damper on Noah's mood when he just got home.*

I heaved a sigh.

"So, how about them... uh, sports teams?" I asked, proud of myself when the question came out sounding somewhat legit. I knew very little about sports, but most guys loved that stuff.

"Sports teams?" Noah gave me a very warranted puzzled look.

"The teams in the, uh, in the game," I said less confidently, stumbling for the right terms. This was still salvageable. "Didn't you watch the game last night?"

Noah's brow rose in amusement as a smile slid across his handsome face. "Which game?"

What the *heck*? People never specified *which* game when I heard them ask this. You just answered yes or no, and then moved on!

"Umm, *the* game." I racked my brain for a sport I'd seen playing on TV before. "Football."

"Emma, the football season hasn't started yet. It begins next week."

"Well, yeah. Duh. Not *football* football, but football." I internally kicked myself for such an easy blunder. Since when did they not play football year-round? Who decided that? "You know, like what we're watching right now—when you kick the ball with your foot? I guess Americans call it *soccer* or something."

Noah stifled what might've been a laugh with a quick cough. "... Emma, *you're* American."

I nodded while metaphorically jumping ship as I realized there was no saving this conversation. Best to just let it go to where things went to die. "Never mind. Forget I asked. So, it's a real shame about the salmon population here in California, don't you think?"

Noah only stared back at me. I pursed my lips to hold in any more verbal diarrhea and used all my focus to stare at the girls kicking a ball back and forth so I wouldn't have to acknowledge how warm my cheeks were getting.

I'd never been much of a blusher before I'd met Noah, but I'd also never so consistently put my foot in my mouth during one conversation.

"The salmon...?" Noah trailed off, trying to follow wherever my crush-drugged brain was taking us.

I cleared my throat and picked at a loose piece of thread on my shorts. "Their numbers are declining..."

Noah sat quietly beside me, and I heard six of my own rapid heartbeats before he made a sound of acknowledgement. "Well, that's a shame. How is it affecting the fisheries?"

I couldn't help perking up, but I looked at Noah to verify if he was serious or about to laugh in my face. Only interest and concern shone back in his gaze. "Horribly. There's cutbacks in the fishing opportunities, and many fishermen's families are affected on the coast."

Noah shook his head. "That's going to have a major trickle-down effect. I suppose we'll have to postpone the fishing date I'd been planning."

Hold up.

Wait a second.

I blinked back up at him as I played his sentence over again in my mind.

"There's still plenty of trout," I blurted, entirely too eager. But it was worth it when Noah laughed and his eyes glinted with amusement.

A drop of water landed with a quiet *plop* on the tip of my nose and broke the moment of me creepily staring at his smile. I went cross-eyed looking at it, then tilted my head back and gazed up at the darkening clouds. The skies opened, and droplets of moisture landed with an increasing tempo against my face.

It happened faster than I could blink.

The skies turned to a darker grey, and rain fell in a torrential downpour. Goose bumps popped up along my arms.

Noah cursed as I yelped, and we scrambled off the bleachers like our butts were on fire.

"Son of a monkey." I fumbled with my water bottle before crossing both arms over my chest. Bad day to wear white.

"It's coming down in sheets," Noah said over the downpour. His fingers met my wet elbow, and I blinked through the onslaught of raindrops to see him squinting. "Let's head for cover."

"It's not that bad. Maybe we can weather it—"

"Come on." Noah tightened his grip on my elbow and pulled me along.

"*Emma!*" a voice called behind us, and I spun around to see Teresa standing behind the fence and looking like a drowned cat as she clung to it. She beckoned me over, and I jerked my head for

Noah to follow before hopping around the puddles already forming in the grass. The rest of the crowd ran the opposite way for cover, and we wove through them. Teresa held a hand above her eyes as she waved us closer. "Hey, they're delaying the game. You guys better go ahead and get out of here."

"Are you coming with us?" I held a hand up to try and block the rain from hitting my eyes as I glanced around. Cold water trickled down my face and neck, sending shivers through my body. "We'll probably just head back to the dorm."

Teresa smiled slyly, and her gaze darted pointedly toward Noah before she winked at me. "The dorm, huh? Nah, you two go ahead. We'll probably head over to Stacie's house."

I offered her my best glare through the pouring rain, but it wasn't very effective when I couldn't keep my eyes open long enough to prove a point.

"Okay, we'll see you later." I waved, and my shoes slushed in the drenched grass as I turned away. Water soaked my socks, and I cringed with each soggy step.

"Nice to meet you, Noah!" Teresa called after us. "Be safe!"

I groaned as I picked up my pace and lost any care for where I placed my Keds in the minefield of puddles forming.

"That's Teresa," I said, not sure if Noah heard me over the rain. "My roommate."

"She seems charming," he said dryly, and I pursed my lips against a smile. "She'll be all right out here?"

"Stacie lives close by," I said as we made it to the sidewalk, where we picked up our pace. Mud clung to my Keds, and I futilely tried to wipe it off against the concrete as we rushed along. "Let's cut across the parking lot to my dorm building."

Noah followed my instructions, leading the way as he overtook my pace. My heart flipped over itself as Teresa's words played over in my head.

Was it wise to take Noah to my dorm?

I rubbed a hand over my chest and followed him.

An Album

ONCE WE REACHED MY BUILDING, I took the stairs two at a time—feeling a burn in my thighs from the short workout when I reached the top—and swiped my student ID to get inside. My shoes sloshed and squelched with each step.

We clambered into the lobby, where we found others who'd taken cover from the rain. I didn't waste any time in wringing out my dripping hair and taking off my soaked shoes. Noah followed suit with his loafers, and I tried not to stare at the water droplets tracing down his jaw and how striking his bone structure was.

I might've failed.

We both stood quietly in the lobby while the air conditioning made goose bumps pop up along my arms. Water dripped from our clothes as I wiped at the droplets trailing down from my hairline, and a shiver racked my body.

"It's really pouring out there. You probably shouldn't chance driving anytime soon." I nodded back toward the hallway that led to my dorm while desperately trying to rub the warmth back into my arms. "Do you want to hang out here?"

Noah hesitated for a beat, and it was long enough for me to second-guess how much he thought I was offering.

"All right." He motioned for me to lead the way as he picked up both pairs of our shoes.

I started down the hall to my dorm before slowing to match Noah's pace. We passed a few girls coming and going from their rooms and exchanged quick hellos.

Noah wasn't talking, and while he was a quiet guy in general, this felt different. Purposefully quiet.

Uncomfortably quiet.

By the time we reached my door, I couldn't take his silence anymore.

"Don't worry, I'm not going to seduce you or anything," I said, trying to put him at ease while I unlocked the door. "Your penis is safe with me."

Wait. *What?*

Noah's eyebrows rose in equal surprise as I winced. I busied myself with leaning a wet shoulder against the door before nudging it open, all while wondering what I'd done so wrong in life that I was cursed with no filter.

"That's... good to know," Noah said, and an extra beat passed before he followed me inside.

Rain battered against the window in torrents, matching the increasing beat of my heart.

I couldn't stop glancing at my bed.

Noah walked the rest of the way in and looked around the room. His eyes immediately went to my side, taking in the pink comforter, Foo Fighters posters, sheet music pinned along the wall, and my treasured pile of Keds next to the bed. I tried not to feel too pleased that he knew which side was mine without asking, but the sheet music may have given it away.

Or maybe it was the pink wooden letters hanging above my bed that spelled *Emma*.

A stuffed elephant pulled my attention from the mountain of

pillows on my bed, and I blanched. Mr. Elephant's googly eyes stared back at me, and my feet inched closer to the bed.

There was no way an older guy could find out I slept with a stuffed animal.

I cleared my throat, pivoting on my heel and finding the stray thread on my comforter incredibly interesting. "So, this is my room. And Teresa's, too."

"So it is," Noah's amused voice said from behind me. "It's nice."

"It's a tiny, cramped dorm room that was made for ants instead of people and probably has mildew growing in places we can't see —but it gets the job done." I sent him a tight smile, and my brain decided now was a good time to start overthinking that I'd invited him to hang out in my dorm for the foreseeable future. A dorm with beds in it.

Crouching as water dripped around me, I dug my storage bin out from under the bed and pulled out a couple bath towels before offering one to Noah. He accepted it with another heart-stopping smile. I started wringing out my hair and wiping my arms and legs. The chill gradually eased, but nothing beat the feel of peeling off my soggy socks.

"I like what you've done with the place." Noah's eyes trailed back over the sheet music and my bookcase as he dried off with a pink towel. I grabbed at Mr. Elephant behind me while he was distracted and stuffed the plushie beneath a pillow before Noah's gaze returned to me. "It's very you."

"Thanks." I wondered if his room had as many knickknacks lying about. I used my toe to subtly nudge a stray dirty sock underneath the bed.

"What's this?" Noah stepped toward my bookcase and pointed at a binder. A picture of myself with bright pink-and-green braces beamed back at us from the binding.

I cringed, definitely regretting inviting a boy into my room.

"Figures you'd go straight for that. It's an old photo album. My mother made me bring it, but I don't— Hey, wait! Don't open it!"

I sprung toward him as he pulled it from the shelf and flipped open the cover. Noah quickly relinquished the album to me.

"Sorry." He held up empty palms as his lips twitched. "I didn't mean to overstep."

I cleared my throat and hugged the binder to my chest while shaking my head. Clumps of damp hair clung to my neck. "No, you're fine. It's just that it's, like, *really* personal. Pictures that should never see the light of day and all that jazz, you know? Not something I think you're ready to see, unless you plan on chancing the rain so you can run for the hills. I'm sure you have a similar album."

Noah tilted his head, and his lips formed a thin line. "I don't have any photos from my childhood. My parents weren't fans of pictures."

Son of a monkey. He sure knew how to play the sympathy card.

"Well, since you had to go and make me feel all guilty and stuff, I guess you can live vicariously through the most traumatic memories of my existence," I said lightly before holding out the binder in a peace offering.

Noah frowned and made no move to accept it. "You don't have to share just because I said that."

"I know. But go ahead, eat your heart out."

He took it, and I moved to perch on the edge of my bed while taking a deep breath. I'd rather avoid seeing Noah's face as he flipped through naked baby pictures, old recitals, and times so long ago my parents had actually smiled when they looked at me. It was just a reminder of what I could never have again.

Noah took it as an invitation, and he settled himself beside me on the bed while cracking the album open. Our clothes were still wet enough to leave marks on the comforter, but I didn't care.

I couldn't help myself, and I watched the hazel in his eyes grow greener as they flitted over the first page. I was mostly naked in the first few pages of photos, as I'd boycotted clothes until the tender age of three, and it didn't escape my notice that Noah was seeing a *lot* more of me than he'd probably bargained for tonight. I, for one, hadn't intended for him to see me naked... yet.

Rain pounded against the lone window between my bed and Teresa's in steady streams, but I felt decidedly cozy sitting next to Noah in my small room.

"You were a mischievous child, I take it?" Noah asked, pointing to a picture of my guilty grin next to the finger-painting mural on our kitchen wall that I'd been so proud of.

My parents hadn't been as thrilled about having a child's interpretation of an elephant astronaut exploring the moon on their kitchen wall.

Scooting closer, I leaned over the page to see nearby evidence of my pudding-covered face and a particularly beautiful shot of me passed out facedown in the grass of our backyard. Buck naked.

"You could say that." I glanced at Noah with a smile. His face was noticeably close to mine, and the butterflies in my stomach perked up. "When I wasn't practicing the piano or sequestered in time-out, that is."

I'd never been more aware of my pulse—of each individual heartbeat thrumming through my body—than I was at that moment. With Noah in my bedroom, gazing back at me with the backdrop of a storm crashing against the window behind him.

He broke my gaze and flipped to the next page. The beginning of my piano recitals. Floofy dresses, bows in my hair, and bangs the size of France—my mother had tried her hardest to turn me into her perfect little marionette.

She'd failed, but I had to give her credit for trying.

"Are those...?"

"Rhinestones on my dress?" I answered when Noah trailed off. "Yes, yes, they are. And yes, at least twelve bows are on that dress. It was my birthday present that year."

My dress had engulfed the piano bench, making me look like a giant cupcake performing for the audience.

Noah snorted. He shifted next to me before pointing at the offending picture. "Oddly enough, I wasn't referring to the rhinestones. I meant the flowers. Stargazer lilies?"

I swallowed and let my eyes linger on the flowers my parents gave me that day. "I told you they were my favorite."

Despite not being decent human beings, my parents had always brought flowers to my recitals. Every single one, and Stargazer lilies were my favorite. Looking back, I knew they did it more for my image than for me, but I always loved seeing the lilies.

"So, this is little Emma Fox." Noah's eyes darted across the pages of my recitals before he flipped to the next page with much of the same. "The piano prodigy."

Lightning flashed in the window behind him, and I admired the way it highlighted his dark hair. I snorted at his ridiculous notion. "Not even close. Though my parents wish—"

Thunder crashed around us, and I jumped like a spooked deer from my perch on the bed. My arms flailed, struggling for purchase as my butt crashed back against the bed—landing practically on top of Noah.

He sat still as a statue beside me, blinking in surprise.

"Sorry," I stammered. The skin of my thigh rested snuggly against his pants. I cleared my throat and told myself to back off, but my legs refused to move. "I'm not a big fan of thunder."

Noah rested a hand on my arm and sent a whole wave of chills through my body when his thumb stroked my skin. "It's okay."

I swallowed and turned away to distract myself with the next picture, but the photo album had fallen to the floor when I'd practically assaulted him in fear. Without the album, there wasn't anything to look at, and my eyes pulled back to Noah's like magnets.

We were close enough that I could see the small flecks of gold around his irises. It was intoxicating, the way his piercing gaze held mine with an intensity that had the butterflies doing somersaults in my stomach.

Noah leaned in, and my brain malfunctioned.

An Accident

MY EYES DROPPED to Noah's lips right as they parted, and it was like time froze. His head moved closer as his hand settled on the mattress behind my butt. Alarm bells went off inside my head. It was too much for my delicate sensibilities to handle. Lightning flashed again, highlighting the flecks of gold in his eyes, and my brain worked a mile a minute.

Did I want to kiss Noah Kincaid? *Absolutely*.

Did the prospect of it happening right now give me stage fright and make me feel like puking? *Yeah, little bit.*

So, what did I do?

I chickened out.

Clearing my throat, I ducked down across Noah's lap and reached for the fallen album. If I had the photos back, I could use them as a barrier between his all-too-inviting lips and my own reckless ones.

What I didn't count on was a follow-up clap of thunder ricocheting through the room with the force of a lion's roar. I jumped out of my skin, head jerking up and meeting the softness of Noah's nose in a woefully-ill-timed headbutt.

Noah grunted in a mixture of surprise and pain, and we sprung apart.

My eyes darted to him in growing dread, and it was blatantly obvious that my head made quite the impression on his nose.

Blood was everywhere.

"Oh no." I watched in dawning horror as blood dripped from his nose like a faucet. "Oh crap, Noah! Are you okay?"

No, no, he very obviously is not *okay, Emma.*

He groaned and rolled back to lie against my bed, both palms covering his volcanic nose. He tilted his head back to ease the bleeding.

I frantically looked around the room for anything to stem the flow of blood until my eyes landed on a roll of paper towels underneath Teresa's bed.

"Oh God, I am *so* sorry!" I sprung off the bed and scooped up the paper towels. I hastily ripped a few squares off before glancing back at the amount of blood and ripping off five more just to be safe. With another leap onto the bed, I accidentally kneed Noah's side in the process and elicited another moan before I pulled gently at his hands. "Hold on, I have towels. Let me—"

His hazel eyes opened to meet mine, filled with a dull sort of pain that made my heart clench. Noah grabbed the paper towels from me and held them to his nose as his eyes closed again.

I hovered awkwardly beside him and reached out to pat his shoulder in comfort before deciding that probably wasn't the right move. Maybe it was best not to touch him at all.

Noah cleared his throat, the sound a little too clogged for my liking, while all I could do was sit there uselessly and watch the blood quickly soak through the paper towels he pressed to his nose.

"Should we go to the hospital?" I shifted my weight back and forth between both knees. "It might be broken. I can call 911 since you probably shouldn't be driving yourself—especially with that crazy storm out there. I'd offer to drive, but I'd have to use your car and I've never so much as driven a go-kart in my life. I wouldn't want to end up driving us both into a flooded ditch where the car locks would malfunction and we wouldn't be able to escape before drowning tragically and your poor, fancy car would—"

"It's not broken," Noah cut off my frantic rambling, and his eyelids fluttered open until he was looking at me steadily. His voice sounded delightfully like he had a stuffy nose, and I made a vow to make fun of him for it later. Just not now. Maybe after he finished bleeding out on my bed. "I'll be fine. I just need a moment."

"Are you sure?" I watched as the red stain spread further through the paper towels. It was making me a little lightheaded to see so much blood. "I have a really hard head. It once knocked out my neighbor's tooth when we were playing tag."

"I don't doubt it," Noah muttered dryly around the wad of paper towels. "I promise it isn't broken, though. I would know. And I'm sorry, my clothes are still wet and now I'm probably getting blood on your sheets."

Noah leaned up, but I planted a hand on his chest and eased him back. "No, no. Don't you dare get up. It's fine. It's just a blanket, and you need something to lean back on."

He miraculously listened as his lean shoulders rested back against the abundance of girly blankets. His pristine hair was tussled, and strands stood up every which way.

I sank back against my headboard and ripped off more paper towels to place in Noah's waiting hand.

"I'm sorry," I said again as my shoulders slumped. I'd wanted Noah's return from Seattle to be a fun celebration that he looked back fondly on, but it was turning out to be the opposite.

"Stop apologizing, Emma." Noah remained calm as he blotted the paper towels carefully against where the blood flow was thankfully slowing down significantly. "It's all right. It was an accident."

"But I hurt you, when you were just trying to..." I trailed off, unsure if we wanted to touch on what'd almost happened moments ago. Noah's eyes met mine again in question, and I cleared my throat before grazing over that touchy topic. "I mean, I pretty much just beat you up."

Noah snorted before tensing and sucking in a breath. I winced in sympathy. He took a few shallow breaths before readjusting the wad of towels.

"You didn't beat me up." Noah gently prodded at the side of his nose. He sent me a teasing look. "And don't start spreading that around campus. I have a reputation to uphold."

I rolled my eyes at his chaffing tone and scooted a little closer until my knee rested against his leg. "And what reputation is that?"

Noah offered me an unimpressed glance, before his eyes gleamed mischievously. "One that's a step up from Hello Kitty enthusiast, don't you think?"

My ears burned at the reminder, and I feared even my future grandchildren would feel the embarrassment of that blunder.

"Not cool, Noah. Not cool." I scowled. "I told you it was laundry day."

"No, don't be embarrassed. I'm glad you wore that underwear," Noah said as he managed a small smile, voice turning nasal as he swapped which hand was holding the paper towels. His free hand found my knee, cupping it gently as I nibbled on my lower lip. "Otherwise, I may have never gotten to know you better."

More like I never would've headbutted him in the face.

I rolled my eyes again and huffed out a breath in disbelief. "You mean the only reason you agreed to that coffee was because you saw my butt? You're not winning yourself any points here, buddy."

Noah's eyebrow rose in challenge, and he took a slow breath before explaining. "First of all, I didn't really see much, so no, that isn't why. Not that you shouldn't be proud of your body, because you have every reason to be."

I must've made a sound of surprise, but Noah didn't stop there.

"I was having a rough morning. Work issues," Noah continued, and his thumb moved against my knee. I didn't dare move. "Then you wiped out on that pavement, showing a good number of the student body your underwear, and I thought there was no way I was having a worse day than you were. So, I agreed to a coffee, because I didn't want to be the reason for your day to get even worse."

I swallowed, realizing how close I'd come to not getting to know this guy outside of sharing two classes together. I never would've thought my cartoon-covered backside would be the catalyst to whatever the world had in store for us. "I take back what I said. You're a pretty cool guy."

He squeezed my knee, the smile remaining firm as he regarded me. "I can't say I've ever been referred to as cool before."

"Well, you are." I cleared my throat and gently pulled my knee out of his grip. "Although I think the loss of blood is making you a little light-headed, because your tongue is looser than usual."

"It's probably because I'm trying not to focus on the pain," Noah said lightly. The skin around his eyes tightened, and I winced.

"Oh, right. Of course. Let me get you some pain meds or something," I said as I slid off the bed and shuffled through my desk drawers until I hunted down my first aid kit.

Well, it was more of a small bin with a ginormous bottle of pain pills and a few Band-Aids, but it got the job done.

I made sure to angle the bin away from Noah's curious eyes as I popped open the bottle of pills. I would never live it down if he saw my Hello Kitty–themed Band-Aids.

Shaking out two pills onto my palm, I made the executive decision to add a third one. Surely a headbutted nose was a good reason to take an extra pill, and I didn't want Noah to feel even the smallest ounce of pain.

"Here, you should take a few of these," I said as I popped the lid back into place and stuffed the bin under my desk before handing the pills to Noah. He accepted them without a fuss, and I headed for the door. "I'll go grab a cup of water."

"No need," Noah said, and I turned with a frown—just in time to see him toss all three pills into his mouth and swallow them dry. As if this were a normal activity for him. As if he hadn't just dry-swallowed three giant horse pills that seemed capable of blocking an entire river on their worst day.

I blinked in horrified amazement, realizing that I had no clue who Noah Kincaid truly was. Everything up until now felt like an illusion.

"Are you a unicorn or something?" I asked bluntly, curious what other vital secrets he'd been hiding from me.

"Pardon?" Noah frowned. I cautiously inched closer to the bed.

"You just swallowed those pills dry," I said, as if he wasn't aware of what he'd just done. "Without water or anything. You didn't even choke or gag or pray to a higher power for divine intervention."

I was growing increasingly used to Noah's blank stare when I said something that threw him off. It was very similar to his look of exasperation. Luckily, I found both incredibly endearing or I would've been insulted.

"Could you tear off another paper towel, please, Emma?" Noah asked, noticeably overlooking my mystification at his impressive swallowing abilities. I couldn't even swallow *air* without choking sometimes.

"Of course." I tugged off another square from the roll and handed it over. Noah leaned across the bed and tossed the soiled paper towels into the waste bin under my desk.

"Here." I stepped forward, moving about some of my pillows and guiding him to lean against them. "Get more comfortable, please."

It felt silly to see Noah lying on my light-pink comforter. The color didn't really match his personality, but it did wonders for his eyes. He moved compliantly, following my nudging until he was lying longways on my bed. I placed a fuzzy pink blanket over his front.

"I'm not an invalid," Noah said as I moved on to fluffing up the pillow beneath his head. "You don't need to fuss over me."

He also sounded super cute when his nose was all stuffed with blood. At least the bleeding had stopped.

"Hush," I said. He reached for the blanket, but I swatted his hand away.

Maybe I liked the way he looked in my bed a little too much.

"Do you sleep on something hard?" Noah leaned up and frowned at the pillows.

I mirrored his frown. What was hard about a mountain of pillows? But realization hit at the same moment Noah stuck his hand into the pile and pulled out a battered pink book.

"What's this?" he asked, and I moved before I could think—leaping forward and snatching my diary from his hand.

"Nothing. Absolutely nothing," I said, not wanting a repeat of the photo album.

Especially since I was pretty sure I'd written a limerick about how beautiful Noah's eyes were in my latest entry.

His brow arched. "That's quite a reaction for nothing."

I swallowed and hid the diary behind my back before tacking on a smile. "It's just a journal. You know, private thoughts. Dreams. Hit lists. That sort of silly stuff."

"You keep a journal?" Noah asked with interest as he shifted the paper towels against his nose. "Is a certain redhead featured on these lists?"

My smile flattened as I recalled a few colorful entries with Blaise's name. "You could say she has a recurring role on them."

He chuckled, the sound coming out stuffy with his nose blocked. He eyed the mountain of pillows closely before switching out one in the back with a bigger pink one in front. I had to admit it actually made a lot more sense after he swapped them.

Until I noticed a very suspicious grey stuffed elephant foot sticking out from underneath the pillow he'd just moved.

Noah had a similar moment of awareness as my heart seized. But before I could leap forward to hide the evidence, he tugged Mr. Elephant out from his hiding place and regarded the plushie cautiously.

As he should; elephants were very dangerous creatures.

My guest sent me a questioning look before glancing back at Mr. Elephant. I sent back my own questioning look, as if wondering what his look could've possibly meant. Noah responded with an eyebrow raise, and I tried to respond back with my own, but it failed miserably as both brows rose and my nose itched.

Noah's stare remained firm, and I feared this one was already a lost cause as I spared another anxious look at Mr. Elephant.

"Um... I have no clue how that got there," I lied through my teeth, trying to play the dumb blonde card as I gave my favorite stuffed elephant the best bewildered look I could manage. *Please forgive me, Mr. Elephant.* "That's so strange. Maybe there's some sort of elephant fairy who leaves them under unsuspecting college students' pillows? Was there any cash with it?"

Mr. Elephant's googly eyes stared back at me from Noah's hold, and I could've sworn he looked betrayed.

"This isn't yours?" Noah sounded a little too surprised for my liking. But I couldn't tell if that was because the plushie was indeed in my bed—so it made sense to be mine—or because he'd already determined that I was the type of college girl to have stuffed animals.

I bit down on my tongue and shook my head as I *denied, denied, denied.* Noah's eyes narrowed before he regarded the plushie again.

"If this isn't yours and Teresa didn't put it here, then I suppose we'll need to involve campus security." Noah's eyebrow rose again in challenge as I tugged lightly on the hem of my shorts. "After all, it means someone was in your room without your knowledge, which is against the dorm codes. They'll need to collect this as evidence."

That did it. I grabbed Mr. Elephant from Noah and hugged him tightly to my chest. "Over my dead body will they take Mr. Elephant from me!"

Noah's smile was far too self-satisfied, despite the blotches of blood under his nose.

"That's what I thought," he murmured victoriously.

My eyes narrowed on his smile as I clutched Mr. Elephant tighter. "You play dirty."

"I simply play to win." Noah leaned back against the pillows and did some weird origami twisting with the paper towel. I watched, unsure what to do now that Noah was comfortable on my bed and wasn't spouting blood out of his nose like a fountain.

Was I supposed to join him on the bed?

A wave of warmth spread through my body just thinking about it.

So, I didn't think twice before placing Mr. Elephant and the diary on my desk. I pulled my mostly dry hair up into a makeshift ponytail and climbed into bed next to Noah. He spared me a quick glance before focusing back on his task as I lay longways beside him. I rested my head against one of the many pillows and watched him turn the flimsy paper towel into two little balls.

He fussed around with his nose again before taking a slow, deep breath. My eyes trailed down to his chest as it rose and fell before Noah rolled over on the lumpy mattress and faced me.

A small smile fought its way onto my face, and I couldn't help the way my lips twitched as Noah's eyes met mine. Two little balls of paper towel jutted out from his nostrils, and it looked so flipping adorable I had to suck my lips in to stop myself from bursting into laughter at his expense.

Noah rolled his eyes toward the ceiling as he waved a hand at me. "Go ahead and laugh. I know you want to."

He didn't have to tell me twice.

My body erupted with giggles, stomach muscles bunching together as I rolled onto my back.

"I'm sorry," I said through the mess of spasms running through my stomach, but just as I'd managed to tame them into submission, they started up again with a vengeance. I snorted into my palm, and my eyes welled up as I fought back the onslaught of giggles. "Noah, I'm so s-sorry. This is so rude. I sh-shouldn't be laughing."

Tears leaked from my eyes as I tried to get ahold of myself. I looked back at Noah, surprised to see a pout forming on his blood-stained lips.

That put a quick stop to my giggles, and they died off quietly as I regarded him fondly.

"Please forgive me?" I whispered. I reached for his hand and wove my fingers between his on the comforter.

My plea was met with silence, and I snickered at his reluctance.

"I had no idea how stubborn you could be," I said just as quietly, followed by another chuckle. I bit my lip and let my eyes trail over his poor nose and endearing pout. "It's just that you look really cute like this."

That got his attention, and Noah gave me a subtle side-eye as I giggled against the pillow.

He didn't seem very impressed by my assessment.

"And handsome, too, of course," I said dutifully, giving his fingers an affectionate squeeze. "Very handsome, in a... bloody... nose-vampire sort of way, if those exist. Wait, no! Handsome like a rugged cattle rancher who got kicked in the face by a calf."

That was flattering, right? Cattle ranchers were both visually appealing and strong. They kept cattle safe and protected, but also wore things like cowboy hats. *Win-win.*

"A calf?" Noah echoed in a voice that I would not call pleased.

Maybe something closer to indignation. "Why a calf? Why not a grown one?"

I gave him a wide-eyed look. "Because if a grown-up cow kicked you in the face, you'd probably be dead. And because I'm not sure if they're flexible enough to do that when they're grown up."

"But they're flexible enough when they're just born?"

I shrugged against the mattress, at a loss for any convincing arguments. "Let me try that again. You look handsome in a good kind of way?"

He blinked slowly, and a soft smile overtook his insulted expression as he gazed back at me.

"Your eyes are very grey," Noah said softly, his own eyes turning curious as he examined mine.

My brows rose, the surprise so tangible I thought they might skyrocket off my face. "Are they?"

"Yes, incredibly grey. Smokier than the smokiest smoke," Noah assured me with an accompanying nod against his pillow as his smile turned decidedly dopey. I tried and failed to follow what he was saying. "Emma the grey-eyed girl. The grey-eyed, gorgeous girl. The gorgeous... grey... goddess."

I opened my mouth, but there were no words. His eyes had taken on a dazed look as he blinked slowly while watching me, and dread pooled in my stomach.

"So grey." He leaned closer, dedicated to studying my bugged-out eyes. "Like a beautiful storm. Or a hippo."

A *what*?

"Hold that thought, Noah." I quickly rolled off my side of the bed and kneeled beside my desk. I popped the lid off the first aid kit and snatched up the bottle of pain meds. Twisting it around until I could read the front, I jolted in horror at the label.

Drowsy.

My heart jump-started into a tizzy, and my eyes raked down the list of warnings and side effects before zoning in on the instructions. Adults ages twelve and up were only supposed to take one pill every twelve hours until symptoms dissipated. I'd given Noah three.

A strangled sound escaped my throat, and I quickly hid the evidence back inside the bin before jumping to my feet.

I'd just drugged Noah Kincaid and tricked him into lying in my bed.

Panic set in swiftly.

"Come back to bed," Noah muttered behind me.

Wh-What?

A crazed chuckle crawled up my throat from a mixture of how much his words warmed me and how much I was going to suffer when he killed me tomorrow morning after finding out what I'd done.

"In a minute, Noah," I promised, my voice cracking halfway through. At a loss for what to do but unable to face the guy I'd drugged, I bustled around the room without any clear intent, moving our shoes around and putting my photo album back on its shelf. I was too ashamed to face Noah, but a quick glance in his direction showed sleepy eyes watching me scuttle around the room aimlessly.

I gulped. He looked more like a lazing lion eyeing his prey than a harmless college guy who was dangerously close to passing out.

"Are you all right?" I asked in concern, afraid his stomach would reject the triple dose of medication. The least I could do was make sure he wasn't feeling worse after I'd drugged him. "Do you feel okay? Do you need water or anything?"

"I need you to come back to bed, beautiful," Noah said, the drowsiness in full effect as he blinked lazily.

My ovaries may or may not have imploded.

"Be right there... honey bunches of oats," I choked back, blanking on a pet name to use and sounding borderline hysterical. I grabbed my toothbrush and dorm keys before booking it out of the room and slamming the door shut behind me.

I needed a moment.

A hot flush crept up my neck as I forced out a strained laugh at yet another predicament I'd found myself in. The hallway was empty, and I felt like a fraud as I quickly shuffled down to the communal bathroom. It wasn't until I reached the sinks that it dawned on me; I hadn't grabbed my toothpaste. But I just shrugged and made do with only water as I tried to calm my blood pressure while giving my molars a thorough scrubbing.

I focused on the facts.

One, Noah was in my bed. There was no way to unmedicate him and safely get him back to his own place. After all, there was a thunderstorm raging outside, and he was way too incapacitated to drive.

Two, Noah was drugged and apparently quite affectionate when under the influence.

Three, Teresa was still busy God knew where, living her best life... which meant we were alone.

Four, Noah wanted me to *come back to bed*.

The toothbrush stilled in my mouth, and I stared back at my flushed reflection. My grey eyes—which were apparently very hippolike—bugged out.

I stalled as long as I dared—brushing five times longer than usual with close to zero effect because my toothbrush bristles were too dull to do anything worth noting—before tiptoeing back down the hallway and sneaking into my own room.

Noah's breathing had evened out when I returned, and the tightening knots in my stomach eased. Him passing out was very much for the best. I debated changing into my pajamas, but my clothes had dried, and I didn't want to make Noah feel even more awkward in the morning, so I switched off the light before crawling into bed beside him.

Noah hummed as my side of the bed dipped, but his eyes remained closed.

I stilled, feeling entirely too creepy watching him sleep. But I'd never had an opportunity to study the guy so openly before.

A hint of freckles scattered across the bridge of his nose—despite the faint bruise I'd put there—had my lips tilting up in reflex. But maybe Noah was right; it didn't *look* broken.

He had a scar near his hairline that was about the size of my pinky toenail, and his brow dipped in concentration even in his sleep.

I felt all kinds of female satisfaction as I soaked him in like a hot fudge sundae on a hot afternoon.

Noah was absolute perfection, even in his imperfections.

I may have spent a little extra time admiring the smooth line of his jaw.

I wanted to touch it.

I tore my eyes away and rested my head on the pillow.

His hand was sprawled out on the comforter between us, and I supposed it couldn't hurt to hold it in mine. We'd already held hands before, so it wasn't like I was taking advantage of the situation...

I reached out and entwined my fingers with his.

That ended up being a mistake, because his hand was all kinds of warm and butterfly-inducing. And maybe I was the one drugged, because his hand didn't feel like nearly enough. I wanted more.

So, I scooted closer and leaned my head on Noah's shoulder before cuddling my legs against his. He smelled like rain and after-shave, and I wanted to eat him up.

I slid my thumb delicately against the skin between his thumb and forefinger. Rain was pattering against the window, and it wasn't long before I was lulled to sleep as well.

It wasn't what I'd imagined would happen when Noah came back from Seattle, but I wasn't complaining.

I never thought I'd be so grateful for thunder.

An Invitation

Dear Police Who Are Possibly Reading This in the Event I Was Arrested,

I swear I didn't mean to drug him. It was an accident. I didn't do anything to his defenseless body while he was passed out in my bed—I swear!

I might've stared a little. I admit it, okay?

But that's not a crime. You can't charge someone for staring. (Right?)

And. There. Was. No. Touching.

Thoughts about touching? Sure.

But you can't throw me in jail for that. I have rights!

Okay, fine, I held his hand. You caught me.

And we might've snuggled a little. Is that a crime? Then sue me!

Wait, don't sue me.

Also—if any non-officers are reading this, please ignore. It's a joke I'm playing on a friend. Not real. Totally didn't happen. (Police, if you're still here… this doesn't count as perjury, okay? I'm pretty sure you have to be under oath for that.)

> *Currently rethinking all my life choices,*
> *Emma*

WHAT I HADN'T EXPECTED Saturday morning was waking up to Teresa's beaming face across the room from me, grinning ear to ear like the cat who caught the canary.

Thrown off by her alarming look, it took my sluggish brain a moment to remember the events of the night before. I jerked around, only to find the bed empty. Sliding a hand across the comforter, it felt cold.

"Prince Charming ducked out of here an hour ago," Teresa offered helpfully.

My head whipped back around, and I cleared my throat to break up the sleep clogging it. "What?"

"He told me to give you this." She slid off her bed and held out a folded piece of paper that I quickly accepted.

"And I picked up our mail this morning. Yours is on the desk," Teresa said conversationally. She nodded toward a small stack of envelopes, and her lips twitched. "Seems like you already picked up some male of your own, though."

I sent her a dry look while unfolding the note.

Noah's penmanship was flawless.

E,

I apologize for falling asleep here last night. The injury must've affected me more than I thought, and I appreciate you looking after me.

Don't worry about my nose. These things happen, and it's not broken.

I have plans with friends this morning, but I'd like to see you again this weekend. Interested in going to the basketball game tomorrow?

Text me,
N

I winced a bit at both his apology and gratitude when it was my fault his nose took a beating and he'd fallen asleep here.

"Well?" Teresa asked impatiently. "Aren't you going to text him?"

I scowled up at her. "You read this?"

She just grinned cheekily back.

I folded the note, frowning. "Did he say anything else when he left?"

Maybe something about calling the police because I drugged him?

"Not a word. All he did was ask me to give you that, and then he was outta here," she said. She grabbed a gym bag and headed for the door with a glance over her shoulder. "And now I'm outta here. I'm gonna get a workout in before we cater this afternoon. Be ready to go at two?"

"Sure," I answered distractedly, unfolding the note and reading it again.

He wanted to see me again. The butterflies sighed happily.

Teresa slipped out of the room before the door auto-locked

with a resounding *click*. I lasted about two seconds before pulling out my phone and texting Noah that I'd love to go to the game with him tomorrow.

With that sent, I let out a breath and mentally went through the events of the night before.

"Could've been worse, Emma," I muttered reassuringly to myself. I set the note on my nightstand. "You could've accidentally murdered him."

Part of me was relieved, too. Maybe Noah never had to know I'd drugged him.

Offering Mr. Elephant my sincerest apology for last night, I placed him back on his throne of pillows before checking my phone for messages. A voicemail and text awaited from my mother, both telling me to check the email she'd sent with videos of some German pianist's recitals to review.

There was another text from Scott to let me know he had a cold and wouldn't be manning the coffee cart this weekend—but not to worry because some girl would be covering for him.

I made a mental note to use the café nearby as my coffee source for the weekend. It was appointed as my backup within the second day of moving here.

I didn't like change.

After skimming through fourteen crude texts from Teresa, I plugged in my phone to charge and got out of bed to flip through the small stack of mail.

Credit card offers, food delivery promotions, and the latest issue of *International Piano*.

It was the letter at the bottom of the meager stack that caught my attention.

A soft plum envelope embossed with lifelike vines.

Emma Fox was written across the front in bold cursive penmanship that used a glossy black ink. I'd never seen my name look so grand before. Each letter had a personality; each loop of calligraphy told a story.

The only thing this envelope was missing was a return address, and my fingers fumbled with it as I flipped it over and broke the wax seal.

The *wax seal.*

The paper inside was soft to the touch and smelled like a bonfire Teresa dragged me to on the beach over the summer. My eyes hungrily darted across the page.

Emma,

Sorry this isn't a more formal invitation. If you knew my manager, you'd understand why I didn't want this going through his official channels.

I have a recital at the Walt Disney Concert Hall in Downtown LA on November 19th, at six o'clock in the evening. It's a new setlist, and this is the most input I've ever had on song choices.

Included are two tickets to the show, along with tickets for the party afterward. I hope to see you there, Emma.

Also, if it doesn't work out with the guy you're talking to, I'd love to see you before then.

Sincerely,
Oliver
P.S. I don't have bodyguards, and I wouldn't have pushed you away.

A phone number was scrawled in the bottom margin.

My lungs found it difficult to breathe. My fingers trembled as the delicate paper wrinkled in my grip, and questions bombarded every corner of my mind.

Was the second ticket for me to bring a friend, or did he assume I'd bring the guy I mentioned?

Was it a test?

What was he expecting to happen at the after-party?

Was that really his number?

How had he gotten my address?

... He wouldn't have pushed me away?

I took a deep breath and flopped back on my bed before watching with detached interest as Mr. Elephant went toppling off his throne.

Oliver Bishop was my childhood crush. The boy I'd named all my Ken dolls after and tried to write my own childish love ballads for. The piano prodigy I'd struggled to mimic while pretending we were boyfriend and girlfriend as I imagined us playing duets together. He was out of reach. Unavailable. A fantasy that wasn't *real*.

But at the moment, he felt entirely reachable, scarily available, and mind-alteringly real.

Not to mention inconceivably interested.

He was pursuing me.

Me!

From the way my heart threatened to lead a mutiny and tear its way out of my chest for a guy who wasn't the one I was dating, I decided that Oliver Bishop could be very, *very* dangerous.

So, I stuffed the invitation in my nightstand drawer, out of sight. November was still a ways away, and that sounded like an issue for Future Emma to deal with.

"It's going to be a *long* semester, Mr. Elephant," I said to the plushie lying facedown on the comforter beside me. I gave him a quick pat on the head. "But at least I'll always have you. Sorry about that whole 'pretending not to know you' thing earlier, by the way. I'm sure you understand."

He didn't respond, and I spent the rest of my morning taking a deeper look into the warning signs of schizophrenia.

A Kiss

MY SCHIZOPHRENIA SEARCH was less than fruitful—though the internet was quite insistent I had cancer—but I was convinced the diagnosis was inevitable. Thankfully, the afternoon arrived before I could self-diagnose, and Teresa and I were off on another catering adventure.

The ride there was not what I would call pleasant.

"So, was he any good?" Teresa asked for the seventh time since we'd left the dorm.

"We didn't have sex, Teresa," I said distractedly, also for the seventh time. I'd zoned out on the drive, unable to get my mind off Oliver's phone number hidden away in my nightstand drawer.

Did I dare call?

"You honestly expect me to believe that Noah slept over because you headbutted him and accidentally overdosed him with drowsy meds?" Teresa asked as we reached the venue, yanking me out of a daydream featuring me calling a certain piano prodigy. She pulled her car into the nearest parking spot and turned off the engine. A beat of silence passed before Teresa hummed. "You know what? Never mind. I believe it. It actually makes more sense that way."

I only felt marginally offended, but it was still disconcerting to know it made more sense that I'd attacked and drugged my romantic partner rather than seduced him.

That didn't exactly reflect well on my character.

"I tried to tell you." I hopped out of the car and into the warm, welcoming California sun. An army of trees loomed over the monstrous country club in front of us, and golf carts lined the circular drive. We were catering a swanky *soiree* of some sort, and I tugged at my simple black shirt to make sure it wasn't too wrinkled.

Mr. Everton's catering van was parked next to a side door, so Teresa and I hurried over to report for duty. Imagine my surprise when we found Mr. Muscles from the breakfast gig unloading the back of the van. I offered him a quick wave while trying to make it look like I was much too busy to help unload boxes.

Not that I was morally above van-unloading or anything. I simply accepted it wasn't my calling.

"Hey, Trent. Is Mr. Everton inside?" Teresa asked Mr. Muscles, and my cheeks warmed when I realized I'd never learned his name.

Trent grunted as he heaved up another box, and I was in awe of the way his veins looked ready to burst out of his muscular arms. Mine were wet noodles compared to that. "Yeah. Fair warning, though. He's in a bit of a mood today. Something about his son popping back up on the radar."

Teresa sent Trent a rueful smile that I didn't understand before giving me the side-eye. "We'll make sure to stay out of the way, then," she said, but I noticed she didn't offer to help him unload either. "And we'll tell him to get lost if we see him around. Right, Emma?"

I nodded along obediently, having no interest in the topic of Mr. Everton's son as my mind had already moved on to what sort of desserts we could be serving today. I spent enough time with children between piano tutoring and the birthday parties we catered that the idea of running into Mr. Everton's son was anything but tempting.

With another wave to Mr. Muscles—*Trent*—Teresa and I bustled our way through the side hall and followed the sharp clanging of pots and pans until we reached the country club's kitchen.

"I think we're both on buffet duty, but let's check over the schedule to be sure." Teresa grabbed my arm and tugged me over to the wall. A crowd of caterers already filled the immaculate kitchen, and there were so many stainless steel appliances I was afraid I'd get smudged fingerprints all over them. I recognized Mr. Everton across the room where he directed a few of the younger teens helping with table setup.

"As long as we're not on van-unloading, we'll be fine," I said, in case she was worried.

Teresa gave me an odd look before focusing on the spreadsheet pinned to the wall. I followed her gaze, skimming the list of our coworkers and what roles they had today.

"Ah, there!" Teresa grinned in triumph, as if finding our names earned her some sort of medal. "Dessert duty for me, and you're on the sides table."

My eyes narrowed to slits as I double-checked. But there was my name, bolded right next to *Sides: Vegetables and Pasta*.

This was an injustice.

"I'll give you two hundred dollars to trade me," I said. I straightened my shoulders and glared at the list of duties. Had Mr. Everton purposefully not put me on the sweets buffet?

Honestly, you drool all over a mountain of cupcakes *one time*.

Teresa snorted. "Emma, you don't have two hundred dollars."

My shoulders slumped, but she made a good point. How had I forgotten I was basically broke? "I meant two dollars. And a hug. And I'll stop accidentally watching Netflix on your profile. I swear, I'll remember to use my profile every time."

Teresa rolled her eyes and stepped back from the bulletin board. "It's not you using my profile that bugs me. It's just that you always seem to watch the weirdest crap, like Russian grandma cooking shows and elephant documentaries. It's messing with my recommendations."

"*Babushkas* have a calming effect on me when they bake, and it doesn't hurt to stay informed about nature." I followed her toward one of the kitchen islands filled with supplies. "Elephants are majestic creatures. Did you know their trunks can typically hold over two gallons of water?"

I wasn't about to admit that the real reason elephant documentaries showed up on her profile was because I put them on for Mr. Elephant in case he got bored while I was away.

Teresa shook her head and pointed to the tub of silverware sitting on the island. She grabbed a napkin before tucking the shiny fork and friends inside and rolling it up into a snug pouch like she'd been born doing it. "Just start rolling, Emma."

I, on the other hand, found my silverware-rolling skills on par with my van-unloading ones.

Nonexistent.

But I hunkered down, pretending I was rolling burritos as we made our way through the tub. Catering typically involved an hour of prep for both cooking and setup. Teresa and I quickly learned to stay far away from the chopping station.

Other college students bustled around our island, preparing the food and buffet trays as I focused on rolling.

"Listen, if Trent was right about Mr. Everton's son being here, then I need to warn you. He's a bit of a handful," Teresa said, but I could only blink back at her. How much trouble could one kid be with so many adults around? "He used to help out here, but then he got in with the wrong crowd and he and the boss had quite the falling out. Touchy subject."

"That sucks," I said, unsure how invested I was expected to be in this story. It sounded like Mr. Everton's son was older than I'd expected, though, if he'd been helping them cater.

"It does, but it's not all bad." She finished another roll and took the one I was fumbling with. "We don't need to use the special locks on the van to stop him from pilfering desserts anymore."

I frowned. The van used to be locked?

"From what I heard, our boss actually kicked him out. I blame those friends of his," Teresa said as I grabbed another napkin and some silverware. "And Mr. Everton must feel awful. If someone I loved fell in with the wrong crowd, I don't know what I'd do."

"Same," I offered sympathetically. This was turning into some juicy gossip. "But what kind of crowd did he get involved in?"

"Drugs. Crime. That kind of stuff." She tossed another rolled napkin into the pile. I played with one of the napkin corners, riveted by the turn this story was taking. It bore a striking resemblance to one of the crime shows we'd seen. A model son turned cocaine dealer. "Totally unexpected. Finn always seemed like a good guy to me."

"Finn?" I asked in reflex as the napkin fell from my grip and landed on the counter. A weight settled in my stomach. Mr. Everton caught me talking to Finn before, and he'd warned me about the boy as if he knew him personally.

Well, maybe Teresa meant a different Finn...

Shut up, Emma.

"Yeah, Finn. Not sure what happened, but over the summer he got busted for a B&E, and Mr. Everton posted bail before dragging him out of the jail cell by his ear." Teresa looked around the room as if she expected Finn to pop out from behind the refrigerators. "I haven't seen him since."

I made a noncommittal sound, crossing both arms as I tried to reconcile the playful magician I'd met with a ruthless criminal.

They didn't mix well.

"It's whatever." Teresa brushed the subject off, grabbing the bin now half-filled with rolled napkins. "Just don't bring it up in front of the boss, or he'll get pissy and take it out on everyone here. Come on, we should take these out to the tables."

I dutifully followed her through the maze of hallways, frowning down at the hardwood floors as my brain worked itself into a scramble.

"Teresa, just to make sure—so I can keep an eye out and be vigilant, of course—what does Finn look like?" I asked, trying to sound casual as I glanced up at her.

"You won't need to worry about him coming inside. Mr. Everton wouldn't allow it," she said as we rounded the corner into a beautiful parlor. "But he's got kind of messy reddish-brown hair, a nice face, and a big smile. Most girls would probably find him handsome."

Okay, no need to panic. There were probably plenty of Finns out there that had chestnut hair and were handsome and not related to Mr. Everton.

"You know, he actually had a sweets obsession rivaling yours," Teresa said as we turned down another hallway. "Like I said, Mr. Everton had to keep the van locked at all times or desserts would go missing. Hell, even *with* the locks, some went missing."

I winced.

Definitely the same Finn.

Macaroni.

An afternoon out for the ridiculously rich and not-so-famous, and I was on macaroni duty.

Not caviar or oysters or even amuse-bouche, but *macaroni and cheese.*

Mind you, it was the super fancy, non-Kraft kind, but how fancy could macaroni really get?

The bread crumbs were a little unsettling. Maybe science had gone too far.

And as one may have guessed, grown adults sipping on cocktails and enjoying the live band weren't exactly interested in dropping by my buffet table for a hearty serving of mac and cheese.

I was ready to pull out Noah's Music Theory flash cards for entertainment after the first twenty minutes.

By the end of the first hour, I was just winning a debate with myself on whether or not I could get away with discreetly playing a phone game underneath the buffet table when my phone burst to life in a flurry of vibrations.

With a subtlety I wasn't known for, I fished it out of my waistband and checked the well-timed text.

NOAH

What's your favorite flavor to add to coffee?

I bit my lip to stifle an untimely squeal. I wanted to tease him a little by saying it was impossible to pick a favorite and depended on the day and my mood, but I was too tickled by the fact Noah texted me that I could only answer honestly.

EMMA

That's easy. Caramel.

And like I should've expected, it took a good sixty-four seconds of me staring at the unchanging screen to realize Noah probably wasn't going to text back anytime soon.

But I wasn't willing to let it go yet.

EMMA

Why do you ask?

His response was instantaneous.

NOAH

Call it curiosity.

"Texting on the job?" a familiar voice tutted from behind me.

I jumped a foot into the air and fumbled for my phone as the little bugger flew from my hands.

I watched in paralyzed horror as it soared through the air, performing an impressive double axel before landing in the macaroni with a wet *plop*.

A few noodles sprayed out of the container, and one landed directly on my cheek as I winced.

"Uh." I tried to think of a viable excuse, blinking down at the phone slowly sinking further into the vat of macaroni. Swallowing, I reluctantly turned around to face Mr. Everton's raised brow. "I can explain."

He frowned, and the exasperation coating his features looked eerily similar to my father's. "That better not be my son you were texting."

"Your son?" I shifted my weight as I debated whether or not Mr. Everton would fire me for touching the food if I tried to save my phone from the macaroni quicksand.

His first rule of catering was you were not allowed to touch the food unless you were wearing gloves.

I'd forgotten my gloves.

"Finn Everton. The boy you were talking to the other week."

Right.

That son.

"It wasn't Finn." I delicately pulled the piece of macaroni off my cheek with a wince. "It was my..."

I trailed off. I didn't exactly have a label for Noah—aside from duet partner.

Friend? *I'd say we were definitely past that.*

Lover? *No, not yet...*

Boyfriend? *Kind of, I guess. But we hadn't exactly made it official. We hadn't even kissed.*

"My... gentleman caller," I said lamely with my cheeks burning.

Mr. Everton sighed. He waved a hand at the macaroni. "Get your phone out of the food, girl. I'll throw the vat out and grab a new batch from the kitchen."

I gazed inside the vat and found a tiny corner of my phone still visible in the gooey pool of noodles.

"Oh. Right. I am *so* sorry, Mr. Everton." I grimaced before sticking my hand into the macaroni and pulling out the suicidal phone.

The noodles were way slimier than I'd expected.

"And Emma?" Mr. Everton scratched at his beard and gave me a dismal once-over before shaking his head. The action was also uncomfortably similar to my father's disappointed look. "Why don't you go take a break and clean up in the bathroom? You have noodles in your hair."

He motioned toward his own mane of brown hair, and I winced.

"Good idea," I said before booking it across the open patio and into the safety of the country club's main building.

After an awkward run-in with a partygoer in the hallway, I ducked into the nearest staff restroom and plucked macaroni noodles out of my hair. Breadcrumbs and sauce remnants were left behind in the tousled mess, but they'd have to wait until I had the chance to shower. Offering the mirror a pitiful excuse for a smile, I flattened a hand down the front of my shirt and took a deep breath.

The afternoon actually wasn't going too badly, all things considered. Ruining one batch of macaroni and humiliating myself in front of my boss was getting off pretty light.

I repeated that to myself three times as I slipped out of the bathroom, determined to believe it.

But when I turned the corner and almost ran into a familiar magician who was strictly prohibited from showing his face anywhere near a certain catering company, it seemed that my luck may have taken a turn for the worse.

I stopped an inch from his lean chest—close enough to catch a whiff of syrupy sweetness as his eyes lit with recognition.

My eyes widened as I hastily took a step back. "Finn, what are you doing here?"

Finn grinned back, leaning against the wall with both hands in his pockets as if we'd run into each other by chance in the park instead of while he infiltrated his dad's catering business. Green eyes twinkled mischievously. "I told you I'd come visit the next time you had a gig."

"But... but I thought you weren't supposed to be here?" I tried not to stare too closely at him. It felt wrong after I'd just been gossiping about him.

His friendly gaze morphed into a puzzled one. "What do you mean? Are you the party-crashing police now?"

I frowned. Maybe it'd be best if we cleared all this up sooner than later.

"You know, funny coincidence. My boss has a son named Finn." I cleared my throat. "He's around your age. Used to help out around here. Apparently has quite a sweet tooth."

Finn's brow rose in interest, and he didn't appear the least bit fazed. "Fancy that. Sounds like he'd be a hit with the ladies."

I barely held back an eye roll, giving up on easing into things as I planted my hands on my hips. "What's your last name, Finn?"

He winked, completely unruffled as his crooked grin appeared. "Tell me yours, and I'll tell you mine."

I narrowed my eyes. "It's Everton, isn't it?"

Finn shrugged a shoulder and pushed off the wall. He scratched the back of his neck. "Guilty as charged. You don't sound too thrilled, though. Is there a problem?"

It was time to rip off the Band-Aid.

"Listen, I don't want to make things awkward, but I might've heard some things about you today from the other workers." I lowered my voice and leaned closer. "They said you're involved in some *stuff*, and you've been to jail...?"

Finn blinked back at me until his smile dimmed.

My frown deepened.

"Don't go telling me you believe everything you hear, Cupcake," Finn said. He reached out and gently flicked the end of my nose. I flinched back, sending him a glare that lacked any heat.

"I'm not accusing you of anything," I said honestly, "but is there something I should know?"

Finn sighed and stuffed his hand back in his pocket. His foot jiggled restlessly against the floor, and I bit my lip to stop from pointing it out. It was kind of cute.

"Okay, so I spent a night behind bars before my ticked-off dad bailed me out the next morning." Finn shrugged, and it rankled me how unaffected he seemed. Then the mischievous smile was back as he leaned forward. "Is this the part where you find my criminal ways disarmingly attractive? Should I get a little closer in case I need to catch you when you swoon?"

I shifted back with a snort as his grin widened.

"I don't think we're in danger of that happening." I crossed my arms and focused on the quasi-interrogation. "Is that what you'd call yourself—a criminal?"

Finn's smile dipped again before vanishing completely. "I'm one of the good guys. I've done some things I'm not proud of, but you can trust me when I say I'm not the bad guy you're building me up to be in your pretty little head right now."

I swallowed around the other questions begging to pop out and settled on a nod for now. Teresa had some strong opinions about Mr. Everton's son, but since when did I blindly trust rumors? I could judge his character myself. Aside from the brutal crime of stealing and eating my cupcake—which I wasn't completely overlooking but was pretty sure the statute of limitations had already passed on—Finn hadn't done anything I would call incriminating. "If you say so."

Finn clapped his hands together. "Good. Now that's enough seriousness for one day. I have something that'll cheer you up."

His smile was back, and I liked it a little too much.

But I couldn't fight off a frown of suspicion.

He looked a little *too* excited. More excited than most teenagers would be at a swanky country club party on a weekend afternoon. Teresa's warnings were still lurking around the back of my mind, and Finn's shining eyes mixed with his jittery legs were as clear as day. Which could only mean...

"I don't do drugs, Finn," I said carefully, glancing sideways down the hallway.

Finn's slack jaw was almost comical when I turned back to him.

He let out a strangled laugh. "I'm not sure whether to be relieved you feel comfortable standing up to me or offended that you think I'd offer you drugs."

My lips pursed. I wondered if he was trying to play off his offer as a joke since I'd already said no. "I remember a detective saying the people most likely to offer you drugs are your friends."

"... Are you talking about McGruff the Crime Dog? The *cartoon?*"

I blushed, fighting back the urge to lower my eyes. "He was based on real statistics..."

He let out another disbelieving laugh. He looked down the hallway as he rubbed a hand over his clean-shaven cheek.

"It's not drugs. Okay, sugarplum?"

I frowned. "Do you have a thing for nicknames?"

"A thing?"

"An obsession or... a fetish or something."

His lips twitched. "I have an obsession, all right."

I needed to get back to my buffet table.

"I promise you'll like it." His smirk foreshadowed all kinds of trouble, and I snorted at the presumptive imp. He moved before I could answer, leaning forward as I tipped back in reflex. "It's a kiss."

My jaw dropped, and it was safe to say I was at a loss for words as my fingers twitched beside my thigh. They weren't sure if they wanted to punch him or applaud his ability to continuously shock me.

Finn's eyes lit up, and his hand reached out and tucked a strand of hair behind my ear so fast my breath hitched.

"I hid it somewhere safe," he murmured. His smirk widened as his fingertip trailed down the shell of my ear, leaving sparks in its wake.

I blinked when his hand pulled back—phantom tingles spreading across my skin—until I saw what he'd apparently retrieved from behind my ear. Sitting innocently on his sun-kissed palm, like a sacrificial lamb awaiting its fate, was a Hershey's Kiss.

Wrapped in tinfoil and shaped perfectly like it'd been 3D printed from my very dreams.

I swallowed and glanced up at Finn's dancing eyes before looking back at the chocolate in his waiting palm. I didn't have to think twice before snatching the treat from his hand and unwrapping the treasure in record time.

Pushing thoughts of sparks and ear tingles out of my mind, I popped the chocolaty goodness into my mouth and tried to focus on anything but the way Finn's smirk made my legs feel like Jell-O.

"Ten points," I said after a moment of satisfaction. I rubbed my stomach as the Kiss made its way down to its new home. I pictured it being very happy there with the butterflies.

"Huh?" Finn asked.

"I'm awarding you ten brownie points," I said, nodding more confidently. "Ten wonderful, chocolate-melting brownie points."

Finn chuckled and rubbed the back of his head. "That means I only need twenty-five more points, right?"

"Plus that cupcake you owe me." I licked at my lips to make sure I got every last drop of the chocolate treat. My fingers were clean, but I was still tempted to lick them just to be safe. Maybe later. "And I think there was a promise of a Milky Way, too."

Finn's grin widened, and I barely blinked before another treat was held in front of me.

A Milky Way.

"You mean this one?" His tone was all kinds of suave, and I felt a laugh bubbling out before I could stop it. I covered my mouth with a hand, trying to stifle it as I glanced from the Milky Way up to him.

I swiped it up before Finn could change his mind and stuffed it in my pants pocket for safekeeping.

"Thanks, Finn."

"Anytime." He tilted his head to the side. "So, what do you think about meeting up outside of these snoozefests sometime? Grab a couple snow cones and hit up some mini golf?"

His directness threw me off, and my mouth opened, then closed before opening again. "You mean like a date?"

Finn's smile widened until the dimples in his cheeks winked back at me. "Yeah, I do."

Oh boy. This was the moment I'd been dreading, but I went with my gut. "I'm actually seeing someone."

Finn's eyes widened comically, and he frowned before shaking himself. "Well, I didn't expect that. But we can still be best friends, right?"

I laughed, surprised by how quickly he bounced back from rejection. If only high school girls everywhere could be like him. "Sure, Finn."

"Unless... Do you think I could take him?" He raised a brow and gazed at me expectantly. Looking down, he made quick work of rolling up his sleeves and flexing the muscles in his arms. I tried not to stare, but his arms looked too lean and smooth to be real. "I've been trying to work out more to balance out all the cupcakes. Is he a big guy?"

"Um." I stalled, gaping at his forwardness but also a little curious myself. Could Finn take Noah? Honestly, the thought of them rolling around on the ground together as they figured out who was stronger... I wasn't opposed to it.

"I'm not sure," I said, which was true. My imagination could guess, but until I saw them battle it out in the flesh, I wouldn't put my money down. "It'd be close, though."

He nodded and then I nodded, and then we both just kind of stood there nodding at each other.

Finn's smile grew even wider.

"I should get back to work," I said when the silence stretched too long. I inched around him toward the door and reminded myself the macaroni wasn't going to serve itself.

"Sure," Finn said, stepping to the side. "You're not getting paid to flirt, after all."

I pretended I didn't hear that as I hurried down the hall, but my smile lasted long after I returned to the macaroni table.

My little macaroni snafu cost my paycheck dearly, and after taking out money for food, I had a measly eight dollars to add to The Noah Fund. It wasn't until Teresa and I trudged down the dorm hallway after catering that I pulled my still-slightly-sticky phone from its home in my waistband. A text from Finn's newly changed name sat unread waiting for me.

POTENTIALLY NOT A CRIMINAL

Did you like the kiss?

I rolled my eyes and barely stopped a smile from breaking out as I typed back.

EMMA

It was delicious.

Just wait until you taste the next one.

EMMA

Finn…

POTENTIALLY NOT A CRIMINAL

Check your back pocket, Cupcake.

Raising my brow at his forwardness, I pulled the Milky Way out of my left pocket as Teresa unlocked our door. The relief was short lived as I slipped my fingers into the other pocket, though. There was a lump that hadn't been there when I'd gotten dressed this afternoon. I pulled it out, and my breath faltered as another Hershey's Kiss sat innocently atop my palm.

I racked my brain for a time when Finn would've had the opportunity to slip this on my person, but it came up blank. It unnerved me that he'd been able to drop something in my pocket without me even being slightly aware of it, even if he was a magician.

Had he touched my butt?

Trailing in behind Teresa, I tossed the Milky Way on my desk and sat on the edge of my comforter. Studying the newest prize, my fingers made quick work of its wrappings before popping the Kiss into my mouth.

This one had caramel in it, and it may have been the best kiss I'd ever had.

Not that Finn deserved to know that.

EMMA

Magicians are sneaky. I'm going to have to keep an eye on you.

POTENTIALLY NOT A CRIMINAL

Please do. I love a challenge. ;)

A Black Coffee

Dear Diary,

    I need help. Here are the facts:

    I'm going on another date with Noah today. (Watching sports still counts as a date, right?)

    Finn is still being all flirty.

    Oliver Bishop gave me his number. Yes, the Oliver Bishop.

    Three guys. One Emma.

    Maybe I should've paid more attention in math class because the numbers just aren't adding up.

                Taking things one day at a time,
                        Emma

POTENTIALLY NOT A CRIMINAL

Third lesson in all things magic: always leave
the audience wanting more.

EMMA

And how do I do that?

Ten Minutes Later

EMMA

Ha. Ha. Very Funny.

SUNDAY ARRIVED with sunny skies and a gentle breeze. A perfect
day to be out lounging on the quad or to take a group down to the
beach. Yet here I was, beyond thrilled to be cooped up in a sweaty,
overcrowded basketball stadium with my new boo.

Noah stopped by my dorm in the early afternoon, and after a
quick chat with Teresa—where I surprisingly only put my foot in
my mouth one time—we found ourselves strolling through
campus on our way to the big game. Teresa told me this was an
exhibition game against our rivals, which was apparently a big
deal. She also gave me a brief refresher on how basketball worked
so I wouldn't make a fool of myself when talking about the
game.

Only time would tell if it worked.

"I like what you've done with your hair," Noah said. He gave
my french braid a light tug.

Teresa had helped me weave red and gold ribbons through it,
and I was quite proud of the end result considering the half hour
we'd spent wrestling with my hair.

I grinned as my fingers ghosted over the braid. "Thanks.

School spirit and all. I brought some face paint in case we wanted to get crazy."

Noah's gaze dropped to the ground, but I had a feeling he was hiding a smile as he looked away. He'd already commented on the golden glitter I'd put around my eyes, and I'd even pulled out the green knee-high socks and a gold Westcroft hoodie I'd gotten during Freshman orientation.

I was so ready for this.

Noah had stuck to his nice slacks with a button-down shirt, but the blazer was conveniently missing.

"Let's see how it goes first without the paint," he said. "If Westcroft is down by twenty points in the second half, we can reconsider."

"I think that's a valid proposal," I said as we trudged up the stadium steps. The lobby was packed with excited students and alumni, and Noah's hand reached for mine as we squeezed through the crowd.

He nodded toward the concession stand across from the doors. "Have you eaten lunch?"

"Kind of, but I could definitely go for a pretzel and cheese right now, as long as they have one without salt." I redirected us to the stand, despite having eaten four Pop-Tarts before Noah picked me up.

"Anything to drink?" Noah asked as we got in line behind a freshman. He let go of my hand to retrieve his wallet and pull out cash.

"I'm not too thirsty. We could just share one?" I looked over the menu board. "I'm down for whatever you like."

Both of Noah's eyebrows rose.

"I mean, as long as you don't have mono or anything," I backtracked in case he had a thing about germs or something. "Because I don't."

"Nor do I," Noah said slowly. He glanced at the one person in front of us with a frown.

"And I promise I don't have herpes of the mouth, either, or anything like that," I said, in case he was jumping to conclusions. "Or herpes anywhere else, just to be clear. I mean, I'm *clean*. Totally STD-free. No diseases have ever been sexually transmitted to me... or nonsexually, of course. Well, unless you count the chicken pox, because I had that once. It was awful. I couldn't stop scratching, and my mother ended up giving me two of her Valium every eight hours until I passed out in her hydrangeas... You know what, *never mind*. That's not important. The point is, I'm clean as a whistle. I promise."

I sucked in my traitorous lips, mentally gluing them shut as heat rose to my cheeks.

I couldn't even blame Noah for just staring back at me.

"That's... good to know," he finally said. He turned toward the concession stand attendant, who was staring at me, and I belatedly realized we were now first in line. "We'll have one pretzel with cheese—no salt—a medium popcorn, and a large Coke, please. Two straws."

Kill me now.

"And a paper bag that would fit over my head, if you have one," I added quietly. I hoped my face wasn't as red as it felt.

"Um, no paper bags," the attendant said. She spared another wide-eyed look toward me before turning to the popcorn machine. I made a new hobby out of studying my tie-dyed Keds.

The weight of my braid disappeared from my back, and it took a moment to realize Noah was holding it. He cleared his throat as his fingers slid down the braid until he was placing it over my shoulder. When the braid brushed against my neck, a shiver ignited as he let go. "I've never had the chicken pox... or any other diseases."

I groaned, fighting the overwhelming urge to make a run for it. "Is it too early to leave? I think there's been enough witnesses to my humiliation."

Noah's lips twitched. His hand brushed down my arm, which

did a great job of splitting my focus from my embarrassment. "The game hasn't even begun yet."

I winced at the reminder. "How long do basketball games last for? Twenty minutes tops? There's a high probability I'll do something even more humiliating before it's over."

Noah chuckled and slipped his hand back into mine as I watched the concession worker fill our popcorn. The electrifying feel of his palm against mine was another distraction. "Never a dull moment with you."

The game passed by in a blur, and I did an awful job of paying attention to the players on the court. I was pretty sure I blacked out for most of the game, but I remembered the little things like Noah's arm resting over the back of my seat, the way he'd offer me the soda before he took a drink, and how he actively listened to every nonsensical bit of fodder my brain came up with while the players ran around the court like chickens with their heads cut off.

The important things.

I didn't seem to care when our team lost horribly or when the girl sitting behind me spilled her popcorn all over our seats or when Noah stepped away to take a call, because when we left the stadium, my hand was nestled comfortably in his again.

"Coffee?" Noah asked as we strolled toward the quad.

I smiled, swinging our arms between us. "Lead the way."

After a woefully-ill-timed hip-bump by yours truly, Noah pulled my hand as he turned left at a fork in the sidewalk. Game day brought more activity to campus than usual, and the tables were packed outside. But the line at the coffee cart wasn't bad, and I made sure to keep my mouth tightly shut during the short wait to prevent a repeat of my earlier herpes monologue.

Scott's familiar face was a welcome distraction once it was our turn.

I tugged on Noah's hand to make him hurry up to the counter. "Oh, Scott! Thank God you're back!"

"Missed me, did you?" Scott teased.

"Like you wouldn't believe," I said in all seriousness, wanting Scott to understand how genuinely valued he was as my coffee guy. "I had to go to the café down the road yesterday, and they have this weird carpet that smells like wet dog. It's so good to have you back."

"The horror." Scott had always been so sympathetic. "What can I get you tonight?"

"Just a double espresso with a scoop of sugar for me, please." I turned toward my trusty sidekick. "Noah?"

"I'll have a black coffee. Good to see you again, Scott." Noah nodded and held out his hand—which Scott quickly shook. I smiled, happy to see a friendship blossoming between the two of them. "Do you still have the item from earlier?"

"Oh, shit," Scott said. He flipped two cups off the stack. "Sorry. I forgot for a sec. Yeah, it's here. I'll get it after making your drinks."

My eyes flickered between the two seemingly innocent men as they exchanged more words than I'd ever seen them exchange during a coffee cart visit before.

"Thank you. I hope it wasn't much trouble," Noah said while I stared.

Scott snorted as he poured a couple shots of espresso into my cup and added sugar before making quick work of filling Noah's cup with coffee. "Are you kidding? Dude, it was nothing. We never use all the fridge space."

"What are you two talking about?" I asked, feeling unusually left out. The coffee cart was basically my kingdom, and they weren't being very respectful to the reigning queen.

Noah was fighting to contain a smile, but he finally looked my way. "It's a surprise."

"A surprise?" I echoed softly, intrigued beyond belief. I both hated and loved surprises. But Noah didn't have the best track record with them if our first date was anything to go by.

Scott crouched behind the counter, and I pulled my wad of bills out from my hoodie pocket as he popped back up in front of us with a to-go container in hand.

"Here you go." Scott held out the secret container to Noah, who accepted it with a nod. My eyes narrowed on both of them, but Noah's gaze was entirely focused on the small pastry offering at the cart—despite never having ordered a pastry in all the weeks I'd known him.

I held out a handful of bills to Scott. "Will this cover our order?"

Scott shook his head and held out our cups. "Already taken care of."

Noah accepted his quickly, balancing it atop the container my fingers itched to crack open as I frowned at Scott. "What do you mean? We haven't paid yet. And don't get any ideas if Noah tries to argue, because I'm paying today."

Scott sent me an apologetic smile as he held out a sleek black card to my date. "Sorry, Emma. I'll remember that for next time, but I already ran his card."

I gaped, looking between the card and Noah's conveniently innocent face as he took it from Scott. "When did you...?"

Scott's no-longer-apologetic smile morphed into a grin. "That was pretty smooth, man. I almost didn't realize the card was in your hand when we shook. I felt like James Bond or something."

My jaw dropped further, and I looked at my date in betrayal.

Noah sighed. He gave his new partner-in-crime a pointed look while studiously avoiding my gaze. "It usually works better if you don't admit to it afterwards."

Scott simply waved us off, and I could only continue to stare open-mouthed as Noah ushered me along the sidewalk. With a huff, I wondered if I could try to slip some money into his pocket without him noticing.

"You're making it exceedingly difficult for me to make up for chewing on your pen, Noah." I couldn't resist pursing my lips at his stubbornness. It rivaled my own, which I'd spent years cultivating.

One side of his lips tilted up in a secret smile. "Maybe it's because I want you to stick around."

Well, that did interesting things to my stomach.

I cleared my throat, feeling some of the wind leave my sails. "Maybe I already have a reason to stick around."

Apparently, he noticed my half surrender, because he took full advantage a moment later as his hand rested on my lower back to lead me through the throng of people.

"I apologize for taking more drastic measures," Noah said, "but I can't in good conscience have you pay during a date I asked you on. Blame it on my Southern upbringing if you need to."

I sighed, but it really wasn't worth arguing over. I'd just have to get craftier in my attempts to pay, too.

"So, what's in the box?" I asked as casually as I could manage, which wasn't very casual at all.

"A surprise."

"A surprise that needs refrigeration?" I asked as we walked through a larger group of students. "Plus a food container. Seems like it might be something perishable."

I risked taking my eyes off the crowded sidewalk to glance up at Noah in time to see his lips twitch. "Are you sure your surname isn't Holmes? With that level of deduction..."

I blinked. He was teasing me.

"I'm just saying, it's probably dangerous for the surprise to go so long outside of the safety of a refrigerator."

A particularly drunk fan bumped into my shoulder, and I pulled on Noah's sleeve to drag him off the crowded sidewalk until we were under the safety of a lonesome tree. Belatedly, I realized it was the same tree he'd brought me coffee underneath earlier in the semester.

"I'm just looking out for the integrity of the surprise," I said.

His head shook in what one might have called disbelief, and his grip visibly tightened on the container. "You don't even know if the surprise is for you yet."

I took a sip of my espresso, nearly burning my tongue as I curled a finger. "Fork it over, Noah."

He opened the container without another word. I blinked as my nostrils flared. An intricate web of caramel topped a slice of something so scrumptious looking that my mouth watered.

"Cheesecake?" I asked hopefully, unable to look away from it.

"Caramel Macchiato Cheesecake," Noah said. He once again proved the lengths of his own willpower by sitting through an entire basketball game while knowing this beauty was waiting in a refrigerator the entire time.

Did the guy have no weaknesses?

I licked my lips and warned myself it was way too early for declarations of love or proposals, but cheesecake had an odd effect of making me feel decidedly romantic. I was tempted to start serenading Noah Kincaid in the middle of the crowded quad.

Then Noah nodded toward the fork lying innocently next to the dessert, so I picked it up and zoned in on the masterpiece between us.

"I hope you don't mind," Noah said, managing to sound both apologetic and amused at the same time while I carefully stabbed off a piece of the decadent fluffiness, "but I only have one fork. It shouldn't be a problem, since we're both diseaseless."

"Very funny," I muttered distractedly. The bite of caramel macchiato heaven touched my tongue, and I barely held back a moan. Noah would have to pry this fork out of my cold, dead hands if he planned on taking it from me.

But that didn't mean I couldn't share.

"Here," I said after swallowing the most delectable bite of cheesecake I'd ever had the pleasure of devouring. I scooped up another—admittedly much smaller—piece and held it toward Noah's mouth. His brow rose. "Your hands are full. Go ahead."

It was true. He was holding both his coffee and the container, which he seemed to realize a moment later.

All hesitation gone, he leaned forward until his lips closed around the bite of caramelly goodness, and I licked my own lips—partially to get any leftover taste from my first bite but mostly because I really, *really* liked the feel of Noah taking a bite from the fork I held.

He hummed as he backed off, using the thumb from his coffee-filled hand to rub along his lower lip and collect a crumb. I'd been tempted to collect it myself.

"Really good surprise," I said as I took another—*slightly* larger —bite myself.

He looked entirely too pleased with himself as I held out another bite for him, but I suppose he kind of earned it, considering this cheesecake tasted like what I assumed the Russian grandmother from my cooking shows made in her old-fashioned kitchen.

It was rich, but still light and fluffy without being underwhelming. I might've fallen a little bit in love with it as we took turns taking bites until we quickly made it through half of the slice.

In a moment of unexpected willpower, I set the fork next to the rest of the cheesecake and let out a hum of content. "Want to save the rest for after our coffee? I know I'll be craving something sweet again."

Noah breathed out a light laugh, but he didn't argue as he closed the container and set it beside the tree trunk.

I sighed happily and took a tentative sip of espresso. Still hot, but not scalding. "Thanks, Noah. That was a wonderful surprise."

"I'm glad you liked it."

We both smiled at each other, and I felt decidedly silly as I fiddled with the strings of my hoodie. But the strong aroma of Noah's plain coffee overshadowed my own sweet drink as he lifted the cup up to hide his smile, and my nose wrinkled at the strength of it.

I tried to contain a grimace, but from the shudder that racked my body, I figured I wasn't successful. "I don't know how you can drink that."

Noah took another sip with his brow furrowed in thought. "It has a rich flavor. It's bold, but not overpowering... although I suppose it's an acquired taste."

"And how exactly do you acquire it?" I did my best to hold in a sneer as I eyed his cup.

"Black coffee isn't quite as excruciating as you seem to think," Noah said, eyes lighting in amusement. His head tilted to the side, and he studied my face so closely I started to rethink my skin-care routine. "If you give it a chance."

Noah's lips turned up slyly, and the look in his eyes could've swallowed me whole as his hand cupped my jaw. My breath caught as his finger brushed my earlobe, sending shivers down my spine. He had the audacity to calmly take a drink of his coffee as I struggled to regulate my breathing.

"Noah, what are you...?"

He moved closer until his chest was crowding mine and my head had to tip back to look at him. Then he leaned in until our breath mingled. My own lips froze as his brushed against them, and my eyes widened in shock before sliding shut.

And then it really sank in that Noah Kincaid was kissing me.

It was chaste and sweet, two soft lips pressed warmly against mine.

Until his moved—and mine joined in the dance. The free-loader butterflies in my stomach awoke from their nap as their wings took flight. Every inch of my skin felt like it'd burst into flame from the pressure of his lips. My hands moved up to his shoulders of their own accord, and Noah's arm found its way around my waist as I closed what little distance remained between us.

When his hand on my jaw slid down to my neck as his lips fused against mine, I could've sworn I floated for a moment as the butterflies worked themselves into a tizzy. Noah was warm and welcoming and all kinds of wonderful.

It was over before I had a chance to fully appreciate his firm lips moving against mine, and Noah pulled back a few inches until he was gazing down at me. He looked equally affected by the kiss—glazed eyes and flushed cheeks—which filled me with such a heady dose of female empowerment that I wanted to beat my fists against my chest and scream out a womanly war cry. Or maybe high-five someone. Or just smile, which was what I ended up doing.

His thumb slid along the skin of my jaw, and a sharp tang lingered on my lips. Licking it off, I tasted the strength and rich-ness of the coffee, but I also tasted *Noah*.

I belatedly realized I'd dropped my mostly full coffee cup onto the grass—a first degree offense if there ever was one—but I somehow couldn't find it in myself to care.

"Consider me converted," I said breathlessly.

That was a lie. Black coffee still sucked, and I wished it would burn in hell for the rest of eternity, but Noah Kincaid tasted pretty darn good. Good enough to mask the bitterness, especially when he was looking at me with eyes that made me feel like I was the most precious thing he'd ever seen.

If someone could bottle that look, it'd be one heck of a drug.

My gaze dropped to where his parted lips curved into a smile. "Actually, hold that thought. Just to be sure..."

I couldn't help myself. I wrapped my hand around the back of his neck—delighting in the feel of goose bumps spreading across his skin where I touched him—before pulling his head back down so I could get another taste.

Noah didn't seem to mind.

A Heart

Sunday night

EMMA

Thanks for taking me to the basketball game today. I had a blast. :)

NOAH (BAE) KINCAID

So did I. Thank you for joining me.

And thanks for the kiss, too.

Or should I say kisses?

No thanks necessary.

You're right, but I'll still thank you again later. ;)

Later that night

EMMA

<image sent>

TERESA

… Did you really just send me an infographic on why Red Vines are better than Twizzlers?

I couldn't live another moment without you knowing the truth.

Oh, Emma. I'm staying over at Stacie's tonight with the team, so I hope you don't get too bored.

Are you kidding? There's still a few hours left of the crime show marathon this weekend. I'm set.

Monday

NOAH

Slade cancelled Music Theory this morning. How does breakfast sound?

EMMA

Oh no! Did he say why? Maybe he got food poisoning from those tacos they were giving out on the quad last night.

And breakfast sounds great.

He sent us an email citing jury duty. There's a café on Melrose Avenue we haven't tried yet if you're interested.

Do you know if they have chocolate chip waffles?

I already called, and they do.

You called ahead to see if they have waffles? Wow. You're a keeper.

NOAH

They'll even add whipped cream in a smiley face pattern if you order from the children's menu.

EMMA

Stop. A woman can only take so much sweet talk.

I'll pick you up in 15?

Yes, sir, and good luck scraping me off the floor from where I melted into a puddle.

Did I mention the café has 18 flavors of macchiatos?

I love it when you talk dirty to me.

Eighteen. Flavors.

You're bad.

Mocha… Caramel… Pumpkin Spice… Vanilla…

Excuse me while I go take a cold shower before you get here.

See you soon, Emma.

Can't wait. <3

Later That Night

EMMA

You still awake?

NOAH

It's only nine o'clock.

Yeah, but I always figured you went to bed early. #OldManLife

NOAH

How old do you think I am?

EMMA

Old enough to have a HANDKERCHIEF that you never use in the BREAST POCKET of your BLAZER.

That's just being practical.

And old enough to actually use the Stocks app on your phone.

People in their twenties should be more actively engaged in their investments.

Not to mention old enough that you probably had a bowl cut at some point in your life.

This is getting personal. Did you text me just to call me old?

Not exactly. Some sorority is hosting a three-legged race at the quad tomorrow. You in?

I'm assuming I would need to wear something casual?

It would be most appreciated, I assure you.

You just want to see me in something other than my blazer, don't you?

Guilty. But now that you mention it, clothing is completely optional.

I'm sure it is. When and where should I meet you?

One o'clock. I'll be the naked girl standing next to our tree in the quad.

Please wear clothes.

EMMA

You're no fun.

NOAH

And we have a tree?

The one I was lying next to when I was
rethinking all my life choices and you brought
me coffee. Also the one you kissed me at.

Right. That tree.

If you can't find it, just look for the naked girl.

Emma...

Sweet dreams, Noah. <3

Good night.

Ten Minutes Later

NOAH

I'm serious, Emma. Please wear clothes.

Wednesday

EMMA

Teresa says you should grow a beard.

NOAH

I'm not growing a beard.

That's what I thought, but she insists that it'll
make you look really handsome.

You don't think I'm handsome?

... Of course I think you're handsome. I don't
just date you because you have fancy pens.

NOAH

That's refreshing. There are so many pen-diggers in the world, I was concerned for a moment.

EMMA

Your jokes are the third reason I decided to date you.

And the fourth?

Your refusal to fish for compliments.

Fifth?

Your webbed toes.

I shouldn't have asked.

Are you claiming they aren't webbed? Pics or it didn't happen.

You're getting sneakier in your attempts to see my feet.

I just find it a little odd that your tongue was in my mouth earlier today, yet you refuse to show me your feet?

I only refused because you were making a big deal out of it.

I wouldn't call trying to wrestle your socks off your feet "making a big deal"…

I'm afraid of what you would consider a big deal.

Nonsense. By the way, this is a great opportunity for you to tell me why you decided to date me, too.

There was another option?

NOAH

EMMA

Excuse me while I pretend these are tears of happiness.

NOAH

I suppose a cameo from Hello Kitty was all the convincing I needed.

Shut up. I hate you a little bit.

Don't hate me for long. I have coffee.

First insults and now bragging?

It's a caramel macchiato with a scoop and a half of sugar.

That's just cruel. You don't even like those…

I'm parked outside your dorm building.

I'll be right down. <3

Thursday

NOAH

Did you finish your homework for Music Theory?

EMMA

Don't think you can cheat off me just because I think you have the lips of an angel, Noah!

I was going to ask if you'd like to work on it together tonight.

Right. Yeah. Um, I did it already.

Five Minutes Later

NOAH

You think I have the lips of an angel?

EMMA

How do I delete a text on someone else's phone? Asking for a friend.

Good question. Do you want to study for the midterm together?

Noah, if you want to come over and make out, all you need to do is ask.

… Pardon?

There's no need to be sneaky about it and ask to "study."

I was being serious. This test is important to you.

So you don't want to make out?

I didn't say that.

I mean, either you do or you don't.

I wouldn't be opposed to it.

Teresa has practice until 9. Wanna come over and show Mr. Elephant why he's not allowed to watch PG-13 movies?

It's a little unsettling how easily I can understand you now.

Your window of opportunity is closing.

I'll be there in 15 minutes.

One Hour Later

TERESA

EMMA!! Why isn't there a sock on the
doorknob?!

EMMA

We're just hanging out! Why did you run out so
fast?

Because I just walked in on you guys
MAKING OUT.

Ugh, sorry, I don't know why I lied. His kisses
make me a little loopy.

Then tell him he's in charge of putting a sock on
the door. He seems responsible enough.

I'm sorry, we're leaving! I thought you had
practice until nine. Sorry, I'm a bad roomie.

You're fine, I'd just rather not walk in on that.
Text me a heads-up when you're gonna be
macking on him in our room.

It won't happen again!

Yes, it will, but with a sock next time.

Okay, fine, with a sock. Does it matter what
color it is?

No.

I have some animal print ones. Would zebra be
too scandalous?

Any sock is fine.

Maybe we can use the green polka-dot toe
sock. It's kind of fun, plus I can't find its pair.

TERESA

The type of sock doesn't matter.

EMMA

One more thing… How did we look together?

What do you mean?

Like me and Noah… kissing. Did it look weird?

What the hell are you talking about? It looked
like two people kissing.

But it didn't look like I was an octopus trying to
suck his face off, right? I don't know what my
form looks like. Did it seem like Noah was
into it?

…

I mean, it felt like he was liking it, but you never
know.

Is he watching you text this right now?

No, he's rearranging the pillows we were
making out on.

You looked good together. Really good. Like
you belong together.

Thanks, roomie. :)

Anytime.

Friday

EMMA

How many of those fancy pens do you even
have?

NOAH

Not that many. Maybe seven.

EMMA

Maybe? You mean you might have an extra ninety-nine-dollar pen lying around that you don't remember buying?

All right, I just checked. Exactly seven.

Hmm. You sure you counted them all? One isn't hiding out in your other blazer pocket or something?

No. Why do you ask?

No reason.

Emma...

Teresa and I might've made a little wager.

And?

I lost.

Truly shocking.

Now I have to stuff as many giant marshmallows into my mouth as I can until I choke.

That doesn't sound safe.

It used to be my favorite game, but I've matured a lot since then.

... Except maybe not, because I'm still really looking forward to it.

I'd like to have a word with Teresa. Was this her idea?

EMMA

Nah, I got to choose my own demise. She knows I have a habit of sabotaging myself. Maybe this wasn't as good of an idea as I thought.

NOAH

It's not too late to back out.

I am a woman of my word, Noah. Now please excuse me while I go stuff my face with copious amounts of stale sugar balls.

Enjoy yourself.

Oh, I plan to.

Twenty Minutes Later

NOAH

Still alive?

EMMA

My tummy hurts.

Should I even ask how many you managed to fit?

Fourteen. You'd have been proud of me.

I'm thrilled. Ice cream to celebrate?

Maybe if I could move.

I'll pick it up. Mint chocolate chip?

Yes, please. How did you know sugar is what I need right now?

I'm learning.

Maybe get some Red Vines, too?

NOAH

I'll stop by the candy aisle. Meet me at our tree?

EMMA

I'll be the one lying next to it in a sugar coma if Teresa can stop laughing long enough to help roll me to the quad.

Tell her I'll bring her a pint of Rocky Road as motivation.

Careful, Noah. A girl might think you're excited to see her.

A girl might be right.

See you soon, handsome. <3

Saturday

NOAH

Super Size Me.

EMMA

Super size you? ... Are we sexting right now?

That's the documentary I couldn't remember the name of last night.

Oh my God. You cheated and googled it, didn't you?

I would never. It came to me over lunch.

It just came to you? Hmm. Questionable.

My friend may have stopped by a drive-thru for a slushie, and it jogged my memory.

EMMA

Sounds like cheating to me. And who the heck only gets a slushie???

NOAH

He's a rare breed. Are you free tonight?

Teresa and I have a catering gig till nine.

Coffee after?

Yes. My treat.

We'll see.

You have to let me pay sometimes, Noah.

We'll see.

Noah.

Emma.

Noah.

I'm leaving for Chicago tomorrow. I'll be there for work till Thursday.

Don't try and change the subject!

I thought my girlfriend might be interested in knowing when I'm leaving the city.

One agonizingly long minute later spent with Emma staring dumbly at her phone before screaming into her pillow

Girlfriend, huh?

It seems appropriate.

EMMA

So that would make you my boyfriend.

NOAH

It would be fitting, all things considered.

You know this means you'll always have to share your fries with me, even if I don't order any, right?

I already do that, and you always order fries.

And I'll want to hold your hand in public.

I'm sure I'll manage.

And you'll have to take cute couple selfies with me using the filters of my choice.

Please, Emma, there's a limit.

Fine. A mutually-agreed-upon filter.

No filters.

:(

No.

But there's a Lion King one...

Emma.

I'll even let you be Simba.

Two Minutes Later

EMMA

Okay, fine, no filters! For now.

NOAH

Deal.

EMMA

Can we go back to you calling me your girlfriend and talking about how much you're going to miss me from Chicago?

I'll be thinking of you the whole time I'm there.

...Well, geez. Are you on campus?

No, I'm at home. Why?

I kinda wanna hunt you down so I can hear you say those words out loud.

<Incoming call from Noah (Bae) Kincaid>

One hour later, after finally hanging up

Don't think I've forgotten about the coffees, by the way. I'm paying! <3

Hours later, at catering

FINN

How's the gig?

EMMA

Pure torture. They have a giant cake with enough sugar to fuel a packed daycare for weeks, and a magician keeps pulling balloon animals out of his butt.

Now that's real talent. Can't say I'm familiar with that trick, but I might need to add it to my repertoire.

EMMA

I think it's sleight of hand, but I can't prove it.

FINN

It'd probably be weird if you tried.

I'm still tempted. How's it going with not catering?

Boring. Hit some waves earlier.

You surf?

Only when I'm not rescuing defenseless cupcakes from predatory caterers.

Too soon.

You ever been surfing?

No, but I once created a giant water slide using five Slip 'N Slides from neighborhood kids. We slid like kings for an afternoon. Surfing seems like the next logical step.

Five Minutes Later

Finn? You still there?

Spaced for a sec. You sure you aren't single?

Finn...

Sorry, sugar. It's just that you're kinda my dream girl.

I'm 100% taken.

Noted, again. And a giant Slip 'N Slide sounds amazing. Maybe I should do that now.

EMMA

It's not worth the grass burns.

FINN

I think you underestimate what I'd do for the craft. Speaking of, please excuse me while I go practice a new balloon animal trick.

Please don't hurt yourself.

Monday

TERESA

Stop texting me a million gifs of baby elephants falling over.

EMMA

I only sent four!

Your bf has been gone for one day, and you're already acting like a lovesick ninny.

Omg, Teresa, they're just elephants.

Find another way to entertain yourself!

Just trying to text my friend.

You already sent me three Celine Dion music videos this morning.

She's a national treasure.

She's Canadian.

We can still treasure her.

You also sent three follow-up reaction videos of you sobbing while listening to them, then crying about how much you miss Noah and trying to sing along.

EMMA

... Was it too much?

TERESA

Find a hobby. Or practice the piano! You love
the piano.

I do. Noah used to play duets with me.

Omg.

He'd put his hand on my knee while we played,
and he'd press the pedals with his
nondominant foot.

You need help.

I miss Noah.

You know our school has a psychologist that
students can use free of charge, right?

Are you saying my schizophrenia fears have
merit??

I give up. Keep the elephant gifs coming.

Great, here's a really cute gif I found of a baby
one taking a bath: <sending gif...>

Five Hours Later

TERESA

Okay, omg, that's enough elephants. What are
you doing tonight?

EMMA

I don't know. Missing Noah, probably. Thinking
about learning how to knit.

TERESA

We're getting you off campus. Let's go play laser tag or something.

EMMA

I have no hand-eye coordination.

You'll be fine. I'll invite the soccer team, and we'll have fun. We're getting your mind off lover boy.

Fine.

Get excited!

I'm so excited.

One Hour Later

FINN

Can I ask for some advice?

EMMA

Ask away. I'm very wise.

If you were having a movie night with friends and were in charge of snacks, what would you get?

Red Vines, Milk Duds, movie theater butter popcorn, cookie dough, whatever drinks everyone likes, gummy bears, and more Red Vines.

Cookie dough?

Preferably raw but could also be cooked. Highly recommended by another movie-watcher.

You sound like an expert. What about chip options? I'm craving something salty.

EMMA

Way too crunchy. They'll mess with the movie ambience.

FINN

And there's nothing a dudes' movie night loves more than "ambience." You're totally welcome to join, btw. We're watching a new action movie, and I know you'll get along great with my friends.

Thanks, but I already made plans for tonight. :(

Hot date?

Lol girls' night with my roomie and her friends.

Jealous. Have fun!

You too. And seriously, don't get the chips.

:(

Tuesday

NOAH

Are you busy?

EMMA

Scott is giving me a rundown on coffee preparation at the cart in case the administration ever takes my application seriously and decides he needs a sidekick. What's up?

Can I call you later?

Of course. Is something wrong?

No. I just want to hear your voice.

<Outgoing call to Noah (Bae) Kincaid>

Wednesday

EMMA

I think I'm being followed.

TERESA

What?

A guy followed me from Music Theory to the library, and now all the way to the coffee cart. He might be a stalker.

Are you sure? Maybe all this schizo talk is making you extra paranoid. The crime shows haven't helped.

I'm not crazy! He's all big and dark and tough-looking with tattoos. Maybe he's a bounty hunter and there's a hit out on me I don't know about?

Sure, because that makes the most sense. Do you feel like you're in danger?

Kind of, and did I mention he's big? Like really big. He could flick me with a single finger and I'd go down.

Well, get away from him! And stay in a populated place.

You're right. He's still following, but I just got to the cafeteria.

Good. Find a security guard and tell them what's going on.

Omg, it's hot fudge sundae day! You need to get down here, Teresa!

What about the creep? Did you tell a guard?

EMMA

That guy? Oh, I think he's fine. He's getting a sundae, too.

TERESA

Please don't befriend your stalker, Emma.

Later that Night

EMMA

high five

NOAH

?

Don't leave me hanging.

Pardon?

Never mind. How's the Windy City?

Windy. I'm back at my hotel for the night. How was Music Theory?

Fine, but I miss our duet practices. Slade broke us up into groups today, and we talked about modulation between keys. Riveting stuff.

That stupid Aaron boy I told you about was in my group again.

I hate him.

You're still holding on to that grudge?

He won't stop making dumb blonde jokes.

Don't let him bother you. He's a child.

He's a jerkface who's just asking to get his nose broken. Maybe my boyfriend will beat him up for me.

NOAH

Luckily, your boyfriend won't have to because he's dating a responsible young woman who doesn't concern herself with those who aren't worth her anger.

Three Minutes Later

EMMA

Yeah, nice try, but I still want to punch him in the face.

NOAH

You'll break your thumb.

Thanks for your faith in me, bae. <3

I thought we agreed on no nicknames.

I only agreed not to call you Ark Boy, and you're not allowed to call me M&M.

I've never called you that.

And you never will. :)

A few hours of texting later

NOAH

It's past midnight. You should get some sleep.

EMMA

It's even later for you!

I'll be fine. I fly back in the morning.

Good. Wanna grab dinner before night class? The diner down the block is doing a happy hour, and I'm craving cheeseburgers.

NOAH

I'd love to. Meet at our tree?

EMMA

At 4!

See you then. Sleep well.

Goodnight. <3

<3

A Phone Call

Dear Diary,

    Noah Kincaid is my boyfriend. I'm his girlfriend. We're dating.

    So... does that mean I can't add Oliver Bishop's number to my phone now?

    I'm kinda regretting stalling on that.

    I mean, it's not like Noah and I are married. And it's not like I'm asking Oliver out or anything. I can have an attractive, talented guy's number in my phone without it being anything scandalous or in poor taste.

    ... Right?

Why do I do this to myself?

Emma

I SHOULD'VE KNOWN things were going too well.

Reality came crashing down on Saturday morning. I was so distracted lounging in bed and writing about Noah in my diary that I answered my phone without checking the caller ID first.

"You're screening my calls again, Emmaline," my mother's voice carried through the phone, ripe with disapproval.

My pen froze against the page, and I quickly flipped the diary shut. "Mother?"

"I just got off the phone with Atticus's teaching assistant," she said thinly. "Blaise Rousseau? She mentioned you two know each other."

My heart dropped out of my chest. "I—yes. We've met."

"She mentioned a few other things, too."

Dread pooled in the pit of my stomach as I wondered what colorful things Blaise had to say about me now. Did she tell my mother about Noah? The dates?

"Really?" I tried for nonchalance while crossing my fingers. "You know, I'm pretty sure the school administration frowns on parents calling their daughter's TA—"

"Why didn't you tell me you were failing out of college?" my mother cut me off, her patience snapping as a bite entered her tone. "Do you know how embarrassing that was for me to hear?"

I swallowed around a lump forming in my throat. *Thanks, Blaise.*

"The ladies at the club have children at Harvard and Yale and Oxford, then my pianist daughter goes and runs off to a small school for something she's been doing her whole life," she prattled on. "That much I can live with—but then she fails the class about piano? Are you purposefully trying to humiliate me?"

"I'm not failing," I said in a rush as I sat up. This was a delicate conversation, and I wasn't about to risk my freedom at Westcroft, but I couldn't help feeling a little relieved it wasn't about Noah. "The first few quizzes were a little rough, but I've brought my grade up since then. I still have plenty of time to study for the midterm."

"But *why* didn't you pass those quizzes? I wonder what could possibly distract you so much that you'd fail at something you've been doing since you could walk."

"Music Theory isn't the same as playing," I said, annoyed by her patronizing tone. "I never took classes like this in high school, and I've only dabbled in composing for fun."

But it was pointless to argue, further proven by my mother's answering sigh. "I thought I raised you better than this. So far this little adventure of yours is a waste. I can't help but assume you're too distracted by college life and its temptations to take your studies seriously."

"I am taking them seriously!"

She hummed. "Then prove it."

"How exactly do you expect me to do that?"

"Ace the midterm, or I'm pulling you out of school, Emma-line," she said, and a chill swept down my spine at the frost in her voice.

Three beeps sounded as she cut the call, and I stared at my phone before tossing it across the bed with a groan.

She was wrong.

And I had plenty of time to worry about the midterm.

I wasn't going to let her get to me.

But a weight settled in my chest the size of Kansas, and a minute later I was texting Noah to set up a study date.

The library was practically deserted by the time I arrived that evening. Saturday night was prime for parties, so it wasn't surprising that I could count the number of library-goers on one hand. Layers of dust on the shelves tickled my nose, and I claimed an empty table near the coffee kiosk for my and Noah's study session. Instead of studying while I waited, I opened a random document on my laptop and used it as a shield to play games on my phone.

It wasn't a minute later that Noah was striding through the door, looking way too good in a midnight-black blazer with his messenger bag slung over one shoulder. I tilted my head to the side as his gaze roamed the open space, thinking he'd make a good-looking college professor if he wanted to.

Noah's eyes landed on me from across the room. There was something about the way his shoulders relaxed when he saw me that did funny things to the butterflies.

I cleared my throat as he walked over, rubbing a hand against my chest as the twitterpated organ sped up.

"Hey, stranger." I flashed a smile as he reached the table. Locking my phone, I turned it facedown on the table to hide the evidence of my virtual coffee shop game.

Noah returned my smile with a tame one of his own, dropped his messenger bag on the table, and slid into the seat across from me. "I should've warned you, but I can only spare about an hour to study."

I propped my chin up with a palm, feeling nosy. "Got plans?"

He nodded as he pulled a notebook and our *Tonal Harmony* textbook from his bag.

I waited for him to expand on said plans but got nothing. That didn't mean I couldn't pry. I cleared my throat, aiming for casual as I gathered my hair and pulled it over one shoulder. "Anything exciting?"

"Just meeting up with friends," Noah said as he flipped through the textbook.

Well. I hesitated, wondering if he was going to invite me to join them. Considering we were dating, it felt like meeting the friends was the next step. He'd already met mine.

When Noah didn't make any move to invite me to tag along, I decided to keep up my nonchalant act instead of begging to join.

"Sounds fun," I said, scratching at my elbow.

He didn't appear to hear me.

"While we're here, we should talk about reworking our duet, too." He paused in his page-flipping and glanced around the table. Not finding what he wanted, he went back to digging through his bag. "What we have so far isn't working."

"Isn't working *how*?"

Noah waved a dismissive hand before lining up three fancy black pens next to his notebook. "Ravel. He's too restrained of a composer to use as our inspirator. Slade's looking for a higher scale of technical risk."

I closed my laptop with a frown. "Ravel is plenty technical, and everyone's doing their own thing. We don't have to cater to Slade's tastes."

That finally got Noah's attention, and he looked up with a downturned tilt to his lips. "Of course we do. He's the professor."

But I wasn't following, and my stare must've shown it. "So?"

"*So*, showing a sharper degree of technique is our best shot at getting the highest grade," Noah said like it was obvious. "I think we should reconsider neoclassical. Someone like Stravinsky."

"No, no, no." I shook my head for emphasis and leaned forward until the table's edge dug into my middle. I lowered my voice, fully aware we were in a sacred library. "We already compromised, remember? Ravel *is* the compromise."

"That was before we knew all the facts," Noah said, not showing the same respect for the library. "Like how it'd risk our grade. Slade doesn't care for the emotional bits."

My lips twisted into a scowl. "And I don't care for pickles on my cheeseburgers, but I'm not letting that affect our decisions."

Noah's eyes narrowed, and a shrewdness entered his gaze that made the hairs on the back of my neck stand up. "Do you take anything seriously?"

"I *am* being serious," I said, thrown off by his sudden cold front. "What's going on with you, Noah? Are you jet-lagged from Chicago or something?"

His eyes flashed before he broke our stare. "I'd rather not talk about Chicago."

My lips parted, and I let my hands fall from the tabletop and into my lap.

What the heck happened in Chicago?

Noah took a deep breath and picked up his pen. "Forget it. We're here to study. The duet can wait."

I didn't move a muscle as he flipped through the textbook. Instead, I took in the tense line of his jaw. The way his eyes squinted at the page without moving. The crease between his brows.

My heart thumped loudly in my chest.

A sharp smack of a dropped book echoed from the bookstacks, and I jerked in my seat as my heart lurched. Grumbling, I glared in the general direction of the dropped book while Noah didn't even flinch.

This wouldn't do.

"Hey," I whispered. I slipped off one of my Keds and slid my sock-covered foot across the carpet before nudging Noah's foot under the table. He barely glanced up. "Why do you even care so much about which style we do? You're auditing the class, so it doesn't matter what grade you get."

"Of course it matters. I'll still show up in the class ranking."

A quiet snort escaped before I could stop it, and I clamped a hand over my nose.

I definitely wasn't fond of the cold Noah I'd gotten a glimpse of today. I missed the one who flirted with me over text all week. The one who'd taken me out for cheeseburgers as soon as he got back from Chicago.

I'd rather not talk about Chicago.

Yes, I wanted the flirty Noah back.

Letting my foot trail up his shoe until it felt his ankle, I traced my toe around the bone there. His expression didn't waver, but his finger twitched against the page.

"You care that much about being ranked in an undergrad course?" I asked.

His foot moved, nudging mine back as he quirked his brow. "You don't?"

We definitely had different levels of competitive drive.

I hooked my foot around his ankle and let it rest there as my heartbeat calmed to a normal rhythm. "I'm more concerned about passing the class in general and keeping my scholarship. Oh, and finding the bakery you bought that caramel macchiato cheesecake from."

Noah's lips twitched, and he rummaged through his bag again before pulling out a stack of flash cards. "You're right. And it's a good reminder that we need to get you ready for the midterm."

I pulled my foot back with a groan, regretting not asking him out for a cup of coffee and a walk around the quad instead of a study date. "You're focusing on the wrong thing."

I couldn't hold back a grin when Noah's toes nudged against my ankle. But I also couldn't help noticing he checked his phone fourteen times in an hour before slipping away to meet his secret friends.

A Friend

Dear Diary,

I think my mother may be evil incarnate, but I'm not allowing myself to think about her until after my midterm.

Besides, there are much better things to think about. Like Noah.

While I might be a tiny bit irritated with him for trying to scrap everything we've done for our duet so far, I can't be too mad. We still have two whole months, so starting over wouldn't be the worst thing to happen.

But I like the sixteen measures we've composed so far. They're thoughtful.

Pensive.

Beautiful.

The breath of silence between two of the notes makes me think of us.

I don't want to scrap it.

The last time we tested playing together, I got goose bumps. Whether it was the piece itself or playing with Noah that caused them, who's to know?

Gotta run,
Emma

FINN THE MAGICIAN

Surfing with a friend Sunday afternoon. Wanna join?

EMMA

Yes! What should I bring?

We'll rent a board and wetsuit for you, so just bring a swimsuit to wear underneath.

I meant snacks. What snacks should I bring?

… I should've known. Bananas are a great surf snack, and we'll hit up a food truck for lunch. I'll text you where to meet.

Can't wait!

OCTOBER WAS FLYING BY, and fall arrived with a vengeance for fuzzy socks and pumpkin spice lattes—both of which I spent copious amounts of time with, along with a certain guy whose kisses were becoming as addictive as my favorite beverage.

Most of my time with Noah was dedicated to working on our duet—when he wasn't determined to quiz me with his flash cards. It was cute how much he cared about keeping my grade up, and I found my procrastination taking a backseat. It helped that the more time we spent studying for Slade's midterm, the more I learned about my new boyfriend.

It was interesting getting to know Noah Kincaid.

Difficult? Yes.

Felt like pulling teeth at times? Sure.

Worth every minute? Totally.

He was an onion, and I just kept pulling back more and more layers—but I was nowhere near the center.

My diary was full of entries detailing our budding romance along with a phone full of photos, though he wasn't the most willing model. Some of my favorite dates were when we'd grab a cup of coffee and just study for a Music Theory quiz or watch one of Teresa's games.

We even made a habit of hanging out in my dorm watching crime shows and doing crossword puzzles—something I'd discovered Noah liked quite a bit.

But it wasn't all sunshine and rainbows.

I'd never seen a guy more glued to his phone. The whole consulting business was new to me, but Noah skipped class, excused himself in the middle of a date, and claimed something had "come up" more times than I could count on both hands and half of my toes.

Part of me was convinced I was the other woman. I'd never been to his place, and he'd only stayed overnight at my dorm once —by complete accident after I'd mistakenly drugged him. He didn't have a ring, but it wasn't like that'd never happened before. I'd never met any of his so-called friends, and he even had the go-to alibi of "business trips." All signs were pointing toward Emma Fox being crowned Most Ignorant Side Chick of the Year at the next student award ceremony.

Which was why I decided to double down and *insist* that we take the party back to Noah's place after we spent Saturday afternoon underneath our tree on the quad. After an hour of flipping through Music Theory flash cards for the midterm, Noah switched to a crossword puzzle while I tried and failed to learn how to juggle.

"Ready to head back to your dorm?" Noah asked. He folded up the completed puzzle and tucked it into his messenger bag. I didn't need to sneak a peek to know the entire puzzle was done in *pen* and there was nothing scratched out.

Overachiever.

I cleared my throat as I collected the fallen apples I'd failed to catch and stuffed them into my bag. "Actually, I was thinking instead of cramming into my tiny, little dorm room tonight for a movie, maybe we could go over to your place instead?"

I watched out of the corner of my eye as Noah's hands froze on his bag.

"You have a kitchen, right?" I asked, going for nonchalance as I pretended to flick a nonexistent ladybug off my backpack. "We could make dinner ourselves and then watch a movie?"

Noah nodded—slower than I would've appreciated, but still.

"That sounds..." He trailed off and flattened a hand over the charcoal tie he'd worn today, before nodding again—somehow even slower this time. "Yes, that should work."

I let out a breath I hadn't realized I was holding. He didn't say no. That was a good sign. Maybe there wasn't a hidden family after all.

I grinned as Noah got to his feet. "Great. I'm excited to see your place. Also—no pressure—but I'm expecting to see an Aurora Ipsilon pen shrine or two. Or maybe a whole room filled with pens in display cases."

Noah chuckled, holding out his hand, which I readily grabbed as we started off toward the student parking lot. "Sadly, my place is severely lacking in any sort of shrines or museum-ready exhibits."

I sighed while swinging our linked hands. "That's a shame."

"I'm parked over by the gym." Noah nodded toward the parking lot. "Did you want another coffee before we leave?"

I shook my head, not leaving any room for temptation. I was already buzzing enough from the anticipation of going to Noah's place that I was a little wary of adding more caffeine to the mix. Wouldn't want to embarrass myself.

Besides, if we stopped by the cart now, Noah would probably find some way to pay for it himself—which didn't do anything to ease the guilt of how slowly I'd been saving up money to repay him for the pen fiasco. I was convinced Noah and Scott had some sort of shifty agreement when it came to coffee payments; I just couldn't prove it.

Yet.

My main theory was that Noah was somehow threatening or blackmailing Scott. I tried my best to assure Scott it was safe to confide in me whenever Noah was absent, but the coffee cart boy simply laughed in my face whenever I tried to gently coax a confession out of him.

When we reached the familiar black Audi, Noah beat me to the passenger door as usual, and we reenacted the dance of me trying and failing to gracefully take a seat before he closed the door. I let out a sigh and tossed my bag to the floor before buckling up as he got in.

As he started the car, Noah pulled out his phone, and there was no way I imagined the tension that blanketed the small space as he typed a message.

"Checking in with a roommate?" I asked lightly, going for casual as I tapped my fingers against my thighs. "Or maybe your... wife?"

Noah shot me an unimpressed look.

"Just trying to lighten the mood," I muttered. I flattened both hands against my skirt and looked out the window.

It was a ten-minute drive from campus, and traffic wasn't too bad. I didn't know where I'd expected Noah to live, but it certainly wasn't the small street of modest duplexes he pulled into.

He parked in one of the driveways, and I followed him up the walkway to the left side of a one-story Spanish-style duplex—doing a double take at the landscaping wrapping around to his side yard. A row of wooden planters stuck out like a sore thumb behind a short hedge. "You have a garden?"

"It's mostly vegetables and other basics. My friend takes care of those, actually," Noah said. "He's got a green thumb but lives in an apartment. Not much space for gardening."

A *friend*.

I snuck a glance up at him. "Is his name Julian, by chance?"

One corner of his lips curved into a smile. "It's Adrian."

"Adrian," I repeated, committing the name to memory.

Noah. Julian. Adrian.

Noah unlocked a bright red front door before holding it open for me, and I slipped past him into the duplex.

It was like walking into a forest when the air freshener assaulted my nose, and I slid off my shoes at the entryway while peeking around the corner at his living space.

A couch. A few not-super-comfy-looking chairs. A coffee table, a couple end tables, and a TV mounted on the wall.

No pictures. No doodads. Just a Rubik's cube on the coffee table with some scattered papers, and a few take-out menus arranged tastefully on the end table.

Maybe it was the distinct lack of *things*, but Noah's living room felt twice as big as one I would've expected in a duplex this size. It could've fit two of my dorm room.

Noah strode to the coffee table. He gathered up the papers and tucked them in a folder. "Work documents. Have a seat."

"Thanks. Nice place."

I admired the cushiness of the taupe carpet under my pink socks as I stepped further inside. Scratching at my elbow, I glanced around at the bare walls. Maybe he hadn't lived here long enough to decorate yet.

Noah tucked the folder under his arm and gave the living room his own assessing look. "I haven't given it much thought, but this is temporary. I'm hardly here, with all the traveling and my work hours."

That made sense, even if it did little to sate my curiosity.

"It's still early for food, so wanna watch a movie first?" I asked. I eyed the menus and wondered if it was too late to suggest takeout so Noah didn't have to witness my nonexistent cooking skills.

"Why don't you pick one out?" Noah handed me a TV remote and pulled his phone from his pocket, checking the screen. "Ah, I have to take this. I'll make sure I have something we can make a meal out of, too."

"Sounds good." I headed for the couch and got comfortable as Noah disappeared through a swinging door that must've been to the kitchen.

"Kincaid," he answered sharply before the door swung shut and muffled the rest of the conversation.

I wasn't too proud to admit that I snooped a little into Noah's Netflix profile—which was disappointingly labeled as simply "Netflix." His list consisted of documentaries and critically acclaimed, award-winning movies sprinkled in with a few foreign films. It was the type of stuff I'd tune into if I was looking to nap an afternoon away. But his recently watched list was the polar opposite, filled with action movies and comedies.

I scrolled through the options, hunting for something interesting—but not *too* interesting, because I was sitting on a perfectly good couch that was just itching to be corrupted—before I settled on a documentary following the migration patterns of pandas.

Perfect.

Noah came back a few minutes later, slipped off his blazer, and joined me on the couch without a word.

I shifted around to get comfortable, pulling my legs up to tuck under my butt. Noah sat a whole cushion away from me, and his jaw was clenched tight enough to cause concern.

I cleared my throat, not liking the abrupt change in mood. "Everything okay?"

He glanced over, and the pinched lines between his brows smoothed out. "Fine. Everything's just fine."

It didn't *sound* fine. "If you need to make a call—"

"No." Noah used a hand to stretch his neck side to side. He shook his head and gestured to the TV. "It's taken care of. Now, what are we watching? Wildlife documentary?"

I frowned, wanting to know what made him tense up like that, but he clearly didn't want to talk about it. So, when he offered a lousy excuse for a smile, I let it go and gave him a brief rundown on the panda shenanigans we had in store for us.

It wasn't ten minutes later that I was snuggled up against Noah's side with his arm around me while we watched a panda test another bamboo stalk to see if it was too dry. Noah relaxed enough to trace his fingers along my shoulder, and it was far too distracting to be healthy.

As interesting as panda eating habits were, the following fifteen minutes felt more like hours because the urge to kiss Noah kept growing stronger. He was right here, we were alone, and my body was hyperfocused on the places his body was touching mine.

"I have a confession," I said after Noah mentioned his concern over a panda getting too close to another panda's territory. I wet my lips, took a deep breath, and hooked a leg over Noah's lap until I was straddling him on the couch. Miraculously, I didn't over-shoot and go flying onto the floor. "I picked this so we could make out during it."

Noah's eyes lit with amusement, and I rested my hands comfortably on his chest.

"You don't mind, right?" I asked as I settled on his lap. The scent of rain tickled my nose in the most pleasing of ways.

Noah's smile was slow to take, but his hand reached out until it was grasping the back of my neck before he pulled my lips down to his.

Good answer.

I melted against him, struggling to stifle a triumphant smile at the success of my seduction technique. I'd come a long way since my first boy-girl party in middle school.

Noah's mouth moved confidently against mine, and I delighted in the feel of his free hand sliding up my thigh before his hold tightened in a way that had me pressing my chest flat against his with my hands happily sandwiched in between us. His chest was warm and firm beneath the dress shirt.

Noah's hand grew bolder, sneaking up inside my top and flattening against my stomach in a way that short-circuited my brain. His other hand slid down from my neck to wrap around my back.

Fire ignited in my veins at his touch, and all my focus zeroed in on his hand against my bare skin as he explored higher. I kissed him harder in response, grabbing on to his tie for leverage.

When his fingers brushed the underside of my bra, I might've accidentally bitten his lip—but when he groaned deep in his chest and his arm around my back pulled me closer, I decided to pretend it was totally intentional.

I was rewarded when his hand moved higher to my breast, sending a warmth skittering over my skin.

The sound of a key unlocking the door had us both freezing as time slowed. But then I heard the doorknob turning, and I jerked back—Noah's grip the only thing that stopped me from falling to the floor. His arm tensed around my back, and my eyes widened to the size of saucers as the front door swung open.

A tall guy around Noah's age strolled in before using his foot to shut the door behind him. His light-brown hair bounced as he hummed a quiet tune, both hands stuffed in the pockets of bright teal medical scrubs. He stopped midhum when he spotted us, eyes widening behind rectangular dark glasses.

I stared back.

"What are you doing here?" Noah spoke first, recovering from our make-out session shockingly quick. My eyes widened further at the sharpness to his tone. There was also the fact that I was still perched on his lap and straddling his thighs in what was no longer a private spit-swapping moment. Thankfully—or maybe not—his hand quickly let go of my breast, as if it'd burned him, and my shirt was once again an Emma's-limbs-only zone.

My cheeks burned, and I wanted to crawl under the couch and disappear.

One of the stranger's brows rose effortlessly—something I was officially jealous of—and his eyes flitted to mine in surprise before darting back to Noah. "Well, hello to you, too. Talk about compromising positions. Who's this?"

"I thought you were coming over for dinner *tomorrow* night?" Noah asked, fingers gripping my side firmly enough that I muffled a squeak.

I fidgeted in Noah's hold as silence fell. Noah looked at the stranger, who stared right back, and the silence stretched to such an uncomfortable length that I briefly wondered if they were either telepathic or deeply in love.

I took advantage of their distraction to slowly slide off Noah's lap—painfully aware of every awkward movement of my body since it was the only motion happening in the quiet room—gripping my skirt to make sure I didn't flash the new arrival as I settled on the couch beside Noah. He didn't seem in a rush to let go of my waist, so I stayed close.

The stranger's lips twisted into an exaggerated frown. "But we *always* have dinner on Sundays."

"Yes, but today is Saturday," Noah said.

My brows knit together as I fought to figure out what the heck was going on.

"Ah, you're right." The new arrival glanced my way. "My apologies. I can be a little scatterbrained when exams are coming up."

"Not a problem. I'll see you tomorrow, then," Noah said as he paused the documentary. I blinked at him. Was he seriously not introducing me to someone who was obviously a friend of his?

"Oh, but I just got here. Although it does look like you're busy with…" The new guy trailed off, and his calculating gaze darted between me and Noah before lingering on me.

Noah's grip tightened around my waist, and all I could do was sit there and look back and forth between the two men. I still hadn't ruled out the possibility that this guy was romantically involved with my boyfriend.

"… date night?" the stranger asked as he pushed up his glasses.

"Julian…" Noah's voice was laced with warning.

"This is Julian?" I asked Noah, finally finding my voice. "Your friend? That Julian?"

Noah muttered under his breath, but Julian perked up. "You've heard of me? I can't say I've been extended the same courtesy, but yes, I'm Julian Carmichael. At your service."

"*Julian,*" Noah repeated, but his friend waved him off.

"I apologize for interrupting. It's easy to confuse days of the week with my profession. You see, I happen to be a doctor," Julian continued confidently. He squinted and crossed both arms over his scrubs. "I'm sure you're familiar with the term."

Who *was* this guy? Had Noah really never told him about me?

"It does ring a bell," I answered carefully, sitting rigidly under Noah's arm as he fake-coughed into his hand.

"What was that, Kincaid?" Julian asked sweetly.

Noah snorted. He actually *snorted*. I was officially in the Twilight Zone. "You're a *vet*, not a doctor. And you're still in school for it."

Julian frowned. "They're basically the same thing."

"You take care of sick puppies," Noah shot back, and my neck twinged from ping-ponging back and forth between them.

His friend turned to me with a small smile, blue eyes shining. "Pretty heroic, isn't it? Those poor, poor puppies who would die without me."

Noah shook his head. "You're shameless."

"Well, there's no shame in saving lives." Julian sent me a wink as he lowered his voice to a whisper. "I think he's just jealous that I look so good in these scrubs. Wouldn't you agree?"

I ignored his wink because I was too busy wondering if I was having a stroke.

"You definitely look like a doctor," I answered diplomatically, taking a closer look at Noah's friend. Everything about him looked rumpled, from the wrinkles in his scrubs to his scuffed sneakers. Light brown and floppy, his hair hung down far enough to kiss his chin. He wouldn't last a minute in my mother's presence before she dragged him to the barber to chop it all off. Intelligence gleamed in his eyes, followed closely by arrogance.

"Vet student," Noah muttered under his breath, pulling me out of my inspection. I jabbed an elbow into his side, and he grunted. "I was making sure you were aware."

"Don't worry, lovebirds. I'll get out of your hair. But since I'd been counting on dinner tonight, I'm sure you won't mind if I grab a quick snack, Noah?" Julian asked with a small smirk as he gestured toward the kitchen door. "Then I can get back to studying."

"Take whatever you need," Noah said. He rubbed his hand up my arm until he could wrap his arm around my tense shoulders. The butterflies in my stomach shivered in delight as his thumb trailed across a patch of exposed skin, and I silently scolded them.

"It's so kind of you to open your home to me," Julian said as he walked toward the kitchen. "Somehow, I never feel like a stranger when I'm here."

Noah sighed and rubbed his temple. I sat there feeling more

confused than I'd been a minute ago. Why was Julian so surprised to see me? Noah said he was close with his friends—wouldn't a girlfriend be something important to mention? There were dozens of possible explanations, but one was still at the forefront of my mind, and I frowned.

"You didn't tell me you had another lover," I murmured to Noah as his friend disappeared into the kitchen. Noah blanched, choking on nothing, and I realized how wrong I was.

Maybe they weren't in love after all.

"He's a friend." Noah battled back a frown as his brow lowered. "Only a friend. I know it seems strange with him walking in like that, but he's basically my brother."

The admission was less than reassuring. I could feel my place in Noah's life shrink further, and my heart clenched. We'd been dating for weeks, and he never once mentioned me on the weekly dinner dates he had with a guy he'd dubbed a brother.

I forced a smile, hoping it didn't look as brittle as it felt. "I'm just teasing you."

He sighed in response and closed his eyes in what I assumed was a plea for patience.

Julian strolled back into the room with a roll of crackers and applesauce, and his eyes zoned in on us immediately.

"Your pantry is pathetic, so I'm going to scavenge for real food at Adrian's. But won't you at least tell me your date's name before I go?" Julian sent a sharp smile Noah's way. "It's only fair, since she knows mine."

Noah took his time responding. I waited another moment for him to introduce me—the clueless butterflies in my stomach greedily anticipating the way he'd refer to me as his *girlfriend*—but he just kept staring pointedly at his friend. An uncomfortable weight settled on my chest.

"I'm Emma," I said, and somehow I managed a small smile despite Noah's silence. "Emma Fox."

"And now you can go," Noah said before his friend could open his mouth.

Julian scrunched his nose at Noah like a displeased child. "Well, somebody's feeling ornery today. Will Emma be joining us for Sunday dinner tomorr—?"

"She has plans," Noah said before Julian got the full question out, and my smile thinned.

"She does?" I asked dryly, staring at the alien that'd replaced my boyfriend. "And *Emma* can speak for herself."

Noah sent me a chastened look, but the resolve in his eyes didn't waver. "You have that fundraiser with Teresa's soccer team."

Oh. Right.

"Teresa? Who's Teresa?" Julian asked with interest as his gaze darted back and forth between us.

"My roommate at school," I said, wondering if I'd be a bad friend if I tried to get out of going. I was much more interested in learning more about Noah's friendship with this guy, especially when Noah was so quick to kick him out.

"Your roommate," Julian echoed, nodding along slowly. "At Westcroft, I'm guessing?"

I nodded as well, curious what sort of information he was fishing for. "That's where Noah and I met."

"And what year are you, Emma?"

I shifted against Noah's side and hoped this wasn't a trick question. "I'm a freshman."

"A freshman." Julian's eyes settled on Noah as his lips twisted into a shit-eating grin. "And you know my boy here is twenty-three, right? I'm a much more youthful twenty-two."

"*Julian.*" Noah sent him a sharp look.

Julian chuckled and held his hands up in surrender as he backed away. "Don't worry, I'm leaving. Have fun, you two. And it was nice to meet you, Emma."

"You too," I said, though I had my doubts if I meant it.

I could feel the room breathe after the door clicked shut behind Julian, but Noah's arm weighed heavily on my shoulders.

"So." I glanced up at him. I wasn't sure whose jaw was clenched tighter—his or mine—but I unglued mine to state the obvious. "That was one of your infamous friends."

Noah's nostrils flared as he watched the closed door. "Yes, that was Julian."

My eyes wandered back to the door, and I frowned.

So, Operation Side Chick had been a complete bust, which was good news for me since I wanted to be the only apple of Noah's eye. But I hadn't expected to discover I was his dirty little secret tonight, either. To my horror, tears welled in my eyes as the truth of that sank in. I kept my gaze firmly averted from Noah's, putting every ounce of focus into stopping even a single tear from escaping.

Noah resumed the panda documentary and sat stiff as a board next to me without another word. I had so many questions to ask him, but I couldn't get them past my tight throat.

I tried to focus on the good news, like how Noah had standing weekly dinners with a good friend. But part of me—the part that was used to being unwanted in my own home—wondered if there would ever be room for me at those dinners, too.

A Moment

IT TOOK ALL my willpower not to bombard Noah with questions.

I thought I'd held out pretty well for the rest of the evening at Noah's place—including an unfortunate first experience cooking together where Noah discovered my embarrassing lack of culinary skills.

Dinner was the definition of a disaster. I'd been so focused on keeping my emotions in check—plus I already had difficulty doing something as simple as boiling water—that I somehow used sugar instead of salt in the recipe and I burned the spaghetti noodles.

But a quiet dinner consisting of eating around the minefield of charred noodles followed by a car ride spent defending my lack of cooking skills to Noah did wonders to distract from the seed of insecurity growing in my stomach.

It wasn't until Noah was walking me down the hallway to my dorm that the little sproutling was overwhelmingly insistent, and I caved. "So... I've met one of your friends."

Noah glanced at me before focusing ahead. "Yes. Julian."

I waited till we passed the last few doors before mine, but he didn't say anything more.

"That's it? Nothing else to say?" I asked, starting to question my own sanity.

Noah frowned. "What else is there to say? That was Julian. You met him."

I pinched my lips and tried to keep this tactful. "Was I *supposed* to meet him?"

Noah stared for a long moment before leaning against the wall next to my door. He rubbed a hand over his jaw and eyed me closely. "It's been a long day, and I'm not following what you're getting at. Spell it out for me?"

Swallowing, I fiddled with my key before putting it in my pocket. "I just got the feeling tonight that you didn't want me to meet him. He didn't even know I existed."

Noah's lips thinned, and he broke our gaze. It felt like a punch to the gut. "I don't know."

"You don't know?" I echoed dryly. I was hoping this talk would calm my suspicions, not light a fire under them. "Noah, what exactly are we doing here? I mean, you're my boyfriend. You've met Teresa, and she's the closest thing I have to family here, but you balk at introducing me to someone you call a brother? Were you nervous he wouldn't approve? I don't want to toot my own horn or anything, but he didn't seem absolutely repulsed by me or anything."

Noah forced out a quiet laugh and shook his head. "No. No, he definitely wasn't repulsed."

"Then... what? Am I reading too much into things? Maybe I'm crazy, but I got the feeling earlier that Julian wasn't supposed to meet me—not just tonight, but *ever*."

Noah still wouldn't meet my gaze, and I wasn't too embarrassed to admit my eyes watered again as the seconds passed and he didn't respond.

He cleared his throat, but his gaze remained steadfastly on the floor. "You're not crazy."

I swallowed again at the softness of his tone, waiting for the other shoe to drop. "So, what does that mean?"

Hazel eyes met mine, and the warmth in them surprised me. "It's not an issue of approval, because you'd pass with flying colors. And even if you didn't meet anyone's approval, it wouldn't change a damn thing about how I feel for you."

My lips parted, but he didn't have to say it like the answer was so obvious. "Well, that could've been something you mentioned earlier. Instead, it felt like you were trying to keep me a secret, like a mistress or something."

"A *mistress*?"

"I mean, you said you didn't have a wife, but Julian obviously hadn't heard of me."

He let out a laugh of disbelief.

"I'm learning very quickly not to keep things from you," Noah muttered. "Because you get these crazy ideas in your head. A *mistress*, Emma?"

"What was I supposed to think?" Insecurity tore away any rational thoughts.

Noah watched me for a beat before he let out a quiet, self-deprecating laugh. "I'm sorry. You're right, I should've explained."

He stepped closer and slid his warm hand into my restless one until he was holding on tightly. The butterflies yelled at me to move because they were confused, but it was impossible to look away from his eyes once they snared mine.

"I told you before that I don't do anything lightly," Noah whispered as his thumb traced my skin. "I never have. If I do something, I give it everything I have. Piano. School. Work. And now *you*."

I swallowed in reflex at the weight he put behind those words.

"I didn't want to risk this by introducing you to Julian," Noah said. "He's the smartest guy I know, but he's notorious for saying stupid things. Hell, he was already teasing about you being too young for me. And he warms up to people a lot quicker than I do. You *just* met, and he was already asking you to dinner."

"To dinner *with you*, and he only invited me because I'm dating you. He was trying to be inclusive, which is more than I can say for how you've been."

Noah's eyes narrowed. "He wasn't being kind. He was trying to get more information from you. Julian makes it his mission to involve himself in everything, but I don't want him to be involved in this."

"So I couldn't even meet him?"

Noah let out a slow breath and rubbed his temple with his free hand. "I've spent the last eight years coming in second place to Julian in most areas of my life, but I couldn't let that happen with you."

For such a smart guy, Noah was an idiot.

I wanted to smack him for being so dumb, but I settled for squinting up at him. "Are you serious? Did you think I would leave you for your friend or something? That's crazy. And you're the last person I would've expected to be insecure. Noah, you're perfect."

He scoffed. "I'm far from perfect."

I opened my mouth to protest, but Noah shook his head and told me to let him finish. His free hand came up and trailed down the line of my jaw until he was tilting my chin to look up at him fully. "I'm not perfect, and I couldn't stand the thought of you looking at him the same way you look at me. You mean too much to me."

I scrunched my nose as my cheeks warmed. Was it that obvious how I looked at him? "I can't mean that much to you if you're hiding me from your friends."

"It's not that." He ran his tongue over the front of his teeth, struggling for words. But then his eyes settled on my lips, and his own curved into a slow smile. "You're my coffee, Emma."

I blinked, positive I'd misheard him. "Wait. What?"

Noah's gaze jumped up to mine, and the smile reached his eyes.

"I'm addicted to you." His smile widened as my grip tightened on his hand. "Think of how much you love coffee. That's how I feel about you."

I felt my jaw go slack.

"You *love* me?" I asked, but it barely came out louder than a whisper.

Noah stared back at me, a flicker of confusion passing over his face before he chuckled. "I do. Yes. I love everything about you. The ramblings, the Jell-O incidents, your musical soul that reaches out to mine—"

I slapped a hand over his mouth, seriously worried for my health if he continued. My brain was already playing his words on repeat.

"Wow," was all I could say. I swallowed around the lump in my throat. That was the most romantic thing anyone had ever said to me. My chest felt tight, and I fought to find any sort of response that didn't involve throwing up on his polished loafers from the elation his words produced. "I, uh, I love you, too."

And I did—I belatedly realized as the butterflies practically vibrated in excitement—with every fiber of my being.

I'd never said that to anyone before; not even my parents.

Noah's lips widened into a smile beneath my palm, and it reached his eyes in a way that had me physically fanning myself. He threw his head back with a laugh, pulling loose from my hold.

I watched the absolute joy take shape on his face, mesmerized, until he calmed down long enough to lean in again.

He traced the underside of my lip with his thumb. "You're my coffee."

His *coffee*.

I swallowed around the growing lump in my throat.

"Okay, shut up or I'm going to start crying," I said with a light shove at his chest, but his face already looked blurry from the tears welling in my eyes. *"Cheese and fries."*

"Did I mention I love the bizarre way you curse, too?" Noah chuckled as he wrapped his strong arms around my waist and pulled me against his broad chest. I tried to keep my eyes focused on his while sniffling back tears. His head tilted down, breath mingling with mine as he placed a kiss on the corner of my mouth. "I love every inch of you."

I breathed in deeply through my nose, trying to get a hold on my heart's frantic beating and my chart-topping blood pressure, but I just ended up getting a noseful of his rain scent. Noah didn't know what he was doing to me.

I wanted to say something sweet and romantic back, but all that my jumbled mind could come up with was that he smelled nice. "Just kiss me already."

That got another big smile as the skin by his eyes crinkled, but it was short-lived as he focused on me—while very noticeably *not* kissing me.

"I'm sorry I tried to hide you," Noah said. His hands slid from my waist to grab ahold of my hips. "I like having you to myself too much, and I've never liked sharing my coffee. But I'm here. I'll be here for as long as you want me, because there's nowhere I'd rather be."

My teary eyes were past any hope of recovery, and I cursed them for not allowing me to see a clear picture of Noah's earnest face. But I saw enough of the emotion swirling in his eyes, and the upward tilt to his lips. He was calm and happy.

I was happy, too.

Painfully happy.

"Noah..." I bit my lip to hide a smile, but it broke through anyway. "What's your opinion on sleepovers?"

His brow wrinkled, offsetting the smile. "Aside from the bloody nose incident, I don't think I've been to one since I was a child—"

"I'm asking if you want to stay the night," I cut in, the words basically tripping over each other to escape my mouth—wishing he hadn't brought up the time I'd accidentally drugged him. I cleared my throat to banish the onslaught of anxious energy. "With me. In my bed. Preferably naked."

Noah's smile softened, and his eyes didn't waver from mine. "I'd love to."

There was a word I'd associated with Noah Kincaid from the start. From the first time he'd stepped through the classroom door and raised a perfectly arched eyebrow at my crazed smile. He seemed to embody it from head to toe, and it wholly described him from the way he wore those impeccable blazers to his flawless Southern manners—all the way down to how he lined up his ninety-nine-dollar pens in a meticulous line exactly one minute before class began.

Perfection.

Noah Kincaid was absolute perfection.

I'd wanted to mess with his impeccable demeanor. Muss up his hair a bit and put a wrinkle in his blazer. Make him arrive ten minutes late for class. Maybe even fill his sandwich with worms just to see if it would faze him.

But as Noah joined me in my room—after I dutifully remembered to place a green polka-dot toe sock on the doorknob and send a warning text to Teresa—and we made our way to the bed, I discovered that his boxers had a few wrinkles in them. That his heart beat just as fast as mine did as we shed each other's clothing, and that I could make involuntary sounds leave his lips that sounded wild instead of thoughtfully formed. Then as the sun was fully setting and his lips felt permanently fused against mine in a duet of our own—when I called out his name and we flew over the edge together in a tangle of sweaty limbs—I decided that maybe Noah Kincaid was human after all.

And hours later, as he held me against the soothing beat of his

heart while whispering sweet nothings that had my own heart tripping over itself, I found a new word that described him even
better.

Mine.

A Bottle of Syrup

BIRDS DIDN'T GENTLY ROUSE me from my sex-induced slumber the next morning. Sunlight wasn't streaming mystically through the blinds, and there was a distinct lack of bacon scent wafting in from a nonexistent kitchen.

All in all, it should've never qualified to be the best morning of my life.

Not even top ten.

But I woke up snuggled against Noah's side with his arm wrapped around my middle. I came into awareness with his warm, bare skin pressed flush to mine. When I blinked my groggy eyes open, it was to find his sleepy hazel ones looking back at me.

I hummed pleasantly, positive there was no better way to wake up. I pressed my lips against his chest in a kiss while subtly checking for a pool of drool—all clear—before following up with another kiss as I worked a trail all the way up to his ear until I could cuddle closer and whisper, "Your penis was inside me last night."

Noah grunted. "For heaven's sake, Emma."

He shook his head and leaned further back against the pillows while giving me a look far too stern for such a decadent morning.

"What?" I asked innocently, basking in the afterglow of such a fun night as my lips stretched into a wide smile. His hand traced down my back while I pressed myself more fully against him. This was something I could get addicted to. "I'm just saying... I'd like you to put it inside me again."

Noah snorted, and his chest shook against mine. The grin spread across his face like a wildfire, and I couldn't resist returning it. His free hand entangled itself in my nest of hair, and he pulled my head toward his until his lips molded to mine in a deep kiss that made me want to melt straight through the mattress.

But he backed off and placed a much shorter, chaster kiss on my lips—then another—before murmuring against them. "Hold that thought, beautiful."

Noah's delectable lips left mine, only to land fleetingly on my forehead before backing off completely. His fingers massaged my scalp before letting go, and then I could only watch in growing confusion as Noah slid me off his front and got up from the bed.

A bed we had just spent most of the night doing dirty things in... A bed that was warm and soft and inviting... A bed that his very willing and enthusiastic girlfriend was lying naked in.

And he just got out like it was nothing.

"You're leaving?" I asked after a long beat of watching him locate his scattered clothing through the rest of my clutter. I hoped the growing sensation in my chest was a sign of indigestion instead of my heart dropping. He probably got a text and had to run off for work. Or maybe there was a tornado, and he was keeping a clear head while preparing for us to find cover.

Or maybe he was just leaving because it was the morning after and that's what people did sometimes. I was an idiot to think he'd want to stick around and hang out.

I tried to push those thoughts down by focusing on his bare, toned butt as he fished for his boxers on the floor.

It worked. I was happy again.

Noah looked over his shoulder with a puzzled smile as he tugged on his boxers, and he let out a breath of laughter.

"I'll be back in thirty minutes, and then I'm going to take you up on that offer," he said with a pointed look. I swallowed at the promise in his eyes while he slid on pants. Then I felt like chopped liver just lying there, so I scooted across the mattress, but Noah reached for my arm before I could get up. He leaned down for another kiss, and my stomach flipped over itself as his lips brushed against mine. "Don't get up. Keep the bed warm for me. Thirty minutes, I promise."

All righty then. I watched him finish dressing before grabbing his phone and wallet off the nightstand. Where did he have to run off to for thirty minutes on a Sunday morning?

Another kiss to my forehead, then he grabbed my dorm key before sweeping out the door. I scooted over to the warm section of the bed he'd left behind and pulled the top sheet over my chest as my brain worked to process the latest events.

I just slept with Noah Kincaid—and I didn't even have to drug him this time!

Life was beautiful.

The excitement coursing through my veins was impossible to contain, and I found myself pulling my blanket over my head and screaming in elation into the makeshift tent. I screamed and squealed and kicked my legs against the bed—

Until the door burst open. I whipped the blanket off my head —clinging the sheet to my chest as Noah's frantic eyes scanned the room.

"Are you okay?" he asked, gripping the doorknob. "I heard screaming."

My cheeks heated, and I readjusted the sheet to cover the blush spreading down my chest.

"I'm good," I answered hoarsely before clearing my throat. "It must've been the girl next door. She sounds okay now, though."

Noah's brow rose, but he accepted my bold-faced lie easily enough and left without another word.

Any embarrassment eased away as I fell back against the pillows and closed my eyes. Mindful of listening ears, I kicked my feet a little less zealously while muffling my squeals with my palm.

I slept with Noah.

A goofy grin fused itself to my face as I mentally replayed the events of the night before, shamelessly embracing the way the memories lit my skin on fire. It wasn't until I opened my eyes that I noticed a certain stuffed elephant staring disapprovingly from his upside-down position atop my bookshelf. I'd been a little careless when removing him from bed the night before.

"Mr. Elephant, don't give me that look," I whispered with a scowl. But still, I tugged the blanket up to cover more of my nakedness as his glare didn't let up. "I have needs, okay? Perfectly acceptable needs."

His stern expression didn't change—never mind that it *never* actually changed—and I frowned.

"Oh, please. You weren't being all holier-than-thou when Noah and I were sucking face the other day. Don't act innocent on me now."

I looked away—effectively ending any rebuttal Mr. Elephant could've had.

My phone showed Noah's thirty minutes had almost passed already—which meant I'd been daydreaming for quite a bit. There was a text from Teresa saying she'd stay away from our dorm until I gave her the all-clear, as well as a few motivational gifs about getting it on.

My personal favorite was the one involving camels.

Below her texts was a *Piano News* notification. *Oliver Bishop Takes the Stage in LA Next Month – Already Sold Out.* I stared at the screen, feeling a little strange seeing a thumbnail of Oliver smiling on a red carpet. After seeing him in jeans and a leather jacket, the tux he wore looked different. Still amazing, but a little out of place.

I chewed on my lip and glanced at my nightstand drawer, where his invitation was tucked away. An invitation with two tickets and a phone number.

An invitation that raised feelings I couldn't even begin to unpack.

Swallowing, I cleared the notification with a jittery finger and scrolled through the others. But there was nothing from Noah, and he'd definitely promised to be back in thirty minutes. I frowned when that actually made my heart drop. God, how pathetic was I? Spend one night with a guy, and suddenly I was the paranoid girlfriend who questioned his promises.

My phone rumbled with a text, and I eagerly swiped without a second thought.

NOAH

Taking a little longer than expected. I'll be back as soon as I can. Don't move. <3

I sank back into the mattress with a sigh before pulling the covers back over my head and trying to ignore how much my cheeks hurt from smiling.

Noah walked through the door exactly fifteen minutes later, carrying a to-go bag and a drink carrier. I sat up with the sheet held against my chest.

"You went to get coffee." I couldn't hide my surprise, and Noah grinned like he was beyond proud of himself. "You trickster! Why didn't you just tell me?"

"It was a surprise." Noah set down the paper bag and handed me one of the to-go cups from the carrier.

I really, *really* liked surprises.

The coffee's rich aroma invaded my nose, and I took the deepest breath possible while he rifled through the bag. It was pure heaven. Then another scent filtered through the divine fragrance of freshly brewed coffee, and I did a double take. "I smell waffles!"

Noah pulled out a bottle of maple syrup with a chuckle and set it on the nightstand. "Good nose."

I could only stare while trying to find my voice, and when I did, my brain could only focus on the most obvious of observations. "You brought waffles?"

"Three containers' worth of waffles."

My heart skipped a couple beats and then stumbled over itself to catch up. "You really shouldn't have done this. There's such a thing as setting the bar too high, you know."

He looked up from the bag, and the smile that lit his face also lit something warm that the butterflies flocked around like a cult. I blinked, pretending my eyelids were a camera shutter that could memorize the moment.

"I need to prove my worth if you're going to keep me around. Did you keep the bed warm for me?" Noah asked.

"Like a furnace." I was entirely too aware of how much clothing I was *not* wearing at the moment. "But I'm a little under-dressed now."

Holding the sheet to my front, I scooted to the edge of the bed, only for Noah to shake his head. His eyes lit with appreciation as he placed a white food container next to the syrup. "No, I like you like this."

I attempted and most likely failed to raise one eyebrow. "Naked?"

Noah's eyes crawled down to where my hand held the sheet against my chest. "Why not? I'm still planning on taking you up on your offer."

"Who knew you were such a *guy*?" I teased before biting my lip to hide the severity of my smile. I scooted back against the pillows and trapped the sheet in place with my arms so I could cup my coffee in both hands. "Does that mean your pants are coming off?"

Noah didn't even blink, but I saw the corner of his lips twitch as his hands went straight to his belt buckle. My jaw went slack as he made quick work of the clasp before sliding the leather smoothly through the buckle, and I sucked in a breath in time to him unzipping.

"I think you mentioned something about seedy background music before?" Noah smiled, and to my utter astonishment he took his time slipping off his pants. They dragged painfully slowly down his hips—flipping my heart upside down—before he stepped out and kicked them up into a smooth catch.

I tried and failed to wolf whistle. Noah took my cup away and put it on the nightstand. Then he proceeded to toss his pants straight at my face. I couldn't help laughing as my world turned dark, and I pulled them down to find Noah climbing into bed beside me.

The bed sheet was still between us, and Noah was still sadly wearing much more clothing than me. But when he leaned in, I eagerly met his lips halfway.

And when his fingers traced lazily up my arm, I might've forgotten about the sheet completely as it slipped down an inch. I felt like I was floating. The feel of his skin under my fingertips was intoxicating. But when his lips kissed down to my neck and I had a prime view of the food container sitting oh-so-innocently behind him, my priorities quickly shifted.

I cleared my throat and delighted in each shiver his touch provoked. "Can we eat the waffles first?"

Noah's lips traced down to my shoulder, making the hairs on the back of my neck stand up as he smiled against my skin. "I need to work on my seduction if you still have waffles on your mind."

"Something would be very wrong if I didn't have waffles on my mind. That's when doctors would need to get involved. Besides, we don't want them to get cold."

He chuckled against my shoulder, and shivers trickled down my arms as his fingers trailed up my bare back.

My breathing stalled when his fingers found a raised patch of skin on my shoulder blade.

"What happened here?" Noah traced a finger over the scar tissue as I shivered. I hated that scar. "I didn't notice it last night."

I swallowed around a lump forming in my throat while scrambling for a believable story. Today was too perfect of a day to ruin with the truth. "Promise not to laugh?"

His lips caressed my shoulder. "I'd never laugh at an injury."

I said the first lie that popped into my head. "I was pretending to be a monkey."

Noah pulled back from my shoulder and nudged my waist until I was facing the other way and he could get a closer look at the reason I rarely wore tank tops.

My mouth babbled on. "I was young, way high up in a tree, and I thought I could make the jump to another branch."

I could practically feel Noah's wince behind me as he traced the tightened skin around the scar.

I licked my lips as a weight settled in my stomach at the evolving lie. "It was a rough landing, and my shoulder took the brunt of it on a sharp rock. Miraculously, there weren't any broken bones."

"A rock did this?"

I nodded, hiding my grimace. It did if the rock was my father. "It never quite healed right."

Silence lingered while I held my breath, until I felt Noah's lips brush against my scar. My whole body turned hot and then cold. I blinked back the tears gathering. His kiss was tender and comforting and made me feel something I never had before.

I felt loved.

"Waffle time?" I asked through a tight throat, absolutely terrified of how potent the feeling was.

Noah pulled back, and I used the reprieve to quickly wipe my eyes as he slid off the bed and grabbed the to-go box before rejoining me. I scooted back around, licking my lips. I eagerly grabbed a fork.

Noah pulled back the top, and the sweet smell of freshly made waffles permeated the room. "I hope I ordered enough."

Little dark dots in the waffles caught my eye, and I froze. "Chocolate chips? I thought the cafeteria didn't have those."

"They don't," Noah said. "I ran to the store. That's where I found syrup, too."

That took a little time to compute, and I stared. "You took chocolate chips to the cafeteria and asked the staff to make waffles with them?"

Noah smiled in answer.

I frowned, feeling a little betrayed. I'd personally asked them three different times to add chocolate chips. "I didn't think they took special requests."

"They didn't want to, but I told them I was in love with a girl and I couldn't go back to her without chocolate chip waffles."

If human bodies were liquefiable, I would've melted on the spot.

"Careful, Noah." I drizzled a generous amount of sugary goodness over the steaming stack of waffles. "This is exactly how you make a girl fall even more in love with you."

He didn't bat an eye at me basically drowning the waffles in syrup, and his hand met my back in a featherlight touch—stroking up and down the bare expanse of skin. "Good. My plan is working."

The waffles were gone in less than ten minutes, and I'd happily eaten two containers by myself. Noah and I spent some time naked-cuddling in bed, sipping on coffees, and avoiding Mr.

Elephant's paternal stare. I was the happiest I'd ever been, and it was honestly making me a little loopy—enough so that I'd told Noah all about my dream where unicorn-shaped waffles frolicked through a forest of Aurora Ipsilons. He found it amusing, which in turn made me even more happy at seeing his smile.

Once Noah gave me the green light to polish off the last bite, we settled into my mountain of pillows and I prepared for a food coma. The day was young, and my heart had never felt lighter, but Noah was unusually quiet as I babbled on about the many health benefits of eating waffles. He stared at the ceiling and randomly chimed in with a word or two whenever I bothered to take a breath.

"What's wrong?" I gently poked at his side when he failed to realize I'd even asked a question. "Regretting last night?"

Noah's gaze met mine head-on at that, and the green in his hazel eyes was so prominent it almost looked like they didn't belong to him. His hand cupped my cheek, and the way his calloused skin brushed against mine did things to my stomach that should've been illegal.

"No, I was just thinking about work for a minute. And the only thing I regret about last night is that it ended." Noah's voice didn't leave a shadow of a doubt as he leaned closer and placed an equally warm kiss on my opposite cheek.

The butterflies were in a full-blown tizzy, but it was too tempting to poke fun at him. "Are you sure it wasn't the part where you fell off the foot of my bed?"

Noah's cheeks tinted a light shade of red, much to my amusement, and his eyes squinted at me in warning.

"Careful with the teasing, beautiful." His own lips twitched as I burst out laughing. "I don't recall you being too upset with what I did once I was down there."

All laughter ceased, and my face flushed twenty shades darker than Noah's. I couldn't resist flicking my gaze to his lips when I recalled the feel of his mouth on me.

"Nope, definitely didn't have a problem with that," I squeaked out. "No complaints here."

Noah's grin was all male, and it reached his eyes in a way that made my toes curl.

"I didn't think so," he drawled. He grabbed another pillow from the mountain and propped it under his head. It took effort not to roll my eyes at his unexpected ego.

But it didn't stop me from snuggling back against him, convinced the smile on my face would become a permanent fixture.

A Midterm

Dear Diary,

Noah and I are together.
Officially.
The man brought me waffles.
I'm in love.

He's waking up. Gotta go!
Emma

Sorry I'm totally bailing, but something came up and I can't surf today. :(Raincheck?

Lame, but I'll accept an IOU.

> Granted.

> Fourth lesson in all things magic: It's not about the size of your wand. It's how you use it.

> That's not... Are you drunk? I don't have a wand.

> It's all in the swish.

IT WAS safe to say Teresa spent the whole weekend at her friend Stacie's house. I would've felt guilty for basically forcing her out and bailing on Finn, but I was a little too busy enjoying myself more than was healthy in the arms of my lover boy.

The eve of Slade's midterm arrived before I knew it, and with it came a hefty dose of heartburn. After my mother's threatening call, Noah and I spent most of our time studying. Well, *mostly* studying—when we weren't doing much more fun things with fewer clothes.

And I refused to feel guilty about that. My dating life wasn't up to my mother.

By now, I knew Noah's flash cards like the back of my hand.

Like how the seventh scale degree of a major scale is typically called the leading tone. Seemed easy enough once I cared to learn.

And that if a major interval is lowered a half step, it doesn't become a diminished interval. It'd be a minor interval.

And, of course, how a Neapolitan chord is really just a major triad built on the lowered second degree of a major or minor scale.

I also learned I had a birthmark in the shape of a turtle on my hand that I'd never noticed before, but that's neither here nor there.

The night before the test, Noah was busy with his consulting gig, so I spent half of the evening flipping through his flash cards and rattling off answers. The other half was spent panicking that no matter how much I studied I'd still end up bombing the midterm and my time at Westcroft would be over before it really began.

Since Teresa was traveling to an away game with the soccer team, she wasn't there to calm me down. Mr. Elephant just ended up getting me more worked up, and by the time my caffeine high crashed well after midnight, I'd had at least two existential crises.

One might've involved pulling Oliver Bishop's invitation from my nightstand and adding his number to my phone.

Then texting him.

Then promptly freaking out about texting him and throwing my phone across the room.

Hopefully Teresa wouldn't notice the dent in the wall above her headboard.

I glanced at my sent messages for the twentieth time in an hour.

EMMA

Hey.

It's Emma, btw. Emma Fox. The crazy girl who cornered you in Westcroft University's music room. You gave me your number. I'm not stalking you or anything. Just wanted to say hey.

Ten Minutes Later

I actually wanted to say more than "hey." Thank you so much for inviting me to your concert! That was really nice of you, and I'd love to see you play again.

Five Minutes Later

Hey... Emma, again. Sorry for the late texts. These aren't booty calls or anything, if that's why you aren't responding. I would die if you thought that. I just have a really important midterm in Music Theory tomorrow, and I'm kinda freaking out, and everyone I would normally freak out with is away, so I guess I thought I'd finally text you. Not that you're a last resort or anything.

Twelve Minutes Later

And I'm sorry for bringing up booty calls. I was hoping that'd be reassuring, but it was just weird—wasn't it? I wasn't sure what to say after you added that little note about not pushing me away in your invitation, but I don't want you to think I'm coming on to you.

Two Minutes Later

Not that you aren't handsome enough to come on to. You're very attractive, and you probably have girls texting you like this all the time. But I'm not trying to sniff around or anything.

Fourteen Minutes Later

I mean, I have a boyfriend who buys me waffles. Okay? I just want to make that clear.

Seventeen Minutes Later

Waffles.

I scrolled through the messages, cringing as my caffeine high faded.

Maybe I'd overdone it a tiny bit?

It wasn't exactly surprising that Oliver wasn't responding at two in the morning, but his lack of answering had goaded me into sending more messages until it was too late to salvage anything. I officially regretted adding his number to my phone.

But one thing was certain: my heart still pitter-pattered when I thought of him, and that was concerning since it wasn't the coffee causing it. Guilt quickly followed, and I wondered what the heck was wrong with me.

Was it normal to have celebrity crushes even when you were in a loving and totally faithful relationship? Maybe there was nothing *wrong* with this.

I could love my boyfriend and still admire a piano god.

Most girls probably didn't text their celebrity crushes, though.

I heaved a sigh and chucked my phone under the blankets before focusing back on Noah's flash cards.

When the pressure grew to be too much and I'd used up the last of my caffeine reserves, I fell asleep surrounded by flash cards and discarded coffee cups.

My laptop sat on the desk playing *Arabesque* on loop.

I awoke to my phone bursting into a flurry of vibrations the next morning. At first, I ignored it—being too tired to even open my eyes. But whoever was calling was persistent, because after a moment of rest, the vibrations would just begin again. When it burst to life after the fourth ignored call, I groaned and fumbled around under the covers for my phone.

"Yeah?" I grunted into it, then cursed myself for not checking if it was my mother before answering.

"Emma, where the hell are you?" Noah asked. There was an urgency in his voice I didn't recognize.

"Noah?" I rubbed at the sleep in my eyes. "What's wrong?"

"Did you just wake up? Class is starting. I just left to come see if you were still in your dorm."

My lungs stopped working.

Did he just say…? I pulled my phone down and briefly noticed an incoming text from Oliver Bishop before checking the time.

8:01 a.m.

Oh my God.

Slade's midterm.

I'd overslept.

Mothercracker.

I gasped before shooting off the bed and pressing the phone to my ear. "Noah, the test! I slept in!"

"It's okay," he said, switching to his soothing voice. I did not feel soothed. "You still have plenty of time."

"I'm late," I cried, fumbling around for my backpack. I stuffed my notes and a handful of flash cards inside before realizing I'd have no use for them on test day. I tossed a few extra pens in instead, just in case. "I'm missing it. I can't fail—"

"Breathe, Emma. Get your things together. I'm halfway to your dorm."

I paused my packing, and my grip tightened on the phone. "What? No, what are you doing? Get back to class! You can't miss the test, either."

"It doesn't matter for me," Noah said dismissively. "I'm auditing, remember?"

"It totally matters." I darted to the closet and dug through the pile of clothes. Pulling up a shirt, I sniffed it before tossing it to the side. "I know you, and you have more pride than that. Even if it's not for credit, you want the *A*."

The line was quiet for a beat until Noah said reluctantly, "I guess you do know me."

"Now go back! I'll change clothes and be right there."

He sighed, sounding torn. "Call me if you need me. I saved you a seat near the door. And remember to *breathe*."

I hung up and threw the phone on my bed before rubbing a hand across my chest to calm my galloping heart.

It didn't work.

All I could think about was missing the test, failing Music Theory, losing my scholarship, and getting shipped back to Kansas on the soonest flight.

Shoving a hand back into the clothing pile, I grabbed a random pair of leggings and a pink sweatshirt before tossing them on my bed. But I needed to take care of my morning breath before changing, so I hunted down my toiletry bag and made a dash for the bathroom.

Halfway down the hall, I realized I forgot my shower shoes and skidded to a stop. After a brief consideration if it was worth it to chance the bathroom tile in bare feet, I doubled back for my flip-flops.

It wasn't until I got back to my dorm and turned the handle that reality reared its cruel head.

The doorknob didn't budge.

"No," I whispered, refusing to believe it. Even my luck wasn't this bad. "No, no, no. *No!*"

I jiggled the handle with each plea even though I knew it was useless.

I was locked out.

Dread settled in the pit of my stomach, and I cautiously looked down at my ensemble. Hello Kitty pajama shorts that *barely* covered my butt, an oversized T-shirt that did little to hide the fact I slept braless, and bare feet.

"No." I stared at my pajama shorts in growing horror. "This can't be happening."

My dorm key was in the room. My phone. My backpack. My shoes. My *bra*.

Everything was unreachable behind a stupid door that auto-locked because school administration took our safety seriously.

But who cared about safety when my sanity was at stake?

Desperate, I glanced up and down the deserted hallway before a lightbulb went off. Crossing my fingers and praying she was here, I ran six doors down from mine to our resident assistant's room. I banged on her door, curling my toes against the dirty carpet.

No answer.

I knocked harder. "Sydney? Are you in there? I'm locked out!"

Nothing.

Each second ticking by was another second I should've been spending on my midterm. Giving up on Sydney magically appearing in her room, I booked it down the hallway and burst into the communal bathroom. Dental hygiene was apparently the only thing I could control this morning. After brushing my teeth at the speed of light, I found a few hair ties strewn about the sinks area. Grabbing one at random, I threw my rat nest up into something that resembled a messy bun.

Leaving my toiletries behind, I ran for the lobby in hopes of a student being on duty at the front desk who could unlock my room. But when I reached the front area, the desk was deserted. They wouldn't open until classes were out.

I didn't have that kind of time.

I looked down at my pajamas and weighed my options.

It usually took five minutes to walk to the music building, but if I ran...

There weren't any other options.

Bracing myself, I beelined for the door.

A few freshmen coming back from breakfast did a double take as I flew past them out the door, and I barely made it past one building before a wolf-whistle sounded.

I kept running, and my bare feet smacked against the pavement with each stride.

By the time I made it to the music building, my breaths came in quick pants.

The coffee cart was sitting right outside the front doors, yards closer than its typical morning spot. I didn't have my phone to check the time, but if there was one thing I needed to make time for before the midterm, it was caffeine.

I just didn't have any money for it.

I ran up to the cart and skidded to a stop beside a student already chatting with Scott.

"Scott, I'm so sorry—" I wheezed, leaning over and pushing on a cramp that squeezed my side. "I don't have—it's locked in my— I'll pay you back—"

"Here." Scott pulled out an already-made cup from behind the counter. His brow pinched in concern, and he secured the coffee in a sleeve. "Noah called and said to have it ready. I put in an extra scoop for good luck. Now *go!*"

I paused at that—eternally grateful to both of them—before accepting the coffee and hobbling toward the door. "Thank you!"

Taking the stairs two at a time quickly caught up to me, and some divine power must've intervened to get me up the last flight. Or maybe it was just the adrenaline.

Jogging down the hallway toward Slade's classroom, I blew into the cup's mouth hole to speed up cooling the coffee.

This was a bad idea.

I made it a few doors down from Slade's when a body darted out of a classroom, and we collided like two runaway trains.

Coffee exploded from my cup, spraying both of us. I hissed at the burn as it hit my arm and chest, and I moved the coffee to my other hand before shaking out the one that'd been hit.

Looking down, I groaned. Coffee splattered across my chest highlighted a certain lack of undergarments I was hoping to hide.

Cheese and fries.

The boy cursed, scowling at the mess on his jacket before looking up. He froze, and his scowl transformed into an apologetic grin when he saw my death glare aimed at him. "Shit, I'm sorry. I was in a rush to piss, and I didn't see you."

How reassuring. I swallowed back a scream before making to walk past him, but he sidestepped to block my path.

"Here, let me—" He pulled the sleeve of his jacket over his hand before wiping at the stain on my shirt. From his angle, it quickly became very, *very* obvious there was nothing substantial separating my skin from the threadbare top.

He could feel *everything*.

My cheeks heated to the point of scalding, and his hand froze on my chest. I felt my heart thundering against my rib cage, which surely wasn't healthy, and I smacked his hand away.

"It's fine. I've got it." I threw away any hope of containing the blush taking over my face as I brushed at the stain myself.

He stared at my chest a beat longer before snapping back to himself. "Oh, right. Yeah. Sorry, again. I'm an idiot."

"It's fine," I said, voice strangled. When my attempts just made the stain spread more, I gave up. I tried to sidestep around him again, but he didn't make any move to go away. "Don't you have to pee?"

His eyes glanced down at my shirt and back before giving his head a shake. "Yeah! Yes, I do. I'll go... do that now."

I pinched the middle of my shirt, fanning it back and forth to try and air it out as I stumbled the last few steps into Slade's room.

The whole class looked up from their tests, and my stomach dropped as Slade's hawklike gaze landed on me from the teacher's desk. He stared for a good five seconds before raising two fingers and beckoning me over with a sigh.

Letting go of my shirt, I tugged on the hem of my shorts to make them as decent as possible as my nerves went haywire. I shuffled over to Slade's desk as my whole face surely turned the color of a stoplight. His expression didn't betray any emotion as I approached.

"Sorry I'm late," I whispered, not wanting to disturb the

students already taking their tests. A quiet buzz of chatter grew in the room, and I held my chin higher as I fought back the urge to make sure my shorts were covering my butt. "But I'm ready for the midterm."

Thankfully, Slade didn't comment on my appearance. He shook his head and pulled a packet of papers from his stack before holding it out. "See that you are, Miss Fox. You have thirty minutes."

A weight eased from my shoulders, allowing me to breathe again. He didn't kick me out.

A few students were still looking my way when I turned around. They were probably waiting for more of a show. I spotted Noah halfway down the first aisle, and my legs felt like Jell-O as I walked toward the empty seat next to him. The snickers trailing behind me did nothing to abate my never-ending blush.

Noah's gaze followed me the whole way as others lost interest, and I summoned all my remaining dignity as I lowered myself into the seat he'd saved for me. My pajama shorts rode up until every inch of my legs was on display, to my mortification. But I didn't even try to fix it; instead I laid the midterm on my desk with the half-spilled cup of coffee and focused on keeping my breathing even.

Noah cleared his throat, and I looked over to see him taking in my disaster of an ensemble before meeting my gaze.

His eyes said everything. *What the hell happened to you?*

I smiled sheepishly before mouthing back. *I'll tell you later.*

I felt his gaze burning into my side as I turned back to the midterm, but I had something more important to focus on than his curiosity.

The test was six pages long, front and back. There were fill-in-the-blank, multiple-choice, and short-answer sections, plus a page comprised of blank staffs to fill in.

And I had to complete all of it in thirty minutes.

Taking a deep breath, I realized I didn't have my backpack—which meant I didn't have my pens.

But I didn't panic. I bit the inside of my cheek to stifle a smile and sneaked a peek at Noah to find him focused on his test again.

I cleared my throat as quietly as possible, inching my bare foot toward Noah's desk to get his attention. He looked over with a quirked brow, and my smile broke through.

"Can I borrow a pen?" I whispered.

One side of Noah's lips lifted into a half smile as he selected one of the five sleek pens from his lineup. He leaned across the aisle, offering it to me.

"Thanks." My fingers brushed against his as I took it, and the butterflies cooed appreciatively.

I tested my grip on the pen, comforted by its weight in my hand. And without any other obstacles, I took a swig from my coffee and flipped back to the first page of the midterm.

With a deep breath, I wrote my name at the top of the page.

The first question was about the four basic triads, and I stifled a snort when I remembered the way Noah explained them using diagrams he made on flash cards. I filled in the four definitions with ease.

The next question asked about circle chord progression, and I smiled. This one clicked when we were quizzing each other in the music room.

After that was identifying intervals, which I'd done ten times over beneath my and Noah's tree.

Then came rhythm and meter, chords, and scales.

My smile widened, and Noah's pen didn't get a second of rest for the remainder of the test.

A Birthday

Dear Diary,

Can you keep a secret?

I mean it. If you tell anyone... let's just say diaries don't hold up well under water torture.

Anyway, about the secret...

I got an A on my Music Theory midterm.

I DID IT!

It happened.

Slade even double-checked and promised he wasn't playing tricks on me. I texted a picture to my mother, so hopefully that's the last I'll hear from her on the matter. Fat chance, though.

But Noah doesn't know yet, so keep your trap shut. I'm gonna surprise him with cheesecake tonight to cele-brate. It's his favorite.

*Also, I need to talk to you about Oliver Bishop
later. It's important.*

I'm so happy,
Emma

Text from the Morning of the Midterm

OLIVER BISHOP

Good luck on your test. Of course I remember
you—how could I forget the girl who thought
we met in a dream? Let me know if you want to
celebrate after acing your midterm. I know a
killer little French place.

LIFE AFTER PASSING Slade's midterm was golden. Noah and I
spent our free time together working on our duet or cooking at his
place or hanging out on the quad by our tree. I'd started sleeping
over at the duplex when we had plans—mostly to avoid the whole
sock-situation with Teresa but also just because I wanted to.

But something I didn't expect was Noah's continued furtive-
ness. After meeting Julian, I'd never seen the vet student again, let
alone any of Noah's other secret friends. While I didn't *feel* like a
dirty little secret anymore, I hated the feeling of uncertainty every
time Noah mentioned meeting up with his friends without
inviting me along.

His phone had a habit of ringing at all times of the night. After
a few weeks of sleepovers, he still excused himself from the room

before answering. I was determined to trust him, but the tiniest grains of doubt crept in no matter how many times he assured me it was business.

I woke up once in the middle of the night, and he was nowhere to be found, only to magically reappear the next morning with a catering-sized traveler of coffee. If it was supposed to distract me... well, it worked.

I took the opposite approach. Aside from texting Finn and *thinking* about texting Oliver back, I basically refused to answer my phone at all. Turns out having a boyfriend was the perfect excuse for screening my mother's calls. And emails. And texts.

The Noah Fund grew slow and steadily. Taking out the damages for a couple more catering snafus, plus food to survive, I was up to a whopping total of eighty-three dollars. Just one or two more catering gigs, and I'd have enough to surprise him with a new pen.

November arrived with a cooling breeze and more pockets of rain, but I found myself unable to keep still because the best day of the year was quickly approaching. November 7th.

My birthday.

I didn't have many fond birthday memories growing up in Kansas. Most were spent performing Chopin and Beethoven for my parents' friends at adult-only parties they hosted. Sometimes there was cake, but my mother watched my figure from an early age, so it wasn't for me. Eventually, my idea of a good birthday was an entire day where my father pretended I didn't exist.

One benefit of traveling over a thousand miles away from home was I could celebrate however I wanted. The possibilities were endless. I could order nineteen cakes and eat them all myself. I could go to a bowling alley and gorge myself on cheeseburgers and fries. I could go to a strip club and look at men's butts.

I wasn't going to do that, but I *could*.

Instead, I dragged Noah to a carnival at the Santa Monica Pier the Saturday night before I turned nineteen. There were booths filled with rigged games, vendors selling odd knickknacks, food trucks lining the street, and even a Ferris wheel. We got our faces painted like cats, ate our body weights in cotton candy, and I even started a little brawl with some twelve-year-olds who hogged the Skee-Ball machines.

It was my favorite birthday party ever.

A finger traced along the shell of my ear and tickled me awake the next morning. I groaned, peeking an eye open to find Noah's warm hazel ones gazing back at me.

"I could get used to waking up like this," Noah said from the comfort of his pillow. His finger traced down my jaw before going back up and curling a loose strand of hair around itself.

I swallowed heavily, blinking to rid the sleep from my eyes as I soaked him in. Bare-chested, disheveled dark hair, and a sleepy smile.

I wanted to eat him right up.

"Me too," I whispered hoarsely.

"Happy birthday, beautiful." Noah's smile grew as he leaned in and pressed his lips to mine in a soft, sweet kiss worthy of an award. If they made awards for kissing, that is.

I didn't even care about morning breath.

My heart skipped a beat, and I barely caught the tail-end of the kiss before he pulled back. I could only watch as he rolled further away, leaned off the bed, and reached into his nightstand's drawer before rolling back. He was closer this time, leaning up on his elbow as he hovered next to me.

Noah placed a light-pink box on the mattress in the barest bit of space between us. It was a small rectangular shape with a soft white ribbon tied around it. My heart stuttered when I realized it looked scarily similar to those jewelry boxes that held bracelets.

I swallowed as I stared at the box. "You didn't have to—"

"I did," Noah said with a smile in his voice. I wanted to look up and admire his smile, but my eyes were riveted to the pink box. "And I wanted to. Open it."

Well, if he insisted.

I reached out and gently untied the ribbon before gingerly picking up the box. There was no wrapping paper on it, and it had a velvety texture. When I flipped open the top with trembling fingers, my breath caught.

Nestled comfortably inside a bed of velvet sat a sleek, elegant pen very closely resembling one of Noah's Aurora Ipsilons.

"It's called an Aurora Talentum," Noah said, while I could only stare at the pen in awe. "More specifically, an Aurora Talentum Finesse Chrome. And it's the ballpoint version, just like mine. It's smaller than the ones I have, so I think it'll be more appropriate for your grip."

His words went in one ear and out the other. I could only stare at the beautiful pen in front of me.

Noah chuckled. "If you don't like it, we can pick out a different one together. I wanted it to be a surprise."

My lips parted, but there were no words.

"Emma?" He cupped my cheek, and his thumb grazed across my skin.

I blinked, greedily devouring the pen with my eyes. "It's pink."

"It is." Noah brushed a strand of hair off my cheek. I kept gazing down at the pen in its super fancy box, willing my brain to make sense of this new development.

"It's expensive." I took an educated guess based on my past web searches.

Noah leaned forward, and his lips met my forehead in a gentle touch. "I wanted to get you something nice."

I shook my head with a snort. He'd definitely done that. This pen had to cost at least as much as Noah's. "I'm still trying to repay you for the other one."

"As far as I'm concerned, that debt was settled when you bought me a cup of coffee," Noah murmured against my forehead before trailing his lips down to place another kiss on my temple. His earthy scent was overwhelming. "You don't owe me anything."

I wanted to scoff at that—I was determined to pay him back, after all—but I was too busy soaking in his soothing scent while focusing on the light-pink color of the pen.

"I love it," I whispered before swallowing around the lump forming in my throat.

Noah had gotten me a pen. A *fancy* pen. One like his, but pink and cute.

It was a lot to digest. The pen sat innocently strapped in the box of velvet, calling out to me like a beacon. I wanted to hold it, use it, love it—but nerves held me back.

"I'm afraid to touch it," I admitted quietly before licking my lips.

Noah chuckled, his lips shaking against my skin before he pulled back with a handsome smile that finally broke my staring contest with the pen. I wondered if they made smile awards, too. I'd nominate him in a second. "Touch it, Emma. Or I'll return it for lack of use."

"No!" Horror clouded my gaze at the thought of him taking this magical instrument away from me. "You can't do that."

"Emma," was all Noah said, with that hint of command in his tone. My toes curled under the sheet. "Just touch it, love."

I gulped as I looked back down at the pink beauty before me. I could feel Noah's eyes on me; they hadn't left since I'd opened the box. I licked my lips in anticipation.

My finger reached out, hesitantly tracing the smooth pink exterior of the pen, and I recalled just how smoothly Noah's pen had written for me.

I shuddered as my fingertip glided across the body of the pen without an iota of resistance, and shivers danced along my skin at the delicious contact.

God, it felt like sex.

Was that even possible?

Really, *really* good sex.

"I think I just had an orgasm," I whispered reverently.

Noah snorted in surprise before covering his mouth with one hand as more laughter erupted. His belly shook, and he rolled onto his back.

"For God's sake," Noah managed to say through his laughter, eyes shining as they looked over at me. I was still in a semistate of shock—both from the highly sensual touching of the pen and from the way he was laughing so openly—and could only gape back at him while I tried to work through the feelings both he and the pen exposed. Noah grinned back at me as I tried not to melt at the strength of the emotion in his eyes. "I love you, Emma Fox."

Maybe I did melt a little. Setting the pen's box between us, I leaned down to plant a full, unyielding kiss on Noah's smiling lips. His molded easily against mine, returning as much as I gave him. I placed a hand on his bare chest, and I pulled back just enough to look into the eyes that held me captive on a daily basis.

"I love you, too, Noah Kincaid."

"Henrietta," I declared proudly with a decisive nod. "I'm going to call her Henrietta."

Noah and I had spent the last hour lounging around in bed. We kissed, whispered sweet nothings, kissed some more, and dozed a little—but I spent most of the time admiring and fussing over my new writing utensil like a new mother would her baby. Noah entertained himself by scrolling through his phone to check something as boring as *stocks* while his finger drew random designs against my side.

It was the perfect birthday.

After fully liberating the pen from its box, I found Noah had even engraved a spot near the top of it.

All my love, Noah

I promptly bawled my eyes out upon seeing it, and Noah did his best to comfort me until I was capable of breathing again without choking on sobs.

I distracted myself by putting the pen to good use, which meant grabbing my diary from my backpack and writing all about my favorite birthday. The pen might as well have been crafted by the gods for how smooth it glided, and I quickly filled up a dozen pages.

Then I took it on a test run against Noah's blank canvas of a chest. I doodled music notes up his arms, hearts over his shoulder, and was currently nibbling on my lip as I created a Hello Kitty masterpiece across his smooth pec.

Noah's finger traced back up my side, creeping underneath my tank top as goose bumps followed his path. I fidgeted a little and grabbed his arm to hold it steady as I fixed Kitty's ears.

"Careful, you're disrupting Henrietta," I murmured, and his finger paused.

"Did you just name your pen?" Amusement was heavy in his voice.

"*Henrietta,*" I corrected him, then frowned when I accidentally gave Hello Kitty an extra ear.

Oh well. Art was in the eye of the beholder, right?

"Your tongue is sticking out," Noah whispered as I moved down to add the whiskers.

"I'm concentrating," I said defensively, belatedly realizing my tongue was in fact poking out as I focused on the drawing.

"We have about an hour before we need to go."

"What do you mean?" I changed my focus to her eyes. "It's Sunday, so we're not going anywhere. We can stay in bed all day, eat Pop-Tarts, and I'll give you more cool tattoos."

"If that's what you want," Noah agreed quickly. Almost *too* quickly. He took a breath that made my pen veer off course again. "But it'd be a shame since I made reservations at that waffle café you like. The one that puts whipped cream and sprinkles on their iced coffee."

Henrietta froze against Noah's chest, and my gaze shot up to his. "You did?"

A smile fought to crack through his poker face. "It's all right. I can always call back and cancel."

"Don't you dare!" I cried. I inadvertently dug Henrietta deeper into his chest before pulling her back. "What time is the reservation?"

Noah's smile broke through. "I was accounting for traffic, but it's not for another hour and a half. You have time to finish your drawings."

His finger trailed up my side, and I shivered. The elected chief of the butterflies—because my stomach was a democracy and not a dictatorship—awoke from his slumber and riled his citizens into a tizzy at the touch.

Noah was taking me out for waffles.

"Have I ever told you how wonderful you are?" I leaned up to smack a kiss on his cheek. "Seriously, you're the best."

Noah chuckled as I settled back down to continue his temporary tattoo. His chest moved in time with his breathing, which was both distracting and detrimental to my already abysmal artistic ability. But I kept all my attention on the pen in my hand, and funny things happened to my stomach when she glided across his skin like roller skates on a rink. The elegant detail on Henrietta was breathtaking, and this strange sense of empowerment fueled my veins as I held her.

Honestly, I was getting a little worked up. My legs shifted restlessly against Noah's as his fingers played with the hem of my tank top, and I cleared my throat while finishing up Hello Kitty's bow.

Noah never missed a thing, and the dry amusement in his voice did little to help my growing dilemma. "Is the pen turning you on again, Emma?"

I froze mid-doodle, avoiding eye contact.

"Well... it's *you* I'm drawing on. So maybe it's you turning me on?" I asked before batting my lashes at his chest.

"Maybe?" Noah's hand slipped further inside my top to grip my hip, and I sucked in my stomach at his cold fingertips. "*Maybe* I'm turning you on?"

His voice ended on a growl, and I squealed out a laugh as he rolled us until he was hovering over me. The movement gave Hello Kitty an unintentional unibrow that stretched across the rest of Noah's chest, but any complaints went flying out the window when Noah grinned down at me.

I swallowed. He looked at me the way I looked at Henrietta.

"Would it be too forward of me to make a move on you right now?" Noah asked as he anchored himself on one elbow above me. His other hand brushed back the curtain of blonde hair that'd gotten in my face, and his gaze dropped to my lips. "I don't want you to think I'm taking liberties because I bought you a gift. You just look so happy, and you've been rubbing up against me, and... well, I'm only a man."

My lips twitched into an amused smile, and I stretched out underneath him to gingerly set Henrietta back into her box on the nightstand. Then I snuggled into Noah's pillow and wrapped my arms around his neck. "You are way more than a man. And I don't see why not. We still have an hour, and they call it birthday sex for a reason."

"Do they?" Noah moved his ankle to cage my legs in as he leaned closer.

"Or so I've heard," I whispered with a smile. I trailed my tongue over my bottom lip before meeting his kiss halfway.

Best. Birthday. Ever.

A Diary

Dear Diary,

Meet Henrietta! My fancy new pen from my equally fancy boyfriend. Doesn't she feel nice?

Noah's taking me out for birthday waffles today. :)

He just hopped in the shower, so I'm stealing a second to write.

Warning: I'm all mushy and sentimental today, so please bear with me.

You know how there's a million little moments that make up your life? Like, say you accidentally smiled at a guy walking into class.

Then you chewed on his pen.

Bought him a coffee.

Failed a quiz... then another quiz.

Somehow ended up on a date.

Played his first duet with him.

Headbutted the guy, then accidentally drugged him.

Okay, that's enough examples. You get the point.

Maybe that's why you're here, Diary. To help me remember those moments. The smiles. The laughs. Even the mortifying things that make me want to crawl into a hole and die.

Looking through my entries from this semester made me realize how lucky I am.

I'm no longer at risk of losing my spot in Music Theory. My scholarship is safe. Noah and I are composing our very own duet, and I almost have enough money saved to finally replace his pen.

But sweetest of all, I have someone to eat waffles with.

I owe everything to that smile,
Emma

A Shower

AFTER PACKING my diary and Henrietta away in my backpack, I rolled off Noah's bed with a groan and arched my back into a stretch until something popped. A moan of sweet relief escaped, followed by a sigh. It'd be heavenly to stay on that cloudlike mattress for the rest of eternity.

Sounds of the shower running carried from down the hall, and I bit the inside of my cheek—tempted to join Noah.

Water conservation was important, after all.

Decision made, I rifled through the two drawers I'd taken over in Noah's dresser and picked out a pair of shorts and a pink hoodie. Tiptoeing down the hall to the duplex's only bathroom with a smile that felt permanently fused to my face, I briefly wondered if it was bad form to surprise someone in the shower.

What if Noah slipped and fell and I was responsible for him breaking a hip?

I paused outside the door, my hand hovering over the knob, before I decided to at least check if it was unlocked first.

I gripped the doorknob, biting my lip and turning slowly—but it didn't budge.

A muffled voice sounded on the other side of the door, and my hand froze. Leaning in, I pressed my ear against the door and listened closely. Noah's voice blended with the sound of the shower, but he clearly wasn't under the spray.

Was he talking to himself?

He really didn't seem like the type to sing in the shower.

I caught the end of a sentence. "... either they have the money today, or we'll have the less nice Pierce brother stop by their place for a visit."

... *What?*

It took effort to close my jaw as my brain worked a mile a minute just to try and understand. Was Noah seriously hiding in the bathroom with the shower on?

I couldn't hear another voice, so he must've been on the phone.

"The west drop spot. Take Adrian with you," Noah said, and the swift command made my hackles rise.

Drop spot? I mouthed in confusion as I pulled back to look at the door. It held no answers.

Money. Drop Spot.

I'd never heard him talk like this before.

So secretive.

Commanding.

While locked in a bathroom.

I pressed closer to the door until my cheek and chest flattened against the textured wood, but Noah's voice was still muffled.

"I can't today. I already made plans... It doesn't matter who they're with... You know you nag worse than most mothers do, right?"

A weight settled in my stomach. He had plans with *me* today. He didn't want this person to know that?

My eyes narrowed, but I pushed back the lingering mistress thoughts.

"*Relax.* She doesn't know anything... No. Not a clue... She's harmless, Julian. Trust me."

I stared at the doorframe and swallowed hard, but he wasn't done yet.

"I told you not to worry about it. Just get this done," Noah said, and the steel in his voice sent a shock up my arm.

I jerked back from the door, stung. The walls of the hallway felt closer than before, and my tongue stuck to the dry roof of my mouth as I tried to swallow again. Shocked back to life, I retraced my steps to the bedroom with my heart thundering in my chest.

Maybe it'd be best to wait and shower by myself.

Noah's words played through my mind on repeat.

Money.

Drop spot.

She doesn't know anything.

Not a clue.

Just get this done.

I stood next to the bed, at a loss and wondering if I should be confronting him right now.

"He was talking about me, right?" I asked the empty room. I tossed my clothes on the bed and rubbed a hand over my chest. The shower was still on, but I barely heard it over my heartbeat in my ears. "There's no way he wasn't talking about me."

She doesn't know anything.

What didn't I know?

Just get this done.

What were they getting done? Something involving money. But wasn't it normal for financial consulting to involve money?

Nothing about that call sounded normal.

My mind raced, grasping for anything tangible.

Noah made a lot of private phone calls, so that wasn't strange.

He just didn't normally hide out in the bathroom, as far as I was aware.

For all I knew, I was stressing over nothing. Maybe there was a simple explanation for all this.

Or maybe not.

But one question was at the forefront of my mind as I perched on the edge of the bed, having lost my appetite for waffles.

What *exactly* did I know about Noah Kincaid?

Thank you so much for reading! This wraps up The Duet Dilemma, but you can join my mailing list at www.maggieevans.com to receive updates on the next books in The Duet Diaries! Subscribers receive a FREE deleted scene of Emma dragging Noah to the Pier for her birthday.

Acknowledgments

I wish I knew where to begin.

Becky, thank you for everything. From cheerleading to advice to beta-reading to rewrites to more rewrites to editing to blurb help and everything in-between, you pushed and supported me every step of the way. Thank you, thank you, thank you.

Claire, thank you for always being there when I needed to vent or bounce ideas around! You truly are the golden sister.

To the rest of my family, thank you for being crazy supportive of my venture into Kindle Vella. Special thanks to Dad, who loves Harry Potter just as much as I do.

Thanks to my writing club, Just Write, for being so amazing! I never would have finished this book (or at least, not for another decade) without your motivation and writing sprints and being there every day. In alphabetical order because I'm a middle child and not trying to play favorites, thank you to angeleumbra, Busy, Dizzo, Jaliza, Jules, Katydid, ladybugtastic, LadySavyss, Ly-luh, Ophelia, Pixelorium, Rae Tina, Rory Stabby Miles, SAM, Shadows_in_shadows, Teslyn, Wetherburn, and everyone else who has been popping in and out of the server. I wish I could add emojis and gifs here.

Thank you to Writer-Bot and her creator, CMR, on discord!

And last but far from least, to my Wattpad and Vella readers. I don't have the words to express how grateful I am for your passionate and everlasting support over the years. I never would've had the courage to do this without you. Thank you!

About the Author

Based in the Midwest, Maggie Evans is a voracious reader always looking for new worlds to explore. Using her own mortifying experiences for inspiration, she has a habit of writing scenes that will make a reader wish secondhand embarrassment wasn't a thing.

She adores coffee with too much sugar, a cozy place to write, and an abundance of book boyfriends.

www.maggieevans.com

 facebook.com/authormaggieevans

 instagram.com/authormaggieevans

www.ingramcontent.com/pod-product-compliance
Lightning Source LLC
Chambersburg PA
CBHW020235010826

48973CB00006B/1524